I'll Be Home
for Christmas

Other Books by Fern Michaels

Published by Kensington Publishing Corporation

I'll Be Home for Christmas

FERN MICHAELS

ZEBRA BOOKS
KENSINGTON PUBLISHING CORP.
http://www.kensingtonbooks.com

ZEBRA BOOKS are published by

Kensington Publishing Corp.
119 West 40th Street
New York, NY 10018

ISBN-13: 978-1-4201-3142-0
ISBN-10: 1-4201-3142-7

First Zebra Books Mass-Market Paperback Printing: October 2012
First Zebra Books Trade Paperback Printing: October 2010

10 9 8 7 6 5 4 3 2 1

Printed in the United States of America

Contents

Merry, Merry

Andi Evans stared at the light switch. Should she turn it on or not? How many kilowatts of electricity did the fluorescent bulbs use? How would it translate onto her monthly bill? She risked a glance at the calendar; December 14, 1996, five days till the meter reader arrived. The hell with it, the animals needed light. She needed light. Somehow, someway, she'd find a way to pay the bill. On the other hand, maybe she should leave the premises dark so Mr. Peter King could break his leg in the dark. Breaking both legs would be even better. Like it was really going to happen.

Maybe she should read the letter again. She looked in the direction of her desk where she'd thrown it five days ago after she'd read it. She could see the end of the expensive cream-colored envelope sticking out among the stack of unpaid bills. "Guess what, Mr. Peter King, I'm not selling you my property. I told that to your forty-seven lawyers months ago." She started to cry then because it was all so hopeless.

They came from every direction, dogs, cats, puppies and kittens, clawing for her attention, their ears attuned to the strange sounds coming from the young woman who fed and bathed them and saw to their needs. They were strays nobody wanted. This was what she'd gone to veterinarian school for. She even had a sign that said she was Andrea Evans, D.V.M. Eleven patients in as many months. She was the new kid on the block, what did she expect? Because she was that new kid, people assumed they could just dump unwanted animals on her property. After all, what did a vet with only eleven patients have to do?

Andi thought about her student loans, the taxes on her house and three acres, the animals, the bills, the futility of it all. Why was she even fighting? Selling her property would net her a nice tidy sum. She could pay off her loans, go to work for a vet clinic, get a condo someplace and . . . what would happen to her animals if she did that? She wailed louder, the dogs and cats clambering at her feet.

"Enough!" a voice roared.

"Gertie!"

Tails swished furiously; Gertie always brought soup bones and catnip. Andi watched as she doled them out, something for everyone. She blew her nose. "I think they love you more than they love me."

"They love what I bring them. I'd like a cup of tea if you have any. It's nasty out there. It might snow before nightfall."

"Where are you sleeping tonight, Gertie?"

"Under the railroad trestle with my friends. Being homeless doesn't give me many choices."

"You're welcome to stay here, Gertie. I told you the cot is yours anytime you want it. I'll even make you breakfast. Did you eat today?"

"Later. I have something for you. Call it an early Christmas present. I couldn't wait to get here to give it to you." Gertie hiked up several layers of clothing to her long underwear where she'd sewn a pocket. She withdrew a thick wad of bills. "We found this four weeks ago. There it was, this big wad of money laying right in the street late at night. Two thousand dollars, Andi. We want you to have it. We watched in the papers, asked the police, no one claimed it. A whole month we waited, and no one claimed it. It's probably drug money, but them animals of yours don't know that. Better to be spent on them than on some drug pusher. Doncha be telling me no now."

"Oh, Gertie, I wouldn't dream of saying no. Did you find it in Plainfield?"

"Right there on Front Street, big as life."

Andi hugged the old woman who always smelled of lily of the valley. She could never figure out why that was. Gertie had to be at least seventy-five, but a young seventy-five as she put it. She was skinny and scrawny, but it was hard to tell with the many layers of clothing she wore. Her shoes were run-down, her gloves had holes in the fingers and her knit cap reeked of mothballs. For a woman her age she had dewy skin, pink cheeks, few wrinkles and the brightest, bluest eyes Andi had ever seen. "Did you walk all the way from Plainfield, Gertie?"

Gertie's head bobbed up and down. "Scotch Plains ain't that far. I left my buggie outside."

Translated, that meant all of Gertie's worldly possessions were in an Acme shopping cart outside Andi's clinic.

"Here's your tea, Gertie, strong and black, just the way you like it. It's almost Christmas; are you going to call your children? You should, they must be worried sick."

"What, so they can slap me in a nursing home? Oh, no, I like things just the way they are. I'm spending Christmas with my friends. Now, why were you bawling like that?"

Andi pointed to her desk. "Unpaid bills. And a letter from Mr. Peter King. He's that guy I told you about. His forty-seven lawyers couldn't bend me, so I guess they're sending in the first string now. He's coming here at four-thirty."

"Here?" Gertie sputtered, the teacup almost falling from her hand.

"Yes. Maybe he's going to make a final offer. Or, perhaps he thinks he can intimidate me. This property has been in my family for over a hundred years. I'm not selling it to some lipstick mogul. What does a man know about lipstick anyway? Who cares if he's one of the biggest cosmetic manufacturers on the East Coast. I don't even wear lipstick. These lips are as kissable as they're going to get, and his greasy product isn't going to change my mind."

"I really need to be going now, Andi. So, you'll tell him no."

"Gertie, look around you. What would you do if you were me? What's so special about this piece of property? Let him go to Fanwood, anywhere but here. Well?"

"Location is everything. This is prime. Zoning has to be just right, and you, my dear, are zoned for his needs. I'd tell him to go fly a kite," Gertie said smartly. "I hear a truck. Lookee here, Andi, Wishnitz is here with your dog food."

"I didn't order any dog food."

"You better tell him that then, 'cause the man's unloading big bags of it. I'll see you tomorrow. Greasy, huh?"

"Yeah. Gertie, I wish you'd stay; it's getting awfully cold outside. Thanks for the money. Tell your friends I'm grateful. You be careful now."

"Hey, I didn't order dog food," she said to the driver.

"Bill says it's a gift. Five hundred pounds of Pedigree dog food, sixteen cases of cat food and two bags of birdseed. Sign here?"

"Who sent it?"

"Don't know, ma'am, I'm just the driver. Call the store. Where do you want this?"

"Around the back."

Andi called the feed store to be sure there was no mistake. "Are you telling me some anonymous person just walked into your store and paid for all this? It's a fortune in dog and cat food. No name at all? All right, thanks."

A beagle named Annabelle pawed Andi's leg. "I know, time for supper and a little run. Okay, everybody *SIT!* You know the drill, about face; march in an orderly fashion to the pen area. Stop when you get to the gate and go to your assigned dishes. You know which ones are yours. No cheating, Harriet," she said to a fat white cat who eyed her disdainfully. "I'm counting to three, and when the whistle blows, *GO!* That's really good, you guys are getting the hang of it. Okay, here it comes, extra today thanks to our Good Samaritan, whoever she or he might be."

"Bravo! If I didn't see it with my own eyes, I wouldn't have believed it. There must be thirty dogs and cats here."

"Thirty-six to be exact. And you are?" Andi looked at her watch.

"Peter King. You must be Andrea Evans."

"Dr. Evans. How did you get in here? The dogs didn't bark." Andi's voice was suspicious, her eyes wary. "I'm busy right now, and you're forty-five minutes early, Mr. King. I can't deal with you now. You need to go back to the office or come back another day." The wariness in her eyes changed to amusement when she noticed Cedric, a Dalmatian, lift his leg to pee on Peter King's exquisitely polished Brooks Brothers loafers.

The lipstick mogul, as Andi referred to him, eyed his shoe in dismay. He shook it off and said, "You might be right. I'll be in the waiting room."

Andi raised her head from the sack of dog food to stare at the tall man dwarfing her. Thirty-six or -seven, brown eyes, brown unruly hair with a tight curl, strong features, handsome, muscular, unmarried: no ring on his finger. Sharply dressed. Pristine white shirt, bold, expensive tie. Very well put together. She wondered how many lipsticks he had to sell to buy his outfit. She debated asking until she remembered how she looked. Instead she said, "You remind me of someone."

"A lot of people say that, but they can never come up with who it is." He started for the waiting room.

"It will come to me sooner or later." Andi ladled out food, the dogs waiting patiently until all the dishes were full. "Okay, guys, go for it!" When the animals finished eating, Andi let them out into their individual runs. "Twenty minutes. When you hear the buzzer, boogie on in here," she called.

Andi took her time stacking the dog bowls in the stainless steel sink full of soapy water. She'd said she was busy. Busy meant she had to wash and dry the dishes now to take up time. As she washed and dried the bowls, her eyes kept going to the mirror over the sink. She looked worse than a mess. She had on absolutely no makeup, her blond hair was frizzy, her sweatshirt was stained and one of her sneakers had a glob of poop on the heel. She cleaned off her shoe, then stacked the dishes for the following day. "When I'm slicked up, I can look as good as he does," she hissed to the animals and let the dogs into their pens. The beagle threw her head back and howled.

"I have five minutes, Mr. King. I told your forty-seven lawyers I'm not selling. What part of 'no' don't you understand?"

"The part about the forty-seven lawyers. I only have two. I think you mean forty-seven letters."

Andi shrugged.

"I thought perhaps I could take you out to dinner . . . and we could . . . discuss the pros and cons of selling your property." He smiled. She saw dimples and magnificent white teeth. All in a row like matched pearls.

"Save your money, Mr. King. Dinner will not sway my decision. You know what else, I don't even like your lipstick. It's greasy. The colors are abominable. The names you've given the lipsticks are so ridiculous they're ludicrous. Raspberry Cheese Louise. Come *onnnnn.*" At his blank look she said, "I worked at a cosmetic counter to put myself through college and vet school."

"I see."

"No, you don't, but that's okay. Time's up, Mr. King."

"Three hundred and fifty thousand, Dr. Evans. You could relocate."

Andi felt her knees go weak on her. "Sorry, Mr. King."

"Five hundred thousand and that's as high as I can go. It's a take it or leave it offer. It's on the table right now. When I walk out of here it goes with me."

She might have seriously considered the offer if the beagle hadn't chosen that moment to howl. "I really have to go, Mr. King. That's Annabelle howling. She has arthritis and it's time for her medication." She must be out of her mind to turn down half a million dollars. Annabelle howled again.

"I didn't know dogs got arthritis."

"They get a lot of things, Mr. King. They develop heart trouble; they get cancer, cataracts, prostate problems, all manner of things. Do you really think us humans have a lock on disease? This is the only home those animals know. No one else wanted them, so I took them in. My father and his father before him owned this kennel. It's my home and their home."

"Wait, hear me out. You could buy a new, modern facility with the money I'm willing to pay you. This is pretty antiquated. Your wood's rotten, your pens are rusty, your concrete is cracked. You're way past being a fixer-upper. You could get modern equipment. If you want my opinion, I think you're being selfish. You're thinking of yourself, not the animals. The past is past;

you can't bring it back, nor should you want to. I'll leave my offer on the table till Friday. Give it some thought, sleep on it. If your decision is still no on Friday, I won't bother you again. I'll even raise my price to $750,000. I'm not trying to cheat you."

Andi snorted. "Of course not," she said sarcastically, "that's why you started off at $200,000 and now you're up to $750,000. I didn't just fall off the turnip truck, Mr. King. Let's cut to the chase. What's your absolute final offer?"

It was Peter King's turn to stare warily at the young doctor in front of him. His grandmother would love her. Sadie would say she had grit and spunk. Uh-huh. "A million," he said hoarsely.

"That's as in acre, right? I have a little over three acres. Closer to four than three."

King's jaw dropped. Annabelle howled again. "You want three million dollars for this . . . hovel?"

"No. Three plus million for the *land*. You're right, it is a hovel; but it's my home and the home of those animals. I sweated my ass off to keep this property and work my way through school. What do you know about work, Mr. Lipstick? Hell, I could make up a batch of that stuff you peddle for eight bucks a pop right here in the kitchen. All I need is my chemistry book. Get the hell off my property and don't come back unless you have three million plus dollars in your hand. You better get going before it really starts to snow and you ruin those fancy three-hundred-dollar Brooks Brothers shoes."

"Your damn dog already ruined them."

"Send me a bill!" Andi shouted as she pushed him through the door and then slammed it shut. She turned the dead bolt before she raced back to the animals. She dusted her hands dramatically for the animals' benefit before she started to cry. The animals crept from their cages that had no doors, to circle her, licking and pawing at her tear-filled face. She hiccupped and denounced all men who sold lipstick. "If he comes up with three million plus bucks, we're outta here. Then we'll have choices; we can stay here in New Jersey, head south or north, wherever we can get the best deal. Hamburger and tuna for you guys and steak for me. We'll ask Gertie to go with us. I'm done crying now. You can go back to sleep. Come on, Annabelle, time for your pill."

Andi scooped up the pile of bills on her desk to carry them into the house. With the two thousand dollars from Gertie and the dog and cat food, she could last until the end of January, and then she'd be right back where she was just a few hours ago. Three million plus dollars was a lot of money. So was $750,000. Scrap that, he'd said a cool million. Times three. At eight bucks a tube, how many lipsticks would the kissing king need to sell? Somewhere in the neighborhood of 375,000. Darn, she should have said two million an acre.

It might be a wonderful Christmas after all.

Peter King slid his metallic card into the slot and waited for the huge grilled gate to the underground garage of his grandmother's high-rise to open. Tonight was his Friday night obligatory dinner with his grandmother. A dinner he always enjoyed and even looked forward to. He adored his seventy-five-year-old grandmother who was the president of King Cosmetics. He shuddered when he thought of what she would say to

Andrea Evans's price. She'd probably go ballistic and throw her salmon, Friday night's dinner, across the room. At which point, Hannah the cat would eat it all and then puke on the Persian carpet. He shuddered again. Three million dollars. Actually, it would be more than three million. The property on Cooper River Road was closer to four acres. He had two hard choices: pay it or forget it.

Who in the hell was that wise-ass girl whose dog peed on his shoe? Where did she get off booting him out the door. Hell, she'd pushed him, shoved him. She probably didn't weigh more than one hundred pounds soaking wet. He took a few seconds to mentally envision that hundred-pound body naked. Aaahh. With some King Cosmetics she'd be a real looker. And she hated his guts.

"Hey, Sadie, I'm here," Peter called from the foyer. He'd called his grandmother Sadie from the time he was a little boy. She allowed it because she said it made her feel younger.

"Peter, you're early. Good, we can have a drink by the fire. Hannah's already there waiting for us. She's not feeling well." Sadie's voice turned fretful. "I don't want her *going* before me. She's such wonderful company. Look at her, she's just lying there. I tried to tempt her with salmon before and she wouldn't touch it. She won't even let me hold her."

Peter's stomach started to churn. If anything happened to Hannah, he knew his grandmother would take to her bed and not get up. He hunched down and held out his hand. Hannah hissed and snarled. "That's not like her. Did you take her to the vet?"

Sadie snorted "He went skiing in Aspen. I don't much care for all those fancy vets who have banker's hours and who don't give a damn. Hannah is too precious to trust to just anybody. Let's sit and have a drink and watch her. How did your meeting go with Dr. Evans?"

"It was a bust. She wants a million dollars an acre. She means it, too. She booted my ass right out the door. I have a feeling she's a pretty good vet. Maybe you should have her take a look at Hannah. One of her dogs squirted on my shoe."

"That's a lot of money. Is the property worth it?"

"Hell yes. More, as a matter of fact. She ridiculed my low-ball offer. Hey, business is business."

"We aren't in the business of cheating people, Peter. Fair is fair. If, as you say, Miss Evans's property is the perfect location, then pay the money and close the deal. The company can afford it. You can be under way the first of the year. I know you had the attorneys do all the paperwork in advance. Which, by the way, is a tad unethical in my opinion. Don't think I don't know that you have your contractor on twenty-four-hour call."

"Is there anything you don't know, Sadie?"

"Yes."

Peter eyed his grandmother warily. God, how he loved this old lady with her pearl white hair and regal bearing. It was hard to believe she was over seventy. She was fit and trim, fashionable, a leader in the community. She sat on five boards, did volunteer work at the hospital and was an active leader in ways to help the homeless. Her picture was in the paper at least three days a week. He knew what was coming now, and he dreaded it. "Let's get it over with, Sadie."

"Helen called here for you about an hour ago. She quizzed me, Peter. The gall of that woman. What do you see in her? I hesitate to remind you, but she dumped you. That's such an unflattering term, but she did. She married that councilman because she believed his PR campaign. She thought he was rich. The man is in debt over his ears, so she left him. Now, she wants you again. She's a selfish, mean-spirited young woman who thinks only of herself. I thought you had more sense, Peter. I am terribly disappointed in this turn of events."

He was pretty much of the same opinion, but he wasn't going to give his grandmother the pleasure of knowing his feelings. She'd been matchmaking for years and was determined to find just the right girl for him.

"We're friends. There's no harm in a casual lunch or dinner. Don't make this into something else."

"I want to see you settled before I go."

"You can stop that right now, Sadie, because it isn't going to work. You're fit as a fiddle, better than a person has a right to be at your age. You can stay on the treadmill longer than I can. You aren't going anywhere for a very long time. When I find the right girl you'll be the first to know."

"You've been telling me that for years. You're thirty-six, Peter. I want grandchildren before . . . I get too old to enjoy them. If you aren't interested in Helen, tell her so and don't take up her time. Don't even think about bringing her to your Christmas party. If you do, I will not attend."

"All right, Sadie!"

Sadie sniffed, her blue eyes sparking. "She just wants to be your hostess so she can network. Men are so stupid sometimes. Tell me about Dr. Evans. What's she like?"

Peter threw his hands in the air. "I told you she

kicked me out. I hardly had time to observe her. She has curly hair, she's skinny. I think she's skinny. She had this look on her face, Sadie, it . . . Mom used to look at me kind of the same way when I was sick. She had that look when she was with the animals. I was sizing her up when her dog squatted on my shoe. The place is a mess. Clean, but a mess."

"That young woman worked her way through school. She worked at a cosmetic counter, did waitressing, sometimes working two jobs. It took her a while, but she did it. I approve of that, Peter. That property has been in her family for a long time. Both her parents were vets, and so was her grandfather. No one appreciates hard work more than I do. Take a good look at me, Peter. I started King Cosmetics in my kitchen. I worked around the clock when your grandfather died and I had three children to bring up. I read the report in your office. I can truthfully say I never read a more comprehensive report. The only thing missing was the color of her underwear. I felt like a sneak reading it. I really did, Peter. I wish you hadn't done that. It's such an invasion of someone's privacy."

"This might surprise you, Sadie, but I felt the same way. I wanted to know what I was up against, financially. For whatever it's worth, I'm sorry I did it, too. So, do we buy the property or not?"

"Are you prepared to pay her price?"

"I guess I am. It's a lot of money."

"Will she hold out?" Sadie's tone of voice said she didn't care one way or the other.

"Damn right. That young woman is big on principle. She's going to stick it to me because she thinks I tried to cheat her."

"You did."

"Why does it sound like you're on her side? What I did was an acceptable business practice."

"I'm a fair, honest woman, Peter. I don't like anything unethical. I wish this whole mess never happened. Why don't you invite Dr. Evans to your Christmas party. If you got off to a bad start, this might shore up things for you. I think you're interested in the young woman. I bet she even has a party dress. And shoes. Probably even a pearl necklace that belonged to her mother. Girls always have pearl necklaces that belonged to their mothers. Things like pearl necklaces are important to young women. Well?"

"Before or after I make the offer?" Jesus, he didn't just say that, did he?

"If you're going to make the offer, call her and tell her. Why wait till Monday? Maybe you could even go over there and take Hannah for her to check over. That's business for her. Then you could extend the invitation."

Peter grinned wryly. "You never give up, do you?"

"Then you'll take Hannah tomorrow."

"For you, Sadie, anything. What's for dinner?"

"Pot roast," Sadie said smartly. "I gave the salmon to Hannah, but she wouldn't eat it."

"Pot roast's good. We settled on the three million plus, then?" His voice was so jittery-sounding, Sadie turned away to hide her smile.

"I'd say so. You need to give Dr. Evans time to make plans. Christmas is almost here. She'll want to spend her last Christmas at her home, I would imagine. She'll have to pack up whatever she's going to take with her. It's not much time, Peter. She has to think about all those animals."

"Three million plus will ease the burden considerably. She can hire people to help her. We're scheduled to go, as in *go*, the day after New Years. I hate to admit this, but I'm having second thoughts about the contractor I hired. I think I was just a little too hasty when I made my decision, but I signed the contract so I'm stuck. Time's money, Sadie. If the young lady is as industrious as the report says, she'll have it under control."

Sadie smiled all through dinner. She was still smiling when she kissed her grandson good night at the door. "Drive carefully, Peter, the weatherman said six inches of snow by morning. Just out of curiosity, do you happen to know what kind of vehicle Dr. Evans drives?"

"I saw an ancient pickup on the side of the building. It didn't look like it was operational to me. Why do you ask?"

"No reason. I'd hate to think of her stranded with those animals if an emergency came up."

"If you want me to stop on my way home, just say so, Sadie. Is it late? Why don't I call her on the car phone on the way?"

"A call is so impersonal. Like when Helen calls. You could tell Dr. Evans you were concerned about the animals. The power could go out. She might have electric heat. You could also mention that you'll be bringing Hannah in the morning. If she doesn't like you, this might change her mind."

"I didn't say she didn't like me, Sadie," Peter blustered.

"Oh."

"Oh? What does oh mean?"

"It means I don't think she likes you. Sometimes

you aren't endearing, Peter. She doesn't know you the way I do. The way Helen did." This last was said so snidely, Peter cringed.

"Good night, Sadie." Peter kissed his grandmother soundly, gave her a thumbs-up salute, before he pressed the down button of the elevator.

As he waited for the grilled parking gate to open, he stared in dismay at the accumulated snow. Maybe he should head for the nearest hotel and forget about going home. What he should have done was bunk with Sadie for the night. Too late, he was already on the road. The snow took care of any visit he might have considered making to Scotch Plains. He eyed the car phone and then the digital clock on the Mercedes walnut panel. Nine o'clock was still early. Pay attention to the road, he cautioned himself.

In the end, Peter opted for the Garden State Parkway. Traffic was bumper-to-bumper, but moving. He got off the Clark exit and headed for home. He could call Dr. Evans from home with a frosty beer in his hand. When the phone on the console buzzed, he almost jumped out of his skin. He pressed a button and said, "Peter King."

"Peter, it's Helen. I've been calling you all evening. Where have you been?"

He wanted to say, what business is it of yours where I was, but he didn't. "On the road," he said curtly.

"Why don't you stop for a nightcap, Peter. I'll put another log on the fire. I have some wonderful wine."

"Sorry, I'm three blocks from home. The roads are treacherous this evening."

"I see. Where were you, Peter? I called your grandmother, and she said you weren't there."

"Out and about. I'll talk to you next week, Helen."

"You're hanging up on me," she said in a whiny voice.

"Afraid so, I'm almost home."

"I wish I was there with you. I didn't get an invitation to your Christmas party, Peter. Was that an oversight or don't you want me there?"

Peter drew a deep breath. "Helen, you aren't divorced. I know your husband well. We play racquetball at the gym. He's a nice guy and I like him. He's coming to the party. It won't look right for you to attend."

"For heaven's sake, Peter, this is the nineties. Albert and I remained friends. We're legally separated. He knows it's you I love. He's known that from day one. I made a mistake, Peter. Are you going to hold it against me for the rest of my life?"

"Look, Helen, there's no easy way to say this except to say it straight out. I'm seeing someone on a serious basis. You and I had our time, but it's over now. Let's stay friends and let it go at that."

"Who? Who are you seeing? You're making that up, Peter. I would have heard if you were seriously seeing someone. Or is she some nobody you don't take out in public? I bet it's somebody your grandmother picked out for you. Oh, Peter, that's just too funny for words." Trilling laughter filled Peter's car.

Peter swerved into his driveway just as he pressed the power button on the car phone, cutting Helen's trilling laughter in mid-note. He waited for the Genie to raise the garage door. The moment the garage door closed, Peter's shoulders slumped. Who *was* that woman on the phone? Jesus, once he'd given serious thought to marrying her. He shook his head to clear away his thoughts.

How quiet and empty his house was. Cold and dark. He hated coming home to a dark house. He'd thought about getting an animal, but it wouldn't have been fair to the animal since he was hardly ever home. He slammed his briefcase down on the kitchen counter. Damn, he'd forgotten the report on Andrea Evans. Oh, well, it wasn't going anywhere. Tomorrow would be soon enough to retrieve it.

Peter walked around his house, turning on lights as he went from room to room. It didn't look anything like the house he'd grown up in. He leaned against the banister, closing his eyes as he did so. He'd lived in a big, old house full of nooks and crannies in Sleepy Hollow. The rug at the foot of the steps was old, threadbare, and Bessie, their old cocker spaniel had chewed all four corners. She lay on the rug almost all her life to wait for them to come home, pooping on it from time to time as she got older. When she died, his parents had buried her in the backyard under the apple tree. Jesus, he didn't think there was that much grief in the world as that day. He thought about the old hat rack with the boot box underneath where he stored his boots, gloves and other treasures. The hat rack and boot box were somewhere in the attic along with Bessie's toys and dog bones. He wondered if they were still intact.

Peter rubbed at his eyes. He'd loved that house with the worn, comfortable furniture, the green plants his mother raised and the warm, fragrant kitchen with its bright colors. Something was always cooking or baking, and there were always good things to eat for his

friends and himself after school. The thing he remembered the most, though, was his mother's smile
when he walked in the door. She'd always say, "Hi,
Pete, how's it going?" And he'd say, "Pretty good,
Mom." They always ate in the kitchen. Dinner hour was
long, boisterous and memorable. Even when they had
meat loaf. He tried not to think about his younger
brother and sister. He had to stop torturing himself
like this. He banged one fist on the banister as he
wiped at his eyes with the other. He looked around.
Everything was beautiful, decorated by a professional
whose name he didn't know. Once a week a florist delivered fresh flowers. The only time the house came
alive was during his annual Christmas party or his
Fourth of July barbecue. The rest of the time it was
just a house. The word nurture came to mind. He
squeezed his eyes shut and tried to imagine what this
perfectly decorated house would be like with a wife,
kids and a dog. Maybe two dogs and two cats.

"Five thousand goddamn fucking square feet of
nothing." He ripped at his tie and jacket, tossing them
on the back of a chair. He kicked his loafers across
the room. In a pique of something he couldn't define,
he brushed at a pile of magazines and watched them
sail in different directions. Shit! The room still didn't
look lived in. Hell, he didn't even know his neighbors. He might as well live in a damn hotel.

On his way back to the kitchen he picked up the
portable phone, asking for information. He punched
out the numbers for the Evans Kennel as his free
hand twisted the cap off a bottle of Budweiser. He
wondered if her voice would be sleepy sounding or
hard and cold. He wasn't prepared for what he did
hear when he announced himself.

"I don't have time for chitchat, Mr. King. I have an emergency on my hands here and you're taking up my time. Call me on Monday or don't call me on Monday." Peter stared at the pinging phone in his hand.

Chitchat. Call or don't call. *Emergency.* Sadie's dire warnings rang in his ears.

Peter raced up the steps. So there was a sucker born every minute. Sadie would approve. He stripped down, throwing his clothes any which way as he searched for thermal sweats, thick socks and Alpine boots. His shearling jacket, cap and gloves were downstairs in the hall closet.

Emergency could mean anything. She was handling it. Oh, yeah, like women could really handle an emergency. Maybe his mother could handle one, or Sadie, but not that hundred pound prairie flower. He raced to the garage where all his old camping gear was stored. Blankets and towels went into the back of his Range Rover. He threw in two shovels, his camp stove, lanterns, flashlights. The last things to go in were Sterno lamps and artificial fire logs. What the hell, an emergency was an emergency.

It wasn't until he backed the 4 by 4 out of the garage that he questioned himself. Why was he doing this? Because . . . because . . . he'd heard the same fearful tone in Dr. Evans's voice that he'd heard in his mother's voice the day Bessie couldn't get up on her legs anymore.

Driving every back street and alley, over people's lawns, Peter arrived at the Evans Kennel in over an hour. Every light appeared to be on in the house and the kennel. There were no footprints in the snow, so that had to mean the emergency was inside the house.

Even from this distance he could hear the shrill barking and high-pitched whine of the animals that seemed to be saying, intruder, intruder.

Peter walked around to the door he'd been ushered out of just hours ago. His eyebrows shot up to his hairline when he found it unlocked. He felt silly as hell when he bellowed above the sound of the dogs, "I'm here and coming through!"

In the whole of his life he'd never seen so many teeth in one place—all canine. "You need to lock your goddamn doors is what you need to do, Dr. Evans!" he shouted.

"You!" She made it sound like he was the devil from hell making a grand entrance.

"Who'd you expect, Sylvester Stallone? You said it was an emergency. I react to emergencies. My mother trained me that way. I brought everything. What's wrong?"

Andi, hands on hips, stared at the man standing in front of her, the dogs circling his feet. She clapped her hands once, and they all lay down, their eyes on the giant towering over them.

"I had to do a caesarean section on Rosie. Her pups were coming out breach. Come here. Mother and puppies are doing just fine, all eight of them. God, eight more mouths to feed." Andi's shoulders slumped as she fought off her tears.

"I'll take two. Three. I love dogs. It won't be so hard. I'm going to meet your price. Three million plus, whatever the plus turns out to be. It's fair. You'll be able to do a lot if you invest wisely. I can recommend a pretty good tax man if you're interested. You might even want to give some thought to taking payments instead of one lump sum. You need to talk to someone. Am I getting girls or boys? Make that four. I'll give one to my grandmother. That's another thing, her cat Hannah is sick. I was going to call you in the morning to ask if you'd look at her. Their regular vet is away on a winter vacation."

"Oh, my. Listen, about this afternoon . . ."

"You don't have to apologize," Peter said.

Andi smiled. "I wasn't going to apologize. I was going to try and explain my circumstances to you. I appreciate you coming back here. It's the thought that counts. Are you serious about the pups?"

Was he? "Hell yes. Told you, I love dogs. Isn't it kind of cold out here for the new mother and my pups?"

"No. Actually, dogs much prefer it to be cooler. I was going to take Rosie into the kitchen, though. I leave the door open, and if the others want to come in, they do. At some point during the night, when I'm sleeping, three or four of them will come in and sleep outside my door. There's usually one outside the bathroom when I shower, too. They're very protective; they know when you're bathing and sleeping you're vulnerable. It's really amazing."

"Bessie was like that. Do you want me to carry the box?"

"Sure. Can I make you some coffee? I was going to have a grilled cheese sandwich. Would you like one or did you have your dinner?"

Peter thought about how he'd pigged out on his grandmother's pot roast. "I'm starved. Coffee sounds good, too. I brought a lot of blankets and towels with me. I thought maybe your heat went out."

"I could really use them. My washer goes all day long, and like everything else in this house, it's getting ready to break down. My furnace is the next thing to go."

Peter's face turned ashen. "Your furnace? Don't you check it? You need to call PSE&G to come and look at it. My parents . . . and my brother and sister died from carbon monoxide poisoning. Turn it off if it's giving you trouble. Use your fireplace. I can bring you electric heaters. Is the fireplace any good?"

Andi stared at the man sitting at her table, a helpless look on her face. "I . . . I'm sorry. I don't know the first thing about the furnace except that it's very old. The fireplace is in good condition; I had it cleaned in September. I'd probably be more at risk using electric heaters; the wiring and the plumbing are . . . old. I guess I just have to take my chances. It's only another two weeks. You said you wanted to . . . start . . . whatever it is you're going to do right after the first of the year."

"Tomorrow when I bring Hannah I'll bring you some of those detectors. I have one in every room in my house. I was away at school when it happened. All you do is plug them in."

"I appreciate that. I won't charge you for Hannah, then."

"Okay, that's fair." He wasn't about to tell her each detector cost eighty-nine dollars. She would need at least four of them for the sprawling house and kennel.

"Want some bacon on your sandwich? Ketchup?"

"Sure."

"I made a pie today. Want a piece?"

Peter nodded. "Your house smells like the house I grew up in. It always smelled like apples and cinnamon. At Christmastime you could get drunk on the smell. Speaking of Christmas, I give a party once a year, would you like to come? I think you'll like my grandmother. It's next Thursday."

"I don't know . . . I hate to leave the animals. I haven't been to a party in so long, I don't think I'll remember how to act. Thank you for asking, though."

"Don't you have a pair of pearls?" he asked, a stupid look on his face.

"What do pearls have to do with it?"

"Your mother's pearls." Jesus, he must have missed something when Sadie was explaining party attire. She was staring at him so intently he felt compelled to explain. "You know, pearls to go with the dress. Your mother's pearls. If you have that, you don't have to worry about anything else. Right? Can I use your bathroom?"

"Upstairs, third door on the right. Don't step on the carpet at the bottom of the steps. Annabelle lies there all the time. She pees on it and I didn't have time to wash it. She chewed all the fringe off the corners. She's getting old, so I can't scold her too much."

Peter bolted from the room. Andi stared after him with puzzled eyes. She scurried into the pantry area where a mirror hung on the back of the door. She winced at her appearance. She didn't look one damn bit better than she had looked earlier. "What you see is what you get," she muttered.

Andi was sliding the sandwiches onto plates when Peter entered the room. "This must have been a nice house at one time."

Andi nodded. "It was a comfortable old house. It fit us. My mother never worried too much about new furniture or keeping up with the neighbors. It was clean and comfortable. Homey. Some houses are just houses. People make homes. Did you know that?"

"Believe it or not, I just realized that same fact today. Every so often I trip down memory lane."

"I don't do that anymore. It's too sad. I don't know how I'm going to walk away from this place. My mother always said home was where your stuff was. Part of me believes it. What's your opinion? By the way, where do you live?"

"In Clark. It's a new, modern house. Decorated by a professional. Color-coordinated, all that stuff. I don't think you'd like it. My grandmother hates it. I don't even like it myself. I try throwing things around, but it still looks the same."

"Maybe some green plants. Green plants perk up a room. You probably need some junk. Junk helps. I'll be throwing a lot away, so you can help yourself."

"Yeah? What kind of junk? My plants die."

"You need to water plants. Get silk ones. All you have to do is go over them with a blow dryer every so often. Junk is junk. Everybody has junk. You pick it up here and there, at a flea market or wherever. When you get tired of it you throw it away and buy new junk."

Peter threw his head back and laughed until his eyes watered. "That's something my grandmother would say. Why are you looking at me like that?"

"I'm sorry. You should laugh more often. You take yourself pretty seriously, don't you?"

"For the most part, I guess I do. What about you?" He leaned across the table as though her answer was the most important thing in the world. She had beautiful eyes with thick lashes. And they were her own, unlike Helen's.

"I've been so busy scrambling to make a go of it, I haven't had the time to dwell on anything. I guess I'm sort of an optimist, but then I'm a pessimist, too, at times. What will be will be. How about some pie? I can warm it up. More coffee?"

"Sure to everything. This is nice. I haven't sat in a kitchen . . . since . . . I left home. We always ate in the kitchen growing up."

"So did we. Are you married?"

"No. Why do you ask? Do you have designs on me?"

"No. I just want to make sure Rosie's pups get a good home. Who's going to take care of them when you work?"

"I already figured that out. I'm going to hire a sitter. I'll have her cook chicken gizzards and livers for them. My mother used to cook for Bessie. She loved it. You're very pretty, Dr. Evans. Why aren't you married?"

"Do you think that's any of your business, Mr. King?"

"As the owner of those dogs, of which I'm taking four, I should know what kind of person you are, marital status included. Well?"

"I was engaged, not that it's any of your business. I wanted to come back here; he didn't. He wanted to work in a ritzy area; I didn't. He was in it for the money. I wasn't. I don't know, maybe he was the smart one."

"No, you were the smart one," Peter said quietly. "It's rare that the heart and mind work in sync. When it does happen, you know it's right."

"Your turn."

Peter shrugged. "I run my grandmother's business. She tells me I'm good at it. She's the only family I have left, and she's up in years. I always . . . take . . . introduce her to the women I, ah, date. I value her opinion. So far she hasn't approved of anyone I've dated. That's okay; she was on the money every single time. Guess I just haven't met the right girl. Or, maybe I'm meant for bachelorhood. Would you like to go out to dinner with me to celebrate our deal?"

"Under other circumstances, I'd say yes, but I have too much to do. I also want to keep my eye on Rosie and the pups. If you like, you can come for dinner tomorrow."

"I'll be here. I'll bring in the towels and blankets and shovel you out before I leave."

"I'll help you. Thanks."

It was one o'clock in the morning when Andi leaned on her shovel, exhaustion showing in every line of her face. "I'm going to sleep like a baby tonight," she panted.

"Yeah, me, too. Tell me, what's it like when you operate on one of the animals, like you did tonight?"

"Awesome. When I saw those pups and when I stitched up Rosie, all the hard years, all the backbreaking work, it was worth every hour of it. Guess you don't get that feeling when you label Raspberry Cheese Louise on your lipsticks."

Suddenly she was in the snow, the giant towering over her. She stretched out her foot, caught him on the ankle and pulled him down in an undignified heap. He kissed her, his mouth as cold and frosty as her own. It was the sweetest kiss of her life. She said so, grinning from ear to ear.

"Sweet?" he asked.

"Uh-huh."

"Didn't make you want to tear your clothes off, huh?"

"You must be kidding. I never do that on a first date."

"This isn't a date." He leered at her.

"I don't do that on pre-dates either. I don't even know you."

"I'll let my hair down tomorrow, and you can *really* get to know me."

"Don't go getting any ideas that I'm easy. And, don't think you're parading me in front of your grandmother either."

"God forbid."

"Good night, Mr. King. You can call me Andi."

"Good night, Dr. Evans. You can call me Peter. What are we having for dinner?"

"Whatever you bring. Tomorrow is bath day. I'm big on fast and easy. What time are you bringing Hannah?"

"How about ten? Our attorney will be out bright and early for you to sign the contract. Is that all right with you?"

"Okay. Good night."

"I enjoyed this evening. Take good care of my dogs."

"I will." Suddenly she didn't want him to go. He didn't seem to want to go either. She watched the 4 by 4 until the red taillights were swallowed in the snow.

He was nice. Actually, he was real nice. And, he was going to give her over three million dollars. Oh, life was looking good.

* * *

The following morning, Andi woke before it was light out. She threw on her robe and raced down the stairs to check on Rosie. "I just want you to know I was having a really, that's as in *really,* delicious dream about Mr. Peter King." She hunched down to check on the new pups, who were sleeping peacefully, curled up against their mother.

While the coffee perked, Andi showered and dressed, taking a few more pains with her dress than usual. Today she donned corduroy slacks and a flannel shirt instead of the fleece-lined sweats she usually wore in the kennel. Today she even blow dried her hair and used the curling iron. She diddled with a jar of makeup guaranteed to confuse anyone interested in wondering if she was wearing it or not. A dab of rouge, a stroke of the eyebrow pencil and she was done. She was almost at the top of the steps when she marched back to her dressing table and spritzed a cloud of mist into the air. She savored the smell, a long-ago present from a friend. She told herself she took the extra pains because it wasn't every day she signed a three-million-plus deal. As she drank her coffee she wondered what the plus part of the contract would net her.

Andi thought about Gertie and her friends under the railroad trestle. Where did they go last night during the storm? Were they warm and safe? As soon as everything was tended to and she checked out Hannah the cat, she would drive into Plainfield and try to locate Gertie and her friends. Now that she had all this money coming to her, she could rent a motel for them until the weather eased up, providing the manager was willing to wait for his money.

The notebook on the kitchen table beckoned. Her list of things to do. Call Realtor, make plans to transport animals. Her friend Mickey had an old school bus he used for camping in the summer. He might lend it to her for a day or so. She could pile Gertie and her friends in the same bus.

Andi's thoughts whirled and raced as she cleaned the dog runs and hosed them out. She set down bowls of kibble and fresh water, tidied up the kennel, sorted through the blankets and towels. The heavy duty machines ran constantly. Her own laundry often piled up for weeks at a time simply because the animals had to come first. She raced back to the kitchen to add a note to her list. Call moving company. She wasn't parting with the crates, the laundry machines or the refrigerator. She was taking everything that belonged to her parents even if it was old and worn-out. The wrecking ball could destroy the house and kennel, but not her *stuff*.

She was on her third cup of coffee when Peter King's attorney arrived. She read over the contract, signed it and promised to take it to her attorney, Mark Fox. Everything was in order. Why delay on signing. The plus, she noticed, amounted to $750,000. That had to mean she had three and three-quarter acres. "Date the check January first. I don't want to have to worry about paying taxes until ninety-seven. Where's the date for construction to begin? Oh, okay, I see it. January 2, 1997. We're clear on that?"

"Yes, Dr. Evans, we're clear on that. Here's my card; have Mr. Fox call me. Mark is the finest real estate attorney in these parts. Give him my regards."

"I'll do that, Mr. Carpenter."

The moment the attorney was out of her parking

lot, Andi added Mark Fox's name to her list of things to do. She crossed her fingers that he worked half days on Saturday. If not, she'd slip the contract, along with a note, through the mail slot and call him Monday morning.

Andi's eyes settled on the clock. Ten minutes until Peter King arrived with his grandmother's cat. She busied herself with phone calls. Ten o'clock came and went. The hands of the clock swept past eleven. Were the roads bad? She called the police station. She was told the roads were in good shape, plowed and sanded. Her eyes were wet when she crouched down next to Rosie. "Guess he just wanted my signature on the contract. My mother always said there was a fool born every minute. Take care of those babies and I'll be back soon."

At ten minutes past twelve, Andi was on Park Avenue, where she dropped the contract through the slot on Mark Fox's door. She backed out of the drive and headed down Park to Raritan and then to Woodland, turning right onto South Avenue, where she thought she would find Gertie and her friends. She saw one lone figure, heavily clad, hunched around a huge barrel that glowed red and warm against the snow-filled landscape. Andi climbed from the truck. "Excuse me, sir, have you seen Gertie?" The man shook his head. "Do you know where I can find her? Where is everyone?" The man shrugged. "I need to get in touch with her. It's very important. If she comes by, will you ask her to call me? I'll give you the quarter for the phone call." She ran back to the truck to fish in the glove compartment for her card, where she scrawled, "Call me. Andi." She handed the card, a quarter and a five-dollar bill to the man. "Get some hot soup and coffee." The man's head bobbed up and down.

Her next stop was Raritan Road and her friend Mickey's house. The yellow bus was parked in his driveway next to a spiffy hunter green BMW.

Mickey was a free spirit, working only when the mood struck him. Thanks to a sizable trust fund, all things were possible for the young man whose slogan was, "Work Is A Killer." She slipped a note under the door when her ring went unanswered. Her watch said it was one-thirty. Time to head for the moving company, where she signed another contract for her belongings to be moved out on December 22nd and taken to storage on Oak Tree Road in Edison. Her last stop was in Metuchen, where she stopped at the MacPherson Agency to ask for either Lois or Tom Finneran, a husband/wife realty team. The amenities over, she said, "Some acreage, a building is a must. It doesn't have to be fancy. I'm going to build what I want later on. Zoning is important. I was thinking maybe Freehold or Cranbury. You guys are the best, so I know you can work something out that will allow me to move in with the animals the first of the year. Have a wonderful holiday."

There were no fresh tire tracks in her driveway and no messages on her machine. "So who cares," she muttered as she stomped her way into the kennel. The kitchen clock said it was three-thirty when she put a pot of coffee on to perk. When the phone shrilled to life she dropped the wire basket full of coffee all over the floor. She almost killed herself as she sprinted across the huge kitchen to grapple with the receiver. Her voice was breathless when she said, "Dr. Evans."

"Andi, this is Gertie. Donald said you were looking for me. Is something wrong?"

"Everything's wrong and everything's right. I was worried about you and your friends out in the cold. I wanted to bring you back here till the weather clears. I signed the contract this morning. For a lot of money. Oh, Gertie, what I can do with that money. You and your friends can come live on my property. I'll build you a little house or a big house. You won't have to live on the street, and you won't get mugged anymore. You can all help with the animals, and I'll even pay you. I'll be able to take in more animals. Oh, God, Gertie, I almost forgot, Rosie had eight puppies. They are so beautiful. You're going to love them. You're quiet, is something wrong?"

"No. I don't want you worrying about me and my friends. I'll tell them about your offer, though. I'll think about it myself. How was . . . that man?"

"Mr. King?"

"Yeah, him."

"Last night I thought he was kind of nice. He came back out here later in the evening and shoveled my parking lot. He was starved, so I gave him a sandwich and we talked. I invited him to dinner tonight. He was supposed to bring his grandmother's cat for me to check and he was a no-show. I even let him kiss me after he pushed me in the snow. You know what, Gertie, I hate men. There's not one you can trust. All he wanted was my signature on that contract. He had this really nice laugh. We shared a few memories. As far as I can tell the only redeeming quality he has is that he loves his grandmother. Oh, oh, the other thing was, he was going to bring me some carbon monoxide things to plug in. He was so forceful I agreed and said I wouldn't charge for Hannah. That's the cat's name. He even invited me to his Christmas party, but he never even told me where he lived. Some invitation, huh? I should show him and turn up in my rubber suit. He acted like he thought I didn't know how to dress and kept mumbling about my mother's pearls. You're still coming for Christmas, aren't you? You said you'd bring all your buddies from the trestle. Gertie, I don't want to spend my last Christmas alone here in this house with just the animals. If they could talk, it would be different. Promise me, okay?"

"I can't promise. I will think about it, though. Why don't you hold those negative thoughts you have for Mr. King on the side. I bet he has a real good explanation."

Andi snorted. "Give me one. Just one. The roads are clear. Alexander Bell invented this wonderful thing called the telephone, and Mr. Sony has this machine that delivers your messages. Nope, the jerk just wanted my signature. I'll never see him again and I don't care. Do you want me to come and get you, Gertie? It's supposed to be really cold tonight."

"We're going to the shelter tonight. Thanks for the offer. Maybe I'll stop by tomorrow. Are the pups really cute?"

"Gorgeous. That's another thing; he said he was taking four, three for him and one for his grandmother. On top of everything else, the man is a liar. I hate liars as much as I hate used car salesmen. You sound funny, Gertie, are you sure you're all right?"

"I'm fine. Maybe I'm catching a cold."

"Now, why doesn't that surprise me? You live on the damn streets. I'll bet you don't even have any aspirin."

"I do so, and Donald has some brandy. I'll talk to you tomorrow, Andi. Thanks for caring about me and my friends. Give Rosie a hug for me."

"Okay, Gertie, take care of yourself."

Andi turned to Rosie, who was staring at her. "Gertie was crying. She's not catching a cold. She's the one who is homeless, and she's the one who always comes through for us. Always. I can't figure that out. She's homeless and she won't let me do anything for her. I hope somebody writes a book about that someday. Okay, bath time!"

Andi ate a lonely TV dinner and some tomato soup as she watched television. She was in bed by nine o'clock. She wanted to be up early so she could begin going through the attic and packing the things she wanted to take to storage. If her pillow was damp, there was no one to notice.

Less than ten miles away, Peter King sat on the sofa with his grandmother, trying his best to console her. He felt frightened for the first time in his life. His zesty grandmother was falling apart, unable to stop crying. "I thought she would live forever. I really did. My God, Peter, how I loved that animal. I want her ashes. Every single one of them. You told them to do that, didn't you?"

"Of course I did, Sadie. I'm going to bring them by tomorrow. Do you want—"

"Do not touch anything, Peter. I want all her things left just the way they were. I wish I'd spent more time with her, cuddled her more. Sometimes she didn't want that; she wanted to be alone. She was so damn independent. Oh God, what am I going to do without Hannah? She kept me going."

"It can't be any worse than when Bessie died. I still think about that," Peter said past the lump in his throat.

"She just died in her sleep and I was sleeping so soundly last night. What if she needed me and I didn't hear her?"

"Shhhh, she just closed her eyes and drifted off. That's how you have to think of it."

"Don't even think about getting me another cat. I won't have it, Peter. Are you listening to me?"

"I always listen to you, Sadie."

"Did you call Dr. Evans?"

"No. She'll understand. She loves animals. She's nice, Sadie. I really liked her. She forced a sandwich on me and I ate it to be polite. I shoveled her parking lot and pushed her in the snow." At Sadie's blank stare, his voice grew desperate. "I kissed her, Sadie, and she said it was a sweet kiss. Sweet! It's too soon to tell, but I think she might be *the one*. Did you hear me, Sadie?"

"I'm not deaf."

"I invited her to the party, but she doesn't want to come. I screwed up the pearl thing. She thought I was nuts." Sadie's eyes rolled back in her head. "Okay," Peter roared, "that's enough, Sadie, pets die every day of the week. People and children grieve, but they don't go over the edge. You're teetering and I won't have it."

Sadie blinked. "Oh, stuff it, Peter. This is me you're talking to. I need to do this for one day, for God's sake. Tomorrow I'll be fine. Why can't I cry, moan and wail? Give me one damn good reason why I can't. I just want to sit here and snivel. You need to make amends to that young veterinarian, and don't go blaming me. I didn't ask you to stay here with me. You didn't even like Hannah and she hated you. Hannah hated all men. I never did figure that out. Go home, Peter. I'm fine, and I do appreciate you coming here and staying with me. It might be wise to send the young lady an invitation. I'd FedEx it if I were you."

"Do you want me to call that guy Donald you're always talking about?"

"Of course not. He's . . . out and about . . . and very hard to reach."

"Why don't you get him a beeper for Christmas."

"Go!"

"I'm gone."

Peter had every intention of going home, but his car seemed to have a mind of its own. Before he knew it he was on the road leading into the driveway of Andi's clinic. What the hell time was it anyway? Ten minutes past ten. It was so quiet and dark he felt uneasy. Only a dim light inside the clinic could be seen from the road. The rest of the house was in total darkness. If he got out to leave a note, the animals would start to bark and Andi would wake up. Did he want that? Of course not, his mother had raised him to be a gentleman. He felt an emptiness in the pit of his stomach as he drove away. He couldn't ever remember being this lonely in his entire life. Tomorrow was another day. He'd call her as soon as the sun came up, and maybe they could go sleigh riding in Roosevelt Park. Maybe it was time to act like kids again. Kids who fell in love when they were done doing all those wonderful kid things. One day out of their lives, and it was a Sunday. Just one day of no responsibilities. He crossed his fingers that it would work out the way he wanted.

Andi rolled over, opening one eye to look at the clock on her nightstand. Six o'clock. How still and quiet it was. Did she dare stay in bed? Absolutely not. She walked over to the window and raised the shade. It was snowing. Damn, her back was still sore. Maybe she could call one of the companies that plowed out small businesses.

She was brushing her teeth when the phone rang. Around the bubbles and foam in her mouth, she managed to say, "Dr. Evans."

"This is Peter King. I'm calling to apologize and to invite you to go sleigh riding. Hannah died in her sleep. I spent the day with my grandmother. I'm really sorry. Are you there?"

"Wait." Andi rushed into the bathroom to rinse her mouth. She sprinted back to the phone. "I was brushing my teeth."

"Oh."

"You should have called me. It only takes a minute to make a phone call." Hot damn, he had a reason. Maybe . . .

"I came by last night around ten, but everything was dark, and I didn't want to stir up the animals so I went home."

He came by. That was good. He said he was sorry. He was considerate. "I went to bed early. It's snowing."

"I know. Let's go sledding in Roosevelt Park. My

parents used to take me there when I was a kid. I have a Flexible Flyer." He made it sound like he had the Holy Grail.

"No kidding. I have one, too. Somewhere. Probably up on the rafters in the garage."

"Does that mean you'll go? We could go to the Pancake House on Parsonage Road for breakfast."

"Will you pull me up the hill?"

"Nope."

"I hate climbing the hill. Going down is so quick. Okay, I'll go, but I have things to do first. How about eleven o'clock?"

"That's good. What do you have to do? Do you need help?"

This was looking better and better. "Well, I have to clean the dog runs and change the litter boxes. I was going to go through the things in the attic. You could see if you can locate someone to plow my parking lot and driveway. Don't even think about offering. I know your back is as sore as mine, and my legs are going to be stiff if we climb that hill more than once. It's going to take me at least two hours to find my rubber boots. Is your grandmother all right? I have some kittens if you're interested."

"It was a real bad day. She doesn't want another cat. Hannah is being cremated so she'll have the ashes. She'll be okay today. Sadie is real gutsy. I know she'll love it when I give her one of Rosie's pups. She'll accept the dog but not a cat. I understand that."

"Yes, so do I."

"What did you have for supper last night? I'm sorry about standing you up. I mean that."

"Tomato soup, a TV dinner and a stale donut. If you do it again, it's all over." She was flirting. God.

She was flirting with him. Peter felt his chest puff out. "Bundle up."

"Okay. See you later."

"You bet. Don't get your sled down; I'll do that."

"Okay." A gentleman. Hmmnn.

Peter kicked the tire of his Range Rover, every curse known to man spitting through his lips. How could a $50,000 year-old truck have a dead battery? He looked at his watch and then at the elegant Mercedes Benz sitting next to it. The perfect vehicle to go sledding. "Damn it to hell!" he muttered.

He was stomping through the house looking for his keys when the doorbell rang. Expecting to see the paperboy, he opened the door, his hand in his pants pocket looking for money. "Helen!"

"Peter! I brought breakfast," she said, dangling a Dunkin' Donuts bag under his nose, "and the *New York Times*. I thought we could curl up in front of a fire and spend a lazy day. Together."

He wanted to push her through the door, to slap the donut bag out of her hand and scatter the paper all over the lawn. What did he ever see in this heavily made up woman whose eyelashes were so long they couldn't be real. "I think one of your eyelashes is coming off. Sorry, Helen, I have other plans. I'm going sledding."

"Sledding! At your age!" She made it sound like he was going to hell on a sled.

"Yeah," he drawled. "Your other eyelash is . . . loose. Well, see you around."

"Peterrrrr," she cried as he closed the door.

He was grinning from ear to ear as he searched the living room, dining room and foyer for his keys. He finally found them on the kitchen counter right where he'd left them last night. She really did wear false eyelashes like Sadie said. He laughed aloud when he remembered the open-toed shoes she had on. "My crazy days," he muttered as he closed the kitchen door behind him.

In the car, backing out of the driveway, he realized his heart was pounding. Certainly not because of Helen. He was going to spend the whole day with Andrea Evans doing kid things. He was so excited he pressed the power button on his car phone and then the number one, which was Sadie's number. When he heard her voice he said, "Want to go sled riding? I'll pull you up the hill. I'm taking Dr. Evans. You won't believe this, but she has a Flexible Flyer, too. So, do you want to come?"

"I think I'll pass and watch a football game. Don't forget to bring Hannah's ashes. I don't want to spend another night without her. I don't care, Peter, if you think I'm crazy. Be sure you don't break your neck. Are you aware that it's snowing outside? I thought people went sled riding when it *stopped* snowing."

"I don't think you're crazy at all. I know it's snowing. I think there's at least three inches of fresh snow. You know how you love a white Christmas. I'll be sure not to break my neck, and I think you can go sledding whenever you want. Mr. Mortimer said I could pick up the ashes after five this afternoon. I'll see you sometime this evening."

"Peter, does this mean you're . . . interested in Dr. Evans?"

"She's a real person, Sadie. Helen stopped by as I was leaving—I'm talking to you on the car phone— and she had open-toed shoes on, and both her eye-lashes were loose at the ends. How could I not have seen those things, Sadie?"

"Because you weren't looking, Peter. Do you think Dr. Evans is interested in you?"

"She agreed to go sledding. She wasn't even mad about yesterday. I like her, Sadie. A lot."

"I love June weddings. Six months, Peter. You have to commit by six months or cut her loose. Women her age don't need some jerk taking up their time if you aren't serious."

"How do you know her age?"

"Well . . . I don't, but you said she put herself through vet school and the whole education process took ten years. That should put her around thirty or so."

"I don't remember telling you that."

"That's because you were rattled over Helen. It's all right, Peter, I get forgetful, too, sometimes. Now, go and have a wonderful time."

Peter pressed the end and power buttons. He de-cided his grandmother was defensive sounding be-cause of Hannah. He wished the next eight weeks were over so he could present her with one of Rosie's pups.

Peter was so deep in thought he almost missed the turnoff to the Evans Kennel. He jammed on his brakes, the back end of his car fishtailing across the road. He took a deep breath, cursing the fancy car again. Shaken, he crawled into the parking lot and parked the car. He wondered again if the Chevy pickup actually worked.

"I saw that," Andi trilled. "It's a good thing there was no one behind you. Where's your truck?"

"Dead battery."

"We can take my truck. It's in tip-top shape. Turns over every time. No matter what the weather is. It was my dad's prized possession. The heater works fine and we can put our sleds in the back." Andi dangled a set of car keys in front of him. She was laughing at him, and he didn't mind one damn bit. "Those boots have to go. When was the last time you went sled riding?"

"Light-years ago. These boots are guaranteed to last a lifetime."

"Perhaps they will. The question is, will they keep your feet dry? The answer is no. I can loan you my father's Wellingtons. Will you be embarrassed to wear yellow boots?"

"Never!" Peter said dramatically. "Does the rest of me meet with your approval?"

Andi tilted her head to the side. "Ski cap, muffler, gloves . . . Well, those gloves aren't going to do anything for your hands. Don't you have ski gloves?"

"I did, but I couldn't find them. Do you have extras?"

"Right inside the yellow boots. I figured you for a leather man. I'm a mitten girl. I still have the mittens my mother knitted for me when I was a kid. They still fit, too. When you go sled riding you need a pair and a spare. I bet you didn't wax the runners on your sled either."

"I did so!"

"Prove it." Andi grinned.

"All right, I didn't. It was all I could do to get the cobwebs off."

"Come on," Andi said, dragging him by the arm into the garage. Neither noticed a sleek, amber-colored Mercury Sable crawl by, the driver craning her neck for a better look into the parking lot.

"Here's the boots. They should fit. I'm bringing extra thermal socks for both of us, extra gloves and mittens. There's nothing worse than cold hands and feet. I lived for one whole winter in Minnesota without central heat. All I had was a wood-burning fireplace."

"Why?"

"It was all I could afford. I survived. Do they fit?"

"Perfectly. You should be very proud of yourself, Andi."

"I am. My parents weren't rich like yours. Dad wasn't a businessman. There's so much money on the books that was never paid. He never sent out bills or notices. I'm kind of like him, I guess."

"My parents weren't rich. My grandmother is the one with the money. My dad was a draftsman; my mother was a nurse. You're right, though; I never had to struggle. Did it make you a better person?"

"I like to think so. When you're cold and hungry, character doesn't seem important. You are what you are. Hard times just bring out the best and worst in a person. Okay, your runners are ready for a test run."

"Do you ski?"

"Ha! That's a rich person's sport. No. I'm ready."

"Me, too," Peter said, clomping along behind her.

"You look good in yellow," Andi giggled.

"My favorite color," Peter quipped.

"That's what my mother said when she presented my father with those boots. The second thing she said was they'll never wear out. My dad wore them proudly. How's your grandmother today?"

"Better. I promised to stop by this evening with Hannah's ashes. My grandmother is a very strong woman. She started King Cosmetics in her kitchen years ago after my grandfather died. I'd like you to meet her."

"I'd like that. Do you want to drive or shall I?"

"I'll drive. Sleds in the back," he said, tossing in both Flexible Flyers.

An hour later they were hurtling down the hill, whooping and hollering, their laughter ringing in the swirling snow.

On the second trek up the hill, Peter said, "Have you noticed we're practically the only two people here except for those three kids who are using pieces of cardboard to slide down the hill?"

"That's because we're crazy. Cardboard's good, so is a shower curtain. You can really get some speed with a shower curtain. A bunch of us used to do that in Minnesota."

Peter clenched his fists tightly as he felt a wave of jealousy river through him. He wanted Andi to slide down a hill on a shower curtain with him, not some other guy, and he knew it had been a guy on the shower curtain next to Andi. He asked.

"Yeah." He waited for her to elaborate, but she didn't.

"Hey, mister, do you want to trade?"

Peter looked at Andi, and she looked at him. "The cardboard is big enough for both of us to sit on. Wanna give it a shot?" he asked.

"Sure. You sit in the front, though, in case we hit a tree."

"Okay, kid." He accepted their offer, then turned to Andi. "Did you notice they waited till we dragged these sleds to the top of the hill?" Peter hissed.

"I don't blame them. I think this is my last run. My legs feel numb."

"Sissy," Peter teased. "Cardboard's easy to drag. We've only been here two hours."

"It seems like forever," Andi said. "I can't feel my feet anymore. How about you?"

"Hey, mister, Where'd you get them yellow boots?" one of the kids asked.

"Macy's. Neat, huh?"

"They look shitty," the kid said.

"That, too. You kids go first and we'll follow."

"Nah, you go first. You might fall off and we'll stop and pick you up. You might break a leg or something. You're old."

Peter settled himself on the slice of cardboard that said Charmin Tissue. "Hang on, Andi, and sit up straight."

They were off. Andi shrieked and Peter bellowed as they sailed down the steep hill. Midway down, the cardboard slid out from under them. They toppled into the snow, rolling the rest of the way down the hill. The kids on the sleds passed them, waving and shouting wildly. Andi rolled up against Peter, breathless, her entire body covered in snow.

"Now *that* was an experience," Peter gasped as he reached for Andi's arm to make sure she was all right.

"I feel like I'm dead. Are we?"

"No. Those little shits are taking off with our sleds!" Peter gasped again.

"Who cares. I couldn't chase them if my life depended on it. Every kid needs a sled. Let them have them."

"Okay. Are you all right?"

"No. I hurt. This wasn't as much fun as I thought it would be. God, I must be getting old. My eyebrows are frozen to my head. They crunch. Do yours?"

"Yep. C'mon, let's get in the truck and go home. The first run was fun. We should have quit after that." He was on his feet, his hand outstretched to pull Andi to her feet. "Ah, I bet if I kissed your eyebrows they'd melt."

"Never mind my damn eyebrows, kiss my mouth, it's frozen."

"Hmmmnn. Aaahhh, oh, yes," Andi said later.

"Was that *sweet?* I have a kiss that's a real wake-up call."

"Oh, no, that one . . . sizzled. Let's try it out," Andi said.

"Oh, look, they're kissing. Yuk. Here's your sleds, mister."

"I thought you stole those sleds. Your timing is incredible. Go away, you can have the sleds."

"My mother ain't never gonna believe you gave us these sleds. You gotta write us a note and sign your name."

"Do what he says." Andi giggled as she headed for the truck, and Peter hastily penned a note.

"Guess you're gonna have to wait for my wake-up call," he said when he caught up to her.

"How long?"

Peter threw his hands up in the air. "I have all the time in the world. You just let me know when you're ready."

"Uh-huh. Okay. That sounds good. I had a good

time today, Peter, I really did. I felt like a kid for a little while. Thanks. Time to get back to reality and the business at hand."

"How about if I drop you off, go pick up Hannah's ashes, take them to my grandmother and come back. We can have dinner together. I can pick up some steaks and stuff. I want to get those carbon monoxide units for you, too."

"Sounds good."

"It's a date, then?"

"Yep, it's a date."

"I'll see you around seven-thirty."

Inside the kennel the animals greeted their owner with sharp barks and soft whines, each vying for her attention. She sat down on the floor and did her best to fondle each one of them. "I smell worse than you guys when you get wet," she said, shrugging out of her wet clothes. "Supper's coming up!"

With the door closed to the outside waiting room, Andi paid no mind to the excessive barking and whining from the animals; her thoughts were on Peter King and spending the night with him. She had at least two hours, once the animals were fed, to shower and change into something a little more *romantic*.

Outside, Helen Palmer watched the dinner preparations through the front window. When she was certain no one else was in attendance, her eyes narrowed. She walked back to the office, a manila folder in hand, the detective's report on one Dr. Andrea Evans that she'd taken from Peter King's car when she'd backtracked from Roosevelt Park where she'd spied on her old lover.

She eyed the messy desk with the pile of bills. On

tiptoe, she walked around the back of the desk to stare down at the piles of bills. With one long, polished nail, she moved the contract to the side so she could see it better. Three million, seven hundred and fifty thousand dollars! For this dump! She tiptoed back to the door and let herself out. Miss Girl Next Door would know there was no manila envelope on the desk. Better to drop it outside where Peter's car had been parked. "She'll think it fell out when he got out of the car. Perfect!" she muttered.

Her feet numb with cold, Helen walked out of the driveway to her car parked on the shoulder of the road in snow up to her ankles. She'd probably get pneumonia and all of this would be for naught. One way or another she was going to get Peter King for herself.

Inside the house, Andi climbed the stairs to the second floor to run a bath. She poured lavishly from a plastic bag filled with gardenia bath salts. It was the only thing she consistently splurged on. She tried to relax, but the dogs' incessant barking set her nerves on edge. What in the world was wrong with them today? Maybe they were picking up on her own tenseness in regard to Peter King. And she was tense.

"I hardly know the man and here I sit, speculating on what it would be like to go to bed with him." The bathtub was the perfect milieu for talking to herself. She loved this time of day when she went over her problems, asked questions of herself aloud and then answered them in the same manner. She wondered aloud about what kind of bed partner he would make. "Shy? No way. Lusty? To a degree. Wild and passionate? I can only hope. Slam, bam, thank you, ma'am?

Not in a million years. A man with slow hands like the Pointer Sisters sang about. Oh, yeahhhhh."

Puckered, hyped and red-skinned, Andi climbed from the tub, towel dried and dressed. She fluffed out her hair, added makeup sparingly. The gardenia scent stayed with her.

Andi eyed the bed. When was the last time she changed the sheets? She couldn't remember. She had the bed stripped and changed inside of eight minutes. "Just in case."

Downstairs, the dogs milled around inside the house, running back and forth to the waiting room and her tiny office area. Susy, a long-haired, fat, black cat, hissed and snarled by the door, her claws gouging at the wood. "Okay, okay, I get the message, something's wrong. Let's do one spin around the parking lot. When I blow this whistle, everyone lines up and comes indoors. Allow me to demonstrate." She blew three short blasts. "Everybody line up! That's the drill. If you don't follow my instructions, you're out for the night. Let's go!" She stood to the side as the dogs and cats stampeded past her. She'd done this before, and it always worked because Beggin Strips were the reward when everyone was indoors. She waited ten minutes, time for everyone to lift their leg or squat, depending on gender. The floodlights blazed down in the parking lot, creating shimmering crystals on the piled-high snow. Now it was speckled with yellow spots in every direction.

Andi blew three sharp blasts on the whistle as she stepped aside. One by one, the animals fell into a neat line and marched to the door. "C'mon Annabelle, you can do it!" Andi called encouragingly. "You can't sit

down in the middle of the parking lot. All right, all
right, I'll carry you. Move it, Bizzy," she said to a cat
with two tails. The cat strolled past her disdainfully.
Andi gave one last blast on the whistle for any stragglers. Satisfied that all the animals were indoors, she
walked over to Annabelle to pick her up. She noticed
the folder then and picked it up. She stuck it under
her arm as she bent to pick up the beagle. "I swear,
Annabelle, you weigh a ton."

Inside, she did one last head count before she doled
out the treats, the folder still under her arm. "My time
now!"

Andi did her best not to look at the clock as she set
the table and layered tinfoil on the ancient broiler.
Candles? No, that would be too much. Wineglasses?
She looked with disgust at the dust on the crystal.
How was it possible that she'd been here almost a
year and a half and hadn't used the glasses, much less
washed them? That was going to change now. The
wineglasses were special, and there were only two of
them. She remembered the day her father had presented the Tiffany glasses to her mother and said,
"When we have something special to celebrate we'll
use these glasses." To her knowledge, nothing special
had ever occurred. Well, tonight was special. She
liked the way they sparkled under the domed kitchen
light. Peter probably used glasses like this to gargle
with every day.

He was late. Again. Her insides started to jump
around. What should she do now to kill time? What if
he didn't show up? "Oh, shit," she muttered. No point
in letting him think she was sitting here biting her
nails waiting for him. Only desperate women did
things like that. In the blink of an eye she had the

dishes back in the cabinet and the wineglasses in their felt sacks with the gold drawstrings. She re-folded the tablecloth and stuck it in the drawer. She eyed the manila folder as she slid the drawer closed. It must have fallen out of Peter's car because it wasn't hers and no one else had been at the kennel today.

Eight o'clock.

Andi moved the folder. She moved it a second time, then a third time. She watched it teeter on the edge of the kitchen counter. She brushed by it and it slid to the floor. Now she'd have to pick up the papers and put them back in the folder. When she saw her name in heavy black letters on the first page, she sucked in her breath. Her heart started to pound in her chest as she gathered up the seven-page report. Twenty minutes later, after reading the report three times, Andi stacked the papers neatly in the folder. From the kitchen drawer she ripped off a long piece of gray electrical tape. She taped it to the folder and plastered it on the door of the clinic. She locked the doors and slid the dead bolt into place. She turned off all the lights from the top of the steps. Only a dim hall light glowed in the house.

She made her way to the attic. The small window under the eaves was the perfect place to watch the parking lot. Sneaky bastard. The report chronicled her life, right down to her bank balance, her student aid, her credit report and her relationships with men. Her cheeks flamed when she remembered one inci-dent where her landlady said Tyler Mitchel arrived early in the evening and didn't leave for three days. The line in bold letters that said *"The lady uses a di-aphragm"* was what sent her flying to the attic. That could only mean someone had been here in her house going through her things. Unless Tyler or Jack or maybe Stan volunteered the information.

"You son of a bitch!"

Headlights arched into the driveway. Andi's eyes narrowed. Down below, the animals went into their howling, snarling routine.

Andi nibbled on her thumbnail as she watched Peter walk back to his car, the folder in his hand. Her phone rang on the second floor. She knew it was Peter calling on his car phone. She sat down on the window seat and cried. The phone continued to ring. Like she cared. "Go to hell, Mr. Lipstick!"

When there were no more tears, Andi wiped her eyes on the sleeve of her shirt. She had things to do. Empty cartons beckoned. She worked industriously until past midnight, packing and sorting, refusing to go to the window. Tears dripped down her cheeks from time to time. At one-thirty she crept downstairs for a soda. She carried it back to the attic and gulped at it from her perch on the window seat. He was still there. He was still there at four in the morning when she called a halt to her activities.

Andi curled herself into a ball on top of the bed with a comforter where she cried herself to sleep. She woke at seven and raced to the window. "We'll see about that!"

With shaking hands, Andi dialed the police, identified herself and said in a cold, angry voice, "I want you to send someone here right now and remove a . . . person from my parking lot. He's been sitting there all night. You tell him he's not to dare set foot on my property until January. If I have to sign something, I'll come down to the police station. Right now. I want you to come here right now. My animals are going crazy. I have a gun and a license to use it," she said dramatically. "Thank you."

Her heart thundering in her chest, Andi raced back to the attic. She knew the dirt and grime on the window prevented Peter from seeing her. She clenched her teeth when she saw the patrol car career into her driveway, the red and blue lights flashing ominously. She just knew he was going to give the officers a box of Raspberry Cheese Louise lipsticks for their wives.

Five minutes later the Mercedes backed out of her parking lot. It didn't look like any lipstick had changed hands. "He's probably going to mail them," she snorted as she raced down the steps to answer the door, the din behind her so loud she could barely hear the officer's voice.

"Do you want to file a complaint?"

"You're damn right I do," Andi screamed.

"All right, come down to the station this afternoon."

"I'll be there."

Andi closed the door and locked it. She tended to the animals, showered and ate some cornflakes before she resumed her packing. "You are dead in the water, Mr. Lipstick," she sniveled as she started to clean out her closet and dresser drawers.

At ten o'clock she called the Finnerans. "You really and truly found something in Freehold! . . . I can move in on Sunday? That's Christmas Eve! . . . Move-in condition! Fifteen acres! A heated barn for the animals. God must be watching over me. How much is fenced in? . . . Great. That's a fair price. . . . The owners are in California. . . . I knew you could do it. . . . Okay. I'll drive down this afternoon and look at it. . . . The last of their things will be out by Saturday. I'm very grateful, Tom." She copied down directions. Her sigh of relief was so loud and long she had trouble taking a deep breath.

Andi's second call was to her friend Mickey. "Can you bring the bus by today? Thanks, Mickey. I owe you one."

Her third call was to her attorney, who admonished her up one side and down the other for signing the contract before he had a chance to go over it. "You're lucky everything is in order. Congratulations. I'm going to set up a payout structure you'll be able to live with." Andi listened, made notes, gave the attorney her new address and told him to check with information for her new phone number.

The phone started to ring the moment she hung up from the attorney. The answering machine clicked on. If it was a patient she'd pick up. A hang up. Mr. Lipstick. "Invade my privacy, my life, ha! Only low-life scum do things like that. Well, you got your property, so you don't have to continue with this charade. It doesn't say much for me that I was starting to fall for your charms." Her eyes started to burn again. She cuddled a gray cat close to her chest, the dogs circling her feet. "So I made a mistake. We can live with it. We'll laugh all the way to the bank. The new rule is, we don't trust any man, ever again."

The elaborate silver service on the mahogany table gleamed as Sadie King poured coffee. "You look like you slept in a barn, Peter. Calm down; stop that frantic pacing and tell me what happened. You've never had a problem being articulate before. So far all I have been able to gather is someone stepped on your toes. Was it Dr. Evans? I'm a very good listener, Peter."

"Yesterday was so perfect it scared me. She felt it, too, I could tell. Somehow, that goddamn investigative report fell out of my car and she found it. When I went back later for dinner, after I left you, she had it taped to the door. Obviously she read it. I called on the car phone, I banged on the door, but she didn't want any part of me. I sat in her parking lot all night long. This morning the police came and ran me off her property. Their advice was to write her a letter and not to go back or they'd run me off. I think I'm in love with her, Sadie. I was going to tell her that last night. I think . . . thought she was starting to feel the same way. My stomach tightens up when she laughs and her laughter shines in her eyes. She gave me her father's boots that were bright yellow, and his gloves. She's so down to earth, so real. I even started to wonder how our kids would look. What should I do? How can I make her understand?"

"A letter isn't such a bad idea. You could enclose it with the invitation to your Christmas party and send it Federal Express or have a messenger deliver it. I'd opt for the messenger because he could deliver it today. If you choose Federal Express she won't get it until tomorrow."

"What's the use, Sadie? I don't blame her. Jesus, the guy even . . . a diaphragm is pretty goddamn personal. I didn't want that kind of stuff. I didn't ask for it either. All I wanted was her financials and a history of the property. I have that same sick feeling in the pit of my stomach I used to get when I was a kid and did something wrong. I could never put anything over on my mother, and Andi is the same way."

"There must be a way for you to get her to listen to you. Apologies, when they're heartfelt, are usually pretty good. Try calling her again."

"I've done that. Her answering machine comes on. I know she's there listening, but she won't pick up. I told you, I don't blame her."

"Maybe you could disguise yourself and ride up on a motorcycle with . . . someone's animal and pretend . . . you know, it will get you in the door. She'll have to listen if you're face-to-face."

"Sadie, that's probably the worst idea you ever came up with. Andi Evans is an in-your-face person. She'll call the cops. They already gave me a warning. I don't want my ass hauled off to jail. They print stuff like that in the papers. How's that going to look?"

Sadie threw her hands up in the air. "Can you come up with a better idea?"

"No. I'm fresh out of ideas. I have to go home to shower and shave. Then I have to go to the office. I have a business to run. I'll stop by on my way home from the office." Peter kissed his grandmother good-bye, his face miserable.

Sadie eyed the urn with Hannah's ashes on the mantel. "Obviously, Hannah, I have to take matters into my own hands. Men are so good at screwing things up, and it's always a woman who has to get them out of their messes. I miss you, and no, I'm not going to get maudlin. I now have a mission to keep me busy."

Sadie dusted her hands before she picked up the phone. "Marcus, bring the car around front and make sure you have my . . . *things.* Scotch Plains. The weather report said the roads are clear." She replaced the receiver.

"They're meant for one another. I know this in my heart. Therefore, it's all right for me to meddle," Sadie mumbled as she slipped into her faux fur coat. "I'm going to make this right or die trying."

Andi had the door of the truck open when she saw Gertie picking her way over the packed-down snow. "Gertie, wait, I'll help you. If you tell me you walked all the way from Plainfield, I'm going to kick you all the way back. You're too old to be trundling around in this snow. What if you fall and fracture your hip? Then what? Where's your shopping cart?"

"Donald's watching it. I wanted to see Rosie and her pups. Can I, Andi?"

"Of course. Listen, I have some errands to run. Do you want to stay until I get back? I can drive you home after that."

"Well, sure."

"Rosie's in the kitchen, and the tea's still hot in the pot. Make yourself at home. I might be gone for maybe . . . three hours, depending on the roads. You'll wait?"

"Of course."

"Gertie, don't answer the phone."

"What if it's a patient?" Gertie asked fretfully.

"If it is, you'll hear it on the machine. Pick up and refer them to the clinic on Park Avenue. My offices are closed as of this morning. I called the few patients I have and told them."

"All right."

"I'll see you by mid-afternoon."

Ninety minutes later, Andi pulled her truck alongside Tom Finneran's white Cadillac. "Oh, it's wonderful, Tom! The snow makes it look like a fairyland. I love the old trees. Quick, show me around."

"Everything is in tip-top shape. Move-in condition, Andi. The owners' things are packed up ready for the mover. All the walls and ceilings were freshly painted a month ago. There's new carpet everywhere, even upstairs. Three bathrooms. A full one downstairs. Nice modern kitchen, appliances are six years old. The roof is nine years old and the furnace is five years old. The plumbing is good, but you do have a septic tank because you're in the country. Taxes are more than reasonable. I have to admit the road leading in here is a kidney crusher. You might want to think about doing something to it later on. Fill the holes with shale or something. It's a farmhouse, and I for one love old farmhouses. A lot of work went into this house at one time. Young people today don't appreciate the old beams and pegs they used for nails back then."

"I love it," Andi said enthusiastically.

"The owner put down carpeting for warmth. Underneath the carpeting you have pine floors. It was a shame to cover them up, but women today want beige carpets. The blinds stay, as do the lighting fixtures and all the appliances. You'll be more than comfortable. Take your time and look around. I'll wait here for you. The owner agreed to an end of January closing, so you'll be paying rent until that time."

"It's just perfect, Tom. Now, show me the barn."

"That's what you're really going to love. It's warm and there's a mountain of hay inside on the second floor or whatever they call it in barns. Good electricity, plumbing, sinks. There's an old refrigerator, too, and it works. The stalls are still intact. You can do what you want with them. There's a two-car garage and a shed for junk. The owner is leaving the lawn mower, leaf blower and all his gardening stuff. Any questions?"

"Not a one. Where do I sign?"

"On the dotted line. You can move in on Sunday at any time. I probably won't see you till the closing, so good luck. Oh, Lois took care of calling the water company, PSE&G and the phone company. Everything will be hooked up first thing Monday morning. You can reimburse us at the closing for the deposits."

Andi hugged the Realtor. She had to remember to send him a present after she moved in.

The clock on the mantel was striking five when Andi walked through the doors of the kennel. "I'm home," she called.

Gertie was sitting at the kitchen table with three of the pups in her lap. "Rosie is keeping her eye on me. It almost makes me want to have a home of my own. Did you give them names?"

"Not yet. Did anyone call?" Andi asked nonchalantly.

"Mr. King called; his message is on the machine. He sounded . . . desperate."

"And well he should. Let me tell you what that . . . lipstick person did, Gertie. Then you tell me what you think I should do. I hate men. I told you that before, and then I let my guard down and somehow he . . . what he did . . . was . . . he sneaked in. I let him kiss me and I kissed him back and told him I liked it. Do you believe that!"

Gertie listened, her eyes glued to Andi's flushed face.

"Well?"

"I agree, it was a terrible thing to do. Andi, I've lived a long time. Things aren't always the way they seem. Everything has two sides. Would it hurt you to hear him out? What harm is there in listening to him? Then, if you want to walk away, do so. Aren't you afraid that you're always going to wonder if there was an explanation? You said he was nice, that you liked him. He sounded like a sterling person to me."

"Listen to him so he can lie to my face? That's the worst kind of man, the one who looks you in the eye and lies. That's what used car salesmen do. Sometimes lawyers and insurance men do it, too. I called the police on him this morning. He sat in my parking lot all night, Gertie."

"How do you know that?"

"Because I watched him. You know what else? I even changed the sheets on the damn bed because I thought . . . well, what I . . . oh, hell, it doesn't matter."

"Obviously it does matter. Your eyes are all red. You really sat up watching him sit in your parking lot! That's ridiculous!"

"I was packing my stuff in the attic. I looked out from time to time," Andi said defensively. "I guess he wasn't who I thought he was. I swear to God, Gertie, this is it. I'm not sticking my neck out, ever again."

"Don't businesspeople do things like that, Andi? I'm not taking sides here, but think for a moment; if the situation was reversed, wouldn't you want to get the best deal for your company?"

"Does that mean he and his company need to know about my love life, that I use a diaphragm? No, it does not. He had no damn right."

"Maybe it's the detective's fault and not Mr. King's. Maybe Mr. King told him to do a . . . whatever term they use, on you, and the man took it further than he was supposed to. That's something to think about," Gertie said, a desperate look on her face.

"Whose side are you on, Gertie? It sounds like you favor that war-paint king."

"I believe in giving everyone a fair hearing."

"Is that why you refuse to call your children and live in a ditch?"

"It's not the same thing, and you know it."

"There's no greater sin in life than betrayal. I could . . . can forgive anything but betrayal."

Gertie's tone turned fretful. "Don't say that, Andi. There's usually a reason for everything if you care enough to find out what it is. I've lived a long life, my dear, and along the way I learned a few things. An open mind is a person's greatest asset in this world."

"I don't want to hear it, Gertie, and my mind just shut down. I know his type; he was just playing with me in case I changed my mind about selling. I would have gone to bed with him, too. That's the part that bothers me. Then, one minute after the closing, it would be good-bye Andi."

"He's not like that at all, Andi. You're so wrong." At Andi's strange look she hastened to explain. "What I meant was . . . from everything you said, from what I've seen in the papers, Mr. King is a gentleman. You said so yourself. I really should be going. Someone's pulling into your driveway. I'm going to walk, Andi. I've been cooped up too long in the shelter." Gertie held up her hand. "No, no, I do not want a ride. You still have packing to do. Thanks for the tea and for letting me hold these precious bundles. When are you going to name them?"

"I was thinking of giving them all Christmas names.

You know, Holly, Jingle, et cetera. Just let me get my coat; it's too cold, and there's ice everywhere. I refuse to allow you to walk home, wherever home may be today."

"I'm walking and that's final," Gertie said, backing out the door. "Besides, I have some thinking I have to do. I do thank you for caring about this old woman. I'll be fine. It's a messenger, Andi, with a letter. I'll wait just a minute longer to make sure it isn't an emergency."

Andi stared after her, a helpless look on her face. She knew how important it was for the seniors to feel independent. She reached for the envelope and ripped at it. "Ha!" she snorted. "It's an invitation to Mr. Lipstick's Christmas party."

"Guess that makes it official. Change your mind and go. Is there a note?"

"Yep. It says he's sorry about the report and all he had requested were the financials, none of the personal stuff. He said he meant to destroy it once he met me, but time got away from him. He also says he had more fun yesterday than he's had in twenty years, and he thinks he's falling in love with me. He's very sorry. Please call."

"So call and put the poor thing out of his misery. That certainly sounds contrite to me. Everyone makes mistakes, Andi, even you. I would find it very heartwarming to hear someone tell me they think they're falling in love with me. Think about that, Andi. Have a nice evening."

"Good-bye, Gertie. Be careful walking."

"I will, my dear."

Andi read the note and the invitation until she had them both memorized. She ran the words over and

over in her mind as she finished packing up the attic.
At one point, as she descended the attic steps, she put
the words to music and sing-songed her way through
her bedroom as she stuffed things in cartons.

Andi stopped only to feed the animals and eat a
sandwich. The telephone continued to ring, the answering machine clicking on just as the person on the
other end hung up. At eleven o'clock she carried the
last of the boxes downstairs to the garage where she
stacked them near the door. By three o'clock she had
her mother's china packed as well as all the pictures
and knickknacks from the living room sealed in bubble wrap. These, too, went into the garage.

At three-thirty, she was sitting at the kitchen table
with a cup of tea, the invitation to Peter King's party
in front of her and his letter propped up against the
sugar bowl. Believe or not believe? Go to the party,
don't go to the party? Call him or not call him? Ignore everything and maybe things would turn out
right. Like thirty-year-old women with thirty-six animals were really in demand. Was Gertie right? Was
she acting like some indignant teenager?

There were no answers in the kitchen, so she
might as well go to bed and try to sleep. Was this how
it felt to be in love? Surely love meant more than a
sick feeling in the stomach coupled with wet eyes
and a pounding headache.

Andi felt as old as Gertie when she climbed the
stairs to the second floor. She blubbered to herself as
she brushed her teeth and changed into flannel paja-
mas. She was asleep the moment she pulled the down
comforter up to her chin.

Even in her dream she knew she was dreaming
because once before, in another lifetime, she'd slid

down the hill on a plastic shower curtain with a col-
league named Tyler. The same Tyler she'd had a two-
year relationship with.

> *She fell sideways, rolling off the frozen plas-*
> *tic, to land in a heap near a monstrous holly*
> *bush. The wind knocked out of her, she strug-*
> *gled to breathe.*
> *"You okay, Andi?"*
> *"Sure. Bet I'm bruised from head to toe,*
> *though. How about you?"*
> *"I'm fine. You really aren't going with me to-*
> *morrow, are you?"*
> *"No. I'll miss you. Let's stay in touch, okay?"*
> *"People promise that all the time; they even*
> *mean it at the time they say it, but it rarely hap-*
> *pens. I'll be in Chicago and you'll be in New*
> *Jersey. I want the big bucks. I could never be*
> *content living in some rural area counting my*
> *pennies and practicing veterinarian medicine*
> *for free. Right now you're starry-eyed at taking*
> *over your family's old practice, but that's going*
> *to get old real quick. You're gonna be the new*
> *kid on the block. Who's going to come to your*
> *clinic? Yeah, sure, you can board dogs, but how*
> *much money is there in that? Not much I can*
> *tell you. Let's go home and make some magic.*
> *We're probably never going to see each other*
> *again. We'll call at first and even write a few*
> *letters, and then it will be a Christmas card*
> *once a year with our name printed on it. After*
> *that it will be, Tyler who? Andi who?"*
> *"Then why do you want to go to bed with me?"*
> *"Because I think I love you."*

"After two years you think you love me? I want to go home and I want to go by myself. I don't want to go to bed with you either because you remind me of someone I don't like. He makes greasy lipstick. I changed the sheets and everything, and then he found out, probably from you, that I use a diaphragm. That was tacky, Tyler, to tell him something that personal."

"I never told him any such thing"

"Liar, liar, your pants are on fire. Get away from me and don't think I'm going to your stupid Christmas party either. Take this damn shower curtain with you, too."

"All right, all right. You came with me, how are you going to get home?"

"I have two feet, I'll walk. When you're homeless that's how you get around; I hope you make your three million plus. Good-bye, Peter."

"My name isn't Peter; it's Tyler."

"Same thing, birds of a feather flock together. All you're interested in is money. You don't care about me. The fact that you're taking this so well is suspect in my eyes. And another thing, I wouldn't let you see me wear my mother's pearls even if you paid me my weight in gold. One more thing, don't for one minute think I'm giving one of Rosie's pups to you to give your grandmother. She'll sneeze from all of that Lily of the Valley powder."

Andi rolled over, her arm snaking out to reach the phone. She yanked it back under the covers immediately. Six-thirty. She'd only had two and a half hours of sleep, and most of that had been dream time. Damn.

Andi struggled to remember the dream as she showered and dressed.

The animals tended to, Andi sat at the table sipping the scalding hot coffee. She frowned as she tried to remember what it was in her dream that bothered her. It didn't hit her until she finished the last of the coffee in the pot. Lily of the Valley. Of course. "When you're stupid, Andi, you're stupid." A moment later the phone book was in her hands. She flipped to the Ks and ran her finger down the listing. She called every S. King in the book until she heard the voice she was expecting. She wasn't sure, but she thought her heart stopped beating when she heard Gertie's voice on the other end of the line. *Sadie King, Peter King's grandmother, was the homeless Gertie.*

Blind fury riveted through her. Shaking and trembling, she had to grab hold of the kitchen counter to steady herself. A conspiracy. If the old saying a fool is born every minute was true, then she was this minute's fool. Of all the cheap, dirty tricks! Send an old lady here to soften me up, to spy on me so I'd spill my guts. You son of a bitch!

Andi fixed another pot of coffee. Somewhere in this house there must be some cigarettes, a filthy habit she'd given up a year ago. She rummaged in the kitchen drawers until she found a crumpled pack pushed way in the back. She lit one, coughed and sputtered, but she didn't put it out.

Promptly at nine o'clock she called King Cosmetics and asked to speak to Peter King. "This is Dr. An-

drea Evans and this call is a one-time call. Tell Mr.
King he doesn't get a second chance to speak with
me. It's now or never."

"Andi, is it really you? Listen I'm sorry—"

"Excuse me, I called you, so I'm the one who will
do the talking. Furthermore, I'm not interested in any
lame excuses. How dare you send your grandmother
to spy on me! How dare you! Homeless my ass! She
said her name was Gertie and I believed her. I didn't
get wise till this morning. It was that Lily of the Valley. *That always bothered me.* Why would a homeless
lady always smell like Lily of the Valley? She should
have had body odor. All those good deeds, all those
tall tales. Well, it should make you happy that I fell
for it. You have to sink pretty low to use an old lady to
get what you want. Don't send her back here again either. My God, I can't wait to get out of here so I don't
ever have to see you or your grandmother again. She
actually had me feeling sorry for her because her
children, *she said,* wanted to slap her in a nursing
home. This is my R.S.V.P. for your party. I'll leave it
up to you to figure out if I'm attending or not."

"What the hell are you talking about. Who's
homeless? My grandmother lives in a penthouse, and
she works to help—"

Andi cut him off in mid-sentence, slamming down
the phone. She zeroed in on Rosie, who was watching
the strange goings-on with puzzlement. Her owner
rarely raised her voice. It was rarer still that she cried.
"Do I care that his grandmother lives in a penthouse?
No, I do not. Do I care that she sneaked in here and . . .
took care of us? No, I do not. I bet that old lady came
here in a chauffeur-driven limousine and parked it

somewhere, and then she trundled over here in her disguise. I am stupid, I admit it. Well, my stupid days are over."

Andi cried then because there was nothing else for her to do.

"Sadie!" The one word was that of a bellowing bull.

"Peter! How nice of you to come by so early. Did you come for breakfast?"

"Sadie, or should I call you Gertie? What the hell were you trying to do, Sadie?"

"So you found out. I only wanted to help. Who told you?"

"Guess!"

"Not Andi? Please, don't tell me Andi found out. So, that was who called this morning and hung up without speaking. I thought it might be Donald."

"Who the hell is Donald?" Peter continued to bellow.

"He covered for me. He's a homeless man I befriended. How did she find out?"

"I have no idea. She said something about you always smelling like Lily of the Valley."

"Yes, I guess that would do it. Was she very upset?"

"Upset isn't quite the word I'd use. She thinks I put you up to it. She thinks we had a conspiracy going to get her property."

"Well, I certainly hope you explained things to her. I'll go right over there and make amends."

"I wouldn't do that if I were you. I couldn't explain; she hung up on me. Don't meddle, Sadie. I mean it."

"She's so right for you, Peter, and you're perfect for her. I wanted you two to get together. When the men found homeless animals, I had them take them to Andi. They told me how nice and kind she was. I wanted to see for myself what kind of girl she was. I want you to get married, Peter, and I don't want you marrying someone like Helen. That's why I did it."

"Couldn't you trust me to find out for myself, Sadie? Why couldn't you simply introduce me or in this case leave me to my own devices? I met her on my own."

"No, I couldn't trust you. Look how long it took you to figure out Helen wore false eyelashes." She watched her grandson cringe at her words. "I just wanted to help so you would be happy. I'm sorry, but I'm not taking all the blame, Peter. You screwed it all up with that report."

"That's another thing. That report was on the backseat. The day we went sledding I didn't have anything in the backseat. I didn't even open the back door. All my stuff was in the trunk. How'd it fall out?"

"It doesn't matter now how it fell out. It did, and Andi found it and read it. End of story," Sadie said.

"I'm not giving up. I like her spunk."

"She hates your guts," Sadie said. "By the way, she isn't going to your party. I was there when the messenger brought your invitation. Peter, I'm so sorry. I just wanted to help. Where are you going?"

"To correct this situation."

"Peter, Andi is very angry. Don't go on her property again unless you want to see yourself and this company on the six o'clock news."

"Then what the hell am I supposed to do?"

"Does that mean you want my advice?"

"Okay, I'll try anything."

"Go to the police station and increase your Christmas donation to the Police Benevolent Association. Then ask them if they'll loan you one of their bullhorns. Talk to her from the road. She'll have to listen, and you aren't breaking any laws. I'm not saying it will work, but it's worth a try."

"Sadie, I love you!" Peter said as he threw his arms around his grandmother.

Peter King, the bullhorn next to him on the front seat, pulled his car to the curb. He felt stupid and silly as he climbed from the car. What to say? How to say it? Apologize from the heart. You know Spanish and French and a smattering of Latin. Do it in four languages. That should impress her. Oh yeah.

Peter took a deep breath before he brought the horn to his mouth. "Dr. Evans, this is Peter King. I'm outside on the road. I want you to listen to me. When I'm finished, if you don't want me to bother you again, I won't, but you need to hear me out. You can't run and hide, and you can't drown this out."

Peter sensed movement, chattering voices and rock music. Disconcerted, he turned around to see a pickup truck full of skis, sleds, and teenagers, pulling a snowmobile, drive up behind his parked car. "Shit!" Like he really needed an audience. Tune them out and get on with it.

"Andi, listen to me. Don't blame my grandmother; she only wanted to help. She wants to see me married with children before she . . . goes. I didn't know she was pretending to be a bag lady, I swear I didn't. As much as I love her, I wanted to strangle her when I found out."

"That's nice, mister," shouted a young girl in a tight ski suit and hair that looked like raffia. "You should always love your mother and grandmother. You're doing this all wrong. You need to appeal to her basic instincts."

"Shut up, Carla," a pimple-faced youth snarled. "You need to mind your own business. Yo, mister, you need to stand tall here and not beg some dumb girl for . . . whatever it is you want out of this scene."

"Listen, Donnie, don't be telling me girl stuff. You're so ignorant you're pathetic. Listen to me, mister, tell her she has eyes like stars and she's in your blood and you can't eat or sleep or anything. Tell her all you want in life is to marry her and have lots of little girl kids that look just like her. Promise her anything, but you better mean it because us women can spot a lie in a heartbeat."

Peter turned around. "She thinks I cheated her or tried, and then I did something really stupid, but I didn't know it was stupid at the time. Well, I sort of knew, but I didn't think anyone would ever find out. How do I handle that one?" he asked the girl with the three pounds of makeup and raffia hair.

"Tell her what you just said to me. Admit it. It's when you lie and try to cover up that you get in trouble."

"Don't listen to Carla, man; that chick in there is gonna think you're the king of all jerks."

"You're a jerk, Donnie. Listen to me, mister, what do you have to lose?"

Peter cleared his throat. "Andi, I'm sorry for everything. I was stupid. I swear to God, I'll never do another stupid thing again. I tried to explain about the business end of things. I want to marry you. I'll do anything you want if you'll just come out here and listen to me or let me come in and talk to you. Sadie says we're meant for each other. She's hardly ever wrong. What's ten minutes out of your life, Andi? I admit I'm dumb when it comes to women. I don't read *Cosmo,* and I don't know diddly squat about triple orgasms and such stuff but I'm willing to learn. I'll use breath mints, I'll quit smoking, I'll take the grease out of the lipstick. Are you listening to me, Andi? I goddamn well love you! I thought I was falling in love with you, but now I know I love you for real."

"Mister, you are a disgrace to the male race," Donnie said.

"Oh, mister, that was beautiful. You wait, she's coming out. Give her five minutes. No woman could resist that little speech. You did real good, mister. My sister told me about triple orgasms. I can explain. . . ."

"Oh, jeez, look, she's coming out. That's who you're in love with?" There was such amazement in the boy's face, Peter grinned.

"Oh, she's real pretty, mister. I know she loves you. You gonna give her something special for Christmas?"

"Yeah, himself," Donnie snorted.

"You know what, kid, they don't come any better than me. You need to get a whole new attitude. Carla, we're looking for teenage models at King Cosmetics. Here's my card; go to personnel and arrange a meeting with me for after the first of the year. Dump that jerk and get yourself a real boyfriend. Here's the keys to my car. My address is in the glove compartment. Drop it off for me, okay? That way she'll have to take me home or else allow me to stay. Thanks for your help. Can you drive?"

"Now you got it, mister. I can drive. Remember now, be humble, and only the truth counts from here on in."

"Got it," he said as he moved toward the house.

Inside the kennel, Andi said, "You got the dogs in a tizzy. I'm in a tizzy. You're out of your mind. I never heard of a grandmother/grandson act before."

"It wasn't an act. Everything I said was true. I do want to marry you."

"I hardly know you. Are you asking me so the three million plus stays in the family?"

"God, no. I feel like I've known you all my life. I've been searching for someone like you forever. My grandmother knew you were the one the moment she met you. She adores you, and she feels terrible about all of this. Can we start over?"

"Well . . . I . . . we're from two different worlds. I don't think it would work. I'm not giving up my life and my profession. I worked too hard to get where I am."

"I'm not asking you to give up anything. I don't much care for the life I move around in now, but it's my job. I can make it nine-to-five and be home every night for dinner. If you're busy, I can even cook the dinner or we can hire a housekeeper."

"I'm moving to Freehold Christmas Eve."

"Freehold's good. I like Freehold. It's not such a long commute. Sunday's good for me. I'm a whiz-bang at putting up Christmas trees. Well?"

"Were you telling me the truth when you said you couldn't eat or sleep?"

"Just look at the bags under my eyes. How about you?"

"I cried a lot. I would have cried more, but the animals got upset so I had to stop."

"So right now, this minute, we're two people who are starting over. All that . . . mess, it never happened. Your money will always be your money. That was a business deal. What we have is personal. So, will you marry me? If you don't have pearls, Sadie will give you hers. This way they'll stay in the family. That kid who took my car knows more than I do. I'll tell you about her later. Was that a yes or a no?"

"It's a maybe. We haven't even gone to bed yet. We might not be compatible."

"Why don't we find out."

"Now? It's morning. I have things to do. How about later?"

"Where we're concerned, later means trouble. Now!"

"Okay. Now sounds good. I put clean sheets on the bed on Sunday. You were a no-show. That didn't do anything for my ego," Andi said.

"I dreamed about it," Peter said.

"You said you didn't sleep."

"Daydreamed. There's a difference. In living color."

"How'd I look?"

"Wonderful!" Peter said. "Want me to carry you upstairs?"

"No. I'm the independent type. I can be bossy."

"I love bossy women. Sadie is bossy. People only boss other people around when they love them. Sadie told me that."

"You are dumb." Andi laughed.

"That, too. I sleep with my socks on," Peter confided.

"Me, too! I use an electric blanket."

"You won't need it this morning." Peter laughed.

"Pretty confident, aren't you?"

"When you got it you got it."

"Show me," Andi said.

"Your zipper or mine?"

"On the count of three," Andi said.

Zipppppppp.

He showed her. And was still showing her when the sun set and the animals howled for their dinner. And afterward, when the kennel grew quiet for the long evening ahead, he was still showing her. Toward midnight, Andi showed him, again and again. He was heard to mutter, in a hoarse whisper, "I liked that. Oh, do that again."

She did.

"I hate to leave. Oh, God, I have to borrow your truck, do you mind?"

"Of course I mind. You sport around in a fifty-thousand-dollar truck and a ninety-thousand-dollar car and you want to borrow my clunker!"

"I'll have someone drive it back, okay? Is this going to be our first fight?"

"Not if I can help it. I do need the truck, though. I have some errands to do, and I'm not driving that bus."

"Are you going to call Sadie?"

"Not today. She needs to sweat a little. Are you going to tell her?"

"Not on your life. Well, did that maybe turn into a yes or a no? What kind of ring do you want?"

"I don't want an engagement ring. I just want a wide, thick, gold wedding band."

"Then it's yes?"

Andi nodded.

"When?"

"January. After I get settled in."

"January's good. January's real good. Jesus, I love you. You smile like my mother used to smile. That's the highest compliment I can pay you, Andi. She was real, like you. I don't know too many real people. When you stop to think about it, that's pretty sad."

"Then let's not think about it," Andi said as she dangled the truck keys under his nose.

"I can't see you till tomorrow. I'll call you tonight, okay? Some clients are in town, and the meetings and dinner are not something I can cancel. You're coming to the party?"

"Yes."

"What about the pearls?" Peter asked fretfully "You have to explain that to me one of these days."

"I have my mother's pearls."

"God, that's a relief."

He kissed her then until she thought her head would spin right off her.

"Bye."

Andi smiled, her eyes starry. "Bye, Peter."

Thursday morning, the day of Peter King's Christmas party, Andi climbed out of bed with a vicious head cold. Her eyes were red, her nose just as red. She'd spent the night propped up against the pillows so her nasal passages would stay open. If she'd slept twenty minutes it was a lot. The time was ten minutes to eight. In her ratty robe and fleece-lined slippers she shuffled downstairs to make herself some hot coffee. She ached from head to toe. Just the thought of cleaning the dog runs made her cringe. She shivered and turned up the heat to ninety. She huddled inside the robe, trying to quiet her shaking body as she waited for the coffee to perk.

Cup in hand at fifteen minutes past eight, she heard the first rumblings of heavy duty machinery in her parking lot. The knock on the door was louder than thunder. She opened the door, her teeth chattering. "What are you doing here? What's all that machinery? Get it out of here. This is private property. Is that a wrecking ball?"

He was big and burly with hands the size of ham hocks, the perfect complement to the heavy duty monster machinery behind him. "What do you mean what am I doing here? I'm here to raze this building. I have a contract that says so. And, yeah, that's a wrecking ball. You gotta get out of here, lady."

"Come in here. I can't stand outside; I'm sick as you can see, and I'm not going anywhere. I, too, have a contract, and my contract says you can't do this. Mine, I'm sure, supersedes yours. So there. I have thirty-six animals here and no place to take them until Sunday. You'll just have to wait."

"That's tough, lady. I ain't comin' back here on Sunday; that's Christmas Eve. I have another job scheduled for Tuesday. Today is the day for this building."

"I'm calling the police; we'll let them settle it. You just go back outside and sit on that ball because that's all you're going to do with it. Don't you dare touch a thing. Do you hear me?" Andi croaked. She slammed the door in the man's face. She called the police and was told a patrol car would be sent immediately.

Andi raced upstairs, every bone in her body protesting as she dressed in three layers of clothing. She had to stop three times to blow her runny nose. Hacking and coughing, she ran downstairs to rummage on her desk for her contract to show the police. While she waited she placed a call to both Peter and Sadie and was told both of them were unavailable. Five minutes later, her electricity and phone were dead.

Two hours later, the electricity was back on. Temporarily. "I don't know what to tell you, ma'am. This man is right and so are you. You both have signed contracts. He has every right to be here doing what he's doing. You, on the other hand, have a contract that says he can't do it. Nobody is going to do anything until we can reach Mr. Peter King, since he's the man who signed both these contracts."

"Listen up, both of you, and watch my lips. I am not going anywhere. I'm sick. I have thirty-six animals in that kennel, and we have nowhere to go. Based on my contract, I made arrangements to be out of here on Sunday, not Saturday, not Friday and certainly not today. Now, which part of that don't you two men understand?"

"The part where you aren't leaving till Sunday. This is a three-day job. I can't afford to lose the money since I work for myself. It's not my fault you're sick, and it's not my fault that you have thirty-six animals. I got five kids and a wife to support and men on my payroll sitting outside in your parking lot. Right now I'm paying them to sit there drinking coffee."

"That's just too damn bad, mister. I'm calling the *Plainfield Courier* and the *Star Ledger*. Papers like stories like this, especially at Christmastime. You better get my phone hooked up again, and don't think I'm paying for that."

The afternoon wore on. Andi kept swilling tea as she watched through the window. The police were as good as their word, allowing nothing to transpire until word came in from Peter King. Her face grew more flushed, and she knew her fever was creeping upward.

Using the police cell phone, Andi called again and again, leaving a total of seven messages on Sadie's machine and nine messages in total for Peter at King Cosmetics. The receptionist logged all nine messages, Mr. King's words ringing in her ears: "Do not call me under *any* circumstance. Whatever it is can wait until tomorrow. Even if this building blows up I don't want to know about it until tomorrow."

At five o'clock, Andi suggested the police try and reach Mr. King at his home. When she was unable to tell them where he lived, the owner of the wrecking equipment smirked. It wasn't until six o'clock that she remembered she had Peter's address on the invitation. However, if she kept quiet she could delay things another day. Besides, his party was due to get under way any minute now. He would probably try and call her when he realized she wasn't in attendance.

The police officer spoke. "You might as well go home, Mr. Dolan. We'll try and reach Mr. King throughout the evening and get this thing settled by morning."

Cursing and kicking at his machinery, Dolan backed his equipment out of the parking lot. The officer waited a full twenty minutes before he left. Andi watched his taillights fade into the distance from the kitchen window. The yellow bus was like a huge golden eye under her sensor light. Large, yellow bus. Uh-huh. Okay, Mr. Peter King, you have this coming to you!

"Hey you guys, line up, we're going to a party! First I have to get the location. Second, you need to get duded up. Wait here." The Christmas box of odds and ends of ribbon and ornaments was clearly marked. Spools of used ribbon were just what she needed. Every dog, every cat, got a red bow, even Rosie. The pups, smaller, skinnier ribbons. "I'm going to warm up the bus, so don't get antsy. I also need to find my mother's pearls. I don't know why, but I have to wear them." Finally, wearing the pearls, wads of tissue stuck in the two flap pockets of her flannel shirt, pups in their box in hand, Andi led the animals to the bus. "Everybody sit down and be quiet. We're going to show Mr. Peter King what we think about the way he does business!"

Thirty-five minutes later, Andi swung the bus onto Brentwood Drive. Cars were lined up the entire length of the street. "This indeed poses a dilemma," she muttered. She eyed the fire hydrant, wondering if she could get past it and up onto the lawn. Loud music blasted through the closed windows. "It must be a hell of a party," she muttered as she threw caution to the wind and plowed ahead.

Andi grabbed the handle to open the door. "Ooops, wait just one second. Annabelle, come here. You, too, Cleo." From her pocket she withdrew a tube of Raspberry Cheese Louise lipstick and painted both dog's lips. Annabelle immediately started to lick it off. "Stop that. You need to keep it on till we get to the party. Okay, you know the drill, we move on three. I expect you all to act like ladies and gentlemen. If you forget your manners, oh, well." She blew her nose, tossed the tissue on the ground and gave three sharp blasts on the whistle. "We aren't going to bother with the doorbell, the music's too loud."

"Party time!"

"Eek!" "Squawk!" "Oh, my God! It's a herd!" "They're wearing lipstick! I don't believe this!"

"Hi, I'm Andrea Evans," Andi croaked. "I think I'd like a rum and Coke and spare the Coke." Her puffy eyes narrowed when she saw her intended lounging on a beautiful brocade sofa, his head thrown back in laughter. He laughed harder when Cedric lifted his leg on a French Provincial table leg. Not to be outdone, Isaac did the same thing. Annabelle squatted in the middle of a colorful Persian carpet as she tried to lick off the lipstick.

"Now, this is what I call a party," Peter managed to gasp. "Ladies and gentlemen, stay or go, the decision is yours. It ain't gonna get any better than this! Wait, wait, before you go, I'd like to introduce you to the lady I'm going to marry right after the first of the year. Dr. Andrea Evans, meet my guests. I don't even want to know why you did this," he hissed in her ear.

"You said you wanted a lived-in house. Myra is going to get sick from all that pâté. Oh, your guests are leaving. By the way, I parked the bus on your lawn."

"No!"

"Yep. Don't you care that your guests are leaving? I'm sick."

"And you're going right to bed," Sadie said, leaning over Andi. "You can forgive me later, my dear. Oh, my, you are running a fever. Isn't this wonderful,

Peter? It's like we're a real family. Your furniture will never be the same. Do you care?"

"Nope," Peter said, wrapping his arm around Andi's shoulders. "Do you want to tell me what prompted this . . . extraordinary visit?"

Andi told him. "So, you see, we're homeless until Sunday."

"Not anymore. My home is your home and the home of these animals. Boy, this feels good. Isn't it great, Sadie? That guy Dolan is a piece of work. It's true, I did sign the contract, but it was amended later on. I don't suppose he showed you a copy of that."

"No, he didn't. It doesn't matter. I thought you'd be angry. I was making a statement."

"I know, and I'm not angry. You did the right thing. You really can empty a room. Look, the food's all gone."

"Do you really love me?"

"So much it hurts."

"I'm wearing my mother's pearls. I think I'd like to go to bed now if you don't mind. Will you take care of Rosie and her pups?"

"That's my job," Sadie chirped. "Peter, carry this child to bed. I'll make her a nice hot toddy, and by tomorrow she'll be fine. Trust me."

Andi was asleep in Peter's arms before he reached the top of the steps. He turned as he heard steps behind him. "Okay, you can all come up and stand watch. By the way, thanks for coming to the party. I really like your outfits and, Annabelle, on you that lipstick looks good."

Peter fussed with the covers under Sadie's watchful eye. "I meant it, Sadie, when I said I love her so much it hurts. Isn't she beautiful? I could spend the rest of my life just looking at her."

"Ha! Not likely, you have to work to support all of us," Andi said sleepily. "Good night, Peter. I love you. Merry Christmas."

"Merry Christmas, Andi," Peter said, bending low to kiss her on the cheek.

"Ah, I love it when things work out," Sadie said, three of Rosie's pups cradled against her bony chest. "I think I'd like five grandchildren. Good night, Peter."

"Thanks, Grandma. It's going to be a wonderful life."

"I know."

A Bright Red Ribbon

Even in her dream, Morgan Ames knew she was dreaming, knew she was going to wake with tears on her pillow and reality slapping her in the face. She cried out, the way she always did, just at the moment Keith was about to slip the ring on her finger. That's how she knew it was a dream. She never got beyond this point. She woke now, and looked at the bedside clock; it was 4:10. She wiped at the tears on her cheeks, but this time she smiled. Today was the day. Today was Christmas Eve, the day Keith was going to slip the ring on her finger and they would finally set the wedding date. The big event, in her mind, was scheduled to take place in front of her parents' Christmas tree. She and Keith would stand in exactly the same position they stood in two years ago today, at the very same hour. Romance was alive and well.

She dropped her legs over the side of the bed, slid into a daffodil-colored robe that was snugly warm and pulled on thick wool socks. She padded out to the miniature kitchen to make tea.

Christmas Eve. To her, Christmas Eve was the most wonderful day of the year. Years ago, when she'd turned into a teenager, her parents had switched the big dinner and gift opening to Christmas Eve so they could sleep late on Christmas morning. The dinner was huge; friends dropped by before evening services, and then they opened their presents, sang carols and drank spiked eggnog afterward.

Mo knew a watched kettle never boiled so she made herself some toast while the kettle hummed on the stove. She was so excited her hands shook as she spread butter and jam on the toast. The kettle whistled. The water sputtered over the counter as she poured it into the cup with the black rum tea bag.

In about sixteen hours, she was going to see Keith. At last. Two years ago he had led her by the hand over to the twelve-foot Christmas tree and said he wanted to talk to her about something. He'd been so nervous, but she'd been more nervous, certain the something he wanted to talk about was the engagement ring he was going to give her. She'd been expecting it, her parents had been expecting it, all her friends had been expecting it. Instead, Keith had taken both her hands in his and said, "Mo, I need to talk to you about something. I need you to understand. This is my problem. You didn't do anything to make me . . . what I'm trying to say is, I need more time. I'm not ready to commit. I think we both need to experience a little more of life's challenges. We both have good jobs, and I just got a promotion that will take effect the first of the year. I'll be working in the New York office. It's a great opportunity, but the hours are long.

I'm going to get an apartment in the city. What I would like is for us to . . . to take a hiatus from each other. I think two years will be good. I'll be thirty and you'll be twenty-nine. We'll be more mature, more ready for that momentous step."

The hot tea scalded her tongue. She yelped. She'd yelped that night, too. She'd wanted to be sophisticated, blasé, to say, okay, sure, no big deal. She hadn't said any of those things. Instead she'd cried, hanging on to his arm, begging to know if what he was proposing meant he was going to date others. His answer had crushed her and she'd sobbed then. He'd said things like, "Ssshhh, it's going to be all right. Two years isn't all that long. Maybe we aren't meant to be with each other for the rest of our lives. We'll find out. Yes, it's going to be hard on me, too. Look, I know this is a surprise . . . I didn't want . . . I was going to call. . . . This is what I propose. Two years from tonight, I'll meet you right here, in front of the tree. Do we have a date, Mo?" She nodded miserably. Then he'd added, "Look, I have to leave, Mo. My boss is having a party in his town house in Princeton. It won't look good if I'm late. Christmas parties are a good way to network. Here, I got you a little something for Christmas." Before she could dry her eyes, blow her nose, or tell him she had a ton of presents for him under the tree, he was gone.

It had been the worst Christmas of her life. The worst New Year's, too. The next Christmas and New Year's had been just as bad because her parents had looked at her with pity and then anger. Just last week they had called and said, "Get on with your life, Morgan. You've already wasted two years. In that whole time, Keith hasn't called you once or even dropped you a post card." She'd been stubborn, though, because she loved Keith. Sharp words had ensued, and she'd broken the connection and cried.

Tonight she had a date.

Life was going to be so wonderful. The strain between her and her parents would ease when they saw how happy she was.

Mo looked at the clock. Five-thirty. Time to shower, dress, pack up the Cherokee for her two-week vacation. Oh, life was good. She had it all planned. They'd go skiing, but first she'd go to Keith's apartment in New York, stay over, make him breakfast. They'd make slow, lazy love and if the mood called for it, they'd make wild, animal love.

Two years was a long time to be celibate—and she'd been celibate. She winced when she thought about Keith in bed with other women. He loved sex more than she did. There was no way he'd been faithful to her. She felt it in her heart. Every chance her mother got, she drove home her point. Her parents didn't like Keith. Her father was fond of saying, "I know his type—he's no good. Get a life, Morgan."

Tonight her new life would begin. Unless . . . unless Keith was a no-show. Unless Keith decided the single life was better than a married life and responsibilities. God in heaven, what would she do if that happened? Well, it wasn't going to happen. She'd always been a positive person and she saw no reason to change now.

It wasn't going to happen because when Keith saw her he was going to go out of his mind. She'd changed in the two years. She'd dropped twelve pounds in all the right places. She was fit and toned because she worked out daily at a gym and ran for five miles every evening after work. She'd gotten a new hairstyle in New York. And, while she was there she'd gone to a color specialist who helped her with her hair and makeup. She was every bit as professional looking as some of the ad executives she saw walking up and down Madison Avenue. She'd shed her scrubbed girl-next-door image. S.K., which stood for Since Keith, she'd learned to shop in the outlet stores for designer fashions at half the cost. She looked down now at her sporty Calvin Klein outfit, at the Ferragamo boots, and the Chanel handbag she'd picked up at a flea market. Inside her French luggage were other outfits by Donna Karan and Carolyn Roehm.

Like Keith, she had gotten a promotion with a hefty salary increase. If things worked out, she was going to think about opening her own architectural office by early summer. She'd hire people, oversee them. Clients she worked with told her she should open her own office, go it alone. One in particular had offered to back her after he'd seen the plans she'd drawn up for his beach house in Cape May. Her father, himself an architect, had offered to help out and had gone so far as to get all the paperwork from the Small Business Administration. She could do it now if she wanted to. But, did she want to make that kind of commitment? What would Keith think?

What she wanted, really wanted, was to get married and have a baby. She could always do consulting work, take on a few private clients to keep her hand in. All she needed was a husband to make it perfect.

Keith.

The phone rang. Mo frowned. No one ever called

her this early in the morning. Her heart skipped a beat as she picked up the phone. "Hello," she said warily.

"Morgan?" Her mother. She always made her name sound like a question.

"What's wrong, Mom?"

"When are you leaving, Morgan? I wish you'd left last night like Dad and I asked you to do. You should have listened to us, Morgan."

"Why? What's wrong? I told you why I couldn't leave. I'm about ready to go out the door as we speak."

"Have you looked outside?"

"No. It's still dark, Mom."

"Open your blinds, Morgan, and look at the parking lot lights. It's snowing!"

"Mom, it snows every year. So what? It's only a two-hour drive, maybe three if there's a lot of snow. I have the Cherokee. Four-wheel drive, Mom." She pulled up the blind in the bedroom to stare out at the parking lot. She swallowed hard. So, it would be a challenge. The world was white as far as the eye could see. She raised her eyes to the parking lights. The bright light that usually greeted her early in the morning was dim as the sodium vapor fought with the early light of dawn and the swirling snow. "It's snowing, Mom."

"That's what I'm trying to tell you. It started here around midnight, I guess. It was just flurries when Dad and I went to bed but now we have about four inches. Since this storm seems to be coming from the south where you are, you probably have more. Dad and I have been talking and we won't be upset if you wait till the storm is over. Christmas morning is just as good as Christmas Eve. Just how much snow do you have, Morgan?"

"It looks like a lot, but it's drifting in the parking lot. I can't see the front, Mom. Look, don't worry about me. I have to be home this evening. I've waited two long years for this. Please, Mom, you understand, don't you?"

"What I understand, Morgan, is that you're being foolhardy. I saw Keith's mother the other day and she said he hasn't been home in ten months. He just lives across the river, for heaven's sake. She also said she didn't expect him for Christmas, so what does that tell you? I don't want you risking your life for some foolish promise."

Mo's physical being trembled. The words she dreaded, the words she didn't ever want to hear, had just been uttered: Keith wasn't coming home for Christmas. She perked up almost immediately. Keith loved surprises. It would be just like him to tell his mother he wasn't coming home and then show up and yell, "Surprise!" If he had no intention of honoring the promise they'd made to each other, he would have sent a note or called her. Keith wasn't that callous. Or was he? She didn't know anything anymore.

She thought about the awful feelings that had attacked her over the past two years, feelings she'd pushed away. Had she buried her head in the sand? Was it possible that Keith had used the two-year hiatus to soften the blow of parting, thinking that she'd transfer her feelings to someone else and let him off the hook? Instead she'd trenched in and convinced herself that by being faithful to her feelings, tonight would be her reward. Was she a fool? According to her mother she was. Tonight would tell the tale.

What she did know for certain was, nothing was going to stop her from going home. Not her mother's dire words, and certainly not a snowstorm. If she was a fool, she deserved to have her snoot rubbed in it.

Just a few short hours ago she'd stacked up her shopping bags by the front door, colorful Christmas bags loaded with presents for everyone. Five oversize bags for Keith. She wondered what happened to the presents she'd bought two years ago. Did her mother take them over to Keith's mother's house or were they in the downstairs closet? She'd never asked.

She'd spent a sinful amount of money on him this year. She'd even knitted a stocking for him and filled it with all kinds of goodies and gadgets. She'd stitched his name on the cuff of the bright red stocking in bright green thread. Was she a fool?

Mo pulled on her fleece-lined parka. Bundled up, she carried as many of the bags downstairs to the lobby as she could handle. She made three trips before she braved the outdoors. She needed to shovel and heat the car up.

She was exhausted when she tossed the fold-up shovel into the back of the Jeep. The heater and defroster worked furiously, but she still had to scrape the ice from the windshield and driver's side window. She checked the flashlight in the glove compartment. She rummaged inside the small opening, certain she had extra batteries, but couldn't find any. She glanced at the gas gauge. Three-quarters full, enough to get her home. She'd meant to top off last night on her way home from work, but she'd been in a hurry to get home to finish wrapping Keith's presents. God, she'd spent hours making intricate, one-of-a-kind bows and decorations for the gold-wrapped packages. A three-quarter tank would get her home for sure. The Cherokee gave her good mileage. If memory served her right, the trip never took more than a quarter of a tank. Well, she couldn't worry about that now. If road conditions permitted, she could stop on 95 or when she got onto the Jersey Turnpike.

Mo was numb with cold when she shrugged out of her parka and boots. She debated having a cup of tea to warm her up. Maybe she should wait for rush hour traffic to be over. Maybe a lot of things.

Maybe she should call Keith and ask him point blank if he was going to meet her in front of the Christmas tree. If she did that, she might spoil things. Still, why take her life in her hands and drive through what looked like a terrible storm, for nothing. She'd just as soon avoid her parents' pitying gaze and make the trip tomorrow morning and return in the evening to lick her wounds. If he was really going to be a no-show, that would be the way to go. Since there were no guarantees, she didn't see any choice but to brave the storm.

She wished she had a dog or a cat to nuzzle, a warm body that loved unconditionally. She'd wanted to get an animal at least a hundred times these past two years, but she couldn't bring herself to admit that she needed someone. What did it matter if that some-one had four legs and a furry body?

Her address book was in her hand, but she knew Keith's New York phone number by heart. It was un-listed, but she'd managed to get it from the brokerage house Keith worked for. So she'd used trickery. So what? She hadn't broken the rules and called the number. It was just comforting to know she could call if she absolutely had to. She squared her shoulders as she reached for the portable phone on the kitchen counter. She looked at the range-top clock. Seven forty-five. He should still be home. She punched out the area code and number, her shoulders still stiff. The phone rang five times before the answering machine came on. Maybe he was still in the shower. He always did cut it close to the edge, leaving in the morning with his hair still damp from the shower.

"C'mon, now, you know what to do if I don't answer. I'm either catching some z's or I'm out and about. Leave me a message, but be careful not to give away any secrets. Wait for the beep." Z's? It must be fast track New York talk. The deep, husky chuckle coming over the wire made Mo's face burn with shame. She broke the connection.

A moment later she was zipping up her parka and pulling on thin leather gloves. She turned down the heat in her cozy apartment, stared at her small Christmas tree on the coffee table and made a silly wish.

The moment she stepped outside, grainy snow assaulted her as the wind tried to drive her backward. She made it to the Cherokee, climbed inside and slammed the door. She shifted into four-wheel drive, then turned on the front and back wipers. The Cherokee inched forward, its wheels finding the traction to get her to the access road to I-95. It took her all of forty minutes to steer the Jeep to the ramp that led onto the Interstate. At that precise moment she knew she was making a mistake, but it was too late and there was no way now to get off and head back to the apartment. As far as she could see, it was bumper-to-bumper traffic. Visibility was almost zero. She knew there was a huge green directional sign overhead, but she couldn't see it.

"Oh, shit!"

Mo's hands gripped the wheel as the car in front of her slid to the right, going off the road completely. She muttered her favorite expletive again. God, what would she do if the wipers iced up? From the sound they were making on the windshield, she didn't think she'd have to wait long to find out.

The radio crackled with static, making it impossible to hear what was being said. Winter advisory. She already knew that. Not only did she know it, she was participating in it. She turned it off. The dashboard clock said she'd been on the road for well over an hour and she was nowhere near the Jersey Turnpike. At least she didn't think so. It was impossible to read the signs with the snow sticking to everything.

A white Christmas. The most wonderful time of the year. That thought alone had sustained her these past two years. Nothing bad ever happened on Christmas. Liar! Keith dumped you on Christmas Eve, right there in front of the tree. Don't lie to yourself!

"Okay, okay," she muttered. "But this Christmas will be different, this Christmas it will work out." Keith will make it up to you, she thought. Believe. Sure, and Santa is going to slip down the chimney one minute after midnight.

Mo risked a glance at the gas gauge. Half. She turned the heater down. Heaters added to the fuel consumption, didn't they? She thought about the Ferragamo boots she was wearing. Damn, she'd set her rubber boots by the front door so she wouldn't forget to bring them. They were still sitting by the front door. She wished now for her warm ski suit and wool cap, but she'd left them at her mother's last year when she went skiing for the last time.

She tried the radio again. The static was worse than before. So was the snow and ice caking her windshield. She had to stop and clean the blades or she was going to have an accident. With the faint glow of the taillights in front of her, Mo steered the Cherokee to the right. She pressed her flasher button, then waited to see if a car would pass her on the left and how much room she had to exit the car. The parka hood flew backward, exposing her head and face to the snowy onslaught. She fumbled with the wipers and the scraper. The swath they cleared was almost minuscule. God, what was she to do? Get off the damn road at the very next exit and see if she could find shelter? There was always a gas station or truck stop. The problem was, how would she know when she came to an exit?

Panic rivered through her when she got back into the Jeep. Her leather gloves were soaking wet. She peeled them off, then tossed them onto the backseat. She longed for her padded ski gloves and a cup of hot tea.

Mo drove for another forty minutes, stopping again to scrape her wipers and windshield. She was fighting a losing battle and she knew it. The wind was razor sharp, the snow coming down harder. This wasn't just a winter storm, it was a blizzard. People died in blizzards. Some fool had even made a movie about people eating other people when a plane crashed during a blizzard. She let the panic engulf her again. What was going to happen to her? Would she run out of gas and freeze to death? Who would find her? When would they find her? On Christmas Day? She imagined her parents' tears, their recriminations.

All of a sudden she realized there were no lights in front of her. She'd been so careful to stay a car length and a half behind the car in front. She pressed the accelerator, hoping desperately to keep up. God in heaven, was she off the road? Had she crossed the Delaware Bridge? Was she on the Jersey side? She simply didn't know. She tried the radio again and was rewarded with squawking static. She turned it off quickly. She risked a glance in her rearview mirror. There were no faint lights. There was nothing behind her. She moaned in fear. Time to stop, get out and see what she could see.

Before she climbed from the car, she unzipped her duffel bag sitting on the passenger side. She groped for a T-shirt and wrapped it around her head. Maybe the parka hood would stay on with something besides her silky hair to cling to. Her hands touched a pair of rolled-up sleep sox. She pulled them on. Almost as good as mittens. Did she have two pairs? She found a second pair and pulled them on. She flexed her fingers. No thumb holes. Damn. She remembered the manicure scissors she kept in her purse. A minute later she had thumb holes and was able to hold the steering wheel tightly. Get out, see what you can see. Clean the wipers, use that flashlight. Try your high beams.

Mo did all of the above. Uncharted snow. No one had gone before her. The snow was almost up to her knees. If she walked around, the snow would go down between her boots and stirrup pants. Knee-highs. Oh, God! Her feet would freeze in minutes. They might not find her until the spring thaw. Where was she? A field? The only thing she knew for certain was, she wasn't on any kind of a road.

"I hate you, Keith Mitchell. I mean, I really hate you. This is all your fault! No, it isn't," she sobbed. "It's my fault for being so damn stupid. If you loved me, you'd wait for me. Tonight was just a time. My mother would tell you I was delayed because of the storm. You could stay at my mother's or go to your mother's. If you loved me. I'm sitting here now, my life in danger, because . . . I wanted to believe you loved me. The way I love you. Christmas miracles, my ass!"

Mo shifted gears, inching the Cherokee forward.

How was it possible, Mo wondered, to be so cold and yet be sweating? She swiped at the perspiration on her forehead with the sleeve of her parka. In her whole life she'd never been this scared. If only she knew where she was. For all she knew, she could be driving into a pond or a lake. She shivered. Maybe she should get out and walk. Take her chances in the snow. She was in a no-win situation and she knew it. Stupid, stupid, stupid.

Maybe the snow wasn't as deep as she thought it was. Maybe it was just drifting in places. She was saved from further speculation when the Cherokee bucked, sputtered, slugged forward and then came to a coughing stop. Mo cut the engine, fear choking off her breathing. She waited a second before she turned the ignition key. She still had a gas reserve. The engine refused to catch and turn over. She turned off the heater and the wipers, then tried again with the same results. The decision to get out of the car and walk was made for her.

Mo scrambled over the backseat to the cargo area. With cold, shaking fingers she worked the zippers on her suitcases. She pulled thin, sequined sweaters—that would probably give her absolutely no warmth—out of the bag. She shrugged from the parka and pulled on as many of the decorative designer sweaters as she could. Back in her parka, she pulled knee-high stockings and her last two pairs of socks over her hands. It was better than nothing. As if she had choices. The keys to the Jeep went into her pocket. The strap of her purse was looped around her neck. She was ready. Her sigh was as mighty as the wind howling about her as she climbed out of the Cherokee.

The wind was sharper than a butcher knife. Eight steps in the mid-thigh snow and she was exhausted. The silk scarf she'd tied around her mouth was frozen to her face in the time it took to take those eight steps. Her eyelashes were caked with ice as were her eyebrows. She wanted to close her eyes, to sleep. How in the hell did Eskimos do it? A gurgle of hysterical laughter erupted in her throat.

The laughter died in her throat when she found herself facedown in a deep pile of snow. She crawled forward. It seemed like the wise thing to do. Getting to her feet was the equivalent of climbing Mt. Rushmore. She crab-walked until her arms gave out on her, then she struggled to her feet and tried to walk again. She repeated the process over and over until she was so exhausted she simply couldn't move. "Help me, someone. Please, God, don't let me die out here like this. I'll be a better person, I promise. I'll go to church more often. I'll practice my faith more diligently. I'll try to do more good deeds. I won't be selfish. I swear to You, I will. I'm not just saying this, either. I mean every word." She didn't know if she was saying the words or thinking them.

A violent gust of wind rocked her backward. Her back thumped into a tree, knocking the breath out of her. She cried then, her tears melting the crystals on her lashes.

"Help!" she bellowed. She shouted until she was hoarse.

Time lost all meaning as she crawled along. There were longer pauses now between the time she crawled on all fours and the time she struggled to her feet. She tried shouting again, her cries feeble at best. The only person who could hear her was God, and He seemed to be otherwise occupied.

Mo stumbled and went down. She struggled to get up, but her legs wouldn't move. In her life she'd never felt the pain that was tearing away at her joints. She lifted her head and for one brief second she thought she saw a feeble light. In the time it took her heart to beat once, the light was gone. She was probably hallucinating. Move! her mind shrieked. Get up! They won't find you till the daffodils come up. They'll bury you when the lilacs bloom. That's how they'll remember you. They might even print that on your tombstone. "Help me. Please, somebody help me!"

She needed to sleep. More than anything in the world she wanted sleep. She was so groggy. And her heart seemed to be beating as fast as a racehorse's at the finish line. How was that possible? Her heart should barely be beating. Get the hell up, Morgan. Now! Move, damn you!

She was up. She was so cold. She knew her body heat was leaving her. Her clothes were frozen to her body. She couldn't see at all. Move, damn you! You can do it. You were never a quitter, Morgan. Well, maybe where Keith was concerned. You always managed, somehow, to see things through to a satisfactory conclusion. She stumbled and fell, picked herself up with all the willpower left in her numb body, fell again. This time she couldn't get up.

A vision of her parents standing over her closed coffin, the room filled with lilacs, appeared behind her closed lids. Her stomach rumbled fiercely and then she was on her feet, her lungs about to burst with her effort.

The snow and wind lashed at her like a tidal wave. It slammed her backward and beat at her face and body. Move! Don't stop now! Go, go, go, go.

"Help!" she cried. She was down again, on all fours. She shook her head to clear it.

She sensed movement. "Please," she whimpered, "help me." She felt warm breath, something touched her cheek. God. He was getting ready to take her. She cried.

"Woof!"

A dog! Man's best friend. *Her* best friend now. "You aren't better than God, but you'll damn well do," Mo gasped. "Do you understand? I need help. Can you fetch help?" Mo's hands reached out to the dog, but he backed away, woofing softly. Maybe he was barking louder and she couldn't hear it over the sound of the storm. "I'll try and follow you, but I don't think I'll make it." The dog barked again and as suddenly as he appeared, he was gone.

Mo howled her despair. She knew she had to move. The dog must live close by. Maybe the light she'd seen earlier was a house and this dog lived there. Again, she lost track of time as she crawled forward.

"Woof, woof, woof."

"You came back!" She felt her face being licked, nudged. There was something in the dog's mouth. Maybe something he'd killed. He licked her. He put something down, picked it up and was trying to give it to her. "What?"

The dog barked, louder, backing up, then lunging at her, thrusting whatever he had in his mouth at her. She reached for it. A ribbon. And then she understood. She did her best to loop it around her wrist, crawling on her hands and knees after the huge dog.

Time passed—she didn't know how much. Once, twice, three times, the dog had to get down on all fours and nudge her, the frozen ribbon tickling her face. At one point when she was down and didn't think she would ever get up, the dog nipped her nose, barking in her ear. She obeyed and moved.

And then she saw the windows full of bright yellow light. She thought she saw a Christmas tree through the window. The dog was barking, urging her to follow him. She snaked after him on her belly, praying, thanking God, as she went along.

A doggie door. A large doggie door. The dog went through it, barking on the other side. Maybe no one was home to open the door to her. Obviously, the dog intended her to follow. When in Rome . . . She pushed her way through.

The heat from the huge, blazing fire in the kitchen slammed into her. Nothing in the world ever felt this good. Her entire body started to tingle. She rolled over, closer to the fire. It smelled of pine and something else, maybe cinnamon. The dog barked furiously as he circled the rolling girl. He wanted something, but she didn't know what. She saw it out of the corner of her eye—a large, yellow towel. But she couldn't reach it. "Push it here," she said hoarsely. The dog obliged.

"Well, Merry Christmas," a voice said behind her. "I'm sorry I wasn't here to welcome you, but I was showering and dressing at the back end of the house. I just assumed Murphy was barking at some wild animal. Do you always make this kind of entrance? Mind you, I'm not complaining. Actually, I'm delighted that I'll have someone to share Christmas Eve with. I'm sorry I can't help you, but I think you should get up. Murphy will show you the way to the bedroom and bath. You'll find a warm robe. Just rummage for whatever you want. I'll have some warm food for you when you get back. You are okay, aren't you? You need to move, get your circulation going again. Frostbite can be serious."

"I got lost and your dog found me," Mo whispered.

"I pretty much figured that out," the voice chuckled.

"You have a nice voice," Mo said sleepily. "I really need to sleep. Can't I just sleep here in front of this fire?"

"No, you cannot." The voice was sharp, authoritative. Mo's eyes snapped open. "You need to get out of those wet clothes. Now!"

"Yes, sir!" Mo said smartly. "I don't think much of your hospitality. You could help me, you know. I'm almost half-dead. I might still die. Right here on your kitchen floor. How's that going to look?" She rolled over, struggling to a sitting position. Murphy got behind her so she wouldn't topple over.

She saw her host, saw the wheelchair, then the anger and frustration in his face. "I've never been known for my tact. I apologize. I appreciate your help and you're right, I need to get out of these wet clothes. I can make it. I got this far. I would appreciate some food, though, if it isn't too much trouble. . . . Or, I can make it myself if you . . ."

"I'm very self-sufficient. I think I can rustle up something that doesn't come in a bag. You know, real food. It's time for Murphy's supper, too."

His voice was cool and impersonal. He was handsome, probably well over six feet if he'd been standing. Muscular. "It can't be suppertime already. What time is it?"

"A little after three. Murphy eats early. I don't know why that is, he just does."

She was standing—a feat in itself. She did her best to marshal her dignity as Murphy started out of the kitchen. "I'm sorry I didn't bring a present. It was rude of me to show up like this with nothing in hand. My mother taught me better, but circumstances . . ."

"Go!"

Murphy bounded down the hall. Mo lurched against the wall again and again, until she made it to the bathroom. It was a pretty room for a bathroom, all powdery blue and white with matching towels and carpet. And it was toasty warm. The shower was obviously for the handicapped with a special seat and grab bars. She shed her clothes, layer by layer, until she was naked. She turned on the shower and was rewarded with instant steaming water. Nothing in the world had ever looked this good. Or felt this good, she thought as she stepped into the spray. She let the water pelt her and made a mental note to ask her host where he got the shower head that massaged her aching body. The soap was Ivory, clean and sweet-smelling. The shampoo was something in a black bottle, something manly. She didn't care. She lathered up her dark, wet curls and then rinsed off. She decided she liked the smell and made another mental note to look closely at the bottle for the name.

When the water cooled, she stepped out and would have laughed if she hadn't been so tired. Murphy was holding a towel. A large one, the mate to the yellow one in the kitchen. He trotted over to the linen closet, inched it open. She watched him as he made his selection, a smaller towel obviously for her hair. "You're one smart dog, I can say that for you. I owe you my life, big guy. Let's see, I'd wager you're a golden retriever. My hair should be half as silky as yours. I'm going to send you a dozen porterhouse steaks when I get home. Now, let's see, he said there was a robe in here. Ah, here it is. Now, why did I know it was going to be dark green?" She slipped into it, the smaller towel still wrapped around her head. The robe smelled like the shampoo. Maybe the stuff came in a set.

He had said to rummage for what she wanted. She did, for socks and a pair of long underwear. She pulled on both, the waistband going all the way up to her underarms. As if she cared. All she wanted was the welcome warmth.

She looked around his bedroom. His. Him. God, she didn't even know his name, but she knew his dog's name. How strange. She wanted to do something. The thought had come to her in the shower, but now it eluded her. She saw the phone and the fire-place at the same time. She knew there would be no dial tone, and she was right. She sat down by the fire in the nest of cushions, motioning wearily for the dog to come closer. "I wish you were mine, I really do. Thank you for saving me. Now, one last favor—find that Christmas ribbon and save it for me. I want to have something to remember you by. Not now, the next time you go outside. Will you do that for . . . ?" A moment later she was asleep in the mound of pil-lows.

Murphy sat back on his haunches to stare at the sleeping girl in his master's room. He walked around her several times, sniffing as he did so. When he was satisfied that all was well, he trotted over to the bed and tugged at the comforter until he had it on the floor. Then he dragged it over to the sleeping girl. He pulled, dragged and tugged until he had it snugly up around her chin. The moment he was finished, he beelined down the hall, through the living room, past his master, out to the kitchen where he slowed just enough to go through his door. He was back in ten minutes with the red ribbon.

"So that's where it is. Hand it over, Murphy. It's supposed to go on the tree." The golden dog stopped in his tracks, woofed, backed up several steps, but he didn't drop the ribbon. Instead, he raced down the hall to the bedroom, his master behind him, his chair whirring softly. He watched as the dog placed the rib-bon on the coverlet next to Mo's face. He continued to watch as the huge dog gently tugged the small yel-low towel from her wet head. With his snout, he nudged the dark ringlets, then he gently pawed at them.

"I see," Marcus Bishop said sadly. "She does look

a little like Marcey with that dark hair. Now that you have the situation under control, I guess it's time for your dinner. She wanted the ribbon, is that it? That's how you got her here? Good boy, Murphy. Let's let our guest sleep. Maybe she'll wake up in time to sing some carols with us. You did good, Murph. Real good. Marcey would be so proud of you. Hell, I'm proud of you and if we don't watch it, I have a feeling this girl is going to try and snatch you away from me."

Marcus could feel his eyes start to burn when Murphy bent over the sleeping girl to lick her cheek. He swore then that the big dog cried, but he couldn't be certain because his own eyes were full of tears.

Back in the kitchen, Marcus threw Mo's clothes in the dryer. He spooned out wet dog food and kibble into Murphy's bowl. The dog looked at it and walked away. "Yeah, I know. So, it's a little setback. We'll recover and get on with it. If we can just get through this first Christmas, we'll be on the road to recovery, but you gotta help me out here. I can't do it alone." The dog buried his head in his paws, but made no sign that he either cared or understood what his master was saying. Marcus felt his shoulders slump.

It was exactly one year ago to the day that the fatal accident had happened. Marcey, his twin sister, had been driving when the head-on collision occurred. He'd been wearing his seat belt; she wasn't wearing hers. It took the wrecking crew four hours to get him out of the car. He'd had six operations and one more loomed on the horizon. This one, the orthopedic specialists said, was almost guaranteed to make him walk again.

This little cottage had been Marcey's. She'd moved down here after her husband died of leukemia, just five short years after her marriage. Murphy had been her only companion during those tragic years. Marcus had done all he could for her, but she'd kept him at a distance. She painted, wrote an art column for the *Philadelphia Democrat,* took long walks and watched a lot of television. To say she withdrew from life was putting it mildly. After the accident, it was simpler to convert this space to his needs than the main house. A ramp and an oversized bathroom were all he needed. Murphy was happier here, too.

Murphy belonged to both of them, but he'd been partial to Marcey because she always kept licorice squares in her pocket for him.

He and Murphy had grieved together, going to Marcey's gravesite weekly with fresh flowers. At those times, he always made sure he had licorice in his pocket. More often than not, though, Murphy wouldn't touch the little black squares. It was something to do, a memory Marcus tried to keep intact.

It was going to be nice to have someone to share Christmas with. A time of miracles, the Good Book said. Murphy finding this girl in all that snow had to constitute a miracle of some kind. He didn't even know her name. He felt cheated. Time enough for that later. Time. That was all he had of late.

Marcus checked the turkey in the oven. Maybe he should just make a sandwich and save the turkey until tomorrow when the girl would be up to a full sit-down dinner.

He stared at the Christmas tree in the center of the room and wondered if anyone else ever put their tree there. It was the only way he could string the lights. He knew he could have asked one of the servants from the main house to come down and do it just the way he could have asked them to cook him a holiday dinner. But he needed to do these things, needed the responsibility of taking care of himself. In case this next operation didn't work.

He prided himself on being a realist. If he didn't, he'd be sitting in this chair sucking his thumb and watching the boob tube. Life was just too goddamn precious to waste even one minute. He finished decorating the tree, plugged in the lights, and whistled at his marvelous creation. He felt his eyes mist up when he looked at the one-of-a-kind ornaments that had belonged to Marcey and John. He wished for children, a houseful. More puppies. He wished for love, for sound, for music, for sunshine and laughter. Someday.

Damn, he wished he was married with little ones calling him Daddy. Daddy, fix this; Daddy, help me. And some pretty woman standing in the kitchen smiling, the smile just for him. Marcey had said he was a fusspot and that's why no girl would marry him. She had said he needed to be more outgoing, needed to smile more. Stop taking yourself so seriously, she would say. Who said you have to be a better engineer than Dad? And then she'd said, *If you can't whistle when you work you don't belong in that job*. He'd become a whistling fool after that little talk because he loved what he did, loved managing the family firm, the largest engineering outfit in the state of New Jersey. Hell, he'd been called to Kuwait after the Gulf War. That had to mean something in terms of prestige. As if he cared about that.

His chair whirred to life. Within seconds he was

sitting in the doorway, watching the sleeping girl. He felt drawn to her for some reason. He snapped his fingers for Murphy. The dog nuzzled his leg. "Check on her, Murph—make sure she's breathing. She should be okay, but do it anyway. Good thing that fireplace is gas—she'll stay warm if she sleeps through the night. Guess I get the couch." He watched as the retriever circled the sleeping girl, nudging the quilt that had slipped from her shoulders. As before, he sniffed her dark hair, stopping long enough to lick her cheek and check on the red ribbon. Marcus motioned for him. Together, they made their way down the hall to the living room and the festive Christmas tree.

It was only six o'clock. The evening loomed ahead of him. He fixed two large ham sandwiches, one cut into four neat squares, then arranged them on two plates along with pickles and potato chips. A beer for him and grape soda for Murphy. He placed them on the fold-up tray attached to his chair. He whirred into the room, then lifted himself out of the chair and onto the couch. He pressed a button and the wide screen television in the corner came to life. He flipped channels until he came to the Weather Channel. "Pay attention, Murph, this is what you saved our guest from. They're calling it The Blizzard. Hell, I could have told them that at ten o'clock this morning. You know what I never figured out, Murph? How Santa is supposed to come down the chimney on Christmas Eve with a fire going. Everyone lights their fireplaces on Christmas Eve. Do you think I'm the only one who's ever asked this question?" He continued to talk to the dog at his feet, feeding him potato chips. For a year now, Murphy was the only one he talked to, with the exception of his doctors and the household help. The business ran itself with capable people standing in for him. He was more than fortunate in that respect. "Did you hear that, Murph? Fourteen inches of snow. We're marooned. They won't even be able to get down here from the big house to check on us. We might have our guest for a few days. Company." He grinned from ear to ear and wasn't sure why. Eventually he dozed, as did Murphy.

Mo opened one eye, instantly aware of where she was and what had happened to her. She tried to stretch her arms and legs. She bit down on her lower lip so she wouldn't cry out in pain. A hot shower, four or five aspirin and some liniment might make things bearable. She closed her eyes, wondering what time it was. She offered up a prayer, thanking God that she was alive and as well as could be expected under the circumstances.

Where was her host? Her savior? She supposed she would have to get up to find out. She tried again to boost herself to a sitting position. With the quilt wrapped around her, she stared at the furnishings. It seemed feminine to her with the priscilla curtains, the pretty pale blue carpet, and satin-striped chaise longue. There was also a faint powdery scent to the room. A leftover scent as though the occupant no longer lived here. She stared at the large louvered closet that took up one entire wall. Maybe that's where the powdery smell was coming from. Closets tended to hold scents. She looked down at the purple and white flowers adorning the quilt. It matched the drapes. Did men use fluffy yellow towels? If they were leftovers, they did. Her host seemed like the green, brown and beige type to her.

She saw the clock, directly in her line of vision, sitting next to the phone that was dead.

The time was 3:15. Good Lord, she'd slept the clock around. It was Christmas Day. Her parents must be worried sick. Where was Keith? She played with the fantasy that he was out with the state troopers looking for her, but only for a minute. Keith didn't like the cold. He only pretended to like skiing because it was the trendy thing to do.

She got up, tightened the belt on the oversize robe and hobbled around the room, searching for the scent that was so familiar. One side of the closet held women's clothes, the other side, men's. So, there was a Mrs. Host. On the dresser, next to the chaise longue, was a picture of a pretty, dark-haired woman and her host. Both were smiling, the man's arm around the woman's shoulders. They were staring directly at the camera. A beautiful couple. A friend must have taken the picture. She didn't have any pictures like this of her and Keith. She felt cheated.

Mo parted the curtains and gasped. In her life she'd never seen this much snow. She knew in her gut the Jeep was buried. How would she ever find it? Maybe the dog would know where it was.

Mo shed her clothes in the bathroom and showered again. She turned the nozzle a little at a time, trying to get the water as hot as she could stand it. She moved, jiggled and danced under the spray as it pelted her sore, aching muscles. She put the same long underwear and socks back on and rolled up the sleeves of the robe four times. She was warm, that was all that mattered. Her skin was chafed and wind-burned. She needed cream of some kind, lanolin. Did her host keep things like that here in the bathroom? She looked under the sink. In two shoeboxes she found everything she needed. Expensive cosmetics, pricey perfume. Mrs. Host must have left in a hurry or a huff. Women simply didn't leave a fortune in cosmetics behind.

She was ready now to introduce herself to her host and sit down to food. She realized she was ravenous.

He was in the kitchen mashing potatoes. The table was set for two and one more plate was on the floor. A large turkey sat in the middle of the table.

"Can I do anything?" Her voice was raspy, throaty.

The chair moved and he was facing her.

"You can sit down. I waited to mash the potatoes until I heard the shower going. I'm Marcus Bishop. Merry Christmas."

"I'm Morgan Ames. Merry Christmas to you and Murphy. I can't thank you enough for taking me in. I looked outside and there's a lot of snow out there. I don't think I've ever seen this much snow. Even in Colorado. Everything looks wonderful. It smells wonderful, and I know it's going to taste wonderful, too." She was babbling like a schoolgirl. She clamped her lips shut and folded her hands in her lap.

He seemed amused. "I tried. Most of the time I just grill something out on the deck. This was my first try at a big meal. I don't guarantee anything. Would you like to say grace?"

Would she? Absolutely she would. She had much to be thankful for. She said so, in great detail, head bowed. A smile tugged at the corners of Bishop's mouth. Murphy panted, shifting position twice, as much as to say, let's get on with it.

Mo flushed. "I'm sorry, I did go on there a bit, didn't I? You see, I promised . . . I said . . ."

"You made a bargain with God," Marcus said.

"How did you know?" God, he was handsome. The picture in the bedroom didn't do him justice at all.

"When it's down to the wire and there's no one else, we all depend on that Supreme Being to help us out. Most times we forget about Him. The hard part is going to be living up to all those promises."

"I never did that before. Even when things were bad, I didn't ask. This was different. I stared at my mortality. Are you saying you think I was wrong?"

"Not at all. It's as natural as breathing. Life is precious. No one wants to lose it." His voice faltered, then grew stronger.

Mo stared across the table at her host. She'd caught a glimpse of the pain in his eyes before he lowered his head. Maybe Mrs. Bishop was . . . not of this earth. She felt flustered, sought to change the subject. "Where is this place, Mr. Bishop? Am I in a town or is this the country? I only saw one house up on the hill when I looked out the window."

"The outskirts of Cherry Hill."

She was gobbling her food, then stopped chewing long enough to say, "This is absolutely delicious. I didn't realize I had driven this far. There was absolutely no visibility. I didn't know if I'd gone over the Delaware Bridge or not. I followed the car's lights in front of me and then suddenly the lights were gone and I was on my own. The car just gave out even though I still had some gas left."

"Where were you going? Where did you leave from?"

"I live in Delaware. My parents live in Woodbridge, New Jersey. I was going home for Christmas like thousands of other people. My mother called and told me how bad the snow was. Because I have a four-wheel drive Cherokee, I felt confident I could make it. There was one moment there before I started out when I almost went back. I wish now I had listened to my instincts. It's probably the second most stupid thing I've ever done. Again, I'm very grateful. I could have died out there and all because I had to get home. I just had to get home. I tried the telephone in the bedroom but the line was dead. How long do you think it will take before it comes back on?" How anxious her voice sounded. She cleared her throat.

"A day or so. It stopped snowing about an hour ago. I heard a bulletin that said all the work crews are out. Power is the first thing that has to be restored. I'm fortunate in the sense that I have gas heat and a backup generator in case power goes out. When you live in the country these things are mandatory."

"Do you think the phone is out in the big house on the hill?"

"If mine is out, so is theirs," Marcus said quietly. "This is Christmas, you know."

"I know," Mo said, her eyes misting over.

"Eat!" Marcus said in the same authoritative tone he'd used the day before.

"My mother always puts marshmallow in her sweet potatoes. You might want to try that sometime. She sprinkles sesame seeds in her chopped broccoli. It gives it a whole different taste." She held out her plate for a second helping of turkey.

"I like the taste as it is, but I'll keep it in mind and give it a try someday."

"No, you won't. You shouldn't say things unless you mean them. You strike me as a person who does things one way and is not open to anything but your own way. That's okay, too, but you shouldn't humor me. I happen to like marshmallows in my sweet potatoes and sesame seeds in my broccoli."

"You don't know me at all so why would you make such an assumption?"

"I know that you're bossy. You're used to getting things done your way. You ordered me to take a shower and get out of my wet clothes. You just now, a minute ago, ordered me to eat."

"That was for your own good. You are opinionated, aren't you?"

"Yep. I feel this need to tell you your long underwear scratches. You should use fabric softener in the final rinse water."

Marcus banged his fist on the table. "Aha!" he roared. "That just goes to show how much you really know. Fabric softener does something to the fibers and when you sweat the material won't absorb it. So there!"

"Makes sense. I merely said it would help the scratching. If you plan on climbing a mountain . . . I'm sorry. I talk too much sometimes. What do you have for dessert? Are we having coffee? Can I get it or would you rather I just sit here and eat."

"You're my guest. You sit and eat. We're having plum pudding, and of course we're having coffee. What kind of Christmas dinner do you think this is?" His voice was so huffy that Murphy got up, meandered over to Mo and sat down by her chair.

"The kind of dinner where the vegetables come in frozen boil bags, the sweet potatoes in boxes and the turkey stuffing in cellophane bags. I know for a fact that plum pudding can be bought frozen. I'm sure dessert will be just as delicious as the main course. Actually, I don't know when anything tasted half as good. Most men can't cook at all. At least the men I know." She was babbling again. "You can call me Mo. Everyone else does, even my dad."

"Don't get sweet on my dog, either," Marcus said, slopping the plum pudding onto a plate.

"I think your dog is sweet on me, Mr. Bishop. You should put that pudding in a little dessert dish. See, it spilled on the floor. I'll clean it up for you." She was half out of her chair when the iron command knifed through the air.

"Sit!" Mo lowered herself into her chair. Her eyes started to burn.

"I'm not a dog, Mr. Bishop. I only wanted to help. I'm sorry if my offer offended you. I don't think I care for dessert or coffee." Her voice was stiff, her shoulders stiff, too. She had to leave the table or she was going to burst into tears. What was wrong with her?

"I'm the one who should be apologizing. I've had to learn to do for myself. Spills were a problem for a while. I have it down pat now. I just wet a cloth and use the broom handle to move it around. It took me a while to figure it out. You're right about the frozen stuff. I haven't had many guests lately to impress. And you can call me Marcus."

"Were you trying to impress me? How sweet, Marcus. I accept your apology and please accept mine. Let's pretend I stopped by to wish you a Merry

Christmas and got caught in the snowstorm. Because you're a nice man, you offered me your hospitality. See, we've established that you're a nice man and I want you to take my word for it that I'm a nice person. Your dog likes me. That has to count."

Marcus chuckled. "Well said."

Mo cupped her chin in her hands. "This is a charming little house. I bet you get the sun all day long. Sun's important. When the sun's out you just naturally feel better, don't you think? Do you have flowers in the spring and summer?"

"You name it, I've got it. Murphy digs up the bulbs sometimes. You should see the tulips in the spring. I spent a lot of time outdoors last spring after my accident. I didn't want to come in the house because that meant I was cooped up. I'm an engineer by profession so I came up with some long-handled tools that allowed me to garden. We pretty much look like a rainbow around April and May. If you're driving this way around that time, stop and see for yourself."

"I'd like that. I'm almost afraid to ask this, but I'm going to ask anyway. Will it offend you if I clean up and do the dishes?"

"Hell, no! I hate doing dishes. I use paper plates whenever possible. Murphy eats off paper plates, too."

Mo burst out laughing. Murphy's tail thumped on the floor.

Mo filled the sink with hot, soapy water. Marcus handed her the plates. They were finished in twenty minutes.

"How about a Christmas drink? I have some really good wine. Christmas will be over before you know it."

"This is good wine," Mo said.

"I don't believe it. You mean you can't find anything wrong with it?" There was a chuckle in Marcus's voice so Mo didn't take offense. "What do you do for a living, Morgan Ames?"

"I'm an architect. I design shopping malls—big ones, small ones, strip malls. My biggest ambition is to have someone hire me to design a bridge. I don't know what it is, but I have this . . . this thing about bridges. I work for a firm, but I'm thinking about going out on my own next year. It's a scary thought, but if I'm going to do it, now is the time. I don't know why I feel that way, I just do. Do you work here at home or at an office?"

"Ninety percent at home, ten percent at the office. I have a specially equipped van. I can't get up on girders, obviously. I have several employees who are my legs. It's another way of saying I manage very well."

"It occurs to me to wonder, Marcus, where you slept last night. I didn't realize until a short while ago that there's only one bedroom."

"Here on the couch. It wasn't a problem. As you can see, it's quite wide and deep—the cushions are extra thick.

"So, what do you think of my tree?" he asked proudly.

"I love the bottom half. I even like the top half. The scent is so heady. I've always loved Christmas. It must be the kid in me. My mother said I used to make myself sick on Christmas Eve because I couldn't wait for Santa." She wanted to stand by the tree and pretend she was home waiting for Keith to show up and put the ring on her finger, wanted it so bad she could feel the prick of tears. It wasn't going to happen. Still, she felt driven to stand in front of the tree and . . . pretend. She fought the burning behind her eyelids by rubbing them and pretending it was the wood smoke from the fireplace that was causing the stinging. Then she remembered the fireplace held gas logs.

"Me, too. I was always so sure he was going to miss our chimney or his sleigh would break down. I was so damn good during the month of December my dad called me a saint. I have some very nice childhood memories. Are you okay? Is something wrong? You look like you lost your last friend suddenly. I'm a good listener if you want to talk."

Did she? She looked around at the peaceful cottage, the man in the wheelchair and the dog sitting at his feet. She belonged in a scene like this one. The only problem was, the occupants were all wrong. She was never going to see this man again, so why not talk to him? Maybe he'd give her some male input where Keith was concerned. If he offered advice, she could take it or ignore it. She nodded, and held out her wineglass for a refill.

It wasn't until she was finished with her sad tale that she realized she was still standing in front of the Christmas tree. She sat down with a thump, knowing full well she'd had too much wine. She wanted to cry again when she saw the helpless look on Marcus's face. "So, everyone is entitled to make a fool of themselves at least once in their life. This is . . . was my time." She held out her glass again, but had to wait while Marcus uncorked a fresh bottle of wine. She thought his movements sluggish. Maybe he wasn't used to so much wine. "I don't think I'd make a very good drunk. I never had this much wine in my whole life."

"Me either." The wine sloshed over the side of the glass. Murphy licked it up.

"I don't want to get sick. Keith used to drink too much and get sick. It made me sick just watching him. That's sad, isn't it?"

"I never could stand a man who couldn't hold his liquor," Marcus said.

"You sound funny," Mo said as she realized her voice was taking on a sing-song quality.

"You sound like you're getting ready to sing. Are you? I hope you aren't one of those off-key singers." He leered down at her from the chair.

"So what if I am? Isn't singing good for the soul or something? It's the feeling, the thought. You said we were going to sing carols for Murphy. Why aren't we doing that?"

"Because you aren't ready," Marcus said smartly. He lowered the footrests and slid out of the chair. "We need to sit together in front of the tree. Sitting is as good as standing . . . I think. C'mere, Murphy, you belong to this group."

"Sitting is good." Mo hiccupped. Marcus thumped her on the back and then kept his arm around her shoulder. Murphy wiggled around until he was on both their laps.

"Just what exactly is wrong with you? Or is that impolite of me to . . . ask?" She swigged from the bottle Marcus handed her. "This is good—who needs a glass?"

"I hate doing dishes. The bottle is good. What was the question?"

"Huh?"

"What was the question?"

"The question is . . . was . . . do all your parts . . . work?"

"That wasn't the question. I'd remember if that was the question. Why do you want to know if my . . . parts work? Do you find yourself attracted to me? Or is this a sneaky way to try and get my dog? Get your own damn dog. And my parts work just fine."

"You sound defensive. When was the last time you tried them out . . . what I mean is . . . how do you know?" Mo asked craftily.

"I know! Are you planning on taking advantage of me? I might allow it. Then again, I might not."

"You're drunk," Mo said.

"Yep, and it's all your fault. You're drunk, too."

"What'd you expect? You keep filling my glass. You know what, I don't care. Do you care, Marcus?"

"Nope. So, what are you going to do about that jerk who's waiting by your Christmas tree? Christmas is almost over. D'ya think he's still waiting?"

Mo started to cry. Murphy wiggled around and licked at her tears. She shook her head.

"Don't cry. That jerk isn't worth your little finger. Murphy wouldn't like him. Dogs are keen judges of character."

"Keith doesn't like dogs."

Marcus threw his hands in the air. "There you go! I rest my case." His voice sounded so dramatic, Mo started to giggle.

It wasn't much in the way of a kiss because she was giggling, Murphy was in the way and Marcus's position and clumsy hands couldn't seem to coordinate with her. "That was sweet," Mo said.

"Sweet! Sweet!" Marcus bellowed in mock outrage.

"Nice?"

"Nice is better than *sweet*. No one ever said that to me before."

"How many were there . . . before?"

"None of your business."

"That's true, it isn't any of my business. Let's sing. 'Jingle Bells.' We're both too snookered to know the words to anything else. How many hours till Christmas is over?"

Marcus peered at his watch. "A few." He kissed her again, his hands less clumsy. Murphy cooperated by wiggling off both their laps.

"I liked that!"

"And well you should. You're very pretty, Mo. That's an awful name for a girl. I like Morgan, though. I'll call you Morgan."

"My father wanted a boy. He got me. It's sad. Do you know how many times I used that phrase in the past few hours? A lot." Her head bobbed up and down for no good reason. "Jingle Bells . . ." Marcus joined in, his voice as off-key as hers. They collapsed against each other, laughing like lunatics.

"Tell me about you. Do you have any more wine?"

Marcus pointed to the wine rack in the kitchen. Mo struggled to her feet, tottered to the kitchen, uncorked the bottle and carried it back to the living room. "I didn't see any munchies in the kitchen so I brought us each a turkey leg."

"I like a woman who thinks ahead." He gnawed on the leg, his eyes assessing the girl next to him. He wasn't the least bit drunk, but he was pretending he was. Why? She was pretty, and she was nice. So what if she had a few hangups. She liked him, too, he could tell. The chair didn't intimidate her the way it did other women. She was feisty, with a mind of her own. She'd been willing to share her private agonies with him, a stranger. Murphy liked her. He liked her, too. Hell, he'd given up his room to her. Now, she was staring at him expectantly, waiting for him to talk about himself. What to tell her? What to gloss over? Why couldn't he be as open as she was?

"I'm thirty-five. I own and manage the family engineering firm. I have good job security and a great pension plan. I own this little house outright. No mortgages. I love dogs and horses. I even like cats. I've almost grown accustomed to this chair. I am self-sufficient. I treat my elders with respect. I was a hell of a Boy Scout, got lots of medals to prove it. I used to ski. I go to church, not a lot, but I do go. I believe in God. I don't have any . . . sisters or brothers. I try not to think too far ahead and I do my best not to look back. That's not to say I don't think and plan for the future, but in my position, I take it one day at a time. That pretty much sums it up as far as my life goes."

"It sounds like a good life. I think you'll manage just fine. We all have to make concessions . . . the chair . . . it's not the end of the world. I can tell you don't like talking about it, so, let's talk about something else."

"How would you feel if you went home this Christmas Eve and there in your living room was Keith in a wheelchair? What if he told you the reason he hadn't been in touch was because he didn't want to see pity in your eyes. How would you feel if he told you he wasn't going to walk again? What if he said you might eventually be the sole support?" He waited for her to digest the questions, aware that her intoxicated state might interfere with her answers.

"You shouldn't ask me something like that in my . . . condition. I'm not thinking real clear. I want to sing some more. I didn't sing last year because I was too sad. Are you asking about this year or last year?"

"What difference does it make?" Marcus asked coolly.

"It makes a difference. Last year I would have . . . would have . . . said it didn't matter because I loved him. . . . Do all his parts . . . work?"

"I don't know. This is hypothetical." Marcus turned to hide his smile.

"I wouldn't pity him. Maybe I would at first. Keith is very active. I could handle it, but Keith couldn't. He'd get depressed and give up. What was that other part?"

"Supporting him."

"Oh, yeah. I could do that. I have a profession, good health insurance. I might start up my own business. I'll probably make more money than he ever did. Knowing Keith, I think he would resent me after awhile. Maybe he wouldn't. I'd try harder and harder to make it all work because that's the way I am. I'm not a quitter. I never was. Why do you want to know all this?"

Marcus shrugged. "Insight, maybe. In case I ever find myself attracted to a woman, it would be good to know how she'd react. You surprised me—you didn't react to the chair."

"I'm not in love with you," Mo said sourly.

"What's wrong with me?"

"There's nothing wrong with you. I'm not that drunk that I don't know what you're saying. I'm in love with someone else. I don't care about that chair. That chair wouldn't bother me at all if I loved you. You said your parts work. Or, was that a lie? I like sex. Sex is wonderful when two people . . . you know . . . I like it!"

"Guess what? I do, too."

"You see, it's not a problem at all," Mo said happily. "Maybe I should just lie down on the couch and go to sleep."

"You didn't answer the second part of my question."

"Which was?"

"What if you had made it home this Christmas and the same scenario happened. After two long years. What would be your feeling?"

"I don't know. Keith whines. Did I tell you that? It's not manly at all."

"Really."

"Yep. I have to go to the bathroom. Do you want me to get you anything on my way back? I'll be on my feet. I take these feet for granted. They get me places. I love shoes. Well, what's your answer? Remember, you don't have any munchies. Why is that?"

"I have Orville Redenbacher popcorn. The colored kind. Very festive."

"No! You're turning into a barrel of fun, Marcus Bishop. You were a bossy, domineering person when I arrived through your doggie door. Look at you now! You're skunked, you ate a turkey leg and now you tell me you have colored popcorn. I'll be right back unless I get sick. Maybe we should have coffee with our popcorn. God, I can't wait for this day to be over."

"Follow her, Murph. If she gets sick, come and get me," Marcus said. "You know," he said, making a gagging sound. The retriever sprinted down the hall.

A few minutes later, Mo was back in the living

room. She dusted her hands together as she swayed back and forth. "Let's do the popcorn in the fireplace! I'll bring your coffeepot in here and plug it in. That way we won't have to get up and down."

"Commendable idea. It's ten-thirty."

"An hour and a half to go. I'm going to kiss you at twelve o'clock. Well, maybe one minute afterward. Your socks will come right off when I get done kissing you! So there!"

"I don't like to be used."

"Me either. I'll be kissing you because I want to kiss you. So there yourself!"

"What will Keith think?"

"Keith who?" Mo laughed so hard she slapped her thighs before she toppled over onto the couch. Murphy howled. Marcus laughed outright.

On her feet again, Mo said, "I like you, you're nice. You have a nice laugh. I haven't had this much fun in a long time. Life is such a serious business. Sometimes you need to stand back and get . . . what's that word . . . perspective? I like amusement parks. I like acting like a kid sometimes. There's this water park I like to go to and I love Great Adventure. Keith would never go so I went with my friends. It wasn't the same as sharing it with your lover. Would you like to go and . . . and . . . watch the other people? I'd take you if you would."

"Maybe."

"I hate that word. Keith always said that. That's just another way of saying no. You men are all alike."

"You're wrong, Morgan. No two people are alike. If you judge other men by Keith you're going to miss out on a lot. I told you, he's a jerk."

"Okayyyy. Popcorn and coffee, right?"

"Right."

Marcus fondled Murphy's ears as he listened to his guest bang pots and pans in his neat kitchen. Cabinet doors opened and shut, then opened and shut again. More pots and pans rattled. He smelled coffee and wondered if she'd spilled it. He looked at his watch. In a few short hours she'd be leaving him. How was it possible to feel so close to someone he'd just met? He didn't want her to leave. He hated, with a passion, the faceless Keith.

"I think you need to swing around so we can watch the popcorn pop. I thought everyone in the world had a popcorn popper. I'm improvising with this pot. It's going to turn black, but I'll clean it in the morning. You might have to throw it out. I like strong black coffee. How about you?"

"Bootblack for me."

"Oh, me, too. Really gives you a kick in the morning."

"I don't think that's the right lid for that pot," Marcus said.

"It'll do—I told you I had to improvise."

"Tell me how you're going to improvise this!" Marcus said as the popping corn blew the lid off the pot. Popcorn flew in every direction. Murphy leaped up to catch the kernels, nailing the fallen ones with his paws. Marcus rolled on the floor as Mo wailed her dismay. The corn continued to pop and sail about the room. "I'm not cleaning this up."

"Don't worry, Murphy will eat it all. He loves popcorn. How much did you put in the pot?" Marcus gasped. "Coffee's done."

"A cupful. Too much, huh? I thought it would pop

colored. I'm disappointed. There were a lot of fluffies—you know, the ones that pop first."

"I can't tell you how disappointed I am," Marcus said, his expression solemn.

Mo poured the coffee into two mugs.

"It looks kind of . . . syrupy."

"It does, doesn't it? Drink up! What'ya think?"

"I can truthfully say I've never had coffee like this," Marcus responded.

Mo settled herself next to Marcus. "What time is it?"

"It's late. I'm sure by tomorrow the roads will be cleared. The phones will be working and you can call home. I'll try and find someone to drive you. I have a good mechanic I'll call to work on your Jeep. How long were you planning on staying with your parents?"

"It was . . . vague . . . depending . . . I don't know. What will you do?"

"Work. The office has a lot of projects going on. I'm going to be pretty busy."

"Me, too. I like the way you smell," Mo blurted. "Where'd you get that shampoo in the black bottle?"

"Someone gave it to me in a set for my birthday."

"When's your birthday?" Mo asked.

"April tenth. When's yours?"

"April ninth. How about that? We're both Aries."

"Imagine that," Marcus said as he wrapped his arm around her shoulder.

"This is nice," Mo sighed. "I'm a home and hearth person. I like things cozy and warm with lots and lots of green plants. I have little treasures I've picked up over the years that I try to put in just the right place. It tells anyone who comes into my apartment who I am. I guess that's why I like this cottage. It's cozy, warm and comfortable. A big house can be like that, too, but a big house needs kids, dogs, gerbils, rabbits and lots of junk."

He should tell her now about the big house on the hill being his. He should tell her about Marcey and about his upcoming operation. He bit down on his lip. Not now—he didn't want to spoil the moment. He liked what they were doing. He liked sitting here with her, liked the feel of her. He risked a glance at his watch. A quarter to twelve. He felt like his eyeballs were standing at attention from the coffee he'd just finished. He announced the time in a quiet voice.

"Do you think he showed up, Marcus?"

He didn't think any such thing, but he couldn't say that. "He's a fool if he didn't."

"His mother told my mother he wasn't coming home for the holidays."

"Ah. Well, maybe he was going to surprise her. Maybe his plans changed. Anything is possible, Morgan."

"No, it isn't. You're playing devil's advocate. It's all right. Really it is. I'll just switch to Plan B and get on with my life."

He wanted that life to include him. He almost said so, but she interrupted him by poking his arm and pointing to his watch.

"Get ready. Remember, I said I was going to kiss you and blow your socks off."

"You did say that. I'm ready."

"That's it, you're ready. It would be nice if you showed some enthusiasm."

"I don't want my blood pressure to go up," Marcus grinned. "What if . . ."

"There is no *what if*. It's a kiss."

"There are kisses and then there are kisses. Sometimes . . ."

"Not this time. I know all about kisses. Jackie Bristol told me about kissing when I was six years old. He was ten and he knew *everything*. He liked to play doctor. He learned all that stuff by watching his older sister and her boyfriend."

She was *that* close to him. She could see a faint freckle on the bridge of his nose. She just knew he thought she was all talk and no action. Well, she'd show him and Keith, too. A kiss was . . . it was . . . what it was was. . . .

It wasn't one of those warm, fuzzy kisses and it wasn't one of those feathery light kind, either. This kiss was reckless and passionate. Her senses reeled and her body tingled from head to toe. Maybe it was all the wine she'd consumed. She decided she didn't care what the reason was as she pressed not only her lips, but her body, against his. He responded, his tongue spearing into her mouth. She tasted the wine on his tongue and lips, wondered if she tasted the same way to him. A slow moan began in her belly and rose up to her throat. It escaped the moment she pulled away. His name was on her lips, her eyes sleepy and yet restless. She wanted more. So much more.

This was where she was supposed to say, *Okay, I kept my promise, I kissed you like I said*. Now she should get up and go to bed. But she didn't want to go to bed. Ever. She wanted . . . needed . . .

"I'm still wearing my socks," Marcus said. "Maybe you need to try again. Or, how about I try blowing *your* socks off?"

"Go for it," Mo said as she ran her tongue over her bruised and swollen lips.

He did all the things she'd done, and more. She felt his hands all over her body—soft, searching. Finding. Her own hands started a search of their own. She felt as warm and damp as he felt to her probing fingers. She continued to tingle with anticipation. The heavy robe was suddenly open, the band of the underwear down around her waist, exposing her breasts. He was stroking one with the tip of his tongue. When the hard pink bud was in his mouth she thought she'd never felt such exquisite pleasure.

One minute she had clothes on and the next she was as naked as he was. She had a vague sense of ripping at his clothes as he did the same with hers. They were by the fire now, warm and sweaty.

She was on top of him with no memory of getting there. She slid over him, gasped at his hardness. Her dark hair fanned out like a waterfall. She bent her head and kissed him again. A sound of exquisite pleasure escaped her lips when he cupped both her breasts in his hands.

"Ride me," he said hoarsely. He bucked against her as she rode him, this wild stallion inside her. She milked his body, gave a mighty heave and fell against him. It was a long time before either of them moved, and when they did, it was together. She wanted to look at him, wanted to say something. Instead, she nuzzled into the crook of his arm. The oversized robe covered them in a steamy warmth. Her hair felt as damp as his. She waited for him to say something, but he lay quietly, his hand caressing her shoulder beneath the robe. Why wasn't he saying something?

Her active imagination took over. One-night stand. Girl lost in snowstorm. Man gives her shelter and food. Was this her payback? Would he respect her in the morning? Damn, it was already morning. What in the world possessed her to make love to this man? She was in love with Keith. *Was. Was* in love. At this precise moment she couldn't remember what Keith looked like. She'd cheated on Keith. But, had she really? *No,* her mind shrieked. She felt like crying, felt her shoulders start to shake. They calmed immediately as Marcus drew her closer.

"I . . . I never had a one-night stand. I would hate . . . I don't want you to think . . . I don't hop in and out of bed . . . this was the first time in two years . . . I . . ."

"Shhh, it's okay. It was what it was—warm, wonderful and meaningful. Neither one of us owes anything to the other. Sleep, Morgan," he whispered.

"You'll stay here, won't you?" she said sleepily. "I think I'd like to wake up next to you."

"I won't move. I'm going to sleep, too."

"Okay."

It was a lie, albeit a little one. As if he could sleep. Always the last one out of the gate, Bishop. She belongs to someone else, so don't get carried away. How right it had all felt. How right it still felt. What had he just said to her? Oh yeah—*it was what it was.* Oh yeah, well, fuck you, Keith whatever-your-name-is. You don't deserve this girl. I hope your damn dick falls off. You weren't faithful to this girl. I know that as sure as I know the sun is going to rise in the morning. She knows it, too—she just won't admit it.

Marcus stared at the fire, his eyes full of pain and sadness. Tomorrow she'd be gone. He'd never see her again. He'd go on with his life, with his therapy, his job, his next operation. It would be just him and Murphy.

It was four o'clock when Marcus motioned for the retriever to take his place under the robe. The dog would keep her warm while he showered and got ready for the day. He rolled over, grabbed the arm of the sofa and struggled to his feet. Pain ripped up and down his legs as he made his way to the bathroom with the aid of the two canes he kept under the sofa cushions. This was his daily walk, the walk the therapists said was mandatory. Tears rolled down his cheeks as he gritted his teeth. Inside the shower, he lowered himself to the tile seat, turned on the water and let it beat at his legs and body. He stayed there until the water turned cool.

It took him twenty minutes to dress. He was stepping into his loafers when he heard the snowplow. He struggled, with his canes, out to the living room and his chair. His lips were white with the effort. It took every bit of fifteen minutes for the pain to subside. He bent over, picked up the coffeepot and carried it to the kitchen where he rinsed it and made fresh coffee. While he waited for it to perk he stared out the window. Mr. Drizzoli and his two sons were maneuvering the plows so he could get his van out of the driveway. The younger boy was shoveling out his van. He turned on the outside lights, opened the door and motioned to the youngster to come closer. He asked about road conditions, the road leading to the main house and the weather in general. He explained about the Cherokee. The boy promised to speak with his father. They'd search it out and if it was driveable, they'd bring it to the cottage. "There's a five-gallon tank of gas in the garage," Marcus said. From the leather pouch attached to his chair, he withdrew a square white envelope: Mr. Drizzoli's Christmas present. Cash.

"The phones are back on, Mr. Bishop," the boy volunteered.

Marcus felt his heart thump in his chest. He could unplug it. If he did that, he'd be no better than Keith what's-his-name. Then he thought about Morgan's anxious parents. Two cups of coffee on his little pull-out tray, Marcus maneuvered the chair into the living room. "Morgan, wake up. Wake her up, Murphy."

She looked so pretty, her hair tousled and curling about her face. He watched as she stretched luxuriously beneath his robe, watched the realization strike her that she was naked. He watched as she stared around her.

"Good morning. It will be daylight in a few minutes. My road is being plowed as we speak and I'm told the phone is working. You might want to get up and call your parents. Your clothes are in the dryer. My maintenance man is checking on your Jeep. If it's driveable, he'll bring it here. If not, they'll tow it to a garage."

Mo wrapped the robe around her and got to her feet. Talk about the bum's rush. She swallowed hard. Well, what had she expected? One-night stands usually ended like this. Why had she expected anything different? She needed to say something. "If you don't mind, I'll take a shower and get dressed. Is it all right if I use the phone in the bedroom?"

"Of course." He'd hoped against hope that she'd call from the living room so he could hear the conversation. He watched as she made her way to the laundry room, coffee cup in hand. Watched as she juggled cup, clothing and the robe. Murphy sat back on his haunches and howled. Marcus felt the fine hairs on the back of his neck stand on end. Murphy hadn't howled like this since the day of Marcey's funeral. He had to know Morgan was going away. He felt like howling himself.

Marcus watched the clock, watched the progress of the men outside the window. Thirty minutes passed, and then thirty-five and forty.

Murphy barked wildly when he saw Drizzoli come to what he thought was too close to his master's property.

Inside the bedroom, with the door closed, Morgan sat down, fully dressed, on the bed. She dialed her parents' number, nibbling on her thumbnail as she waited for the phone to be picked up. "Mom, it's me."

"Thank God. We were worried sick about you, honey. Good Lord, where are you?"

"Someplace in Cherry Hill. The Jeep gave out and I had to walk. You won't believe this, but a dog found me. I'll tell you all about it when I get home. My host tells me the roads are cleared and they're checking my car now. I should be ready to leave momentarily. Did you have a nice Christmas?" She wasn't going to ask about Keith. She wasn't going to ask because suddenly she no longer cared if he showed up in front of the tree or not.

"Yes and no. It wasn't the same without you. Dad and I had our eggnog. We sang 'Silent Night,' off-key of course, and then we just sat and stared at the tree and worried about you. It was a terrible storm. I don't think I ever saw so much snow. Dad is whispering to me that he'll come and get you if the Jeep isn't working. How was your first Christmas away from home?"

"Actually, Mom, it was kind of nice. My host is a very nice man. He has this wonderful dog who found me. We had a turkey dinner that was pretty good. We even sang 'Jingle Bells'."

"Well, honey, we aren't going anywhere so call us either way. I'm so relieved that you're okay. We called the state troopers, the police, everyone we could think of."

"I'm sorry, Mom. I should have listened to you and stayed put until the snow let up. I was just so anxious to get home." Now, *now* she'll say if Keith was there.

"Keith was here. He came by around eleven. He said it took him seven hours to drive from Manhattan to his mother's. He was terribly upset that you weren't here. This is just my opinion, but I don't think he was upset that you were stuck in the snow—it was more that he was here and where were you? I'm sorry, Morgan, I am just never going to like that young man. That's all I'm going to say on the matter. Dad feels the same way. Drive carefully, honey. Call us, okay?"

"Okay, Mom."

Morgan had to use her left hand to pry her right hand off the phone. She felt sick to her stomach suddenly. She dropped her head into her hands. What she had wanted for two long years, what she'd hoped and prayed for, had happened. She thought about the old adage: Be careful what you wish for because you might just get it. Now, she didn't want what she had wished for.

It was light out now, the young sun creeping into

the room. The silver-framed photograph twinkled as the sun hit it full force. Who was she? She should have asked Marcus. Did he still love the dark-haired woman? He must have loved her a lot to keep her things out in the open, a constant reminder.

She'd felt such strange things last night. Sex with Keith had never been like it was with Marcus. Still, there were other things that went into making a relationship work. Then there was Marcus in his wheelchair. It surprised her that the wheelchair didn't bother her. What did surprise her was what she was feeling. And now it was time to leave. How was she supposed to handle that?

Her heart thumped again when she saw a flash of red go by the bedroom window. Her Jeep. It was running. She stood up, saluted the room, turned and left.

Good-byes are hard, she thought. Especially this one. She felt shy, schoolgirlish, when she said, "Thanks for everything. I mean to keep my promise and send Murphy some steaks. Would you mind giving me your address? If you're ever in Wilmington, stop . . . you know, stop and . . . we can have a . . . reunion. . . . I'm not good at this."

"I'm not, either. Here's my card. My phone number is on it. Call me anytime if you . . . if you want to talk. I listen real good."

Mo handed over her own card. "Same goes for me."

"You just needed some antifreeze. We put five gallons of gas in the tank. Drive carefully. I'm going to worry so call me when you get home."

"I'll do that. Thanks again, Marcus. If you ever want a building or a bridge designed, I'm yours for free. I mean that."

"I know you do. I'll remember."

Mo cringed. How polite they were, how stiff and formal. She couldn't walk away like this. She leaned over, her eyes meeting his, and kissed him lightly on the lips. "I don't think I'll ever forget my visit." *Tell me now, before I leave, about the dark-haired, smiling woman in the picture. Tell me you want me to come back for a visit. Tell me not to go. I'll stay. I swear to God, I'll stay. I'll never think about Keith, never mention his name. Say something.*

"It was a nice Christmas. I enjoyed spending it with you. I know Murphy enjoyed having you here with us. Drive carefully, and remember to call when you get home."

His voice was flat, cool. Last night was just what he'd said: *It was what it was.* Nothing more. She felt like wailing her despair, but she damn well wasn't going to give him the satisfaction. "I will," Mo said cheerfully. She frolicked with Murphy for a few minutes, whispering in his ear, "You take care of him, you hear? I think he tends to be a little stubborn. I have my ribbon and I'll keep it safe, always. I'll send those steaks FedEx." Because her tears were blinding her, Mo turned and didn't look at Marcus again. A second later she was outside in the cold, bracing air.

The Cherokee was warm, purring like a kitten. She tapped the horn, two light taps, before she slipped the gear into four-wheel drive. She didn't look back.

It was an interlude.

One of those rare happenings that occur once in a lifetime.

A moment in time.

In a little more than twenty-four hours, she'd managed to fall in love with a man in a wheelchair—and his dog.

She cried because she didn't know what else to do.

Mo's homecoming was everything she had imagined it would be. Her parents hugged her. Her mother wiped at her tears with the hem of an apron that smelled of cinnamon and vanilla. Her father acted gruff, but she could see the moistness in his eyes.

"How about some breakfast, honey?"

"Bacon and eggs sound real good. Make sure the . . ."

"The yolk is soft and the white has brown lace around the edges. Snap-in-two bacon, three pieces of toast for dunking and a small glass of juice. I know, Morgan. Lord, I'm just so glad you're home safe and sound. Dad's going to carry in your bags. Why don't you run upstairs and take a nice hot bath and put on some clothes that don't look like they belong in a thrift store."

"Good idea, Mom."

In the privacy of her room, she looked at the phone that had, as a teenager, been her lifeline to the outside world. All she had to do was pick it up, and she'd hear Marcus's voice. Should she do it now or wait till after her bath when she was decked out in clean clothes and makeup? She decided to wait. Marcus didn't seem the type to sit by the phone and wait for a call from a woman.

The only word she could think of to describe her bath was *delicious*. The silky feel of the water was full of Wild Jasmine bath oil, her favorite scent in the whole world. As she relaxed in the steamy wetness, she forced herself to think about Keith. She knew without asking that her mother had called Keith's mother after the phone call. Right now, she was so happy to be safe, she would force herself to tolerate Keith. All those presents she'd wrapped so lovingly. All that money she'd spent. Well, she was taking it all back when she returned to Delaware.

Mo heard her father open the bedroom door, heard the sound of her suitcases being set down, heard the rustle of the shopping bags. The tenseness left her shoulders when the door closed softly. She was alone with her thoughts. She wished for a portable phone so she could call Marcus. The thought of talking to him while she was in the bathtub sent shivers up and down her spine.

A long time later, Mo climbed from the tub. She dressed, blow-dried her hair and applied makeup, ever so sparingly, remembering that less is better. She pulled on a pair of Levi's and a sweater that showed off her slim figure. She spritzed herself lightly with perfume, added pearl studs to her ears. She had to rummage in the drawer for thick wool socks. The closet yielded a pair of Nike Air sneakers she'd left behind on one of her visits.

In the kitchen her mother looked at her with dismay. "Is that what you're wearing?"

"Is something wrong with my sweater?"

"Well, no. I just thought . . . I assumed . . . you'd want to spiff up for . . . Keith. I imagine he'll be here pretty soon."

"Well, it better be pretty quick because I have an errand to do when I finish this scrumptious breakfast. I guess you can tell him to wait or tell him to come back some other time. Let's open our presents after supper tonight. Can we pretend it's Christmas Eve?"

"That's what Dad said we should do."

"Then we'll do it. Listen, don't tell Keith. I want it to be just us."

"If that's what you want, honey. You be careful when you're out. Just because the roads are plowed, it doesn't mean there won't be accidents. The weatherman said the highways were still treacherous."

"I'll be careful. Can I get anything for you when I'm out?"

"We stocked up on everything before the snow came. We're okay. Bundle up—it's real cold."

Mo's first stop was the butcher on Main Street. She ordered twelve porterhouse steaks and asked to have them sent Federal Express. She paid with her credit card. Her next stop was the mall in Menlo Park where she went directly to Gloria Jean's Coffee Shop. She ordered twelve pounds of flavored coffees and a mug with a painted picture of a golden retriever on the side, asking to have her order shipped Federal Express and paying again with her credit card.

She spent the balance of the afternoon browsing through Nordstrom's department store—it was so full of people she felt claustrophobic. Still, she didn't leave.

At four o'clock she retraced her steps, stopped by Gloria Jean's for a takeout coffee and drank it sitting on a bench. She didn't want to go home. Didn't want to face Keith. What she wanted to do was call Marcus. *And that's exactly what I'm going to do. I'm tired of doing what other people want me to do. I want to call him and I'm going to call him.* She went in search of a phone the minute she finished her coffee.

Credit card in one hand, Marcus's business card in the other, Mo placed her call. A wave of dizziness washed over her the minute she heard his voice. "It's Morgan Ames, Marcus. I said I'd call you when I got home. Well, I'm home. Actually, I'm in a shopping mall. Ah . . . my mother sent me out to . . . to return some things . . . my dad was on the phone, I couldn't call earlier."

"I was worried when I didn't hear from you. It only takes a minute to make a phone call."

He was worried and he was chastising her. Well, she deserved it. She liked the part that he was worried. "What are you doing?" she blurted.

"I'm thinking about dinner. Leftovers or Spam. Something simple. I'm sort of watching a football game. I think Murphy misses you. I had to go looking for him twice. He was back in my room lying in the pillows where you slept."

"Ah, that's nice. I Federal Expressed his steaks. They should get there tomorrow. I tied the red ribbon on the post of my bed. I'm taking it back to Wilmington with me. Will you tell him that?" Damn, how stupid could one person be?

"I'll tell him. How were the roads?"

"Bad, but driveable. My dad taught me to drive defensively. It paid off." This had to be the most inane conversation she'd ever had in her life. Why was her heart beating so fast? "Marcus, this is none of my business. I meant to ask you yesterday, but I forgot. Who is that lovely woman in the photograph in your room? If it's something you don't care to talk about, it's okay with me. It was just that she sort of looked like me a little. I was curious." She was babbling again.

"Her name was Marcey. She died in the accident I was in. I was wearing my seat belt, she wasn't. I'd rather not talk about it. You're right, though—you do resemble her a little. Murph picked up on that right away. He pulled the towel off your head and kind of sniffed your hair. He wanted me to . . . to see the resemblance, I guess. He took her death real hard."

She was sorry she'd asked. "I'm sorry. I didn't mean to . . . I'm so sorry." She was going to cry now, any second. "I have to go now. Thank you again. Take care of yourself." The tears fell then, and she made no move to stop them. She was like a robot as she walked to the exit and the parking lot. Don't think about the phone call. Don't think about Marcus and his dog. Think about tomorrow when you're going to leave here. Shift into neutral.

She saw his car and winced. Only a teenager would drive a canary yellow Camaro. She swerved into the driveway. Here it was, the day she'd dreamed of for two long years.

"I'm home!"

"Look who's here, Mo," her mother said. That said, she tactfully withdrew, her father following close behind.

"Keith, it's nice to see you," Mo said stiffly. Who was this person standing in front of her, wearing sunglasses and a houndstooth cap? He reeked of Polo.

"I was here—where were you? I thought we had a date in front of your Christmas tree on Christmas Eve. Your parents were so worried. You look different, Mo," he said, trying to take her into his arms. She deftly sidestepped him and sat down.

"I didn't think you'd show," she said flatly.

"Why would you think a thing like that?" He seemed genuinely puzzled at her question.

"Better yet," Mo said, ignoring his question, "what have you been doing these past two years? I need to know, Keith."

His face took on a wary expression. "A little of this, a little of that. Work, eat, sleep, play a little. Probably the same things you did. I thought about you a lot. Often. Every day."

"But you never called. You never wrote."

"That was part of the deal. Marriage is a big commitment. People need to be sure before they take that step. I don't believe in divorce."

How virtuous his voice sounded. She watched, fascinated, as he fished around in his pockets until he found what he was looking for. He held the small box with a tiny red bow on it in the palm of his hand. "I'm sure now. I know you wanted to get engaged two years ago. I wasn't ready. I'm ready now." He held the box toward her, smiling broadly.

He got his teeth capped, Mo thought in amazement. She made no move to reach for the silver box.

"Aren't you excited? Don't you want to open it?"

"No."

"No *what?*"

"No, I'm not excited; no, I don't want the box. No, I don't want to get engaged; and no, I don't want to get married. To you."

"Huh?" He seemed genuinely perplexed.

"What part of *no* didn't you understand?"

"But . . ."

"But *what,* Keith?"

"I thought . . . we agreed . . . it was a break for

both of us. Why are you spoiling things like this? You always have such a negative attitude, Mo. What are you saying here?"

"I'm saying I had two long years to think about us. You and me. Until just a few days ago I thought . . . it would work out. Now, I know it won't. I'm not the same person and you certainly aren't the same person. Another thing, I wouldn't ride in that pimpmobile parked out front if you paid me. You smell like a pimp, too. I'm sorry. I'm grateful to you for this . . . whatever it was . . . hiatus. It was your idea, Keith. I want you to know, I was faithful to you." And she had been. She didn't make love with Marcus until Christmas Day, at which point she already knew it wasn't going to work out between her and Keith. "Look me in the eye, Keith, and tell me you were faithful to me. I knew it! You have a good life. Send me a Christmas card and I'll do the same."

"You're dumping me!" There was such outrage in Keith's voice, Mo burst out laughing.

"That's exactly what you did to me two years ago, but I was too dumb to see it. All those women you had, they wouldn't put up with your bullshit. That's why you're here now. No one else wanted you. I know you, Keith, better than I thought I did. I don't like the word *dump*. I'm breaking off our relationship because I don't love you anymore. Right now, for whatever it's worth, I wouldn't have time to work at a relationship anyway. I've decided to go into business for myself. Can we shake hands and promise to be friends?"

"Like hell! It took me seven goddamn hours to drive here from New York just so I could keep my promise. You weren't even here. At least I tried. I could have gone to Vail with my friends. You can take the responsibility for the termination of this relationship." He stomped from the room, the silver box secure in his pocket.

Mo sat down on the sofa. She felt lighter, buoyant somehow. "I feel, Mom, like someone just took fifty pounds off my shoulders. I wish I'd listened to you and Dad. You'd think at my age I'd have more sense. Did you see him? Is it me or was he always like that?"

"He was always like that, honey. I wasn't going to tell you, but under the circumstances, I think I will. I really don't think he would have come home this Christmas except for one thing. His mother always gives him a handsome check early in the month. This year she wanted him home for the holidays so she said she wasn't giving it to him until Christmas morning. If he'd gotten it ahead of time, I think he would have gone to Vail. We weren't eavesdropping—he said it loud enough so his voice carried to the kitchen. Don't feel bad, Mo."

"Mom, I don't. That dinner you're making smells soooo good. Let's eat, open our presents, thank God for our wonderful family and go to bed."

"Sounds good to me."

"I'm leaving in the morning, Mom. I have some things I need to . . . take care of."

"I understand."

"Merry Christmas, Mom."

Mo set out the following morning with a full gas tank, an extra set of warm clothes on the front seat, a brand new flashlight with six new batteries, a real shovel, foot warmers, a basket lunch that would feed her for a week, two pairs of mittens, a pair of fleece-lined boots, and the firm resolve never to take a trip without preparing for it. In the cargo area there were five shopping bags of presents that she would be returning to Wanamaker's over the weekend.

She kissed and hugged her parents, accepted change from her father for the tolls, honked her horn and was off. Her plan was to stop in Cherry Hill. Why, she didn't know. Probably to make a fool out of herself again. Just the thought of seeing Marcus and Murphy made her blood sing.

She had a speech all worked out in her head, words she'd probably never say. She'd say, *Hi, I was on my way home and thought I'd stop for coffee.* After all, she'd just sent a dozen different kinds. She could help cook a steak for Murphy. Maybe Marcus would kiss her hello. Maybe he'd ask her to stay.

It wasn't until she was almost to the Cherry Hill exit that she realized Marcus hadn't asked if Keith had shown up. That had to mean he wasn't interested in her. *It was what it was.* She passed the exit sign with tears in her eyes.

She tormented herself all of January and February. She picked up the phone a thousand times, and always put it back down. Phones worked two ways. He could call her. All she'd gotten from him was a scrawled note thanking her for the coffee and steaks. He did say Murphy was burying the bones under the pillows and that he'd become a coffee addict. The last sentence was personal. *I hope your delayed Christ-*

mas was everything you wanted it to be. A large scrawled "M." finished off the note.

She must have written five hundred letters in response to that little note. None of which she mailed.

She was in love. Really in love. For the first time in her life.

And there wasn't a damn thing she could do about it. Unless she wanted to make a fool of herself again, which she had no intention of doing.

She threw herself into all the details it took to open a new business. She had the storefront, she'd ordered the vertical blinds, helped her father lay the carpet and tile. Her father had made three easels and three desks, in case she wanted to expand and hire help. Her mother wallpapered the kitchen, scrubbed the ancient appliances, and decorated the bathroom while she went out on foot and solicited business. Her grand opening was scheduled for April first.

She had two new clients and the promise of two more. If she was lucky, she might be able to repay her father's loan in three years instead of five.

On the other side of the bridge, Marcus Bishop wheeled his chair out onto his patio, Murphy alongside him. On the pull-out tray were two beers and the portable phone. He was restless, irritable. In just two weeks he was heading back to the hospital. The do-or-die operation he'd been living for, yet dreading. There were no guarantees, but the surgeon had said he was confident he'd be walking in six months. With extensive, intensive therapy. Well, he could handle that. Pain was his middle name. Maybe then . . .

maybe then, he'd get up the nerve to call Morgan Ames and . . . and chat. He wondered if he dared intrude on her life with Keith. Still, there was nothing wrong with calling her, chatting about Murphy. He'd be careful not to mention Christmas night and their lovemaking. "The best sex I ever had, Murph. You know me—too much too little too late or whatever that saying is. What'd she see in that jerk? He is a jerk, she as much as said so. You're a good listener, Murph. Hell, let's call her and say . . . we'll say . . . what we'll do is . . . *hello* is good. Her birthday is coming up—so is mine. Maybe I should wait till then and send a card. Or, I could send flowers or a present. The thing is, I want to talk to her now. Here comes the mailman, Murph. Get the bag!"

Murphy ran to the doggie door and was back in a minute with a small burlap sack the mailman put the mail in. Murphy then dragged it to Marcus on the deck. He loved racing to the mailman, who always had dog biscuits as well as Mace in his pockets.

"Whoaoooo, would you look at this, Murph? It's a letter or a card from you know who. Jesus, here I am, thinking about her and suddenly I get mail from her. That must mean something. Here goes. Ah, she opened her own business. The big opening day is April first. No April Fool's joke, she says. She hopes I'm fine, hopes you're fine, and isn't this spring weather gorgeous? She has five clients now, but had to borrow money from her father. She's not holding her breath waiting for someone to ask her to design a bridge. If we're ever in Wilmington, we should stop and see her new office. That's it, Murph. What I could do is send her a tree. Everyone has a tree when they open a new office. Maybe some yellow roses. It's ten o'clock in the morning. They can have the stuff there by eleven. I can call at twelve and talk to her. That's it, that's what we'll do." Murphy's tail swished back and forth in agreement.

Marcus ordered the ficus tree and a dozen yellow roses. He was assured delivery would be made by twelve-thirty. He passed the time by speaking with his office help, sipping coffee and throwing a cut-off broom handle for Murphy to fetch. At precisely twelve-thirty, his heart started to hammer in his chest.

"Morgan Ames. Can I help you?"

"Morgan, it's Marcus Bishop. I called to congratulate you. I got your card today."

"Oh, Marcus, how nice of you to call. The tree is just what this office needed and the flowers are beautiful. That was so kind of you. How are you? How's Murphy?"

"We're fine. You must be delirious with all that's happening. How did Keith react to you opening your own business? For some reason I thought . . . assumed . . . that opening the business wasn't something you were planning on doing right away. Summer . . . or did I misunderstand?"

"No, you didn't misunderstand. I talked it over with my father and he couldn't find any reason why I shouldn't go for it now. I couldn't have done it without my parents' help. As for Keith . . . it didn't work out. He did show up. It was my decision. He just . . . wasn't the person I thought he was. I don't know if you'll believe or even understand this, but all I felt was an overwhelming sense of relief."

"Really? If it's what you want, then I'm happy for you. You know what they say, if it's meant to be, it will be." He felt dizzy from her news.

"So, when do you think you can take a spin down here to see my new digs?"

"Soon. Do you serve refreshments?"

"I can and will. We have birthdays coming up. I'd be more than happy to take you out to dinner by way of celebration. If you have the time."

"I'll make the time. Let me clear my deck and get back to you. The only thing that will hinder me is my scheduled operation. There's every possibility it will be later this week."

"I'm not going anywhere, Marcus. Whenever is good for you will be good for me. I wish you the best. If there's anything I can do . . . now, that's foolish, isn't it? Like I can really do something. Sometimes I get carried away. I meant . . ."

"I know what you meant, Morgan, and I appreciate it. Murphy is . . . he misses you."

"I miss both of you. Thanks again for the tree and the flowers."

"Enjoy them. We'll talk again, Morgan."

The moment Marcus broke the connection his clenched fist shot in the air. "Yessss!" Murphy reacted to this strange display by leaping onto Marcus's lap. "She loves the tree and the flowers. She blew off what's-his-name. What that means to you and me, Murph, is maybe we still have a shot. If only this damn operation wasn't looming. I need to think, to plan. I'm gonna work this out. Maybe, just maybe we can turn things around. She invited me to dinner. Hell, she offered to pay for it. That has to mean something. I take it to mean she's interested. In *us,* because we're a package deal." The retriever squirmed and wiggled, his long tail lolling happily.

"I feel good, Murph. Real good."

* * *

Mo hung up the phone, her eyes starry. Sending the office announcement had been a good idea after all. She stared at the flowers and at the huge ficus tree sitting in the corner. They made all the difference in the world. He'd asked about Keith and she'd responded by telling him the truth. It had come out just right. She wished now that she had asked about the operation, asked why he was having it. Probably to alleviate the pain he always seemed to be in. At what point would referring to his condition, or his operation, be stepping over the line? She didn't know, didn't know anyone she could ask. Also, it was none of her business, just like Marcey wasn't any of her business. If he wanted her to know, if he wanted to talk about it, he would have said something, opened up the subject.

It didn't matter. He'd called and they sort of had a date planned. She was going to have to get a new outfit, get her hair and nails done. Ohhhhh, she was going to sleep so good tonight. Maybe she'd even dream about Marcus Bishop.

Her thoughts sustained her for the rest of the day and into the evening.

Two days later, Marcus Bishop grabbed the phone on the third ring. He announced himself in a sleepy voice, then waited. He jerked upright a second later. "Jesus, Stewart, what time is it? Five o'clock! You want me there at eleven? Yeah, yeah, sure. I just have to make arrangements for Murphy. No, no, I won't eat or drink anything. Don't tell me not to worry,

Stewart. I'm already sweating. I guess I'll see you later."

"C'mon, Murph, we're going to see your girlfriend. Morgan. We're going to see Morgan and ask her if she'll take care of you until I get on my feet or . . . we aren't going to think about . . . we're going to think positive. Get your leash, your brush and all that other junk you take with you. Put it by the front door in the basket. Go on."

He whistled. He sang. He would have danced a jig if it was possible. He didn't bother with a shower— they did that for him at the hospital. He did shave, though. After all, he was going to see Morgan. She might even give him a good luck kiss. One of those blow-your-socks-off kisses.

At the front door he stared at the array Murphy had stacked up. The plastic laundry basket was filled to overflowing. Curious, Marcus leaned over and poked among the contents. His leash, his brush, his bag of vitamins, his three favorite toys, his blanket, his pillow, one of his old slippers and one of Marcey's that he liked to sleep with, the mesh bag that contained his shampoo and flea powder.

"She's probably going to give us the boot when she sees all of this. You sure you want to take all this stuff?" Murphy backed up, barking the three short sounds that Marcus took for affirmation. He barked again and again, backing up, running forward, a sign that Marcus was supposed to follow him. In the laundry room, Murphy pawed the dryer door. Marcus opened it and watched as the dog dragged out the large yellow towel and took it to the front door.

"I'll be damned. Okay, just add it to the pile. I'm sure it will clinch the deal."

Ten minutes later they were barreling down I-95. Forty minutes after that, with barely any traffic on the highway, Marcus located the apartment complex where Morgan lived. He used up another ten minutes finding the entrance to her building. Thank God for the handicapped ramp and door. Inside the lobby, his eyes scanned the row of mailboxes and buzzers. He pressed down on the button and held his finger steady. When he heard her voice through the speaker he grinned.

"I'm in your lobby and I need you to come down. Now! Don't worry about fixing up. Remember, I've seen you at your worst."

"What's wrong?" she said, stepping from the elevator.

"Nothing. Everything. Can you keep Murphy for me? My surgeon called me an hour ago and he wants to do the operation this afternoon. The man scheduled for today came down with the flu. I have all Murphy's gear. I don't know what else to do. Can you do it?"

"Of course. Is this his stuff?"

"Believe it or not, he packed himself. He couldn't wait to get here. I can't thank you enough. The guy that usually keeps him is off in Peru on a job. I wouldn't dream of putting him in a kennel. I'd cancel my operation first."

"It's not a problem. Good luck. Is there anything else I can do?"

"Say a prayer. Well, thanks again. He likes real food. When you go through his stuff you'll see he didn't pack any."

"Okay."

"What do you call that thing you're wearing?" Marcus asked curiously.

"It's my bathrobe. It used to be my grandfather's. It's old, soft as silk. It's like an old friend. But better yet, it's warm. These are slippers on my feet even though they look like fur muffs. Again, they keep my feet warm. These things in my hair are curlers. It's who I am," Mo said huffily.

"I wasn't complaining. I was just curious. I bet you're a knockout when you're wearing makeup. Do you wear makeup?"

Mo's insecurities took over. She must look like she just got off the boat. She could feel a flush working its way up to her neck and face. She didn't mean to say it, didn't think she'd said it until she saw the look on Marcus's face. "Why, did Marcey wear lots of makeup? Well, I'm sorry to disappoint you, but I wear very little. I can't afford the pricey stuff she used. What you see is what you get. In other words, take it or leave it and don't ever again compare me to your wife or your girlfriend." She turned on her heel, the laundry basket in her arms, Murphy behind her.

"Hold on! What wife? What girlfriend? What pricey makeup are you talking about? Marcey was my twin sister. I thought I told you that."

"No, you didn't tell me that," Mo called over her shoulder. Her back to him, she grinned from ear to ear. Ahhh, life was lookin' good. "Good luck," she said, as the elevator door swished shut.

In her apartment with the door closed and bolted, Mo sat down on the living room floor with the big, silky dog. "Let's see what we have here," she said, checking the laundry basket. "Hmmm, I see your grooming is going to take a lot of time. I need to tell you that we have a slight problem. Actually, it's a large, as in *very large,* problem. No pets are allowed in this apartment complex. Oh, you brought the yellow towel. That was sweet, Murphy," she said, hugging the retriever. "I hung the red ribbon on my bed." She was talking to this dog like he was a person and was going to respond any minute. "It's not just a little problem, it's a big problem. I guess we sleep at the office. I can buy a sleeping bag and bring your gear there. There's a kitchen and a bathroom. Maybe my dad can come down and rig up a shower. Then again, maybe not. I can always come back to the apartment and shower. We can cook in the office or we can eat out. I missed you. I think about you and Marcus a lot. I thought I would never hear from him again. I thought he was married. Can you beat that?

"Okay, I'm going to take my shower, make some coffee and then we'll head to my new office. I'm sure it's nothing like Marcus's office and I know he takes you there with him. It's a me office, if you know what I mean. It's so good to have someone to talk to. I wish you could talk back."

Mo marched into the kitchen to look in the refrigerator. Leftover Chinese that should have been thrown out a week ago, leftover Italian that should have been thrown out two weeks ago and last night's pepper steak that she'd cooked herself. She warmed it in the microwave and set it down for Murphy, who lapped it up within seconds. "Guess that will hold you till this evening."

Dressed in a professional, spring-like suit, Mo gathered her briefcase and all the stuff she carried home each evening into a plastic shopping bag. Murphy's leash and his toys went into a second bag. At the last moment, she rummaged in the cabinet for a water bowl. "Guess we need to take your bed and blanket, too." Two trips later, the only thing left to do was call her mother.

"Mo, what's wrong? Why are you calling this early in the morning?"

"Mom, I need your help. If Dad isn't swamped, do you think you guys could come down here?" She related the events of the past hours. "I can't live in the office—health codes and all that. I need you to find me an apartment that will take a dog. I know this sounds stupid, but is it possible, do you think, to find a house that will double as an office? If I have to suck up the money I put into the storefront, I will. I might be able to sublease it, but I don't have the time to look around. I have so much work, Mom. All of a sudden it happened. It almost seems like the day the sign went up, everybody who's ever thought about hiring an architect chose me. I'm not complaining. Can you help me?"

"Of course. Dad's at loose ends this week. It's that retirement thing. He doesn't want to travel, he doesn't want to garden, he doesn't know what he wants. Just last night he was talking about taking a Julia Child cooking course. We'll get ready and leave within the hour." Her voice dropped to a whisper. "You should see the sparkle in his eyes—he's ready now. We'll see you in a bit."

Once they reached the office, Murphy settled in within seconds. A square patch of sun under the front window became his. His red ball, a rubber cat with a hoarse squeak and his latex candy cane were next to him. He nibbled on a soup bone that was almost as big as his head.

Mo worked steadily without a break until her parents walked through the door at ten minutes past noon. Murphy eyed them warily until he saw Mo's enthusiastic greeting, at which point he joined in, licking her mother's outstretched hand and offering his paw to her father.

"Now, that's what I call a real gentleman. I feel a lot better about you being here alone now that you have this dog," her father said.

"It's just temporary, Dad. Marcus will take him back as soon as . . . well, I don't know exactly. Dad, I am so swamped. I'm also having a problem with this . . . take a look, give me your honest opinion. The client is coming in at four and I'm befuddled. The heating system doesn't work the way he wants it installed. I have to cut out walls, move windows—and he won't want to pay for the changes."

"In a minute. Your mother and I decided that I will stay here and help you. She's going out with a Realtor at twelve-thirty. We called from the car phone and set it all up. We were specific with your requirements so she won't be taking your mother around to things that aren't appropriate. Knowing your mother, I'm confident she'll have the perfect location by five o'clock this evening. Why don't you and your mother visit for a few minutes while I take a look at these blueprints?"

"I think you should hire him, Mo," her mother stage-whispered. "He'd probably work for nothing. A couple of days a week would be great. I could stay down here with him and cook for you, walk your dog. We'd be more than glad to do it, Mo, if you think it would work and we wouldn't be infringing on your privacy."

"I'd love it, Mom. Murphy isn't my dog. I wish he was. He saved my life. What can I say?"

"You can tell me about Marcus Bishop. The real skinny, and don't tell me there isn't a skinny to tell. I see that sparkle in your eyes and it isn't coming from this dog."

"Later, okay? I think your real estate person is here. Go get 'em, Mom. Remember, I need a place as soon as possible. Otherwise I sleep here in the office in a sleeping bag. If I break my lease by having a pet, I don't get my security deposit back and it was a hefty one. If you can find something for me it will work out perfectly since my current lease is up the first of May. I'm all paid up. I appreciate it, Mom."

"That's what parents are for, sweetie. See you. John . . . did you hear me?"

"Hmmmnn."

Mo winked at her mother.

Father and daughter worked steadily, stopping just long enough to walk Murphy and eat a small pizza they'd had delivered. When Mo's client walked through the door at four o'clock, Mo introduced her father as her associate, John Ames.

"Now, Mr. Caruthers, this is what Morgan and I came up with. You get everything you want with the heating system. See this wall? What we did was . . ."

Knowing her client was in good hands, Mo retired to the kitchen to make coffee. She added some cookies to a colorful tray at the last moment. When she entered the office, tray in hand, her father was shaking hands and smiling. "Mr. Caruthers liked your idea. He gets what he wants plus the atrium. He's willing to absorb the extra three hundred."

"I'm going to be relocating sometime in the next

few weeks, Mr. Caruthers. Since I've taken on an associate, I need more room. I'll notify you of my new address and phone number. If you happen to know anyone who would be interested in a sublease, call me."

Caruthers was gone less than five minutes when Helen Ames bustled through the door, the Realtor in tow. "I found it! The perfect place! An insurance agent who had his office in his home is renting it. It's empty. You can move in tonight or tomorrow. The utilities are on, and he pays for them. It was part of the deal. It's wonderful, Mo—there's even a fenced yard for Murphy. I took the liberty of okaying your move. Miss Oliver has a client who does odd jobs and has his own truck. He's moving your furniture as we speak. All we have to do is pack up your personal belongings and Dad and I can do that with your help. You can be settled by tonight. The house is in move-in condition. That's a term real estate people use," she said knowledgeably. "Miss Oliver has agreed to see if she can sublease this place. Tomorrow, her man will move the office. At the most, Mo, you'll lose half a day's work. With Dad helping you, you'll get caught up in no time. There's a really nice garden on the side of the house and a magnificent wisteria bush you're going to love. Plus twelve tomato plants. The insurance man who owns the house is just glad that someone like us is renting. It's a three-year lease with an option to buy. His wife's mother lives in Florida and she wants to be near her since she's in failing health. I just love it when things work out for all parties involved. He didn't have one bit of a problem with the dog after I told him Murphy's story."

* * *

Everything worked out just the way her mother said it would.

The April showers gave way to May flowers. June sailed in with warm temperatures and bright sunshine. The only flaw in Mo's life was the lack of communication where Marcus was concerned.

Shortly after the Fourth of July, Mo piled Murphy into the Cherokee on a bright sunshiny Sunday and headed for Cherry Hill. "Something's wrong—I just feel it," she muttered to the dog all the way up the New Jersey Turnpike.

Murphy was ecstatic when the Jeep came to a stop outside his old home. He raced around the side of the house, barking and growling, before he slithered through his doggie door. On the other side, he continued to bark and then he howled. With all the doors locked, Mo had no choice but to go in the same way she'd gone through on Christmas Eve.

Inside, things were neat and tidy, but there was a thick layer of dust over everything. Obviously Marcus had not been here for a very long time.

"I don't even know what hospital he went to. Where is he, Murphy? He wouldn't give you up, even to me. I know he wouldn't." She wondered if she had the right to go through Marcus's desk. Out of concern. She sat down and thought about her birthday. She'd been so certain that he'd send a card, one of those silly cards that left the real meaning up in the air, but her birthday had gone by without any kind of acknowledgment from him.

"Maybe he did give you up, Murphy. I guess he isn't interested in me." She choked back a sob as she buried her head in the retriever's silky fur. "Okay, come on, time to leave. I know you want to stay and wait, but we can't. We'll come back again. We'll come back as often as we have to. That's a promise, Murphy."

On the way back to her house, Mo passed her old office and was surprised to see that it had been turned into a Korean vegetable stand. She'd known Miss Oliver had subleased it with the rent going directly to the management company, but that was all she knew.

"Life goes on, Murphy. What's that old saying, time waits for no man? Something like that anyway."

Summer moved into autumn and before Mo knew it, her parents had sold their house and rented a condo on the outskirts of Wilmington. Her father worked full-time in her office while her mother joined every woman's group in the state of Delaware. It was the best of all solutions.

Thanksgiving was spent in her parents' condo with her mother doing all the cooking. The day was uneventful, with both Mo and her father falling asleep in the living room after dinner. Later, when she was attaching Murphy's leash, her mother said, quite forcefully, "You two need to get some help in that office. I'm appointing myself your new secretary and first thing Monday morning you're going to start accepting applications for associates. It's almost Christmas and none of us has done any shopping. It's the most wonderful time of the year and last year convinced us that . . . time is precious. We all need to enjoy life more. Dad and I are going to take a trip the day after Christmas. We're going to drive to Florida. I don't want to hear a word, John. And you, Mo, when was the last time you had a vacation? You can't even remember. Well, we're closing your office on the twentieth of December and we aren't reopening until January second. That's the final word. If your clients object, let them go somewhere else."

"Okay, Mom," Mo said meekly.

"As usual, you're right, Helen," John said just as meekly.

"I knew you two would see it my way. We're going to take up golf when we get to Florida."

"Helen, for God's sake. I hate golf. I refuse to hit a silly little ball with a stick and there's no way I'm going to wear plaid pants and one of those damn hats with a pom-pom on it."

"We'll see," Helen sniffed.

"On that thought, I'll leave you."

At home, curled up in bed with Murphy alongside her, Mo turned on the television that would eventually lull her to sleep. She felt wired up, antsy for some reason. Here it was, almost Christmas, and Marcus Bishop was still absent from her life. She thought about the many times she'd called Bishop Engineering, only to be told Mr. Bishop was out of town and couldn't be reached. "The hell with you, Mr. Marcus Bishop. You gotta be a real low-life to stick me with your dog and then forget about him. What kind of man does that make you? What was all that talk about loving him? He misses you." Damn, she was losing it. She had to stop talking to herself or she was going to go over the edge.

Sensing her mood, Murphy snuggled closer. He licked at her cheeks, pawed her chest. "Forget what I just said, Murphy. Marcus loves you—I know he does. He didn't forget you, either. I think, and this is just my own opinion, but I think something went

wrong with his operation and he's recovering somewhere. I think he was just saying words when he said
he was used to the chair and it didn't bother him. It
does. What if they ended up cutting off his legs? Oh,
God," she wailed. Murphy growled, the hair on the
back of his head standing on end. "Ignore that, too,
Murphy. No such thing happened. I'd feel something
like that."

She slept because she was weary and because
when she cried she found it difficult to keep her eyes
open.

"What are you going to do, honey?" Helen Ames
asked as Mo closed the door to the office.

"I'm going upstairs to the kitchen and make a
chocolate cake. Mom, it's December twentieth. Five
days till Christmas. Listen, I think you and Dad made
the right decision to leave for Florida tomorrow. You
both deserve sunshine for the holidays. Murphy and I
will be fine. I might even take him to Cherry Hill so
he can be home for Christmas. I feel like I should do
that for him. Who knows, you guys might love Florida
and want to retire there. There are worse things, Mom.
Whatever you do, don't make Dad wear those plaid
pants. Promise me?"

"I promise. Tell me again, Mo, that you don't mind
spending Christmas alone with the dog."

"Mom, I really and truly don't mind. We've all
been like accidents waiting to happen. This is a good
chance for me to laze around and do nothing. You
know I was never big on New Year's. Go, Mom. Call
me when you get there and if I'm not home, leave a
message. Drive carefully, stop often."

"Good night, Mo."

"Have a good trip, Mom."

On the morning of the twenty-third of December, Mo woke early, let Murphy out, made herself some bacon and eggs and wolfed it all down. During the night she'd had a dream that she'd gone to Cherry Hill, bought a Christmas tree, decorated it, cooked a big dinner for her and Murphy and . . . then she'd awakened. Well, she was going to live the dream.

"Wanna go home, big guy? Get your stuff together. We're gonna get a tree, and do the whole nine yards. Tomorrow it will be a full year since I met you. We need to celebrate."

A little after the noon hour, Mo found herself dragging a Douglas fir onto Marcus's back patio. As before, she crawled through the doggie door after the dog and walked through the kitchen to the patio door. It took her another hour to locate the box of Christmas decorations. With the fireplaces going, the cottage warmed almost immediately.

The wreath with the giant red bow went on the front door. Back inside, she added the lights to the tree and put all the colorful decorations on the branches. On her hands and knees, she pushed the tree stand gently until she had it perfectly arranged in the corner. It was heavenly, she thought sadly as she placed the colorful poinsettias around the hearth. The only thing missing was Marcus.

Mo spent the rest of the day cleaning and polishing. When she finished her chores, she baked a cake and prepared a quick poor man's stew with hamburger meat.

Mo slept on the couch because she couldn't bring herself to sleep in Marcus's bed.

Christmas Eve dawned, gray and overcast. It felt like snow, but the weatherman said there would be no white Christmas this year.

Dressed in blue jeans, sneakers and a warm flannel shirt, Mo started the preparations for Christmas Eve dinner. The house was redolent with the smell of frying onions, the scent of the tree and the gingerbread cookies baking in the oven. She felt almost light-headed when she looked at the tree with the pile of presents underneath, presents her mother had warned her not to open, presents for Murphy and a present for Marcus. She would leave it behind when they left after New Year's.

At one o'clock, Mo slid the turkey into the oven. Her plum pudding, made from scratch, was cooling on the counter. The sweet potatoes and marshmallows sat alongside the pudding. A shaker of sesame seeds and the broccoli were ready to be cooked when the turkey came out of the oven. She took one last look around the kitchen, and at the table she'd set for one, before she retired to the living room to watch television.

Murphy leaped from the couch, the hair on his back stiff. He growled and started to pace the room, racing back and forth. Alarmed, Mo got off the couch to look out the window. There was nothing to see but the barren trees around the house. She switched on more lights, even those on the tree. As a precaution against what, she didn't know. She locked all the doors and windows. Murphy continued to growl and pace. Then the low, deep growls were replaced with high-pitched whines, but he made no move to go out his doggie door. Mo closed the drapes and turned the floodlights on outside. She could feel herself start to tense up. Should she call the police? What would she say? My dog's acting strange? Damn.

Murphy's cries and whines were so eerie she started to come unglued. Perhaps he wasn't one of those dogs that were trained to protect owner, hearth and home. Since she'd had him he'd never been put to the test. To her, he was just a big animal who loved unconditionally.

In a moment of blind panic she rushed around the small cottage checking the inside dead bolts. The doors were stout, solid. She didn't feel one bit better.

The racket outside was worse and it all seemed to be coming from the kitchen area. She armed herself with a carving knife in one hand and a cast iron skillet in the other. Murphy continued to pace and whine. She eyed the doggie door warily, knowing the retriever was itching to use it, but he'd understood her iron command of *No*.

She waited.

When she saw the doorknob turn, she wondered if she would have time to run out the front door and into her Cherokee. She was afraid to chance it, afraid Murphy would bolt once he was outside.

She froze when she saw the thick vinyl strips move on the doggie door. Murphy saw it, too, and let out an ear-piercing howl. Mo sidestepped to the left of the opening, skillet held at shoulder height, the carving knife in much the same position.

She saw his head and part of one shoulder. "Marcus! What are you doing coming in Murphy's door?" Her shoulders sagged with relief.

"All the goddamn doors are locked and bolted. I'm stuck. What the hell are you doing here in my house? With my dog yet."

"I brought him home for Christmas. He missed you. I thought . . . you could have called, Marcus, or sent a card. I swear to God, I thought you died on the operating table and no one at your company wanted to tell me. One lousy card, Marcus. I had to move out of my apartment because they don't allow animals. I gave up my office. For your dog. Well, here he is. I'm leaving and guess what—I don't give one little shit if you're stuck in that door or not. You damn well took almost a year out of my life. That's not fair and it's not right. You have no excuse and even if you do, I don't want to hear it."

"Open the goddamn door! Now!"

"Up yours, Marcus Bishop!"

"Listen, we're two reasonably intelligent adults. Let's discuss this rationally. There's an answer for everything."

"Have a Merry Christmas. Dinner is in the oven. Your tree is in the living room, all decorated, and there's a wreath on the front door. Your dog is right here. I guess that about covers it."

"You can't leave me stuck like this."

"You wanna bet? Toy with *my* affections, will you? Not likely. Stick *me* with your dog! You're a bigger jerk than Keith ever was. And I fell for your line of bullshit! I guess I'm the stupid one."

"Morgannnn!"

Mo slammed her way through the house to the front door. Murphy howled. She stooped down. "I'm sorry. You belong with him. I do love you—you're a wonderful companion and friend. I won't ever forget how you saved my life. From time to time I'll send you some steaks. You take care of that . . . that big boob, you hear?" She hugged the dog so hard he barked.

She was struggling with the garage door when she felt herself being pulled backward. To her left she heard Murphy bark ominously.

"You're going to listen to me whether you like it or not. Look at me when I talk to you," Marcus Bishop said as he whirled her around.

Her anger and hostility dropped away. "Marcus, you're on your feet! You can walk! That's wonderful!" The anger came back as swiftly as it had disappeared. "It still doesn't excuse your silence for nine whole months."

"Look, I sent cards and flowers. I wrote you letters. How in the damn hell was I supposed to know you moved?"

"You didn't even tell me what hospital you were going to. I tried calling till I was blue in the face. Your office wouldn't tell me anything. Furthermore, the post office, for a dollar, will tell you what my new address is. Did you ever think of that?"

"No. I thought you . . . well, what I thought was . . . you'd absconded with my dog. I lost the card you gave me. I got discouraged when I heard you'd moved. I'm sorry. I'm willing to take all the blame. I had this grand dream that I was going to walk into your parents' house on Christmas Eve and stand by your tree with you. My operation wasn't the walk in the park the surgeon more or less promised. I had to have a second one. The therapy was so intensive it blew my mind. I'm not whining here, I'm trying to explain. That's all I have to say. If you want to keep Murphy, it's okay. I had no idea . . . he loves you. Hell, *I* love you."

"You do?"

"Damn straight I do. You're all I thought about during my recovery. It was what kept me going. I even went by that Korean grocery store today and guess what? Take a look at this!" He held out a stack of cards and envelopes. "It seems they can't read English. They were waiting for you to come and pick up the mail. They said they liked the flowers I sent from time to time."

"Really, Marcus!" She reached out to accept the stack of mail. "How'd you get out of that doggie door?" she asked suspiciously.

Marcus snorted. "Murphy pushed me out. Can we go into the house now and talk like two civilized people who love each other?"

"I didn't say I loved you."

"Say it!" he roared.

"Okay, okay, I love you."

"What else?"

"I believe you and I love your dog, too."

"Are we going to live happily ever after even if I'm rich and handsome?"

"Oh, yes, but that doesn't matter. I loved you when you were in the wheelchair. How are all your . . . parts?"

"Let's find out."

Murphy nudged both of them as he herded them toward the front door.

"I'm going to carry you over the threshold."

"Oh, Marcus, really!"

"Sometimes you simply talk too much." He kissed her as he'd never kissed her before.

"I like that. Do it again, and again, and again."

He did.

The Christmas
Stocking

Chapter One

Los Angeles, California
October, Two Months Before Christmas

It was a beautiful five-story building with clean lines, shimmering plate glass and a bright yellow door. A tribute to the architect who designed the building. An elongated piece of driftwood attached to the right of the door was painted the same shade of yellow. The plaque said it was the Sara Moss Building. The overall opinion of visitors and clients was that the building was impressive, which was the architect and owner's intent.

The young sun was just creeping over the horizon when Gus Moss tucked his briefcase between his knees as he fished in his jeans pocket for the key that would unlock his pride and joy, the Sara Moss Building named after his mother.

Inside, Gus turned off the alarm, flicked light switches. He took a moment to look around the lobby of the building he'd designed when he was still in school studying architecture. He thanked God every day that he'd been able to show his mother the blueprints before she'd passed on. It was his mother's idea to have live bamboo plants to match the green marble floors. It was also her idea to paint clouds and a blue sky on the ceiling. The fieldstone wall behind the shimmering mahogany desk was a must, she'd said. Fieldstones he'd brought to California from Fairfax, Virginia, in a U-Haul truck. There was nothing he could deny his mother because he was who he was because of her.

There was only one picture hanging in the lobby: Sara Moss standing next to a sixty-foot blue spruce Christmas tree that she had his father plant the day he was born. That tree was gone now from the Moss Christmas Tree Farm, donated to the White House by his father the same year his mother died. Over his objections.

He'd gone to Washington, DC, that year and took the Christmas tour so he could see the tree. He'd been so choked up he could hardly get the words out to one of the security detail. "Can you break off a branch from the back of the tree and give it to me?" For one wild moment he thought he was going to be arrested until he explained to the agent why he wanted the branch. He'd had to wait over two hours for one of the gardeners to arrive with a pair of clippers. He'd had a hard time not bawling his eyes out that day but he'd returned to California with the branch. Pressed between two panes of glass, it now hung on the wall over his drafting table. He looked at it a hundred times a day and it meant more to him than anything else in the world.

Gus stared at the picture of his mother the way he did every morning. As always, his eyes grew moist and his heart took on an extra beat. He offered up a snappy salute the way he'd always done when she was right about something and he was wrong. At this point in his daily routine, he never dawdled. He sprinted across the lobby to the elevator and rode to the fifth floor where he had his office so he could settle in for the day.

As always, Gus made his own coffee. While he waited for it to drip into the pot, he checked his appointment book. A light day. He really liked Fridays because they led to the weekend. Still, it was the middle of October and business tended to slow down as a rule. He wished it was otherwise, because the approaching holiday season always left him depressed. He told himself not to complain; he had more business than he could handle the other ten months of the year. When you were named "Architect of the Year" five years running and "Architect to the Stars" six years running, there was no reason to complain. His burgeoning bank balance said his net worth was right up there with some of Hollywood's finest stars. He wasn't about money, though. He was about creating something from nothing, letting his imagination run the gamut. *Architectural Digest* had featured eleven of his projects to date and called him a "Wonder Boy."

Everyone in the business who knew or knew of Gus Moss were aware that when the new owners moved into one of his custom-designed houses, Gus himself showed up wearing a tool belt and carrying a Marty Bell painting, his gift to the new owners, that he hung himself.

Gus loved this time of the day, when he was all alone with his coffee. It was when he let his mind go into overdrive before the hustle and bustle of the day began. He ran a loose ship, allowing his staff to dress in jeans and casual clothing, allowing them to play music in their offices, taking long breaks. He had only three hard and fast rules. Think outside the box, never screw over a client and produce to your capability. His staff of fourteen full-time architects, four part-timers and an office pool of seven had been with him from day one. It worked for all concerned.

As Gus sipped his coffee he let his mind wander. Should he go to Tahoe for some skiing over Christmas? Or should he head for the islands for some sun and sand and a little snorkeling? And who would he ask to accompany him? Sue with the tantalizing lips, Carol with the bedroom eyes or Pam the gymnast with the incredible legs? None of the above. He was sick of false eyelashes, theatrical makeup, spiky hair, painted on dresses and shoes with heels like weapons. He needed to find a nice young woman he could communicate with, someone who understood what he was all about. Not someone who was interested in his money and had her own agenda. At thirty-seven, it was time to start thinking about settling down. Time to give up takeout for homecooked. Time to get a dog. Time to think about having kids. Time to think about putting down roots somewhere, not necessarily here in California, land of milk and honey, orange blossoms and beautiful women.

Gus settled the baseball cap on his head, the cap he was never without. Sometimes he even slept with it on. It was battered and worn, tattered and torn but he'd give up all he held dear before he'd part with his cap that said Moss Farms on the crown. He settled it more firmly on his head as he heard his staff coming in and getting ready for the day.

Gus finished his coffee, grabbed his briefcase and headed for the door. He had a 7:15 appointment with the Fire Marshall on a project he was winding up. He high-fived several members of his staff as he took the steps to the lobby where he stopped long enough to give Sophie, the Moss Firm's official receptionist/ greeter, a smooch. "How's it going this morning, Sophie?"

"Just fine, Gus. When will you be back?"

"By nine-thirty. If anything earth shattering happens, call me on the cell. See ya."

As good as his word, Gus strode back into the lobby at 9:27. Out of the corner of his eye he noticed an elderly couple sitting on a padded bench between two of the bamboo trees. Sophia caught his eye and motioned him to her desk. "That couple is here to see you. They said they're from your hometown. Their names are Peggy and Ham Bledsoe. They don't have an appointment. Can you see them? They're here visiting a daughter who just graced them with their first grandchild."

Gus grinned. "I see you got all the details. Peggy and Ham here in California! I can't believe it."

"We're of an age, darling boy. Go over there and make nice to your hometown guests."

Gus's guts started to churn. Visiting with Peggy and Ham meant taking a trip down Memory Lane and that was one place he didn't want to travel. He pasted a smile on his face as he walked over to the patiently waiting couple. He hugged Peggy and shook Ham's hand. "Good to see you, sir. Miss Peggy, you haven't changed a bit. Sophie tells me you're grandparents now. Congratulations! Come on up to the office and have some coffee. I think we even have sticky buns. We always have sticky buns on Friday."

"This is a mighty fine looking building, Augustus. The lady at the desk said it's all yours. She said you designed it."

"I did," Gus mumbled.

"Mercy me. I wish your momma could have seen this. She was always so proud of you, Augustus."

They were in the elevator before Gus responded, "Mom saw the blueprints. She suggested the field-stone and the bamboo trees. Did you see the picture?"

"We did, and it is a fine picture of Sara. We tell everyone that tree ended up in the White House," Ham said.

Gus was saved from a reply when the elevator came to a stop and the doors slid open. Peggy gasped, her hand flying to her mouth. "This is so . . . so grand, Augustus."

Gus decided he didn't feel like making coffee. He was too nervous around this couple from home. He knew in his gut they were going to tell him something he didn't want to hear. He pressed a button on the console. "Hillary, will you bring some coffee into my office. I have two guests. Some sticky buns, too, okay?"

Gus whirled around, hoping to delay the moment they were going to tell him why they were *really* here. "So, what do you think of California?"

"Well, we don't fit in here, that's for sure," Peggy said. "We're simple people, Augustus. All those fancy cars that cost more than our farm brings in over ten years. The stores with all those expensive clothes where they hide the price tags made my eyes water. Our son-in-law took us to Ro-day-o Drive. That was the name of it, wasn't it, Ham? Hollywood people," she sniffed. "I didn't see a mall or a Wal-Mart anywhere."

Will you just please get to it already. Gus licked at his dry lips, trying to think of something to say. "I just finished up a house for Tammy Bevins. She's a movie star. Would you like to see a picture of the house?"

"No," the Bledsoes said in unison. Gus blinked and then blinked again just as Hillary carried in a tray with an elegant coffeepot with fragile cups and saucers. Linen napkins and a crystal plate of sticky buns were set in the middle of a long conference table.

"Will there be anything else, Gus?"

"Nope, this is fine. Thanks, Hillary. Hey, how's the new boyfriend?"

"He's a hottie." Hillary giggled. "I think I'll keep this one." Gus laughed.

Peggy Bledsoe pursed her lips in disapproval. "Shouldn't that youngster be calling you Mr. Moss?"

"Nah. We're pretty informal around here, Miss Peggy. Sit down. Cream, sugar?"

"Black," the Bledsoes said in unison.

Gus poured. He filled his own cup and then loaded it with cream and four sugars. *I hate coffee with cream and sugar. What's wrong with me?* He leaned back in his chair and waited.

"We stopped by the farm before we left, Augustus. Your father isn't doing well. I don't mean healthwise. The farm has gone downhill. Business is way off. Last year he sold only two hundred Christmas trees. This year if he sells half that he'll be lucky."

Gus was stunned. Moss Farms was known far and wide for their Christmas trees. People came from

miles around to tag a tree in September. Normally his
father sold thirty to fifty thousand trees from November first to Christmas Eve. He said so.

"That was before your momma died and you lit
out, Augustus. Sara was the heart and soul of that
farm. She did the cider, she did the gingerbread, she
managed the gift store. She did the decorations, she
made the bows for the wreathes and the grave blankets. She even worked the chain saw when she had to.
All that changed when she passed on. You should
have gone back, Augustus. That farm is falling down
around your father's feet. The fields need to be
thinned out," Peggy snapped.

Gus snapped back before he could bite his tongue.
"I did go back. Pop didn't want me there. Told me to
get out. I call three times a week—the answering machine comes on. He never calls me back. I send
money home and he sends it back."

Ham drained the coffee in his cup. "I don't think
he's going to sell *any* trees this year. The Senior Citizens group rented the old Coleman property and are
setting up shop. Tillie Baran is spearheading the effort. They ordered their trees from North Carolina.
They're going all out to raise money to refurbish the
Seniors' Building. Just last week at our monthly
meeting, Tillie said her daughter is coming home
from Philadelphia to take over the project. Little Amy
has her own publicity company. That means she's the
boss. When you're the boss, you can take off and help
your momma," he said pointedly.

"You wouldn't believe how good that little girl is
to her momma," Peggy said with just a trace of frost
in her voice.

Gus reached for a sticky bun he didn't want. "And

you think I should go home to help my father and save the day, is that it? Like little Amy Baran is. doing."

"The thought occurred to us," Peggy said. "I think your momma would want you to do that."

Before Gus could think of something to say, Ham jumped into the conversation. "Tillie went out to the farm and asked your father if he would sell her the trees at cost if he wasn't going to promote his own farm. It would have been a good way to thin out the fields but he turned her down flat. So now the Seniors have to pay a trucking company to bring the trees from North Carolina."

Gus searched for something to say. "Maybe the farm is getting too much for him. It's possible he wants to retire. It sounds to me like he's had enough of the Christmas tree business."

"Moss Farms is his life, Augustus. Your father can at times be a cantankerous curmudgeon," Peggy said. "He's all alone. With no business, he laid everyone off."

Gus felt sick to his stomach. He thought about his teenage years on the farm when his father worked him like a dog. That was when his father thought he was going to stick around and run the farm, but his mother was determined he go to college to make something of himself. How he'd hated the fights, the harsh words he heard late at night. All he wanted was to get away from the farm, to do what he was meant to do—create, design and see his creative designs brought to life. All he'd done was follow his mother's dream for him. He wanted to explain to the Bledsoes that he wasn't an uncaring son. He'd done his best where his father was concerned but his best wasn't good enough. He reached for another sticky bun he didn't want. He hated the sugary sweet coffee. He wished he could brush his teeth. Even as he decided that silence was a virtue at this point in time, he asked, "More coffee?"

"No, thank you, Augustus. We have to be going. It was nice to see you again."

"Yes, it was. Nice to see you too. I'm glad you stopped by. I'll take you down to the lobby."

"What are all those movie stars *really* like?" Ham asked.

"Just like you and me. Underneath all the glitz and glamour, they're real people. The glitz and glamour is what they do to earn a living. When they go home at night, they're just like you and Miss Peggy."

Peggy snorted to show what she thought of that statement.

The ride down to the lobby was made in silence. Gus stepped aside to allow the couple to walk out first. "Have a safe trip home. It was nice seeing you. Have a nice holiday." He extended his hand to Ham who ignored it. Gus shoved his hands into the pockets of his jeans. His gut was still churning.

"Just how rich are you, Augustus?" Peggy asked.

Stunned, Gus thought about the question and how his mother would respond. She'd say if a person had the guts to ask such a personal question, they deserved whatever answer you wanted to give. "Filthy rich!" he said cheerfully.

Peggy snorted again. Ham held the door open for his wife before he scurried through. Neither one looked back. Gus wondered how all this was going to play out back home when the Bledsoes returned.

Gus took the stairs to the fifth floor, his head buzzing. When he reached the fifth-floor landing, he sat down on the top step and dropped his head into his hands. For one wild moment he thought he could smell pine resin on his hands. He fought with his breathing to calm down. When his heartbeat returned to normal he let his thoughts drift. He thought about his dog Buster, his faithful companion during his childhood. He thought about Bixby, his buddy all through high school and college. He wondered where Bix was these days. He made a mental note to go on the Net to look him up.

Gus felt his eyes fill with moisture. The Bledsoes were right—his father was a hard man. A cranky curmudgeon pretty well nailed it. Because he'd been big for his age, six foot three at the age of twelve, his father thought him capable of a man's work—to his mother's chagrin. No amount of interference on her behalf could change his father's mind. He'd worked him from sunup until sundown. He'd get sick late at night and his mother would always be there promising his life would get better. And it did when he went off to college.

Gus's head jerked upright as he wondered if he hated his father or if he just didn't like him. More likely the latter, since he didn't hate anyone. He simply wasn't capable of hating anyone.

An hour later, Gus untangled himself and opened the door that led to his office. He felt like he was stepping onto foreign territory since his thoughts were back at Moss Farms. Nothing had changed in his absence. The tray with the coffee service and the leftover sticky buns was still in the middle of the conference table. The pine branch was still hanging over his drafting table. How strange that the Bledsoes hadn't asked what it was or why a dried pine branch was hanging on his wall. Everyone who entered the office asked sooner or later.

He decided right then and there that he didn't like the Bledsoes any more than he liked his father.

The phone on his desk rang. He picked it up and made small talk with a client who wanted to take him to dinner. "How about a rain check, Karl? I have to go out of town for a while. Let's pencil in the first week of the New Year. Okay, glad it works for you. I'll be in touch."

Gus whipped his day planner out of his backpack. He flipped through the pages to see what pressing matters had to be taken care of. Nothing that couldn't wait, he decided.

Five minutes later he made an announcement over the intercom. "Look alive, people, this is your boss. I'd like to see all of you in my office, STAT."

They came on the run the way they always did. When the boss called a special meeting it was of paramount importance. Gus Moss never sweated the small stuff.

Gus wasted no time. "Look, guys, I need to go out of town for a couple of months. Actually, I have to go home. My father needs me." He wondered if it was a lie or wishful thinking on his part. "Can you guys handle things?"

"Surely you jest," Derek Williams quipped. "It will be a vacation for all of us with you gone. We'll party up a storm and drink a toast to you every night."

Gus grinned. They wouldn't do any such thing and they all knew it.

"Hey, man, you said you were going to watch Cyrus for me while I go to Costa Rica next month." It was Max Whitfield, who was Gus's right hand.

"Damn! Okay, okay, I'll take him with me if that's okay. He can run the farm all day. You okay with that, Max?"

"Oh no, my dog does *not* fly in the cargo hold. Dogs die on airplanes."

"Then I'll drive. Works for me if you're okay with it. I promise to coddle him just the way you do. I'll give him an apple and a carrot every day. I'll make sure to give him his vitamins and will give him only bottled water, just the way you do. What I won't do is dress him up in those designer duds you deck him out in."

Max, a string bean of a man, eyeballed his boss and then nodded. "When are you leaving?"

"In the morning. Bring the dog to the office and I'll take off from here. You guys sure you can handle things?"

"Yes, Dad," the little group said in unison.

"Swear you won't call us a hundred times a day," Derek said.

"I don't think you have to worry about that. Okay, it's all set then. Hillary, cancel the rest of my appointments. Reschedule."

Gus looked around at his loyal staff. A lump formed in his throat. They were the best of the best. He made a mental note to double their Christmas bonuses. He could do that tonight at home and hand them out in the morning. Loyalty was one thing he never skimped on. A long time ago his mother had told him a person was only as good as the people who worked for them. At the time he hadn't understood what that meant. He knew now, though.

Time to go cross-country.

Back to his childhood memories.

Back to his father's house.

He hoped he was up to the challenge.

Chapter Two

A week later and three thousand miles away in Philadelphia, Pennsylvania, thirty-four-year-old career woman Amy Baran was on an emotional high as she packed her already overstuffed briefcase. She looked around her cluttered office and sighed. One of these days she really had to give some thought to organizing things. She knew it wasn't going to happen because she loved living in clutter, loved that she could instantly lay her hands on anything she needed.

Amy Baran owned a small public relations firm in the heart of the Main Line District. It employed two full-time staff members; two part-time moms whose schedules she worked around; a receptionist-slash-secretary; and a battle-scarred, bushy-haired orange tabby cat named Cornelia she had found half-starved in the basement of the building she rented. If anyone reigned supreme at the Baran Agency, it was Cornelia who greeted clients by purring and strutting her stuff.

Cornelia knew how to turn on the computer, flush the john and even open the box of Tender Vittles when someone left it sitting on the kitchen counter.

"You going to miss me, Linda?"

"Does Cornelia need whipped cream on her catnip? Of course I'm going to miss you. That was a silly question, Amy. But things slow down at this time of year and you're only a cell phone call away. You said your mom has a fax machine, so I think we're good to go in case something crops up. In a way, I envy you. Going home for the holidays is always kind of special and going all out on your mom's project to help the Seniors is the icing on top as far as good feelings go. If anyone can make it work, you can."

Amy flopped down on her swivel chair, her long legs stretched out in front of her. "Easy to say, Linda. Mapping out a PR campaign to sell cosmetics or corn flakes is a lot different from selling Christmas trees. I know zip about Christmas trees other than you put them in a stand, string lights and ornaments and flick the switch. Instant gratification."

"You got a plan, boss?"

Amy laughed, the sound ricocheting off the walls. "Sort of, kind of. I'm thinking three tents. One for the stuff Mom wants to sell. You know, ornaments, lights, gift wrap, the big red velvet bows. I ordered tons of stuff a week ago when Mom hit me with this. I jumped right on it. Mom's got the Seniors lined up to work the store, as she calls it. They're going to be serving gingerbread and hot mulled cider the way they used to do at Moss Farms. I told you about that wonderful place from my childhood. I hate it that Mr. Moss let the farm go to ruin. I have such nice memories of going out there with my father. He always made it a special event. One year it actually snowed the day we went to pick up the tree. I was so excited I could hardly sleep the night before. Memories are wonderful, aren't they?"

Linda flicked the long braid that hung down to the middle of her back. "Memories are super as long as you don't dwell on them. Maybe you'll meet Prince Charming when you go home. I see it now: He appears out of nowhere, asks you to help him pick out the perfect tree. You do, and then he asks you to deliver it and help him set it up. You agree. You fall into his arms in front of the tree and voila, you now have a boyfriend!"

"In your dreams! I don't have time for boyfriends. I'm trying to build this business and working sixteen hours a day is more than any guy can understand. All in good time."

Linda eyed her boss. She would never understand how someone as personable, as pretty, as intelligent as Amy didn't have men falling all over her. "Your clock is ticking, Amy. There's more to life than building a business."

Amy sniffed as she fiddled with the comb that controlled her long, dark, curly hair. She fixed her green eyes on Linda and said, "You're a year older and I don't see you in any hurry to settle down."

"Yeah, well, at least I have a prospect. George loves me and would marry me in a heartbeat if I said the word. I'm thinking about it. I want us to have enough money saved up to put a down payment on a house. There's no way I'm going to live in an apartment with kids. I want lots of kids and so does George. By next year we'll have saved enough for a starter house. It's my plan. You don't even have a prospect, much less a plan, Amy."

Linda was right even though she didn't want to admit it. She longed for Mr. Right but so far he had eluded her. Maybe Linda was right and she needed to cut back on the hours she worked and get some kind of personal life. Or she could go to the Internet and sign up on one of those match-making sites. *Like that was really going to happen.*

Amy shrugged as she continued to stuff her briefcase. She had to sit on it so she could lock it. "I don't know why I'm taking all this. Better to be prepared for anything and everything. Okay, okay, I'll work on my social skills and try to snag a guy when I get home. You realize single guys do not buy Christmas trees. They buy artificial ones. Families, moms and dads and kids, buy trees. Having said that, I will do my best to find a man who will meet with your approval. If I come back empty-handed, I will explore one of those dating sites, okay?"

"Yeah. Look, if you need me, give me a call. I can take the train and be there in three hours. I'm going to miss Corny," Linda said as she scooped up the tabby to settle her in the carryall. She pulled the zipper.

Amy took a last look around. "It feels right, Linda. Going home, I mean. I hate leaving you for two whole months but like you said, I'm just a phone call away. You don't think I'm making a mistake, do you?"

"Am I hearing right? The famous Amy Baran is asking me if she's making a mistake? The short answer is, no. Look, my mom passed away. I'd drop everything, even George, to have her back calling me to help out.

You always have to give back, Amy. If you don't, you're just a shell of a person. I expect you to be an authority on Christmas trees when you get back. I can go on the Net and research Christmas tree farms and send out some query letters asking if they want to use our services next year. That's assuming you pull this off and raise the money you need."

You don't know my mother, Linda. "Good idea. You know what bothers me the most is the trucking fees. We're starting out in debt. I don't like that. If bad weather sets in, the trees might not be cut in time. I'm at growers' and truckers' mercies. Mom did all the initial contacting. I wish she had left it up to me instead of going with the first person she contacted. You need to shop around to get the best price. Well, I gotta be going. I packed everything up last night. Yes, yes, I will call you along the way and will call you when I get to Mom's house. I'll miss you, Linda. Two months is a long time," Amy said wistfully.

Linda threw her arm over her boss's shoulder. "I think you're going to be too busy to miss this place. Go on now before we both start blubbering."

Amy picked up Cornelia's carrying case and threw it over her shoulder. The briefcase weighed a ton and she probably wouldn't even open it once she got to Virginia. Her mother always said she overcompensated for everything. Her mother also said she was anal retentive, was an overachiever and needed to think inside the box instead of outside. So much for her loving mother.

Amy settled Cornelia on the passenger seat before she unzipped the carryall. Cornelia poked her head up just long enough to see her surroundings before she curled up to sleep. Amy slipped a disc into the player and settled down to make the trip to Fairfax, Virginia.

Four hours later with four stops along the way, Amy pulled into her mother's driveway on Little Pumpkin Lane. She leaned back and closed her eyes for a moment. She was home. The house where she'd grown up. A house of secrets. The house where she'd been lonely, sad, angry. So many memories.

Now why had she expected her mother to be standing in the doorway waiting to greet her? Because that's what mothers usually did when an offspring returned home for a visit. A stupid expectation, Amy decided as she climbed out of the car. She left Cornelia in the car while she unloaded her bags and the boxes of things she'd brought with her. Four trips later, Amy carried Cornelia into the house and settled her and her litter box in the laundry room. She called her mother's name, knowing there would be no answer. Her mother was a busy lady who did good deeds twenty-four/seven. All she did was sleep at the house. It was like that while she was growing up, too. Tillie Baran for the most part had always been an absentee mother with various housekeepers picking up her slack. When the housekeepers went home, her father took over, making sure she ate a good dinner, brushed her teeth, helped her with her homework and tucked her into bed at night. For some reason, though, she'd never felt cheated.

All of that changed when her father died of a heart attack in the lobby of the Pentagon on the day after she graduated from college. If her mother had grieved, she hadn't seen it. Armed with her substantial inheritance, Amy had relocated to Philadelphia where she worked for a PR firm to get her feet wet before she opened her own small agency.

She called home once a week, usually early Sunday morning, to carry on an inane conversation with her mother that never lasted more than five minutes. She returned home for Easter, Thanksgiving and Christmas—just day trips, because her mother was too busy to visit. For the past two years, though, she hadn't returned home at all. Her mother didn't seem to notice. No matter what, though, Amy kept up with her early Sunday morning phone calls because she wanted to be a good daughter.

And now here she was. Home to do her mother's bidding. For the first time in her entire life her mother had asked for her help. She couldn't help but wonder if there was an ulterior motive to this particular command performance.

Amy carried her bags, one at a time, to her old bedroom on the second floor. It all looked the same, neat as always, unlived in, smelling like lemon furniture polish. A cold, unfeeling house. Her mother's fault? Her father's?

Amy hated the house. She thought about her cozy five room town house, chockful of doodads, knickknacks and tons of green plants that she watered faithfully. In the winter she used her fireplace every single evening, not caring if the soot scattered from time to time or if the house smelled like woodsmoke. She had bright-colored, comfortable furniture and she didn't mind if Cornelia slept on the couch or not. Her garage was full of junk and she loved every square inch of it. There simply was no comparison between her mother's house and her own. None at all.

Amy stopped in the hallway and opened the door to her father's old room. It still smelled like him after all these years. How she'd loved her father. She looked around. It was stark, nothing out of place. A man's room with rustic earthy colors. She opened the closet the way she always did when she returned home. All her father's suits hung neatly on the double racks, exactly two inches apart. His shoes were still lined up against the wall. This was a room that didn't include her mother. Amy had always wondered why. She backed out of the room, closing the door behind her.

She had no interest in checking her mother's room. Instead, she opened the door to her room. A bed, a dresser, a bookshelf and two night tables on each side of the twin bed. The drapes were the same; so was the bedspread. She hated the patchwork design.

Long ago she'd taken everything from this room, even the things she no longer wanted. There was nothing here that said Amy Margaret Baran ever resided in this room. It was a guest room, nothing more. Well, she didn't do guest rooms. In a fit of something she couldn't explain, Amy carried her bags back down the hall and opened the door to her father's room a second time. She would sleep here for the next two months. The bed was king-size, and there was a deep reading chair and a grand bathroom, complete with a Jacuzzi.

As Amy unpacked her bags she wondered if her father's spirit would visit her. She didn't know if she believed in such things or not but she had an open mind. If it happened, it happened. If not, her life would go on.

She set her laptop on her father's desk, her clothes hanging next to her father's. The picture of her and her father on her sixteenth birthday—taken by the housekeeper whose name she couldn't remember—went on the night table next to the house phone. She looked around as she tried to decide what she should do next. She walked over to the entertainment center that took up a whole wall. Underneath was a minifridge. She opened it to see beer and Coca-Colas. She wondered when the drinks had been added. She popped a Coke and looked for the expiration date. Whoever the housekeeper was, she was up-to-date.

Amy settled herself in the lounge chair and sipped her drink. All she had to do now was wait for her mother.

Cornelia leaped into her lap and started to purr. Amy stroked her, crooning words a mother would croon to a small child. Eventually her eyes closed and she slept, her sleep invaded by a familiar dream.

. . . She knew it was late because her room was totally dark and only thin slivers of moonlight showed between the slats of the blinds. She had to go to the bathroom but knew she wouldn't get up and go out to the hall because she could hear the angry voices. She scrunched herself into a tight ball with her hands over her ears but she could still hear the voices. . . .

Chapter Three

Exhausted from his long trip, Cyrus antsy to get out and run, Gus pulled up to the entrance of Moss Farms and looked at the dilapidated sign swinging on one hinge from the carved post. A lump rose in his throat. A few nails, new hinges, some paint, and it would be good as new. The lump stayed in his throat as he put his Porsche Cayenne into gear and drove through the opening.

Gus ascended a steep hill lined with ancient fragrant evergreens, their massive trunks covered in dark green moss. His mother always said it was so fitting because their name was Moss.

At the top of the hill, Gus shifted into park and got out of the car to look down at the valley full of every kind of evergreen imaginable. He saw the Douglas firs; the blue spruce field; and to the left of that, the long-needle Scotch pine. He shaded his eyes from the sun to better see the fields of balsam fir, Fraser firs and Norway Spruce. To the left as far as the eye could see were the fields of white pines and the white firs. The Austrian pines looked glorious, and the three fields of Virginia pines seemed to go on to infinity. Thousands and thousands of trees. The lump was still in his throat when he tried to whistle for Cyrus, who came on the run.

Gus coasted down the hill to the valley where his old homestead rested. It looked as shabby and dilapidated as the entrance sign. *What does my father do all day?*

Gus wasn't disappointed at the lack of a welcoming committee. He really hadn't expected his father to run out and greet him. Still, it would have been nice. He parked the car at the side of the house and climbed out. He whistled for Cyrus, who was busy smelling everything in sight. "Hey, Pop!" he bellowed. Cyrus stopped his sniffing long enough to lift his head to see what was going on.

A tall man with a shaggy gray-white beard appeared out of nowhere. He was wearing a red plaid jacket with a matching hunting cap. "No need to shout, son. There's nothing wrong with my hearing. You on your way to somewhere or are you visiting?"

Gus licked at his lips. *What happened to, "Nice to see you, son" or "Good to see you, son"? Maybe a handshake or a hug.*

"I came for a visit. I thought I'd help with the trees this year. Looks kind of dead around here. What's going on, Pop?"

"Like you said, it's dead around here. I let everyone go. I'm retired now."

"Just like that, you retired? Why didn't you tell me?"

"Didn't much think you'd care. Nice looking dog. Not as nice as old Buster, though. Buster was one of a kind."

Gus jammed his hands into his pockets. "Why would you think I wouldn't care? If you needed my help, all you had to do was ask. Are you just going to let those trees grow wild? That's just like throwing money down the drain."

"You're a little late in coming around, son. When I needed you, you were in California making fancy houses for fancy people. When you left here, you said you didn't want to be a farmer. I took you at your word."

Gus flinched. The old man had him there. He didn't want to be a farmer; he wanted to do exactly what he was doing. *Well, I'm here now, so I'll just have to make the best of it.*

"I'm here to help. The first thing I'm going to do is fix the steps on the front porch before you kill yourself. Then I'm going to hire some people to thin the fields and then I'm going to set up shop and sell Christmas trees. I'll find someone to operate the Christmas store and then when you're back on your feet, you can take over."

"Don't need your help, Augustus. If that's why you came here, you can just climb into that fancy rig of yours and drive back to California and all those fancy people you like so much."

Gus dug the heels of his sneakers into the soft ground and rocked back. "I kind of figured you'd say that, Pop. So, let me put it another way. I came home to protect my investment, *my half* of Moss Farms. The half Mom left to me. If you don't want me staying in the house, I can get a room at a hotel in town.

It doesn't matter to me. The farm does matter. So, Pop, like it or not, I'm going to go to work."

"Won't do you any good. Some group of women in town will be selling trees this year. A lady all prissy and dressed up came out here to ask me to sell her my trees. She wanted them at cut-rate prices. I said no. You want to go up against her, go ahead. I always said you were a smart aleck," Sam Moss said as he turned to lumber away. "Stay in the house if you want; I don't care, just pick up after yourself."

"Yeah, Pop, you always did say that. And a bunch of other things that were even worse," Gus called to his father's retreating back. If the old man heard his son's words, he didn't show it. Gus wished he was a kid again so he could cry. Instead, he straightened his shoulders and climbed back into the Porsche, with Cyrus right behind him.

Gus backtracked and headed for town and a used car lot, where he bought a secondhand pickup truck the owner said he could drive off the lot with the promise that one of his workers would drive the Porsche back to Moss Farms by midafternoon.

With Cyrus riding shotgun, Gus drove to Home Depot, where he loaded up the back of the truck with a new chain saw, hammers, nails, lumber, paint and anything else he thought he would possibly need. When he checked his loading sheet and was satisfied, he drove to the unemployment office and posted a notice for day workers paying five dollars over minimum wage. All calls would go to his cell phone so as not to bother his father. The *Fairfax Connection* took his ad and promised to run it for a week. Again, he asked for day workers to run the Christmas store his mother had made an institution.

Gus made two more stops, one at a florist he remembered his mother liking. There he explained what he needed and was promised wholesale prices. The order, the nice lady said, would be delivered by the end of the week. His last stop was a gourmet shop, where he again explained his needs and was promised delivery in seven days.

On his way home, Gus pulled into a roadside stand where his mother used to buy fresh cider. Within thirty minutes, he signed a contract for a daily delivery of fresh cider, and for an extra hundred dollars the owner agreed to rent him a top-of-the-line cooler. His arms loaded down with vegetables, fresh apples, eggs and some frozen food, along with some dog food, he completed his shopping, and headed back to Moss Farms, feeling like he'd put in a hard morning's work. He was on a roll and he knew it. It was the same kind of feeling he always got when he presented a finished set of blueprints to a client. He loved the feeling.

As he drove along in his new pickup truck, Gus wondered about the dressed-up prissy woman who wanted to buy trees from his father. Competition was a good thing, a healthy thing. Maybe he needed to come up with a jingle or something to be played on the radio. For sure he was going to need to do some advertising. Well, hell, he had a workforce back in California. He'd give them a call and let them run with it. Creative minds needed to be put to use. He made a mental note to order a fax machine.

"I'm paying my dues again, Mom," he whispered.

"I know, son, I know," came back the reply.

Gus almost ran off the road as he looked around,

his eyes wild. Cyrus let his ears go flat against his head. He whined as he tried to get closer to Gus. *I must be either overtired or overstimulated.* He tried again. "Did you just talk to me, Mom? Or was I hearing things?"

The tinkling laugh he'd loved so much as a kid filled the car. "In a manner of speaking, Gussie. I told you I'd always be there for you when you needed me."

"Where . . . where are you, Mom?"

"Right beside you where I've always been. You just haven't needed me before. I'm so proud of you, coming back like this. Your father is a hard man, Gus. Be patient and things will work out."

"He gave our tree to the White House. I went there and got a branch. I hated him for that, Mom."

"I know. I saw you there. I don't want you to hate your father. He has difficulty showing affection. He loves you."

"Well, Mom, he has a hell of a way of showing it." Gus wondered if he was losing his mind. Was he so desperate for family affection he was imagining all this? he asked.

He heard the tinkling laugh again. "No, you aren't losing your mind. You're opening your mind. It goes with the upcoming season, Gus. You really need to fix that sign," Sara Moss said, as Gus pulled into the entrance of Moss Farms.

Gus stopped the truck. "I'm going to do it right now. I have everything in back of the truck. Mom, did you . . . what I mean is . . . ?"

"I saw the plaque on your office building. That was so wonderful of you, Gus. I felt so proud of you. Go along now. Do what you have to do."

Gus climbed out of the truck, looked around. Then he shook his head to clear his thoughts. Cyrus was still whining. "Will you come back, Mom?"

"Only if you need me. Remember now, be patient with your father."

Gus didn't know if he should laugh or cry. He looked at his watch. High noon. His shoulders straightened and his step was firm as he rummaged in the back of the new pickup for the tools he would need.

By one o'clock, Gus had the sign fixed with a new coat of paint. By two-thirty, he had the front steps fixed, sanded and painted. He jacked up the front porch with a two-by-four and had it back in place by three-thirty. By five o'clock he had the kitchen cleaned to his satisfaction. At six o'clock he was washing bed linens for his bed and was in bed between the clean sheets and blankets by eight-thirty. And he hadn't seen his father once since coming back from town. He was asleep the moment his head hit the pillow because he knew he had to get up at four, eat and head out to the fields, because that's what a farmer did.

Chapter Four

Amy jerked awake when Cornelia stirred in her lap. At the same moment, the front door slammed shut.

Her mother was home.

Groggy from the short nap, Amy combed her hair with her fingers, tightened the velvet bow at the back of her head, then knuckled her eyes as she steeled herself for what she knew would probably be an unpleasant encounter with her mother. She waited at the top of the steps to see if her mother would call her name, acknowledge her presence in some way. Such a silly thought. Evidently Cornelia was of the same opinion as she hissed and snarled, circling Amy's ankles. She bent down to pick up the unhappy cat and descended the steps. She called her mother's name twice before she entered the kitchen.

Tillie Baran waved airily as she babbled into the cell phone clutched between her ear and her cheek. She was opening a container of yogurt and sprinkling something that looked like gravel over the top. A bottle of mineral water was clutched under one arm as she juggled everything and still managed to sound animated to whomever was on the other end of the phone. Amy thought it was an awesome performance.

She eyed her stick-thin mother. She was, as usual, dressed impeccably. There wasn't a hair out of place. There never was.

Finally, the call ended. Amy reached for the cell phone and, in the blink of an eye, danced away and turned it off. "I need to talk to you, Mom. Without this stupid thing ringing off the hook."

"Oh, honey, don't do that. It's my lifeline to the world. I have to charge the battery for at least thirty minutes."

Amy wagged her finger. "No, no. Either we talk or I'm outta here. What's it going to be, Mom? I sure hope you aren't going to tell me this is one of your projects that you gave up on."

"Good Lord, why would you say such a thing, Amy? Everything is ready to go for the Seniors. All you have to do is set things up and make it work. I'm depending on you to pull this off. I'm working on the New Year's Gala the Rotary is sponsoring. I have so much to do and not enough hours in the day." All this was said as Tillie shoveled the yogurt and gravel into her mouth. After every bite she swigged from her water bottle.

"What exactly is ready to go, Mom? By the way, did you see that study someone did about people who talk on cell phones all day the way you do?"

"I don't believe I saw that, Amy?"

"You can get a brain tumor. Go to the library and look it up."

For the first time in her life Tillie Baran was at a loss for words. "You can't be serious."

"I'm serious. Now, what's there to set up?"

"The Christmas trees, of course. I ordered them. They will arrive on the Tuesday before Thanksgiving. I told you I rented the Coleman property."

"Mom, you rented a piece of land. A corner property on a major highway. Did you give any thought to a structure of some sort? It gets bitter cold around here in November. Who did you hire to work, to make the wreathes, the grave blankets and all the stuff you have to do to get something like this under way? You're going to need a guard at night so people don't steal the trees. Where are you going to sell all the extras you told me about?"

Tillie looked puzzled for a moment. "That's your job, dear."

"No, Mom, that's not my job. It was your job. You said you had it ready to go and all I had to do was the PR stuff to get it off the ground. Are the Seniors going to help? Do you know how heavy a Christmas tree is? Who is going to work the chain saw to trim off the bottoms? Who's going to drill the holes in the trunks? Mom, did you think this through?"

"Good heavens, Amy, of course I did. We had seven different meetings about the trees. You're over-reacting, aren't you?"

Amy watched as her mother tugged at the jacket of her Chanel suit. She noticed a worried look in her mother's eyes. "No, Mom, I'm not. Who is going to unload the trees from the trucks when they're delivered, and don't tell me the Seniors, because they won't be able to lift them. I hope you don't expect me to do it. How about you? Are you going to be helping?"

The worried look was becoming more intense. "I have this gala . . . there are so many details . . . hire people," she said vaguely. "The university . . ."

"Mom, the kids are studying for finals. They go home for the holidays. No one is going to want to stand out in the cold to sell trees and make six bucks an hour. It doesn't work that way these days. Kids spend all their time with their iPods."

"I'm sure you'll think of something, dear. I really have to go now. Can I please have my phone back?"

"NO!" Amy bellowed at the top of her lungs. "This is where the rubber meets the road, *Mother.* Either you sit down and hash this out with me or I'm leaving. I'll leave it up to you to explain how you failed. I won't be here to scrape the egg off your face either."

"You're just like a bulldog. Your father was that way," Tillie complained, but she did sit down and fold her hands.

"Don't go there, Mom. Right now I'm pretty damn angry, so tread lightly. Did you pay a deposit to the Colemans?"

"Of course not. We have to pay them $2,000 the day after Christmas."

"What? Why didn't you get them to donate the land? This is for the Seniors. Couldn't you have gotten a better rate?"

"They said they wouldn't take a penny less. I had no other choice."

"Did you look for a better place? You didn't, did you? You took the easy way out. Okay, we're now

$2,000 in debt. What kind of deal did you make for the trees?"

Tillie started to wring her hands. "Well . . . it's $40 a tree. We have to sell them for $100 each. Some of the bigger trees will cost more. I ordered twenty thousand and put down a deposit of $5,000."

"Oh my God! If you don't sell all of them, you, Mrs. Baran, are on the hook for the balance. You do know that, don't you? I assume you signed an order for them. Did you sign it as Tillie Baran?"

"I did do that. And the lease with the Colemans."

"That's just great, Mom. Why didn't you talk to me first? Right now you, *personally,* are $797,000 in debt, and we haven't even started. If there's something else, you better tell me now."

"Well . . . I did hear something today when I was having lunch with the secretary of the Chamber of Commerce. It seems . . . appears . . . it just might be gossip . . . but the rumor is Sam Moss is gearing up to reopen his farm to sell his trees this year. They're saying his fields need to be thinned out and he's going to sell each tree for . . . $40. Of course I never listen to rumors. I even made a trip out to his farm and the old geezer ran me off. I offered to buy his trees for $40 each. Which just goes to show you can't trust a man. Never ever!"

Amy jerked upright. She'd think about that last comment later. "Old geezer. Mr. Moss is as old as you are, Mom. That means he's sixty-four. He probably called you an old biddy. This is a disaster. Are you listening to me, Mom?"

"Of course I'm listening. Are you listening to me? I told you, it's just a rumor. Sam Moss is an angry, bitter old man. If he is indeed going forward, it's out of spite. He always hated how Sara got so involved with the Seniors."

"What about you, Mom? If Mr. Moss is bitter, what are you? You're a robot, a machine that goes twenty-four/seven. I never see you laugh or cry. You're always on automatic, you never stop. Well, you better stop now and think about this little project you just dumped on me. Either we partner on it or I'm bailing out on you. That means you failed. *You,* not me, Mom. Now, how important is all that to you?"

Tillie cleared her throat, then licked at her dry lips. "The Seniors are counting on me. I promised we would raise enough to refurbish the Seniors' Building before the town condemns it. I gave my word. It . . . it is important. I've never failed at any of my events. What . . . what should I do, Amy?"

Amy threw her arms in the air. "I don't know. I'm not a magician. I have a few ideas but I don't know if they'll work. We need to sit here and map out a plan of action, so don't get any ideas about leaving me holding the bag with the mess you created. See this," Amy said, holding up her mother's cell phone. She walked over to the sink, turned on the water and let it cascade over the phone. "Don't even think about getting another one. Mine will be enough for both of us. Now, let's sit here and talk. First I'm going to make some coffee and order some food. I'm up for Chinese. From here on in, Mom, you are going to keep this refrigerator filled with food. I do not exist on yogurt and water. I want you to think of this little project as me saving you from a life of humiliation. Starting right now, it is my way or the highway, with me driving down it."

Tillie sniffed. She knew she was beaten. She kicked off her shoes and settled down with the paper and pencil Amy placed in front of her. She needed to have the last word. "You are just as mean and hard as your father."

After ordering dinner from Ginger Beef Chinese Food over on Telegraph Road, Amy spooned coffee into the paper cone on the coffeemaker. "We aren't going to go there, Mom, but rest assured before I leave here we will revisit the issue of your husband and my father, because it is long overdue."

Tillie bit down on her lip as she played with the cup and spoon that her daughter set in front of her. If she had anything to say about it, that particular little talk was never going to happen.

Amy risked a glance at her mother, wishing she could feel something other than aggravation. Her mother was copping an attitude. Well, she would just have to deal with it. How strange that this was turning into a role reversal. She felt like the mother admonishing a wayward child. She hoped she could remain tough and stern and not let her mother stomp all over her.

"Let's get our home base settled before we tackle anything else." Amy didn't wait for her mother to agree or disagree. She forged ahead. "We are going to have three meals a day. That means either your housekeeper makes it or you and I take turns. We will sit here at this very table and eat together and discuss what's going on with what I am now calling Tillie's Folly. There will be no more yogurt or that rabbit poop stuff you sprinkle on top of it. This refrigerator will be filled with meat, fish and chicken. We will have cheese, fruit and vegetables, along with bread and English muffins. And eggs. Good food. You, Mother, will be working alongside me, so I suggest you get yourself some warm boots, flannel-lined slacks, some heavy sweaters and a good warm hat. The first time I see a cell phone hanging off your ear, our deal is off and you can sink or swim. Do we have a deal, Mom?"

Tillie squirmed in her chair. "Yes, we have a deal. When did you get like this?"

"Do you really care, *Mother?*"

"No, I suppose I don't."

It was Amy's turn to squirm. There was a lot to be said for honesty.

"All right, let's get to it. We have an hour before our dinner arrives. Now, this is what I've been thinking. Give me your input and don't be shy about it. I don't care how bizarre something sounds. We might be able to make it work."

Tillie licked her lips. "Were you trying to scare me before when you said I was liable for all . . . for all those bills?"

Amy leaned across the table. "Read my lips, Mom. You signed the work orders. That means you are liable."

"That . . . that would wipe out my nest egg. I would have to get a job."

"That's what it means, Mom. Look at it this way, 'tis the season of miracles—or almost, anyway."

Chapter Five

Sam Moss sat on the top of the newly repaired steps that led to the front porch. There was a time when the porch held pumpkins with lit candles, cornstalks and a few scarecrows. So long ago. Now the porch was empty, just the way he was empty.

It was full dark now, an hour past supper. The only thing he'd eaten today was a frozen TV dinner at lunchtime that tasted like cardboard because the pot of stew he'd made wasn't done cooking. Sometimes he wondered why he even bothered.

Out of the corner of his eye he could see a line of headlights heading out of the fields. The drivers of the vehicles wouldn't see him sitting on the steps because the big blue spruce at the corner of the house blocked the view of the porch. Gus's workers, that's how he thought of them, wouldn't be gazing about anyway. They'd be in a hurry to get home to their families and a warm supper. Gus would be the last one to come down the road.

His son had been home six full days, and what the boy—which was how he thought of his son, the boy—had accomplished stunned him. In all of his sixty-four years he had never seen such single-minded determination to get the farm up and running. A river of guilt rushed through him at what he was allowing to go on. What *really* bothered him was the boy hadn't asked him for a penny. He knew from the talk in town that Gus was paying his workers more than a decent wage plus overtime. He'd never in his life paid over-time to an employee. Sara always said he was behind the times, a fuddy-duddy with tunnel vision. If she were here right now, sitting on the steps right next to him, she'd give him a poke on the arm and say, "See, Sam, I told you our son is the best of the best." Like he didn't know that.

How he wished he was more like Sara, who was so outgoing and loved by everyone. *Was* outgoing. *Was* loved by everyone. Especially by Gus. That hurt, but he'd accepted that the boy liked his mother more than him. Because of that, without really meaning to, he'd been extra hard on him. In his own defense, he'd said things like, hard work never hurt anyone, hard work builds character. He'd truly believed that because of him, Gus was the man he was today. Until yesterday afternoon, when it started to rain and Gus had come in for a slicker. They'd eyeballed each other until Gus finally said, "Yeah, I know, Pop, working in freezing rain won't kill me, and it will build my character. Well guess what, if your next line is 'I'm the man I am today because of you,' think again. I'm the man I am because of Mom. Not you. Never you." Then he'd stomped out in the cold rain to continue working the fields, to correct what his father had let go to wrack and ruin.

"So, I'm a horse's patoot," Sam Moss muttered as he got up to go into the house.

He'd cooked a pot of stew earlier in the day. It was the one thing he did well. It was simmering on the stove now, ready to be eaten. If he got into the kitchen in time, he could casually mention the stew and even set the table. Maybe they could talk. Maybe he could offer . . .

Sam removed the red plaid mackinaw and hung it on the hook by the back door. He was setting the table when Gus walked in. "Made some stew today. You're welcome to sit down and eat. Got some frozen bread warming in the oven," he said gruffly.

"No, thanks. I'm too tired to eat. Maybe later. Since you seem to be talking to me today, one of my guys told me he heard in town that you're going to be selling trees for $45 each to clear the fields. I sure as hell hope you're talking about *your half* of the farm and not my half. I'll be selling mine at market value. You better get it in gear, Pop, or you're going to look like . . ."

"A horse's patoot?"

Gus reared back. "I was going to be a little more blunt and say a horse's ass. That's if the rumor is true. If it isn't true, I'll take back my opinion." Without another word, Gus left the room.

Sam turned away to hide his grin. The boy had grit, he had to give him that. He ladled the fragrant stew into his bowl and sat down to eat.

Sam's mind roamed as he ate. He now knew his son's habits at the end of the workday. He showered, slept for three hours, came downstairs to eat, did some paperwork and went back to bed. It was during Gus's three-hour nap that Sam went out to the fields to check the day's work. After his inspection, on the walk back to the house, he always felt like puffing out his chest. The boy had grit *and* promise. He frowned as he broke a piece of bread off the loaf on the table. He really hadn't expected the rumor he started to get back to Gus so quickly. He still couldn't believe he'd purposely started it. How stupid of him to think people would flock to buy the trees Gus cut down at a giveaway price. Gus's trees. He had to remember that.

Upstairs, Gus stood in the bathroom, staring at himself in the mirror. Who the hell was that wild-looking guy with the six-day growth of beard staring back at him? His face was windburned and his eyes were bloodshot. The beard itched. He was so cold he thought he'd snap in two before he could get into the hot shower. Nothing, not even rousing sex, felt as good as the hot water running over his body. He let his shoulders droop as he turned this way and that in an effort to get warm. Stew. Hot stew. He couldn't remember when he smelled something half as good. Made by his father, who had issued an invitation. Maybe he was finally coming around. Or maybe his father thought he was going to fall on his face. Maybe he thought he didn't have the stamina to carry through on his plan. *Who the hell knew what the old man thinks.* Still, an invitation was an invitation. His mouth started to water at the thought of the savory stew and crusty bread.

Bone tired, Gus stepped out of the shower, dressed and headed downstairs. He was stunned to see a place set for him at the table. There was even a napkin. Salt, pepper and butter were in the middle of the table. He helped himself. He'd dined in five-star restaurants, eaten gourmet food, but nothing had ever tasted as good as what he was eating. He had two bowls of the delicious stew, drank a bottle of beer and ate half the loaf of bread. Beyond stuffed, Gus cleaned up, transferred the contents of the pot into a huge bowl and set it in the refrigerator. He wrapped the leftover bread in foil.

With no idea where his father was, Gus turned off the light and switched on the night-light over the stove before he headed upstairs where he turned on his laptop and proceeded to go shopping at L.L. Bean. He ordered thermal underwear, flannel shirts, foot warmers, hand warmers, several wool watch caps and four pairs of boots. He ordered his own slicker, two shearling jackets, heavy corduroy trousers and a dozen pairs of wool socks. He completed his order and hit the button for overnight delivery.

With the temperatures in the low forties, he wanted to be prepared.

His eyes drooping, his stomach full, Gus fell into bed. He slept soundly until the shrill of the alarm woke him at four o'clock. He groaned, rolled over, tussled with Cyrus for a few minutes, then climbed out of bed to get dressed. He sniffed. Was that coffee and bacon he smelled? He wondered if his father was making breakfast for himself. Or for him. *Nah, lightning doesn't strike twice. Yesterday had to be a fluke.* How could he possibly be hungry after all he'd eaten last night? Yet he was starved, his stomach rumbling.

Cyrus loped ahead of him and sprinted down the stairs. By the time Gus reached the kitchen, Cyrus was gobbling eggs and bacon from a bowl that used to belong to old Buster.

Gus blinked. The table was set. On his mother's place mats. A plate full of eggs, bacon, sausage and toast waited for him along with a huge mug of coffee. Next to his plate was a large thermos. "Looks good," Gus said, sitting down. He bowed his head and said a prayer the way his mother taught him to do before he dived in. It did not go unnoticed by his father.

Sam Moss raised his head and looked directly at his son. "Can you use another set of hands out there?"

Gus stopped chewing long enough to stare at his father. "I can use all the help I can get to clear the white pine field. How are you at taking orders?"

" 'Bout as good as you are, Augustus. I can learn."

"We're clearing *my* half of the fields. If you want me to work on *your* half, you're going to have to ask me, Pop. That's how this has to work."

"Let's work on your half first. Don't expect big things out of me, Augustus. I haven't done any manual labor for a long time. I'm out of shape. I'll work your half of the farm. I don't have a problem with that."

"I hope not, because I'm going to work you the way you worked me."

The old man stroked his beard with a gnarled hand. "Payback time, eh? I worked you as a kid until you dropped to try to make a man out of you. Now you're going to work this old man to prove . . . what?"

Gus stood up. "To prove to me you're good enough to be my father. We're running late. Time is money. Remember those words?"

"Yep." Sam pulled his mackinaw from the hook. He followed Gus and Cyrus out the door.

"Who's cleaning up that mess in the kitchen?" Gus called over his shoulder.

"The new housekeeper who starts today. I even gave her a menu for tonight."

Gus hunched into his jacket as he headed for the pickup truck. He was grinning from ear to ear in the darkness.

Chapter Six

It was ten o'clock when Amy pushed her chair away from the table. Earlier, she'd kicked off her shoes, and now she contemplated her pedicure as she tried to make sense out of her resentful mother. She hated being hard-nosed, but she really didn't have many options under the circumstances. She eyed her mother now as she tried to think of something nice to say. The words eluded her.

"Are we done here, Amy?"

"For now, Mom. Do you at least understand what a problem you created? I don't know if I can pull this off. I just wish you had consulted me when you first came up with the idea. It's a wonderful idea and if it works it will benefit the Seniors." *There, that was something nice. Now they wouldn't go to bed angry with each other.*

"But you don't think it will, is that it? Say it, Amy. Say what you're thinking. Let's get it all out in the open before we go any further."

"I don't think we should go there, Mom. Let's go to bed, sleep on it and tackle it again in the morning. I have some savings I can use. I still have most of Dad's insurance left. My business is doing well, so I can cut some corners. I'm going to call the people you ordered the trees from and see if I can cancel the order in the morning. I just want you to know this is a seat-of-the-pants operation as of this moment."

"I have things to do tomorrow. My day planner is full," Tillie snapped.

"Not anymore it isn't," Amy snapped. "You're mine now, Mother. From now till December 26, you will be working right alongside me. I want your word. Your word, Mom."

"But . . . I can't possibly . . . I have plans . . . commitments. I don't know you anymore, Amy Margaret Baran."

Amy bit down on her lower lip to try to stem the words she was thinking about, but they spewed out of her mouth because they were long overdue. "Like I know you, Mom! You stopped being my mother when I was four years old. Housekeepers cooked for me, washed my clothes, fed me, put me to bed. I lost count of how many we had. God knows what would have happened to me if it wasn't for Dad. You were never here. You didn't even show up at my high school graduation. You never talked to my teachers. You showed up five hours late for my college graduation. I still can't believe you showed up for your husband's funeral. You were never here for Christmas. Dad and I always got the tree and decorated it. Oh, you posed in front of it, then off you went. Dad bought the presents. Dad wrapped the presents. Dad taught me to roller skate. Dad taught me to ride a bike, and he taught me how to drive. I've always wanted to know, Mom. *Where were you all that time?*"

"Not now, Amy. I'm very tired right now. Let's just both agree that I was a horrible mother and let it go at that."

Amy did her best to blink away her tears. "At least we can finally agree on something."

Amy gathered her books and ledgers and all the notes she'd made earlier together in a nice, neat pile. She set them on the counter out of the way. Her shoes in her hands, she made her way to the second floor, where she threw herself on the bed and had what she intended to be her last cry where her mother was concerned.

Down the hall and across the room, Tillie Baran sat down on the edge of the bed, her shoulders shaking, tears rolling down her cheeks. She should have told her. Why didn't she? Why didn't she defend herself against her daughter's onslaught of hateful words? Because she was guilty, that's why. Too little, too late. The best she could hope for now was a civil relationship with her daughter until this Christmas tree fiasco she'd created was over and done with.

Tillie could see her reflection in the mirror across the room. She looked haggard, and she looked every one of her sixty-four years. She was old, and she had no purpose in life except to do what she called good deeds. If the truth were known, she didn't even really do good deeds. She had ideas for good deeds that other people carried out with a lot of hard work, then she got the credit for those good deeds. She heard her name on the local radio and TV news, and it was always her picture in the paper, never the drones who brought her ideas to fruition. In a million years she never thought her daughter would bring her to task the way she had down in the kitchen just moments ago.

Tillie knew she had to make things right with her daughter, somehow, some way, without damaging her thoughts and memories of her father. How could she possibly tell her daughter that three years into her marriage she'd found out her husband was a philanderer, that he needed a string of women to make his life happy. A wife at home tending the fires was just for photo ops in his political life as a roving ambassador to different countries. With offices in the Pentagon and access to the White House, there had been no shortage of young women to entertain and Aaron Nathaniel Baran entertained them all.

How well she remembered a well-meaning friend telling her she thought she should *know* about her husband's outside social activities. She'd gone into shock, became depressed and had a full-blown nervous breakdown. Amy had been five when she finally crawled out of her misery and started a life of her own. A life that didn't include her husband and the little girl who adored him. So long ago, and yet it was just like it was yesterday. The pain was the same today as it was then, only magnified now with Amy's attitude.

Tillie Baran knew she had some serious soul-searching to do. She wondered if it was too late to redeem herself in her daughter's eyes. Respect was all she could hope for. Love was simply out of the question and with no other options available to her, she would have to accept whatever Amy was willing to give her.

As Tillie prepared for bed, a plan started to form in her mind. Tomorrow, if Amy cut her some slack, she'd go out to Moss Farms and try to sweet-talk Sam. If she had to, she would trade on her old friendship with Sara and Sam. Then again, maybe she wouldn't do that. That was the way the old Tillie would have done it. This new Tillie was going to have to be up front and businesslike.

Tillie stared at herself in the mirror as she removed her makeup. *Why do I need all this glop?* If Amy's dire predictions came to pass, she wouldn't be able to afford it anyway. She didn't think twice about sweeping her arm across the vanity. She watched as bottles, jars and tubes slid into the wastebasket. She didn't feel anything one way or the other. Tomorrow morning she would wash her face and put on some moisturizer and that would be that.

Bedtime reading. No novels tonight. Tonight it would be her latest brokerage statement and how she could make things right for Amy, for the Seniors and possibly herself. She shivered with guilt and humiliation when she recalled her daughter's tone and the expression on her face. That had to be right up there with the moment when she'd confronted her husband about his infidelities and his *so what* attitude.

It was almost midnight when Tillie slid the brokerage statement into the current folder. Obviously, she was going to have to sell the house, which was nothing more than a status symbol anyway. She'd get a town house somewhere and maybe she could get a job as a tour guide. She'd be good at that, she thought. She'd start clean, with no debts. A ripple of fear skittered around in her stomach at the mere thought. She said a small prayer then, asking God to give her the strength to follow through on her plans.

Tillie tossed and turned all night long. In the end she finally gave up, showered, smeared on some moisturizer and dressed in clothes she dug out of a trunk and smelled like mothballs. Old clothes, the kind she used to wear before she became a social gadabout. Corduroy trousers, wool socks, a heavy sweater and a pair of ankle-high boots she had to clean before she could put them on. She couldn't remember why she'd saved all these clothes. Maybe she knew one day she would need them. "I guess this is the day," she muttered to herself as she made her way downstairs to the kitchen where she would have made coffee if she had any. But since she didn't, she reached for her daughter's heavy jacket and left the house.

Tillie couldn't remember the last time she'd been out and about at four-thirty in the morning.

What would Sam Moss say when he opened the door to see her standing there? Well, she'd find out soon enough.

She stopped at the first fast-food establishment she came to, a Wendy's, and ordered two coffees to go. As Tillie sipped at the hot brew, she thought about the last time she'd gone to see Sam Moss and how it had turned out. Maybe Sam would be in a better mood.

Ten minutes away, Sam Moss was explaining to his son Gus that he would join him as soon as he picked up the new blades for the chain saw. "Henry doesn't open his shop till five o'clock. He told me he has two used saws. I want to take a look at them, and if he gives me a guarantee, I'll take them. I'll meet you in the Fraser fir field."

Gus waved, and a minute later was gone.

Sam sat down at the kitchen table, a second cup of coffee in front of him. He could see the clock on the wall across from the table. He was finishing the last of his coffee when he heard a knock on the kitchen door. He opened the door and then took a step backward. "Kind of early to be visiting, isn't it, Tillie?"

"Yes, it is early to be visiting. I was thinking about that on the drive out here. I wasn't sure . . . what I mean is, you all but ran me off the last time I was out here. I need to talk to you, Sam. Actually, the truth is, I need your help. I thought I could trade on our old friendship. It's cold out here, can I come in?"

Sam wiggled his nose. "You smell like mothballs, Tillie. Of course you can come in. Would you like some coffee?"

Tillie was glad she had left the coffee from Wendy's in the car.

"Yes, that would be nice. The smell . . . well, that's part of my problem. Do you think you can ignore it?"

Sam turned away, his mind racing. This visit couldn't be a good thing. He poured coffee into a mug and set it down in front of his old friend. That wasn't quite true; Tillie had been his wife's friend more than his. She'd always been nice to him, though. Sara had loved going to the Senior Citizen meetings and helped plan the social calendar with Tillie. He sat down across from her. He should apologize to her for running her off his property the last time she'd been out here to the farm. There was something different about her today, and it wasn't just the mothball smell.

"I've managed to get myself into some trouble, Sam. I know if I tell you, you won't go spreading my business all over town. That was one of the things I always liked about you—you didn't gossip like the rest of us. I'm here for advice and if you can see your way clear to helping me, that will be fine, but if not, I'll settle for the advice. Will you hear me out?"

Sam poured himself some more coffee before he settled down to listen. When Tillie finally wound down it was five-thirty. "All these years, and you never told your daughter about her father? Why, Tillie?"

Tillie shrugged. "She loved him, Sam. When I had my nervous breakdown, I abandoned her. He was all she had. He might have been a lousy husband but he was a good father to Amy. I screwed up. Everything she said about me is true. I don't know how to undo all those years. For now, I can do everything she wants me to do, but what about afterward? I'm going to cancel the tree order, pay for my mistake, sell my house and get something smaller. I don't need that big house. I should be okay if I get a job. I need some of your trees, Sam. I need you to sell them to me at cost. It's the only way I can make this work. It's not for me, Sam, it's for the Seniors." Tillie's eyes filled with tears. She swiped them away with the back of her hand. "The young can be so cruel, Sam. What Amy said was all true, it was how she said it that burned to the quick. By the way, how is that son of yours who lives in California? Sara was so proud of him. Did you two make peace?"

It was Sam's turn to open up. When he finished, Tillie stared at him wide-eyed. "Oh, Sam, how wonderful for you. He came back to help you. That means he's forgiven you. That's what it means, isn't it?"

"Your girl came to help you. Do you think she's forgiven you?"

Tillie shook her head. "No. She's doing what she thinks a daughter should do. I guess your son is doing the same thing. How did we get to this place in time, Sam? We should be taking cruises, buying little treasures in gift stores, going to afternoon matinees, going to friends for dinner." A lone tear rolled down her cheek. "We let it happen, Sam. We can't blame anyone else but ourselves. It's almost light out. I have to get back to the house. Will you think about what I asked and get back to me? I don't have a cell phone any longer. Amy took it away and ran it under the water because she said it was growing out of my ear. Call me at home even if the answer is no."

Sam nodded, stood up, then stunned himself by saying, "Would you like to go out to dinner this evening?"

Tillie jammed a fur-lined hat on her head. "Sure, Sam. I'd like that. Is it a date?"

Sam had to think about the question. A date was where you got dressed up, rang the lady's doorbell. "Yep," he said. "Just don't wear those clothes."

"Okay," Tillie said as she opened the kitchen door. "It might be better if I met you wherever it is you want to go for dinner. Amy doesn't need to know all my business."

Sam nodded, understanding perfectly. "Do you like the Rafters?"

"I do. I'll meet you there at seven. Or is that too late?"

"No, that will work for me, Tillie. I'll have some answers for you tonight."

Tillie didn't know why she did what she did at that

moment. She stood on her toes and kissed Sam's cheek. Later she thought it was because she was just so relieved to have finally told someone her problems, someone who had actually listened. "I'll see you this evening. Have a nice day, Sam."

Have a nice day, Sam. She'd kissed his cheek. He could still smell her mothballs. Sam Moss laughed then, a belly laugh that was so deep the floor under his feet rumbled.

When he hit the Fraser fir field at seven-thirty, Gus looked at his father suspiciously. "Did something happen, Pop?"

"No, why do you ask?"

"You smell like mothballs."

Sam burst out laughing as he picked up one of the chain saws and moved off. When had he last heard his father laugh? Never, that was when.

Chapter Seven

The scents emanating from the kitchen were tantalizing as Amy set the table. She was so tired she could hardly see straight. All that aside, she'd put in a productive day's work along with her mother who was chirping about this and that, finally winding down with, "I'm sorry, Amy, but I'm going out to dinner. I guess I should have told you sooner but my head is just swimming with all we've done today."

Amy looked at her mother, at the flowered dishes on the table, the lit candle, the wineglasses just waiting for her to pop the cork. She sniffed at the aromas coming from the stove, the mixed salad and the baby carrots in the warming bowl. That was when she really noticed her mother. She smelled good. Her hair was pulled back from her face into a bun. She wore no makeup other than a little lipstick. She wore flannel slacks with a bright yellow sweater and low-heeled shoes. She looked like a matron, so unlike Amy's always-fashionable mother that her daughter could hardly wrap her mind around the new Tillie Baran she was seeing.

What could she say other than, "Okay. I guess we'll be eating this stuff for the rest of the week. By the way, thanks for going shopping. You certainly were up and out pretty early this morning."

"Umm, yes. The early bird gets the worm, that kind of thing. You said you wanted me here in the kitchen at eight o'clock, so I had to take care of some business early to be back here on time. We *old* people don't sleep much."

Amy reared back. This was the first time in her memory that she could remember her mother using the word *old* in reference to herself. Other people were old, not Tillie. Maybe this was where she was supposed to say, "*You're not old, Mom.*" She turned away to fiddle with the lid on the pot roast. "Don't stay out too late."

Tillie laughed, a delightful sound. Amy realized she'd never actually heard her mother laugh out loud. How in the world was that possible? She'd seen her smile but that was it. There must be a man lurking somewhere in the picture. "You smell good," she blurted.

"Do you think so? I have to be going. I'm sorry I didn't tell you sooner about my plans, Amy. Everything looks and smells delicious. I'll look forward to the leftovers tomorrow."

Amy poured herself a cup of coffee and sat down to think about her mother and all that had transpired during the day. Her mother had behaved like a trooper to her surprise. She did everything Amy suggested, even more. She followed through on every single detail by making copious notes. The things they'd accomplished in a mere ten hours boggled her mind. They'd opened a business bank account, with both of them depositing sizeable checks to activate it. They'd ordered two large tents that would be set up on the Coleman property over the weekend. The power company promised electric hookup first thing Monday morning. Portable heaters were ordered along with all the Christmas decorations from the Curiosity Barn. The wholesaler she'd contacted had promised delivery of the wreath wires, the lath, the florist wires, the speciality bows and everything else she needed for assembling the wreaths and grave blankets. Trial and error was the order of the day as she tried to figure out where to get a barrel and the netting for the trees. Several Seniors had come to the rescue, and there was now a huge metal rain drum sitting on her mother's back porch. The bails of netting would be delivered on Tuesday along with tree trimmers and chain saws.

She was going to have at least fifty volunteers but no real workers. Tomorrow she would go on the hunt for actual employees. Tonight she had to get started on her PR campaign.

Damn, she was tired. Detail tired, not physically tired. Maybe she needed to get dressed and go for a run to clear her thoughts.

Amy looked at the dinner she'd prepared. Just the thought of mashing the potatoes and making gravy left her weak in the knees. She'd do that when she served leftovers. Instead she made herself a sandwich with the meat and ate it, along with a second cup of coffee. The minute she finished eating, she tidied up the kitchen, wrapped everything up, turned on the dishwasher and then stared at the huge chart she'd pasted to the kitchen wall. The big red X in the middle of the chart glared at her. *I can pull this off. I really can. All I need are Christmas trees.* The grower her mother had signed on with was not an easy man to deal with even after she threatened him. Finally, in desperation, she'd told him to keep the five-thousand-dollar deposit and cancel the order. He in turn threatened to sue Tillie. That's when she told him to get in line with all the other people waiting to sue Tillie Baran. He'd squawked and threatened some more, but at the end of the conversation he'd agreed to cancel the order. She'd been lightheaded with her victory, but the elation was short-lived. Now she had to find Christmas trees, and the only place that had what she needed was Moss Farms. Maybe Mr. Moss would remember her and agree to sell her some trees. If not, this whole thing was going to go down the drain.

Well, that wasn't going to happen, not on her watch.

Amy looked at the kitchen clock. It was only 6:45. She could drive out to the farm in fifteen minutes. Mr. Moss would be done with his dinner and settled in for the evening. Maybe he would be more agreeable to her than he was with her pushy mother. Then again, maybe the cranky old man would run her off his property the way he'd run her mother off. *Oh well, nothing ventured, nothing gained. If he won't help, maybe out of the kindness of his heart he'll steer me in the right direction.*

Without stopping to think about it anymore, she reached for her jacket and was out of the house before she could change her mind.

* * *

Gus Moss stepped out of the shower, towel dried and pulled on a pair of beat-up sweatpants and his first Tulane sweatshirt, which was full of holes. He stared at himself in the mirror and burst out laughing. He'd shaved his beard yesterday and he now looked like himself. He slicked his curly hair back but knew the moment it dried it would be all over the place. *Maybe I'll get a buzz cut over the weekend. If I can find the time.*

Cyrus, who dogged him everywhere he went, barked sharply. "Yeah, yeah, I know, Cyrus, we're running behind schedule, but Pop threw me for a loop when he said he wouldn't be here for dinner. Did you see him, Cyrus? He looked like a dandy, all duded up and wearing aftershave! I think he's stepping out on me is what I think. Okay, okay, let's see what Mrs. Collins left us for dinner."

Everything, including Cyrus's dinner, would be in the warming oven. It was the best move his father could have made. With all the different smells, Gus liked coming into the house. He liked the sweet-smelling sheets and clean blankets Mrs. Collins put on his bed. He liked that there was a fire blazing in the kitchen fireplace when he came in from work. He liked the whole gig. Cyrus liked it too. The dog had made friends with Gus's father. Out of the corner of his eye he'd see Gus's father scratch Cyrus behind his ears and call him Buster from time to time. He knew at night that the retriever spent part of the night with him and part of the night with his father. He grinned at the thought.

"Here we go, big guy. You get chicken, mashed potatoes, a little gravy, lots of broccoli and even a buttered roll. I get the same thing, but just a little broccoli because I hate it. That berry pie looks pretty good, too." Cyrus woofed, gobbled down his food and then went to the door. He knew when he got back he'd get his dessert.

Gus filled his plate twice, saving just enough room for a slice of pie. When he finished, he leaned back in the captain's chair at the head of the table and let his mind go back over the day's work. Another week of hard work with his crew and he'd be ready to cut the trees to go on sale the day after Thanksgiving. He felt so proud of himself he decided he would have an extra large slice of pie—as soon as Cyrus pawed at the door to get in. While he waited he added two more logs to the fire. A shower of sparks raced up the chimney.

Outside, Cyrus was barking his head off. Gus listened to the tone. It wasn't a playful bark, or an I-treed-a-racoon bark, or an Okay, I'm-done-and-ready-for-dessert bark. This was a bark that meant there was an intruder on the premises. He reached up and turned on the outside floodlights. The entire backyard was suddenly bathed in a blinding white light and Cyrus was escorting a young woman to his back door. *Cyrus must like her,* Gus thought, because his tail was swishing back and forth at the speed of light.

Gus opened the door and stared at the young woman in the purple hat and scarf. She smiled. He smiled— and fell in love on the spot.

His love opened her mouth and spoke. Suddenly he wanted to shower her with diamonds and rubies. Maybe pearls. "I know it's late, but is it possible to speak with Mr. Moss?"

"Uh, sure. I'm Mr. Moss. Gus Moss. Come in, come in."

His love spoke again. "I'm sorry. I meant the other . . . Mr. Moss senior."

"Oh, *that* Mr. Moss. He isn't here. Will I do?"

Cyrus, never known for his patience, barked and pawed at the kitchen counter where the pie was. "Excuse me. Cyrus is relentless. He won't give up until he gets his pie. I was just about to have some. Will you join me?"

Amy stared at the good-looking young man. She thought her blood was boiling in her veins. "You know what, I think I will join you. I have a sweet tooth."

His love had a sweet tooth. "Me too. All my teeth are sweet." Gus grimaced, showing his teeth. His love laughed.

"Is that good for a dog?" Amy asked, pointing to the pie Gus just put in Cyrus's bowl.

"His owner refuses to give him dog food. I'm just dog sitting old Cyrus. People food seems to agree with him. Do you want ice cream on your pie?"

"Well, sure. What good is pie without ice cream? Do you have any coffee to go with that pie?" He watched, mesmerized when the purple hat and scarf came off, then the jacket. Lean and trim. Just the right kinds of curves. His love was perfect, and she was standing right there in his father's kitchen.

"Absolutely. Big slice or little slice?"

His love laughed again, a tinkling sound that sent shivers up Gus's spine. "Oh, a big slice. If you're going to eat pie and ice cream, you need a big piece to really enjoy it. I haven't had pie in a long time. What kind is it?"

"Berry. What should I call you?" Gus said, turning his back on her to cut the pie.

"I'm sorry; my manners are atrocious. Amy Baran. Nice to meet you, Gus Moss. I didn't know Mr. Moss had a son. I used to come out here every September with my dad to tag a tree. Then we'd come back around Thanksgiving to take the tree home. It was the highlight of my life back then. Dad would always give me ten dollars to spend in the Christmas shop. I felt so grown-up when I'd sit down to eat the gingerbread and cider. Then I really grew up, and we didn't do it anymore. Your mother always took time with the kids. Where were you?"

"Out in the fields I guess." *Amy Baran*. This was the young woman Peggy and Ham Bledsoe talked about. The same Amy Baran who returned home to help her mother. His competitor. He turned around, his expression blank. "Nice to meet you, Amy Baran." Gus extended his hand and she grasped it. It was no wishy-washy handshake either. She gave as good as she got.

Gus ate his pie as he tried to figure out what this . . . *spy* was doing sitting in his kitchen. He decided his eyes were bigger than his stomach. Suddenly, the pie and ice cream lost their appeal. He set the dish down on the floor for Cyrus. Amy continued to eat. She appeared to be enjoying every mouthful.

"So what did you want to see my father about?"

"To buy some trees. A lot of trees. My mother told me she heard in town that your father is selling all his trees this year for $45 to thin out his fields. We'd be happy to buy about ten thousand. For buying that many we'd like a discount of maybe 5 percent. It's for the Seniors. No one will be making money off this deal, and that includes me and my mother. My mother asked me to come home to help out and to map out a PR campaign to sell the trees. I have to admit it was all a good idea, but my mother didn't think it through and made some major goofs. It was left to me to pick up the pieces. When do you think I can talk to your father? Or do you make the decisions? That was certainly good pie. I enjoyed it."

"The housekeeper made it. I'll pass on the compliment. That would be a loss of $55 a tree to Moss Farms. I don't know who started that rumor. Moss Farms is in business to *make* money, not give it away. What are you planning on selling them for? A hundred bucks a pop? That's a lot of money, Miss Baran. So you would still make a 25 percent return on the investment if I sold to you at $80 a tree."

"Yes, it is a lot of money, but it's for the Seniors' Building. There's no other place to get funding. As it is, the building was left to the Senior Citizens in a member's will. Are you following me here?"

"I'm on the same page. Only half the fields will be ready to harvest. The half you're talking about is overgrown. They haven't been fertilized or irrigated. There are a lot of dead trees in those fields. I don't have enough help to get them in shape for this season. Ah, I see by your expression that you aren't following me. Let me explain. My father let the farm go to wrack and ruin. I came home last week from California to help out. A lot of people his age don't want to hear from their whippersnapper sons, who think they know more than they do. My father . . . my father felt the same way. Push came to shove and, Miss Baran, I exercised my option to take over the half of the farm left to me by my mother, that wonderful lady who was always so nice to you. *My* trees will be ready to cut Thanksgiving week. If my father sells to you, you are going to have a lot of disgruntled customers. As they stand now, I wouldn't pay twenty bucks for one of them. Business is business, and time is money. I learned that at my father's knee," Gus snapped.

Amy's jaw dropped as she tried to absorb what Gus Moss was telling her. Her back stiffened. "Let me be sure I understand what you've just said. As far as you know the $45 per tree is a rumor. Moss Farms is divided into two parts. You own half, your father owns half. You are working your tree fields, and your father's are nothing but garbage. You're willing to sell your trees to me for $80 a tree, which is a 20 percent discount to the Seniors. Did I get that all right?"

"That's about it. We'll trim the base, clip the straggly branches, drill the hole in the trunk and net the trees. We'll divide the lot into three categories—small, medium and large trees. You can sell them for whatever you want. We'll even deliver them to your site. That's all gratis. Labor is expensive. It's the best I can do."

"Well, that isn't good enough, Mr. Moss. This is for charity, for the Senior Citizens of our town. Your father is a senior citizen, and so is my mother. One day you and I will be seniors. Shame on you, Gus Moss. I wouldn't do business with you if you paid me my weight in gold. Who do you think you are?"

His love was angry. Well, he was angry too. "I'm an architect. I'm not a tree farmer. I came here to help my father and to protect my interest in this farm. I put my personal life on hold to come here to do this and to make it work. And it is working. My fields are ready to go."

"Helloooo, Mr. Moss. I did the same thing. I'm going to make it work, but for all the *right* reasons. Not to make money for myself and to protect my investment."

The purple hat was suddenly on her head, the muffler whipping past his nose as she wrapped it around her neck. "You . . . you . . . *Scrooge.* Shame on you, Gus Moss. I hope you enjoy your ill-gotten gains. Thanks for the pie." The door slammed behind Amy. Cyrus let out a shrill bark and slammed against the back door as he tried to understand the young woman's angry tone.

Gus flopped down on the chair he'd been sitting on during Amy Baran's tirade. *Scrooge! Scrooge!* She'd called him, Gus Moss, a scrooge.

Chapter Eight

The Rafters was a secluded restaurant perched high on a hill. In the fall and winter when the trees were bare, the nation's capitol could be seen in the distance. It wasn't necessarily the kind of eatery where one went to be seen—just the opposite, as it afforded privacy and small rooms where one could dine without worrying about people stopping by to say hello. It was rumored that more than one senator and congressmen had dalliances in the private rooms. The owners of the establishment, the ladies Harriet and Olivia Neeson, were quick to deny all such rumors.

Sam Moss had called ahead for a reservation and was assured by Harriet, who had been a dear friend of his wife, Sara, that she would reserve the best table in the house.

Sam and Tillie were halfway through the meal when Sam realized he was enjoying himself. He liked the witty, sharp-tongued Tillie Baran. He knew he was going to be sorely disappointed if this outing turned out to be solely about Christmas trees.

It had been ages, years actually, since he'd dined out. He always felt like a fish out of water sitting down in a restaurant by himself. When Sara was alive, they ate out every Saturday and Sunday to give her a break from cooking. He'd liked the fact that they both got slicked up. Sara preferred to say they got dressed up. Before his date with Tillie he'd dithered about what to wear and had trouble deciding if he should get dressed up. Finally, he settled on one of his vintage sport jackets. He was glad now that he hadn't gone the suit-and-tie route, because Tillie was dressed casually. She smelled so good he kept sniffing her over the delectable aromas emanating from the kitchen. Yes sireee, he was enjoying himself.

Tillie looked up from her pecan-crusted salmon she was eating and said, "I can't help but notice how you keep sniffing, Sam. Do I still smell like moth-balls?"

"No, no. I'm trying to decide which smells better, the aromas from the kitchen or your perfume. It's been a long time since I smelled perfume. The truth is, I haven't been out with a lady since Sara died."

Tillie pushed her plate away. "I can top that, Sam. I haven't been with a man in twenty-eight years. What I mean is, I haven't . . . never mind. It must have been very hard on you when Sara passed away. My husband . . . it was different. I know you and Sara were very happy."

Sam saw that his dinner companion was becoming agitated. "That was all a long time ago. Life goes on whether we like it or not. Let's talk about more pleasant things."

"How about we get down to business and talk about trees?" Tillie said bluntly.

"I can do it, Tillie, but it's going to pose a big problem for me. Unless we can come up with some way . . . Look, I'm on shaky ground where my son is concerned. We're being civil to one another but our relationship is very strained. He hasn't forgiven me for a lot of things I really don't want to go into right now. What that means to you is, he is working his half of the farm. He hired people to thin out the trees. He did some irrigating and fertilizing. His half. My half of the fields is in poor shape. If we can find a way to get the trees thinned and cut, I'll donate as many as you want to the Seniors' fund-raiser."

"Sam! Really! You'll donate as many as we can sell? That's wonderful. We'll just have to find people to help us. We have over seventy members to our chapter. The members have sons, nephews, grandchildren. Surely we can convince them to help us."

Sam toyed with his wineglass. "We have to do it at night, Tillie."

Tillie reared back in her chair. "At night! Right off, I see that as a problem. Why?"

Sam looked embarrassed. "I don't want Gus to know. Right now the boy doesn't have a very high opinion of me. Like I said, we're on shaky ground. He left his business to come here to help me. I reacted like the old fool I am, said and did a lot of things Sara would deplore, but I did them anyway. He wants to prove to me he can get the farm back on its feet. He just might succeed at the rate he's going. It's too late to get my fields in shape, so while I'm donating them to you, you won't be able to charge much for them. That means they aren't going to be perfect trees. If I donate them to you, whatever you do sell them for will be all profit. Perhaps less than you planned, but you'll make something. If you can get the volunteers, I think we can make it work. Maybe you can bill them as Charlie Brown trees." Sam guffawed at what he thought was his witticism.

"Why are you doing this, Sam?" Tillie asked suspiciously. "When I came out to see you weeks ago you all but ran me off your property."

"I'm sorry about that. I wasn't in a good place mentally at the time. Then Gus came home with a major attitude. I had to fall back and regroup. At my age it's damn hard to admit when you're wrong, especially to your son. There are things . . . I don't know if I can ever make right."

Tillie reached across the table to take Sam's hand in her own. "I know all about that, Sam. I really do. Amy and I are in the same position. I think we're two old fools that stepped off the road and are trying to find it again. My daughter is so . . . efficient, so smart. She's detail oriented. She follows through. That's important, as she pointed out to me. She doesn't like me, Sam. She as much as said I wasn't mother material. Do you know how hard that was to hear? Worse, she's right. She ran my cell phone under water. She said it was growing out of my ear." This last sentence was said with such outrage, Sam burst out laughing. He squeezed her hand.

"My son doesn't like me either. He needs to show me up, prove that he can run the farm and make money. He's trying to show me that even though he hates it, he's good at it. Does that make sense?" Tillie nodded. "I understand he's a damn fine architect and makes tons of money out there in California. Gets all kinds of awards. Sara would have been so proud of him. He never forgave me for donating 'his' tree to the White House. Sara always said when it got to a proper growth, she was going to donate it to the White House in Gus's name. She was so proud of that tree. Gus thinks I did it for spite."

Tillie was aghast. "And you never told him?"

"No, I never told him, just the way you never told your daughter about your husband."

"Not only are we old fools, Sam, we're stupid old fools. Why do we always think we know best just because we're older? Do you think we can pull this off, Sam? Won't your son hear or notice the activity out in your . . . your half of the fields?"

"No. What he considers my half is down more in the valley. We can drive in from the back end. He's busy working *his half*. He goes to bed at eight o'clock and sleeps so soundly the house could fall down around him and he wouldn't hear it. How are you going to explain it to your daughter?"

"I'll think of something. It's the season of miracles, isn't it? Every morning when Amy gets to the site she'll see whatever we put there during the night. She did tell me this was a seat-of-the-pants operation. I think she's right. A mysterious Good Samaritan delivers trees in the middle of the night. She'll find a way to run with that. She's a PR person and will play that up to the public. *I think she's right.* Can we really do this, Sam? I'm starting to get excited."

Sam stared across the table at his dinner partner, saw the sparkle in her eyes, felt her hand squeeze his again. He was starting to get excited himself. "Yes, we can do it. When you go home, start making phone calls. I'll do the same. We'll start work tomorrow night. We'll all meet at the back entrance at eight-thirty and take it from there. Do you care for dessert?"

"No, Sam, I don't think so. I think we should go home and get to work. I have one small question. If we work all night, when are we going to sleep?"

Sam threw his head back and laughed again. "We might have to pretend we're sick. Old people get sick all the time. We can say we got our flu shots and like a lot of people, got sick."

"Oooh, Sam, you're so devious. I think that might work. I don't see your son or my daughter fussing over either one of us, do you?"

Sam grinned from ear to ear. "Nope." He squeezed Tillie's hand. When she squeezed back, he laughed again. "Okay, partner, let's hit the road and get to work. I think we should do this again sometime, Tillie."

"I'd like that, Sam. I really would. It was a lovely dinner. Thank you."

Amy was sitting at the kitchen table nursing a glass of wine she really didn't want. Every time she thought about Gus Moss, her cheeks burned. The man was a scrooge. An out-and-out California guy who thought only about money. The arrogance of the man!

Amy was startled out of her reverie when she noticed her mother standing in the doorway. "Did you have a nice time wherever you went, Mother?"

"I suppose so. Dinner is dinner. You eat, you chat, you pay the check. Dinner. Is something wrong? You look angry."

"I am angry. After you left, I drove out to Moss Farms to talk to Mr. Moss, only he wasn't there. His know-it-all son was there. Mr. Moneybags Moss. I offered to buy his trees and asked for a discount. The best he could do was 20 percent. We can't operate and make money at that rate. We had words. I called him a scrooge. I think I might have screamed that. He gave me some pie that was very good. He's in charge of the farm these days. He was so arrogant, Mom. But boy was he good-looking. I'm really pissed off right now."

Tillie felt so weak in the knees she had to sit down. Her daughter poured a glass of wine for her, which she drained in one long gulp. "I see."

Amy bolted off her chair and started pacing the kitchen from one end to the other. "What do you see, Mother?"

"That . . . that you're upset. I'm . . . ah . . . feeling a little slow today. I got a flu shot the other day and for some reason I always get sick afterward. That happens to a lot of people my age for some reason. I could . . . ah . . . be laid up for as long as a week. I'm sorry, Amy. I'll do what I can, even if I have to do it in bed. It's not easy getting old. Not that you would understand that."

"Oh, I understand, Mother. It's called a cop-out. Good night. I'll see you in the morning. I'll make breakfast if you can see your way to getting out of bed."

Tillie felt her shoulders stiffen. "I'll do my best, Amy," she said coolly.

Tillie poured herself another glass of wine as she contemplated what the coming days would bring. "This is all my fault," she mumbled to the silent room. "All my fault."

Chapter Nine

The silvery flakes of frost on the windows of Amy's car alarmed her. She hoped she was dressed warm enough. To her way of thinking it was too cold for this time of year. They shouldn't have a frost until Thanksgiving, but then what did she know about weather conditions? Not a whole lot, she decided as she climbed into her car to head to the Coleman site, where the tent people would be erecting the tents three days ahead of schedule. Nothing was working right. Everything had a glitch. Even her mother was under the weather. Sometimes, life wasn't fair.

She had to find some Christmas trees or she was going to fizzle like a dead firecracker. She'd been talking a good game to her mother but it wasn't working for her. Someone, somewhere had to have some Christmas trees they were willing to sell for a discount for a worthy cause. She'd beaten the bushes, banged the drum, and the tree growers had laughed at her. None to spare, she'd been told. Orders were placed months in advance, not weeks like she was doing. If push came to shove, she might have to resort to dealing with the crook her mother had signed on with. If she didn't pull this off, she'd be a failure in her eyes, and her mother's as well. Amy thought about her bank balance as she drove to the Coleman site. It wasn't exactly robust, but it was healthy. She'd dipped into it for deposits, and now it looked like she might have to do more than dip the second time around.

She thought about Gus Moss and how nice it had been sitting in the kitchen at Moss Farms. Everything had gone so well until she told him what she wanted. Such a scrooge. Why couldn't people be more generous? Money wasn't the answer to everything. Christmas was supposed to be a time for giving, for helping one's fellow man. What was it Gus Moss had said? *Time is money, business is business.* Maybe that was her problem, she was taking this personal. The tired old cliché of all PR people came to mind. Fight fire with fire. Preempt your opponent. Strike first. Amy shivered. Was she a match for Gus Moss? Probably not. What she knew about Christmas trees would fill a thimble, whereas Gus Moss could write the book on the subject. One of the sharpest PR people she'd ever come across told her she had to subscribe to his credo: Dazzle them with rhetoric and baffle them with bullshit, and you win the game. Like she was really going to do that? Not in this lifetime.

Amy swerved into the vacant lot and was surprised to see three trucks and men hustling about, driving stakes into the ground. She was pleased to see that the tents were made from a shiny white plastic that would lend itself well to the red and green Christmas colors, colors that would stand out and draw attention. Another plus was the site, which was a corner property with an entrance from both roads and more than ample parking. She would have plenty of room to line up her trees if she ever got any to line up.

Amy watched the workers for a few minutes before she drove off down the road to a Burger King, where she bought a honey biscuit and two cups of coffee to go.

Back at the site she opened her laptop and logged on. Time to find some Christmas trees. An hour later, Amy was jolted from her search by a knock on the car window. She looked at the bill, winced and wrote out the check. She went back to her search as the men drove off. She looked at the tents and was impressed. At least she'd done one thing right.

It was midmorning when a whoop of pleasure echoed in the car. A man named Ambrose McFlint had trees for sale in McLean, Virginia. The banner ad running across the flat screen said the trees were reasonably priced, and free delivery went with the deal. Within minutes, Amy had the car in gear and she was headed for McLean.

Ten miles away Gus Moss was tagging trees he judged ready to be cut in two weeks' time. Orange tags were tied onto the branches for the first cutting. Red tags meant the second cutting. Purple tags were balled trees to be dug out with the backhoe, but only when the trees were paid for.

As Gus tromped from the Douglas firs to the Balsam firs to the Virginia pines, he let his mind run wild to the young woman he'd shared dessert with last night. Even though he was bone tired, he hadn't slept well, tossing and turning all night long. He couldn't get Amy Baran's expression out of his mind. She'd been shocked, dismayed at his callousness. Then she'd added insult to injury and called him a scrooge. Would it kill him to sell her a few trees at a healthy discount for the Seniors' cause? All his life he'd been a generous person, so why was he suddenly turning into a skinflint? He didn't have to prove anything to anyone except maybe his father. The why of it simply eluded him.

"Jack, Bill, come over here," he called to two of his workers. "See this grove of Virginia pine? I want you to trim the trees, cut away the brush and tag them with these red tags. We'll cut these trees the Tuesday before Thanksgiving and deliver them after dark. Don't look at me like that and don't ask any questions. Just do it."

"All of them? There must be over two hundred," Jack, his foreman, said.

"Yeah, all of them. We'll stagger the deliveries, fifty at a time. I'll pay you overtime."

Gus felt his shoulders lighten a bit as he prowled his fields. An anonymous donation of two hundred trees should take him out of the scrooge category.

Every so often Gus glanced over his shoulder to look for his father, but he was nowhere to be seen. He'd had to make his own breakfast that morning. He felt a grin stretch across his face. His father must have had a really busy night. He'd heard him come in, heard him going up and down the stairs all night long. Obviously he wasn't the only one who hadn't had a good night's sleep.

As he worked through the day, all he could think of was Amy Baran. He suddenly loved the color purple. *Where is she? What is she doing right now?* He wished he knew.

He wondered what she would do if he called her up and asked her out to dinner. He nixed that idea as soon as it popped into his head. He knew in his gut Amy Baran would never go out with someone she considered to be a scrooge. *So why did I even think about it?*

It was noon when Gus made his way back to the farmhouse. He needed some hot soup and a cup of strong, black coffee. He looked up when he felt something brush his cheek. Rain? He was stunned when he realized what he felt was a snowflake. Thick gray clouds scudded across the sky. Snow this early? He hoped not.

Gus almost swooned at the delicious scents that assailed him the moment he and Cyrus entered the kitchen. A fire was roaring in the fireplace. *The only thing missing is the girl with the purple hat and scarf,* Gus thought as he washed his hands. He ladled soup into a bowl, cut a chunk of crusty bread and fell to it. He was careful to only eat two bowls of soup; otherwise, he'd be sluggish all afternoon. The strong, black coffee made his eyeballs stand at attention. As he sipped the brew he walked around the house calling his father's name. He craned his neck to stare out the window. His father's truck was gone. He must have gone to town for something. He shrugged.

Gus set his dishes in the sink, gave Cyrus a rawhide chew, put on his jacket and hat and was out of the house, all within five minutes. Instead of walking out to the white pine field, he climbed into his pickup. If the weather held he could clear at least two rows of the beautiful white pines that would bring him top dollar. As he bumped along the rutted fields his thoughts returned to Amy Baran. He felt like a sixteen-year-old again with his first crush.

On the seat next to him, Cyrus growled as he fought with his chewie, which wasn't crumbling to his satisfaction. "You see, Cyrus, you have to work for everything in this life. There's no free lunch, even though Miss Amy Baran seems to think there is." Cyrus ignored him as he continued fighting with the rawhide bone.

Gus stood in awe as he gazed at the white pine grove. How beautiful, how pungent it smelled. Suddenly, he didn't want to cut the trees. They were just too majestic. Even though his father hadn't fertilized or irrigated the beautiful trees, they had survived. All the grove needed was to be thinned out. Maybe he would cut every third one instead of all of them. It broke his heart that once the magnificent specimens were cut, decorated by someone in a house that was probably too warm, the tree would slowly die and be discarded. *You live, then you die,* he thought bitterly.

Angrily, Gus walked among the stately trees, tying long, yellow strips onto the branches. Long strips of the bright yellow tape meant the trees were not to be touched.

Why, he asked himself, was he so angry? Was he angry that his mother died, that his father let everything go to hell, that he'd killed *Gus's birth tree* by cutting it down and donating it to the White House? Or was he angry at the young woman in the purple hat and scarf for calling him a scrooge and hurting his feelings? All of the above, he decided as the chain saw in his hand came to life. He worked then like there was a devil on his shoulder, cutting away the thick undergrowth and dead branches. He broke a sweat but continued until it was too dark to see what he was doing. He was sweating profusely and every bone in his body ached as he drove back over the same bumpy fields. He looked down at his watch and was surprised to see that it was six-thirty. His father would be waiting dinner for him.

His father wasn't waiting for him when he opened the kitchen door. The table wasn't set either. The huge pot of soup was still simmering on the warming burner. The oven showed a golden roast chicken dinner complete with stuffing and mashed potatoes and gravy. Cyrus barked.

Gus shed his outer clothing, and that's when he noticed the red blinking light on his father's answering machine. No voice mail for Sam Moss. Gus pressed the button to listen to the message. His eyebrows shot up to his hairline when he heard the sweet, melodious voice of his love. "Mr. Moss . . . ah, Gus, this is Amy Baran. I'm . . . ah, calling you to apologize for calling you a scrooge last night. I was upset when I called you Scrooge. At the time I meant it because I was angry. I don't mean it today because I'm no longer angry. Even though we're competitors of sorts, I hope you sell all of your trees and that you make a lot of money. Again, I'm sorry for my rude behavior."

"Well, hot damn! Did you hear that, Cyrus?" Gus slapped at the kitchen table as he danced a little jig while Cyrus nipped at his ankles. His love apologized. She wasn't angry with him. Maybe now he could call her for a date. He played the message again and listened to the end of it. A frown built between his brows. She hoped he sold all his trees and made a lot of money. She thought this was all about money. She thought he was a money-hungry Christmas tree salesman. How could she think that about him? It was never about the money.

A niggling voice whispered in his ear, a voice he didn't want to hear. *Sure it's about the money. It's about proving to your father you can do in two months what he didn't do in the last ten years. This is your way of getting back at him. It all translates to money—$$$. Who are you kidding, Gus Moss?*

You didn't put it behind you. You're kidding yourself if you think you've moved on. You haven't. You are a scrooge.

The phone found its way to Gus's hand. He dialed Information and asked for the number to the Baran residence. His shoulders slumped when he heard the voice mail click on. "This is Gus Moss, a.k.a. Scrooge. I just want to say I accept your apology and would like you to know I'm really a stand-up guy. I'd like to invite you to dinner if you have some free time. If you're agreeable, we should probably schedule it before we both get busy selling Christmas trees. The apology wasn't necessary. I would have said the same thing if I had been standing in your shoes. I think you should give me an opportunity to defend myself. I hope you have a nice evening."

Chapter Ten

It was eight-thirty when Amy Baran dialed Gus Moss's phone number. She hated herself for what she was about to do but she had no other choice. Ripples of anxiety raced up and down her arms. "Gus, this is Amy Baran. I just got your message. I appreciate the return phone call. Listen, I was just about to go out to Tony's to grab a pizza. Would you like to join me?" *Liar, liar, pants on fire.*

Gus looked down at his worn sweatpants, then at the oven where his dinner sat. He'd been in no hurry to eat earlier. "Well, sure. Thirty minutes?"

"That works for me. I'll meet you there."

"Wear that purple hat and scarf, okay?"

Amy laughed, a jittery sound, but Gus didn't pick up on her nervousness. He was beyond excited as he raced upstairs to change his clothes, with Cyrus right behind him, nipping at his heels. It took him four minutes to change into acceptable clothes for a pizza date. He used up another five minutes filling a plate for Cyrus. Two minutes later he was out the door. It only took a minute for him to realize how cold it was. He cranked on the heater and sailed down the road.

Gus was ten minutes early when he parked his truck and headed for the pizzeria. It was warm and steamy, the rich scent of garlic and cheese wafting about. The place was full of chattering customers chomping down on Tony's pizza. He looked around at the red leather booths for a sign of Amy. He saw her in the back. She waved. He grew light-headed as he made his way to the booth.

She smiled.

He smiled.

She motioned for him to sit opposite her.

He obliged.

"I took the liberty of ordering. I got the works except for anchovies. If you want them, now's the time to ask. I hope you like Corona."

"I do. Like Corona and no, I don't like anchovies. I guess we have something in common. I love pizza. Three food groups you know." He needed to stop acting like a young teenager and act like the successful man he was. He struggled for something to say that sounded intelligent. "It's cold out." *Wow, that was brilliant.*

"I felt some snow flurries when I got out of the car. Usually it doesn't get this cold this early. How do you handle this cold coming from California?"

"I bought a lot of warm clothing. The truth is, today I was so cold I was numb. How was your day?"

Amy picked at the napkin in her hands. It was almost shredded. Here it was, the question she'd been dreading. "Listen, I want you to know something about me, Gus. By nature I am not a devious person. I have ethics. I'm pretty much up front and in your face if anything. I called you back . . . under false pretenses. I was sincere about the apology the first time I called you. I'm not going to beat around the bush. I need your Christmas trees. I went out to McLean to a guy who said he would sell me some. It didn't work out. I'm asking you to help me. Well, not me really, the Seniors." She was so frustrated, so embarrassed, her eyes filled with tears. She blinked them away. She squared her shoulders. "I was wondering . . . hoping you would consider the two of us pooling our efforts to help the Seniors. I know you want to make money, so here is my proposition. I'll take on your loss as my own personal debt. It might take me a few years to pay it off, but I will pay it off."

Gus stared at the agitated woman sitting across from him. Whatever he'd been expecting, this wasn't it. Her eyes looked luminous with unshed tears. He wanted to bolt over to her side of the booth and wrap his arms around her. He grappled for something to say. "Why is this so important to you?"

Amy brushed at the corners of her eyes. "I'm not sure. If you absolutely need an answer, the only thing I can say is I'm trying to . . . to . . . prove to my mother that I turned out okay even though she was never around when I did things she should have patted me on the head for. I suppose that sounds silly to you. I don't know, maybe it's a girl thing. I never got . . . what I mean is . . . I always wanted her approval. I never got it. So, while it is about the Seniors, it's all about me, too. Does any of this make sense to you?"

Well hell yes, it made perfect sense to him. Wasn't

he living through the exact same thing? Maybe they were soul mates. He nodded, his eyes sober as he handed her a paper napkin. "It makes sense," he said quietly. "I'm doing exactly what you're trying to do. So, do you have an idea, a plan?"

Amy leaned across the table. Her eyes sparkled with hope. "Does that mean you'll help me?"

Gus didn't trust himself to speak. He nodded.

"Well, I thought I could . . . I have a campaign all worked out. That's my speciality. It's what I do for a living. I'll have to get rid of the tents, suck up the deposit and relocate to your farm. People, according to Mom, don't know you're back in business, so I can make that happen. I'll work alongside you. I'll do whatever you want. You don't have to worry about me carrying my weight. I'll work around the clock if that's what you want. We can draw on the Seniors to set up your store. I can make the wreaths and grave blankets. This will free up your people to handle the trees. Does . . . do you think . . . ?"

Gus leaned back in the booth to allow the waiter to set a steaming pizza in the middle of the table. "Okay."

Amy's face lit up like a neon sign. "Do you mean it, Gus? What . . . what about time is money and business is business? Are you sure?"

Was he? Suddenly he realized he'd never been more sure of anything in his life. He nodded. "Let me ask you a question. What happens if when this is all over and done with, your mother and my father don't understand what we're all about?"

Amy sat up straighter in the booth. "Then, Gus Moss, it's their loss, not ours."

Ah, his love thought just the way he did. He nodded again. He stretched his arm across the table. "Okay, partner, let's put our heads together, but first we eat this pizza."

His love laughed, her eyes sparkling like diamonds. She squeezed his hand. Gus felt like he was on fire. He watched as she loaded her pizza with hot peppers, just the way he liked his. He said so. They both laughed in delight.

Gus Moss was in love. It never once occurred to him that Miss Amy Baran might be using him for his Christmas trees. He told himself his heart would know if that was the case.

Amy Baran tried to still her pounding heart. It never once occurred to her that Gus Moss might be using her and her PR campaign to sell his Christmas trees. If that were the case, she told herself, her heart wouldn't be pounding the way it was.

At one point, Gus moved to the other side of the booth, where they talked in low whispers about everything and anything. Without realizing it, he reached for Amy's hand. She exerted a little pressure to show she didn't mind this closeness.

It was eleven-thirty when Gus paid the check and walked Amy to her car. He wanted to kiss her so bad his teeth ached with the feeling. Something told him this wasn't the time.

Suddenly he was jolted forward when Amy grabbed the lapels of his shearling jacket and pulled him to her, where she put a lip-lock on him that made his world rock right out from under him. When she finally released him, she smiled. "I'll see you at six o'clock tomorrow morning, Gus Moss." She leaned forward and whispered in his ear. "Dream about me, okay?"

Gus stood statue-still as he watched his love drive away. His fist shot upward. "Yessss!"

Sam Moss looked down at the oversize watch on his wrist, a gift from Gus a few years ago. It was almost midnight, and his well-meaning Seniors were pooped to the nth degree. Tillie, at his side, looked like she was going to collapse any minute, but she was still wearing her game face. "This isn't working, Tillie. They mean well, their minds want to do this but their bodies aren't willing. I think we need to fall back and regroup."

"I know, Sam. Can we go someplace where it's warm and talk about it? I'm worried about some of them. Let's all go over to the all-night diner and decide what we're going to do. I didn't think getting old was going to be this devastating. My daughter was right, making arrangements via cell phone and doing the actual work are two different things. I owe her an apology. Actually I owe her more—"

"Shhh," Sam said as he put his finger near her lips. "We'll figure something out. I'll talk to the men, you talk to the ladies. If nothing else, we have enough branches and limbs to make a good many wreaths and grave blankets. Three and a half hours, and all we managed was to cut down six trees, and even with all our manpower we can't get the trees into the trucks. You're right, Tillie, we're old. Where in the hell did all the wisdom we're supposed to have go?"

How sad he sounds, Tillie thought. She tried then to do what all women had done since the beginning of time—bolster up the big man standing next to her.

"I think, Sam, we transferred our wisdom to our children because they turned out to be know-it-alls."

Her words had the desired effect. Sam guffawed as he drew her to him with his arm. Tillie felt light-headed. "Let's get our work crew and head for the diner. Breakfast, dinner, whatever, is on me. Snap to it, little lady. I'll meet all of you at the diner."

Tillie found herself giggling. *Dear God, have I ever giggled like this? Never, as far as I can remember.* Suddenly, she felt warm all over as she herded the female Seniors to cars for transport to the diner. She felt guilty as she realized not one of them would have given up, even knowing they weren't carrying their weight.

"Look, we didn't really fail. We're going to rethink this. When we're warm with some good food, we'll come up with a better idea." Tillie wondered if what she was saying was true.

They were a weary, bedraggled group as they trooped into Stan's Diner, which was open twenty-four hours a day. Two police officers were paying for take-out coffee and Danish. Otherwise, the diner was empty.

The women all headed for the restrooms to wash the pine resin off their hands. Tillie sat down, her shoulders slumping. How had it come to this? She hoped she was strong enough not to cry.

Within minutes, Sam and the weary male Seniors blew into the diner. Stan, the owner, greeted them, his eyes full of questions. Sam took him aside to speak with him. Within minutes, the waiters had the tables pushed together and Stan had his marching orders. Hot chocolate, tea and coffee were brought. Taking into consideration the Seniors' health, Sam ordered Egg Beaters omelets, turkey bacon, oven-baked potatoes and toast.

When they were all seated with hot drinks in front of them, Tillie looked around. Her friends, and they were her friends, looked shell-shocked. She wondered if she looked the same way. Probably. She decided she really didn't care how she looked. She had to give her friends some hope, some encouragement. She couldn't let them return to their homes thinking that just because they were old, they were failures. With a nod from Sam, she used her spoon to tap her water glass for attention.

"I want you all to listen to me. Like Sam said, our minds are willing but our bodies aren't in tune. This was an overwhelming project. Most of us don't see well at night. That's strike one. Strike two is we aren't twenty, thirty, forty or fifty. We simply cannot do the things we used to do even though we want to do them. Strike three is the cold weather. We aren't used to manual labor. Been there, done that. We all had good intentions but they aren't working for us. I'm going to turn it over to Sam now in case he has some ideas. I, for one, am not giving up."

The Seniors clapped their approval of Tillie's little speech.

Sam stood up and looked around the long table. "I have an idea but I don't know if it will work. When I go home tonight, I'm going to wake up my son and *talk* to him. I think most of you know about . . . about how things are with me. I'm going to ask him to help us. The boy has a lot of ill feeling toward me. I'm going to try and make that right. Will it work? I don't know. I've never . . . I've never had to actually ask him for anything. It's going to be a new experience for both of us. If Augustus turns his back on me, I am prepared to donate whatever you would have netted from selling trees to the Senior project."

"But if you donate the money that means we still failed," Ian Conover said. "We wanted to earn the money, Sam. If your son turns his back on you, can you handle it? No man wants to see his son turn against him."

"I'm prepared for that, Ian. Nothing can be worse than all the years since Sara died. I'm going to do my best, and if my best isn't good enough, then so be it."

The Seniors clapped and raised their mugs to toast their leader.

Sam Moss walked into the kitchen at one-thirty in the morning. Cyrus greeted him with a soft woof of pleasure. His son was asleep at the kitchen table. Sam took a minute to stare at his Gus, remembering the day he was born. He'd been so crazy with happiness, he'd left the hospital, raced home to plant a tree and named it Gus's tree. Then he headed for Wheeler's Hardware store and bought a child's John Deere tractor for his newborn son. That was probably his first mistake. He should have bought him an easel or a drafting board.

Sam sighed as he hung up his jacket and hat. If there was a committee that handed out a prize for the most mistakes made by a father, he'd win it hands down. He poured himself a cup of the strong, bitter coffee that was still in the pot. He sat down at the table to wait for his son to wake up. One taste told him the coffee was bad, so he threw it out and made a fresh pot. He was into his second cup when Gus woke up.

"Dad!"

"It's me, son. I've been sitting here wondering if by some chance you were waiting up for me. I seem to recall that was my job. It's funny how things turn around when you least expect it. Were you waiting up for me? I want to talk to you about something, Gus."

"I was waiting for you. I guess I'm not used to you going out at night. Yeah, I remember the nights I came home and you and Mom were sitting here pretending you weren't waiting for me. I need to talk to you about something too. How would you feel about me donating all my trees to the Seniors?" he blurted. "I had a pizza with Amy Baran this evening, and they really are in a bind. Nothing worked out for them. She brought me up short. She told me she would partner up with me, do the public relations campaign, and she would make the grave blankets and wreaths herself. She said the Seniors would man the shop, bake the gingerbread and hand out the cider. She has some really grand ideas. It will put Moss Farms back on the map, Dad.

"I want to apologize to you about that . . . my-half-of-the-farm crap I spouted when I first got here. This is your farm. It was always yours and Mom's. I came here to help you, Dad. Then you dug in your heels, and I, in turn, dug in my heels. I let old . . . hurts and memories take over. So, if you're okay with Moss Farms working with the Seniors, I'll stay on through the holidays and give it all I've got."

Sam Moss could feel his insides start to shake. He knew how hard it was for his son to say what he'd just said. He nodded. He finally managed to get the words out. "I regret the things I've done, Gus—for so many things that went wrong. I was selfish. I wanted a chip off the old block. I wanted you to love this farm the way your mother and I loved it."

Gus reached down to scratch Cyrus behind the ears. "I do love the farm, Dad. I just don't want to farm it. There are other people who can do it better than I ever could. All I ever wanted was for you to be proud of me. You never ever, by thought, word or deed, indicated that you were. Mom said you were, but I thought she was just saying what she knew I wanted to hear. I'm a damn good architect, Dad."

"Come here, son," Sam said, going into the living room. He opened a chest that served as a coffee table. Gus looked down and saw copies of all his awards, stacks of *Architectural Digest* where his designs were featured, piles and piles of newspapers that carried his picture and write-ups about him. "Does this answer your question, son?"

Gus was so stunned he didn't know what to do or say. He knew in his gut this was as close as he was going to get to a real, gut-wrenching apology. The words "I'm sorry" simply were not in Sam Moss's vocabulary. He decided he could accept that. "Yeah, Pop, except for one thing. If you were so damn proud of me, if you loved me, why did you chop down my tree and give it to the White House? Mom said an hour after I was born you planted my tree. Then you chopped it down and sent it away."

Sam Moss dropped down on his knees to rummage in the bottom of the chest until he found an envelope. He held it out to Gus. Gus read his mother's letter addressed to the White House and the reply that was sent to her accepting her offer of Gus's tree for display during the Christmas season. "Why did you let me think . . . why didn't you tell me . . . ?"

"That's where I am guilty, son. I wasn't in a good mental place that year. Your mother and I were invited to the White House. Your mother wanted it to be a surprise for you. It was what she wanted. If it means anything to you at this point, I tried arguing her out of it. I dearly loved that old tree. Another year or so and it would have gotten straggly looking. Just so you know."

And then his father said the magic words Gus had waited a lifetime to hear. "No father could be prouder of his son than I am of you. I'm sorry, son."

Chapter Eleven

Operation Christmas Tree, as Gus referred to it, kicked into high gear the following Monday morning. His work crew, numbering twelve, arrived at the crack of dawn. Sam's crew of Seniors arrived minutes later. Both Moss Senior and Moss Junior issued orders like the generals they pretended to be. OCT was under way.

Tillie stepped forward and led the Senior Ladies to the gift shop where they proceeded to set up shop opening box after box of ornaments, ribbons, Christmas toys, bells and everything else she had ordered at the last minute for opening day.

Amy arrived breathless, wearing sturdy work boots, tight-fitting jeans, a bomber jacket and a bright orange hat and scarf. Gus Moss fell in love all over again. When she waved her clipboard at him and winked, he thought he would go out of his mind. Suddenly, all he wanted to do was cuddle, to snuggle, to hold her hand, to whisper in her ear. What he didn't want to do was go out in the tree fields and wield a chain saw. When she winked and waved again, he groaned and climbed into his truck.

Sam and Tillie poked each other and grinned at these goings-on.

"Seven days to Thanksgiving, then the fun starts," Sam said happily. "It gets pretty wild around here, Tillie. Are you sure you're up to it?"

"We'll soon find out. Did you have anything in mind for Thanksgiving, Sam? If you don't, I have an idea."

"Let me hear it, little lady."

"We always have a turkey dinner at Seniors' head-quarters, as you know. Adeline McPherson makes the best turkeys in the county. I'm sure you know that too. Let's do the dinner out here at the farm. I know Addy would be more than happy to work in your kitchen and you have those two, big double ovens. We'll invite everyone—Gus's crew, their families, all the Seniors and us. I think it would be a good incentive and a great way to kick things off. Everyone will be in the mood to give 100 percent on Friday morning when the trees go on sale. You'll have to pay for it, Sam. Can you see your way clear to doing that?"

Sam beamed. It had been a long time since anyone asked for his opinion or for a donation to anything. Giving his trees away simply didn't fit into this particular equation. "It would be my pleasure. You sounded like my Sara just then, Tillie."

Tillie looked up at Sam, a stricken look on her face.

"What? What's wrong? What did I say?" Sam asked anxiously.

"I'm not Sara, Sam. I'm me, Tillie. Please don't compare or confuse us. I have to go now, the ladies need me. Lunch will be promptly at noon. We need to keep to a schedule."

Sam ambled off, scratching his head. "That was kind of blunt, Mom, don't you think?" Amy asked.

"Well . . . I just don't . . . I wouldn't want . . . Never mind. What's on your agenda for today?"

Amy settled her knit cap more firmly on her head as the wind kicked up. "I'm going into town. I have appointments lined up through the whole day. My first stop is the local radio station. I already contacted the stations in the District, and one of them agreed to play my jingle and advertise for Moss Farms every hour on the hour. It's all free, Mom. The station manager's parents live in an assisted living facility, and she's all for anything that benefits senior citizens. On Wednesday two billboards are going up where you can see them from I-95. I had to pay for those but got a 40 percent discount. Local TV is in the bag, all four channels. A new Christmas sign is going up at the entrance to the farm tomorrow. It's an eye popper—bright red.

"Tomorrow I pick up the Christmas Stocking. For a hundred bucks the Canvas Shop made this twenty-foot stocking out of bright red canvas. It's going to be weatherproof. We'll hang it from the tree next to the gift shop. I'm going begging today, asking for donations to fill the stocking. Everyone who comes out here to buy a tree gets to fill out an entry form, and Sam or Gus will pick the winner at noon on Christmas Eve. We're not actually going to put the donations in the stocking, but we will have a scroll next to the stocking so people can see which store donated what item. I think this is a biggie, Mom. It's going to draw people like crazy. The radio and television stations will be announcing who gave what. Free advertising for the donors. Win–win!"

Tillie looked at her daughter in amazement. "Oh, Amy, that's wonderful. In a million years I never could have come up with an idea like that. I am so proud of you. You're right, it's a biggie." Impulsively, she reached out and hugged her daughter.

Amy grew light-headed. This was the closest her mother had ever come to showing any kind of affection toward her. She hugged her back, and suddenly her world was right side up. Feeling shy at this show of affection, she waved her arms about. "I think we make a good team. We're going to make so much money for your Seniors they might be able to add that new wing to the building you were talking about."

"Well, my dear, Sam and I can't take credit for anything. It was you and Gus who brought all this together. Sam, me, the Seniors are just the elves. You two are Mr. and Mrs. Santa. I think he *really* likes you, Amy," Tillie whispered.

"How . . . how can you tell?"

"Silly girl. Open your eyes. Good luck, honey. I'll see you when I see you. Lunch is at noon if you make it back in time."

Honey. Her mother had called her honey. Another first. She said Gus *really* liked her. Mothers never lied to their children. She wondered if that was a myth made up by some disgruntled mother who had lied to her child and then tried to salvage the lie. She discounted the thought immediately.

As Amy made her way to her car she knew, just knew, it was going to be a dynamite day.

* * *

Sam Moss was thinking the same thing as he chugged his way over the frozen fields in his battered pickup truck. He couldn't remember the last time he'd felt this alive, this good. He looked down at the cell phone on the seat next to him. A gift from Gus, who had said, "You need to get with it, Dad. I'll program it for you, and you just hit the button. It's a new world out there, and you need to join it." Sam snorted when he remembered Tillie telling him her daughter ran her cell phone under the faucet because it was growing out of her ear. Well, if his son said he needed a cell phone, then he needed a cell phone. He stopped the truck as he diddled and fiddled with the gadget in his hands. Finally, he simply called Information for the number to the butcher shop in town.

"Elroy, Sam Moss. I want you to come out here and fill my three freezers. A whole side should see us through the holidays. On second thought, maybe a side and a hindquarter. And I want to order six fresh turkeys for Thanksgiving. Big turkeys, twenty-five pounds each. Go on that fancy computer of yours and send everything else times ten that Sara used to order."

Sam listened to the voice on the other end of the phone. "Well, hells bells, Elroy, I want it now, like today. Why else do you think I called you? Be sure you come out here for your tree now. They go on sale the day after Thanksgiving. I just might throw it in for free if I don't get voted down. I'm not really in charge anymore. My son, Gus, is issuing the orders these days."

Sam listened again. "You're right, Elroy, it's the best feeling in the world."

Sam pressed the Off button. He wished there was someone else to call, but he didn't have many friends these days. Then again, he didn't want the darn thing to grow out of his ear. He guffawed at the thought.

Sam blew the horn on the old truck, and waited. It took the golden streak two and a half minutes to arrive and hop into the truck. Cyrus barked happily as he tried to nuzzle Sam's neck. Sam laughed all the way out to the Norway spruce field.

Life was suddenly so good he was scared.

Gus was waiting for him, the chain saw that he never seemed to be without in his hands. "Dad, I've been waiting for you." He pointed to the narrow row of trees. "I think these particular trees can use another year of growth. What do you think? I don't want to tag and cut them if they won't sell. I say we tag them, let the buyers choose the ones they want, then cut them. Two hundred bucks for one of these beauties. By the way, I just got a call on my cell from someone at Super Giant. The supermarket chain wants to order a thousand Christmas wreaths and five hundred grave blankets for their different stores. Ten minutes ago a call came in from a Boy Scout troop asking to buy two hundred trees to sell for a fundraiser. I said we'd donate them. You okay with that, Dad?"

His son wanted his opinion. Sam wondered if it was a test of some kind. "That's pretty pricey for a tree, don't you think? I don't have a problem with the Scouts or the supermarkets. I just hope we can handle it."

Sam rubbed the whiskers on his chin as he pondered the situation. "The only people willing to pay that kind of money are the Beltway's politicos. I say we sock it to them good. Mark them at $250, and they'll kill themselves trying to get one so they can brag about how much they paid for their Christmas trees. Good thinking, son."

Gus looked at his father and burst out laughing. "Okay, Dad, you're the boss."

Sam thought he was going to black out at the kind words. He had to get past the moment and think about all this later. He could hardly wait to talk to Tillie and tell her. He had to think about *that* later, too. "You sweet on that little gal, Amy?"

A smart-ass retort rose to Gus's lips, but he stifled it. "She's okay, Dad. She's got a good work ethic."

"Well, that sure as hell doesn't sound very romantic, son. Do I need to take you into the woodshed and explain the facts of life? I asked you if you were sweet on her. I'm kind of sweet on her momma. You wanna run with that one, son?"

Son of a gun! "Yeah, Dad, I am kind of sweet on that little gal. You want to run with that one?"

Sam threw his arm around his son. Father and son started to laugh like two lunatics as they slapped each other on the back.

"I'm going over to the balsam fir field. Is it okay if Cyrus goes with me?" Sam gasped as he wiped at his wet cheeks.

Gus nodded. Banner days like this were something he'd only dreamed of.

Chapter Twelve

Gus Moss hung up the dish towel just the way his mother had taught him. He looked around at the tidy kitchen. It was hard to believe they'd fed over seventy people today. Seventy happy people, who left the cleanup to Gus and Amy.

It was eight o'clock now, time to sit down with a nice glass of wine and stare into the fire. At least for a little while. Then the mad rush would begin in less than twelve hours. "Thanks for helping with the dishes. I don't mind the dishes as much as the pots and pans." *Such a titillating conversation,* Gus thought.

Amy flopped down on the couch. "You want to hear something, Gus? I've never been this tired in my whole life. I'd never admit it to my mother, though. Right now she thinks I walk on water. It's such a good feeling, but, God, I am beat. Eating all that food sure didn't help. Aren't you tired?"

Gus grinned. "If I leaned up against the wall, I'd go right to sleep. The only thing that keeps me going is the same thing that drives you. I don't want to disappoint my father. I can design houses in my sleep. I can't swing a chain saw in my sleep." He yawned to make his point.

"That's a great fire. I use my fireplace every day during winter." She yawned, then Gus yawned. A second later, they were both asleep, Amy's head on Gus's shoulder.

Sam Moss returned an hour later and covered up the couple with an afghan his wife had made one winter when the snow was so deep they were snowbound for over a week. If memory served him right, she'd made two afghans that week. He smiled at the sleeping couple, wondering what the future held in store for both of them. Gus lived and worked in California. Amy lived and worked in Philadelphia. No matter what he thought or wanted for them, he wasn't about to stick his nose into his son's affairs. He'd learned a bitter, hard lesson, and he wasn't going there ever again.

In the kitchen, Sam poured the last of the coffee into a cup and cut a slice of pumpkin pie. He had no idea how he could still be hungry after all he'd eaten today. He needed to think, and he always thought best when he was eating, which just proved Sara had been right when she said that meant he could do two things at one time.

Sara. He'd promised himself that he was going to do some hard thinking. He wondered what Sara would think if she knew what he was feeling where Tillie Baran was concerned. He wondered if she was proud of him for the way things were turning out with Gus. He wished he knew.

"You had a nice turnout today, Sam."

Sam whirled around, but no one was in the kitchen. He was so tired now he was hearing voices. A voice from beyond. *Maybe I've overdone it. Time to go to bed.*

"It's time to move on, Sam. I want you to be as happy as our son is right now. Are you listening to me, Sam?"

Sam didn't trust himself to speak. He nodded.

"Then clean up your mess and go to bed."

"Are you sure it's okay, Sara?" Sam whispered.

"It is very okay. I'm proud of you, Sam. Now, get on with your life."

Sam jolted forward when he felt Cyrus stick his wet nose against his hand. "Thanks for waking me up, boy. I was dreaming there for a minute. Want some pie?" Cyrus woofed softly.

Sam moved by rote then as he washed his plate and cup. He couldn't shake the feeling that he had spoken to his dead wife. He never dozed off while he was eating. *Is it possible Sara just visited me? Or is it wishful thinking?*

Sam stopped in the living room to check on his sleeping son. Out for the count. His chest puffed out with pride. A little late, but Sara had always said it was never too late to make things right.

As he climbed the stairs to the second floor he decided Sara had indeed visited him and told him to get on with his life. A tired smile lit up his face. She was proud of him. He knew in his old heart that it didn't get any better than that.

The weather cooperated the following morning. The storm clouds of the day before had moved on. It was cold and brisk, with a hint of snow flurries to come, perhaps later in the day.

Gus woke first and wondered why he felt so cozy and warm. Then he saw Amy burrowed under his arm. A loud sigh escaped his lips, loud enough to wake Amy. She didn't wake in stages either. She bolted wide awake, looked at him with wide eyes and burst out laughing. "I hope you respect me this morning."

"We didn't . . ." Flushing a bright red, Gus jumped off the couch and held out his hand for her to grasp. He pulled her to him and kissed her the way she'd kissed him once before. When he finally broke free, he said, "If that didn't make your teeth rattle, I have to tell you that was my best shot."

Amy tweaked his cheek. "Oh, my teeth are rattling all right. But . . . I know you can do better. You know how I know this, Gus Moss?"

Somehow, Gus managed to get his tongue to work. He sounded like a bullfrog in acute distress. "How?"

"Because the next time, I'll cooperate and give it 110 percent. I only gave you 50 percent this time. Now you have something to look forward to." Gus watched her, his mouth hanging open as she sashayed out of the room.

"Promises, promises," Gus muttered as he made his way upstairs to his bathroom. She was right, though, it was definitely something to look forward to.

The only lull in business that day happened shortly after lunch when Gus's crew returned to the fields with the flat-bed U-Haul to replenish the eight-foot trees. The gift shop absorbed the lull with the antique cash register ringing constantly. Children came back for seconds for the gingerbread men and the hot cider. To the children's delight, Sam's old-fashioned Victrola, sitting outside on the back porch, played "Jingle Bells."

Cyrus, decked out in Buster's old reindeer ears, the bells on his collar tinkling when he walked, allowed himself to be petted and chased by the little ones. When the cars left the compound, trees tied to their roofs, one of the Seniors handed out little cellophane bags to the children. The bags said REINDEER TREATS in bright red letters. The children squealed and giggled as their trip to Moss Farms ended on a happy note.

It was clear to everyone that the Moss Christmas Tree Farm was back in business.

Tillie worked the kitchen, making coffee and sandwiches that she handed out during free moments, which were few and far between.

The cash register continued to ring. Sam said it was the sweetest sound in the world.

Amy looked up from the work table, where she was busy making wreaths and grave blankets. "Gus! How's it going out there?"

"I don't have much to judge by, but to my mind it's the biggest day after Thanksgiving I can remember. I gave up counting a couple of hours ago. I just stopped to get some coffee. Your mother is like a chicken on a hot griddle."

Amy giggled. "She's having the time of her life. Trust me."

"So is my dad. Two people are waiting for their blankets. They asked me how much longer it will be."

"I know. I can't make them fast enough. I'm not

too proud to tell you I need some help. I ran out of wreaths two hours ago. We need more of an assembly line here. I can't do the wiring and the bows. My hands are raw from the wire."

"You need to wear gloves," Gus said as he took her hands in his. They were black from the resin and bark, and he could see specks of blood on the palms of her hands. How well he remembered the days when he'd done the same thing. His mother had always put something called Bag Balm on his hands and wrapped them in warm flannel at night when he went to bed. Then he would wake and do it all over again. To this day he still had scars on his hands from the baling wire.

"There's no easy way to do it, Amy. Can you work with gloves?"

"I'm not complaining, Gus. It's too awkward working with gloves. I have to be able to feel the wire. I just said I could use some help. Someone to make the bows and tie them on will make things go a little faster. I hate the idea that people will go somewhere else for their wreaths and blankets. You know, time is money. Don't worry about me."

"I'll see if I can find you some help. I don't think any of us were prepared for such a busy day. Your ad campaign is really working. Your mother told me she ran out of patches for the Christmas Stocking. Everyone wants the plasma TV Zagby's donated. Whoever wins that stocking is going to need a truck to haul it off. That was one of the best ideas I ever heard of."

Amy glowed with Gus's praise. "Okay, I have to get back to work. I'm going to need some more greenery in about ten minutes."

"Okay, see you later." Amy's mind raced as she worked the wire through the wreath hoop and then threaded it back through the pine boughs. The Seniors all had arthritis and while they might try to help her, they would do more harm to themselves. Where could she find someone willing to cut their hands to shreds to help the Seniors?

Volunteers.

At four-thirty, just as it was starting to get dark, Amy had a brainstorm. She stopped what she was doing, not caring if two dozen people were waiting for her creations. She stepped out of the barn and made an announcement: "Leave your name in the store, and we'll deliver your blanket or wreath." There was a little grumbling, but for the most part, people were understanding. "I'll try to get them to you by Sunday afternoon. Mr. Moss and the Seniors appreciate your business and your patience."

Back in the barn, Amy whipped out her cell phone. An hour later she'd called every church in town asking the priests and ministers if they could send their youth groups to help after school next week. She promised to make donations to each church. All promised to get back to her later in the evening.

Amy looked at her work table. She was fresh out of greenery. Time to take a break. She wanted to wash her hands, which would probably be a mistake since the thick resin was coating the cuts. She didn't care. All she wanted right now was to soak her hands in soothing warm water and sip a hot drink through a straw. She was just closing the door when Gus pulled up in his pickup, the trailer full of greens.

"I'm going to pretend I didn't see you. I'm going

into the house to get some coffee and wash my hands. I think I might have a lead on some volunteers."

"I'll join you. I'll pretend I didn't get here." In the time it took his heart to beat twice, Gus scooped her up in his arms and carried her across the compound to the kitchen, where he sat her down on one of the kitchen chairs.

Tillie stopped what she was doing long enough to pour her daughter a cup of coffee.

"Put a slug of something in it, Mom."

That's when Tillie noticed her daughter's ravaged hands. She wanted to cry. She looked up at Gus, who could only shrug.

"I had no idea what a hard business this is," Tillie said softly. She quickly ran a dishcloth under warm water. She gently wrapped it around her daughter's hands.

Gus eyed both women. "This is only day one, ladies. We have thirty-three more days to go. It won't get any easier."

"I'm no quitter," Amy said vehemently.

"And neither am I," Tillie said with spirit.

"So what's the lead you have?" Gus asked.

"I called all the churches in the area and asked the priests and ministers if they would ask their youth groups to come out and help after school. They all promised to get back to me this evening. I just hope I can stay awake long enough to take the calls. If it works out, we can build up an inventory. If that doesn't work, I'm all for using that liquid cement to glue the boughs together. I'll make it work . . . so will both of you stop looking at me like that?"

"What's for dinner?" Gus asked as he slipped back into his jacket.

"Stew and fresh bread. Addy made it all this morning. Store-bought pie."

"Works for me." Gus grinned as he headed out the door.

"What's the deal here, Mom?"

"Everyone eats here, we're taking turns cooking. Breakfast, lunch and dinner. We close the gates at five-thirty. Everyone goes home to sleep in their own beds. Sam and I pick everyone up in the morning and we do it all over again. Are you coming home with me, Amy?"

"Of course. Why would you think otherwise?"

"Well . . . you didn't . . ."

"Mom, I was so tired yesterday I fell asleep on the couch. No one woke me up. Don't read into something that isn't there, okay?"

"Okay. Just thirty-three more days to go. We can do this, can't we, Amy?"

Amy closed her eyes. "We have to do it. Thanks for the coffee, Mom."

"Oh, Amy, I almost forgot. A reporter from the newspaper was here earlier to take pictures of the Christmas Stocking. They're going to run it in tomorrow's paper on the front page. Above the fold! Isn't that great?"

"Super, Mom! Just super!" Amy said wearily as she headed back to the barn.

Hours later, the workday finally ended, and Amy, a can of Bag Balm in hand, followed her mother to the car. She waved to Gus and Sam. "Burn rubber, Mom!"

"Gotcha, kiddo. Heigh-ho, heigh-ho, it's off to home we go, with only thirty-three more days to go! Heigh-ho, heigh-ho. I can't wait to go home."

Amy laughed hysterically. Tillie wondered if she

should slap her daughter. She decided she was too tired to do anything but drive. Then she, too, started to laugh. "This is where the rubber meets the road, Amy. A month ago if someone had told me this would be happening, I would have laughed in their face."

"Yeah, me too. You can't sing worth a damn, Mom."

"I know. Sad, isn't it?"

"Boo hoo." Amy giggled. "I meant it back there when I said I was no quitter."

"I know, Amy. I'm no quitter either. We'll do it." She looked over at her daughter, who was suddenly sound asleep. *How pretty she is,* Tillie thought. *How dedicated. How warm and caring my daughter is.* Then she cried for all the lost years.

Chapter Thirteen

Amy's alarm buzzed at six o'clock. A second later, the local radio station came to life with a rousing rendition of "Jingle Bells." Then the announcement for Moss Farms invaded her bedroom. She pulled the covers over her head, but she could still hear the cheerful voice announcing the latest gift to go in the Christmas Stocking, a gift certificate to the China Buffet for a free dinner for two every week for a full year.

Amy swung her legs over the side of the bed. She smiled in spite of herself. Her PR campaign had taken off like a rocket. Instead of the television and radio announcers doing a countdown of days left till Christmas, they started the top of each hour by announcing the latest contribution to the Christmas Stocking. Estimates were running high as to the value of the contents. Fifty thousand dollars' worth of merchandise and gift certificates seemed to be the magic number. Amy thought it was much higher, because shops and business professionals dropped by with gift certificates on a daily basis. Just yesterday a local plastic surgeon stopped on his way to the office to drop off a gift certificate for a free face-lift. She'd giggled over that all morning, as did all of the Senior ladies.

Then there was the mystery gift that the announcers played up every day. A gift valued at ten thousand dollars. The different stations had call-in periods during which people called in trying to guess what the mystery gift was and who had donated it. So far no one had come close to guessing the mystery gift was a seven-day Carnival Cruise for a family of four.

Just three more days, Amy thought as she lathered up under the shower. Three more days and she could sleep until the New Year. Then it was back to her own world in Philadelphia. Gus Moss would be returning to his life in California, and her mother and Sam would probably start "keeping company" once they wound down from this little adventure. And it *was* an adventure. Tillie was dressed and waiting by the front door with a cup of coffee and a Pop-tart. Amy wolfed it down and could have eaten another one. "Three more days, Mom!"

"Don't talk with your mouth full, Amy," Tillie said in a motherly tone.

Amy looked up at her mother. No one had ever said that to her before. Then again, maybe she never talked to anyone with her mouth full. "Let's go. Time is money, Mom. Pastor Mulvaney is sending out three college kids from his choir to help me this morning. I've got kids coming this afternoon too. We have a great inventory now for all the people who stop by at the last minute."

They quickly walked to the car and climbed in. Tillie settled herself behind the wheel and backed out of the driveway. "I'm going to miss you when you leave, Amy."

"I'll come home more often, Mom. You know what, I think Sam is going to be taking up a lot of your time once Christmas is over."

"I hope so. I really like him. We're comfortable together. You know, that old sock-and-shoe routine. He told me yesterday that he's making plans to take every single person who worked at the farm, their families and even the schoolkids who volunteered on a cruise at the end of January. Just four days. He said the cruise line gave him a great deal. You and Gus are invited, of course."

"Hmm," was all Amy could think to say.

"I know this is none of my business, Amy, but I'm going to ask you anyway. Are you and Gus . . . are you going to stay in touch?"

That was the question Amy had been asking herself for days. She tried for a blasé attitude. "Don't know, Mom. California is across the country. I'm thinking, 'out of sight, out of mind.'"

"Does that bother you?"

Amy was tempted to fib to her mother but couldn't. "Yes," she mumbled over the rim of her coffee cup. "Oh, look, it's starting to snow."

"Then do something about it," her mother snapped. Amy looked over at her mother, who looked grim and determined.

"Just like that! Do something! Takes two to tango, Mom."

Tillie took her eyes off the road for a moment. "Yes, just like that. Haven't you learned anything in the last two months? It's all about communication, giving off mixed signals, ignoring the obvious, being afraid to say what's on your mind and in your heart. Like Sam says, you snooze, you lose. I say, go for the gusto!"

"Is that what Sam says?" Amy drawled. "Gusto, eh?"

"Yes, that's what Sam says, and that's what I say. I can't believe I'm giving you relationship advice."

"Yeah, me too. You're pretty hip these days, Mom."

"I know. I want my cell phone back. I think I earned it."

"I got you one for Christmas. It's purple. It takes pictures and everything. You can even text message. Play your cards right and I might throw in an iPod."

Tillie turned on the right-turn signal and swerved into Moss Farms. She drove slowly over the old road and came to a stop at the top of the rise. "That's one kick-ass Christmas stocking, daughter! I like sitting here looking at it every morning. Did you ever call those people from *Money* magazine who called you?"

"Nope. I'm playing hard to get. C'mon, Mom, time to get to work. What's on the menu today?"

"Addy said she was making waffles for breakfast, corn chowder for lunch and pepper steak for dinner. With buttered noodles. Does that work for you?"

"It does," Amy said, hopping out of the car. She loved this time of the day, when she could sit next to Gus eating breakfast. They weren't too tired to talk about anything and everything, unlike at the close of the workday, when they were red-eye tired with only one thought—sleep.

"Morning, everyone," Amy said cheerfully.

Gus looked around to see who "everyone" was. She must be referring to Cyrus and him. "Good morning to you, too, Miss Baran."

"Three more days!" Amy said as she filled her

plate with waffles from the warming oven. Gus poured coffee for her, and Cyrus dogged her steps, no doubt hoping for a sliver of bacon. She obliged.

"It will be over before you know it," Gus said, trying to be as cheerful as Amy sounded. He knew he wasn't pulling it off. He was simply too damn tired to be cheerful at this hour of the morning.

"Are you and your dad going to put up a Christmas tree here in the house?"

"I don't think so. He didn't say anything about it. Are you and your mom putting up a tree?"

Amy eyed the man she secretly thought of as her destiny and laughed, a forced sound. "Not if I can help it. I don't want to see a pine tree of any kind until next year and maybe not even then. I think I turned into a grinch. It's snowing out. Looks like it might lead to some of the serious white stuff. You know, an accumulation." Such a scintillating conversation.

Gus groaned. "Do you know what snow means, Amy?"

"Yeah, I have to shovel Mom's driveway."

"No, it means all the procrastinators will be trooping out here to buy a tree in the snow. Snow means Christmas. People get the spirit the minute the snow starts to fall."

"I can help with that, Gus. We have a good amount of inventory in the barn. For the most part, I think my end is done. I can't imagine selling 200-some wreaths and 125 grave blankets over the next few days. Tell me what you want me to do and I'm all yours."

Gus jerked to attention. "Do you mean that?"

"Uh . . . well, yes. Just tell me what you want me

to do. I can bale the trees. I can saw off the bottom branches and I can drill the holes. I don't have the upper-body strength to lift the trees."

"Oh, I thought . . . what I mean is . . ."

Tillie's words rang in Amy's ears. *Then do something about it. Go for the gusto!* "You thought I meant I was all yours as in us, as in a team, as in a couple. . . . I did mean that. I meant the other part too. What are you going to do about it, Gus Moss?" she asked boldly. Surely that counted as going for the gusto.

Gus decided to take the high road. "What do you *want* me to do about it?"

Amy stood up and stomped her foot. "I want you to tell me whatever the hell you want to tell me. I'm too tired to play games. I like you. I am very attracted to you. You're a great kisser, and you said yourself you were a stand-up kind of guy. I see us as a couple. I can see myself married to you with a bunch of kids. Well?"

Cyrus barked so loud Amy thought her eardrums had ruptured.

Amy felt her eyes start to burn. So much for saying what was on her mind. She was going to strangle her mother as soon as she found her. She shrugged into her jacket. "Your silence tells me all I need to know. You can just kiss my . . . my . . ."

"Mouth? I'd be happy to oblige, but do you see that SUV out there with all those squealing kids? Jeez, they even brought the dog with them. I told you, it's a family thing the minute it starts to snow. I will kiss you later, and you said it all better than I ever could. Start thinking about moving out to the Golden State. Five kids, two dogs, a cat, a bird and some hamsters. You okay with that?" Gus called over his shoulder as he rushed out the door. "I'll design us a house around you, Amy Baran."

Amy stood rooted to the floor. "I think that was a proposal of sorts. Don't you, Cyrus? If so, I'll take it." She wrapped her muffler around her neck and marched outside to greet the family with the squealing kids and barking dog.

"We want four trees," Amy heard the father say. She watched as the mother rolled her eyes as she did her best to herd the six kids to the gift shop. "Don't forget the four wreaths and the four grave blankets." Amy laughed. She knew immediately who was the boss of this rambunctious family. She continued to laugh as the dog chased Cyrus, trying to get his reindeer ears.

The rest of the day was no better. By four o'clock three inches of snow covered the ground. The trees were coated with it, which only made them heavier. At five o'clock, when Gus closed the gate at the entrance, Amy thought she would collapse. She knew if she closed her eyes even for a second she'd be out for the rest of the night.

While she waited for the Seniors to come in for supper, Amy drank three cups of black coffee, one after the other. She was so wired from all the caffeine she'd consumed that she thought she was going to explode. The minute Gus walked in the door, she eyeballed him and said, "So when are we getting married?"

"How about tomorrow?"

"I'm too tired."

Gus laughed. "Did you just propose to me? I thought I was supposed to do the asking."

"You did. This morning. I'm just . . . I'm just confirming it. I'm a detail kind of gal. You should know that about me." Suddenly, Amy looked around and was stunned to see the room was full of Seniors, her mother and Gus's father.

"We're getting married," Gus said.

Everyone clapped. Even Amy.

"When?" the Seniors asked.

"New Year's Day," Gus said.

Amy yawned. "Works for me," she said before she slid to the floor and was out like a light.

"Looks like your daughter might be spending the night, Tillie. Guess I'll be driving you home after supper."

Tillie smiled. What was the point in telling Sam she'd driven to the farm this morning? There were all kinds of being tired. She smiled up at Sam. "I'd really appreciate that, Sam. I was going to put my tree up tonight as a surprise for Amy. Maybe if you aren't too tired, you could help me."

Gus sidled up to his father. "Go for it, Dad; that's the best offer you're ever going to get." He bent over to pick up Amy. Cyrus barked as he slung the sleeping girl over his shoulder. She felt like a rag doll. The Seniors clapped again. Gus felt like a caveman as he made his way through the gauntlet of helpers to the living room.

Gus covered the sleeping girl and built up the fire. He was staring into the flames, his thoughts a million miles away, when one of the Seniors brought two plates of food, one for him and one for Cyrus.

Harvey Jenkins poked his head into the living room. "We're going to put a tree up for Sam if you don't mind, Gus. Is there anything special you want in the way of ornaments, or should we use some from the gift shop?"

"I have no idea where Mom kept the ornaments, Harvey. Just put some lights on the tree and use the ornaments from the shop. I appreciate it. You've all done so much already. This is above and beyond what any of us expected."

"Can't have Christmas without a tree in your living room. We want to do it. We'll have it up in no time and be out of your way. You can sit here and enjoy it. It's snowing pretty heavy out there right now. Most of us are staying the night, because if it snows all night we won't be able to get back here. Sam said it was okay. We'll be upstairs if you need us. Later on, that is," the old man said gruffly.

"Okay," Gus said as he leaned back in his father's favorite chair. He was asleep the moment his eyes closed. He didn't open his eyes again until six o'clock the next morning. He could smell bacon and coffee, but it was the sight of the beautiful tree in the corner of the living room that made him suck in his breath. This was the tree he'd never had as a kid. All lit up with shiny ornaments and a ton of gaily wrapped packages nestled under it. He had to blink his eyes several times to ward off the tears. How beautiful, how awesome, how generous of the Seniors. He knew he would remember this moment for the rest of his life.

He turned around to see the Seniors watching him like a cluster of precocious squirrels, big smiles on their faces. "Does it look like the kind your momma used to put up?" Addy asked.

Gus had no trouble with the lie he was about to tell. "Exactly," he said, going over to hug each one of them. He loved how they fussed over him, patting him on the arm, on the back, then hugging him.

"Wake up Amy. I hope she likes it," Harvey said.

"Hey, sleepy head, wake up," Gus said, poking Amy on the arm.

Amy bolted upright. She looked around in a daze. "Did I sleep for three whole days? Is it Christmas? It's gorgeous. It takes my breath away. Oh, Gus, it's just beautiful."

"The Seniors did it while we both slept. Thank them, not me. I couldn't have done that even on my best day. But to answer your question, you did not sleep for three days, and it is not Christmas."

"Oh, well, we'll manage somehow," Amy said as she ran over to the Seniors, who hugged and kissed her. "It's like having a bunch of mothers, fathers and grandparents all rolled into one." She winked at Gus. "I don't think it gets any better than this."

Time lost all meaning as Gus, his crew, Amy and the Seniors got their second wind as the countdown to the noon hour on Christmas Eve began. Sam's Victrola continued to play Christmas carols over the jury-rigged sound system as all the Christmas tree procrastinators showed up to buy their trees at the last minute while the kids romped in the snow and chased Cyrus all over the compound.

Christmas Eve morning, Sam and Tillie arrived with what Gus called sappy expressions on their faces. All Amy could do was giggle. She'd never seen her mother so happy. Gus said the same thing about his father. All morning, as they worked side by side, they kept poking each other and pointing to their parents.

"I don't know why I say this, but I think the two of them are up to something," Gus said as he picked up a twelve-foot tree to shove into the barrel. Amy pulled it out from the other side and tied the bailing plastic in a knot. Two of Gus's crew plopped it on top of an SUV, its engine still running. They both waved as the car drove out of the compound, the kids inside bellowing "Jingle Bells" at the top of their lungs.

"One more hour and it's all over. Then all we have to do is deal with the media and the drawing, and the rest of the day is ours. Did I mention lunch? Addy said Dad's freezers are about empty, so lunch and dinner will be a surprise."

"I wonder who's going to win the contents of the stocking," Amy said. "I hope it's someone who can use a face-lift."

"The snowblower is what everyone is talking about. Whoever wins is going to need an eighteen-wheeler to cart it all away." He grew serious when he turned to Amy. "This was . . . an experience I wouldn't trade for anything in the world. If you hadn't showed up that night in your purple hat and scarf, I don't know which direction I would have gone in. I feel so damn good right now. All thanks to you, Amy Baran." Amy blushed as she squeezed Gus's arm.

"I wouldn't trade it either, but you did all the hard work. All my wreaths and blankets sold. We have two trees left. I think that says it all. Look, here comes the media, and it's starting to snow again. I guess we better get ready."

"What does that mean, get ready?"

"That means we comb our hair and get ready to smile. I'll do that while you close the gates. Business is officially over."

Gus loped off. As he struggled through the snow with the huge, slatted, iron gate, he looked up at the sign he'd repainted when he first arrived. He blinked, then rubbed the snow from his eyelashes. It was a different sign. This one said, MOSS & SON CHRISTMAS TREE FARM. A lump the size of a lemon settled in his throat.

The snow was too deep; the damn gate wasn't going to close. Suddenly, it started to move. "Need some help, son?"

Maybe he should have answered, but he couldn't get his tongue to work. Suddenly, he was eight years old, running to his dad because he couldn't close the gate by himself. His father's words were crystal clear in his memory. "You need some help, son?"

Gus threw himself at his father, and together they toppled into a snowdrift. "Yeah, Dad, I need some help."

"Then let's put our shoulders to the wheel and close this gate. The media people will have to open and close it on the way out. We're done here."

How easy it all was when you worked together. Gus wished he could think of something profound to say but he couldn't come up with the words. Then again, maybe actions and not words were all that was necessary.

His father's arm around his shoulder, Gus walked with his father back to the compound.

The Victrola was still playing, the Seniors were

bundled up in their winter gear, and Amy and her mother were standing between the giant Christmas Stocking and the mile-long scroll that Amy was starting to unroll. Cameramen snapped and snapped their pictures, close-ups of the awesome scroll and the giant stocking. Amy pointed to the glittering letter on the stocking. An obliging cameraman focused his camera and took his shot.

MERRY CHRISTMAS TO ONE AND ALL!

In smaller letters, each Senior's, each worker's, each volunteer's name was listed. At the bottom, it said, THANKS FOR YOUR SUPPORT. The names Sam, Tillie, Amy and Gus ran across the toe of the stocking.

"I think this is the most exciting moment of my life," Tillie whispered to Sam.

"I *know* it's the second most exciting moment of my life," Sam whispered back. "The first was the day Gus was born."

Gus smiled. If he had been a bird, he would have ruffled his feathers and taken wing. Since he was a mere mortal, he punched his father lightly on the arm as he moved forward to stand by Amy, who was getting ready to pick the winner from the bulging stocking.

A microphone was shoved in Amy's face as she stood on top of a ladder and dug deep into the stocking for one of the entries. "And the winners are . . . Janet and Ed Olivetti!"

The Seniors buzzed. Gus caught phrases as they chirped and chittered among themselves. *They sure*

*can use it. . . . Ed was laid off the whole summer. . . .
Two kids in college . . . two more getting ready to go . . .
and the littlest one with major health problems . . .*

After the media packed up and left, Gus turned to
Amy and said, "Now."

"Okay." Amy turned to the assembled Seniors and
proclaimed, "Listen up, people. There was an unan-
nounced gift not listed on the Christmas Stocking
scroll. Let me tell you about it."

She took a piece of paper out of her pocket and
read, "In honor of all the effort put in by the Senior
Citizens, a prizewinning architectural firm has donated its services to supervise the building of an additional wing."

Before anyone could react, Gus turned to his father and said, "Please, Dad, can we turn off your Victrola?"

"I can do better than that." Within minutes, Sam
had the old contraption and the scratchy records in
his hands. With a wild flourish, he dumped the machine and the records in the trash. "As a very wise
person said to me just recently, it's time to move on. I
could use a little Bing Crosby or Nat King Cole.
Now, let's have some lunch."

Gus reached up to help Amy down from the ladder.

"Merry Christmas, Amy."

"Merry Christmas, Gus."

"Do you realize in seven days I'll be calling you
Mrs. Moss?"

"Yep," Amy said linking her arm with her soon-to-
be-husband's. "Until then, you won't mind if I sleep
the days away."

"Not as long as I'm sleeping alongside you."

Gus opened the door to the kitchen. Everyone shouted, "Merry Christmas!"

"To one and all!" Amy and Gus called out in return.

Epilogue

Amy Baran slipped into her mother's wedding gown, which fit her to perfection. "I didn't know you saved your gown. You never said . . ."

"I never said a lot of things, Amy. I was happy the day I wore that gown. What came after . . . well, it no longer matters. A wedding gown is something you save for your daughter. You look beautiful. Do you have something old, something new, something borrowed, and something blue?"

"I do. The Seniors were more than helpful. Mom, I am so happy. I wish there was a way for me to thank you for asking me to come home. I did what you said, I went for the gusto. I hope Gus doesn't think I'm pushy."

"He doesn't think any such thing. He loves you. Sam told me he talks about you in his sleep. He's a fine young man, Amy. Sam . . . Sam can be stubborn, but he finally came around. We've had such long talks. He's become a good friend. A really good friend."

"Is that your way of asking me if I approve?"

"I guess. This room we're standing in was Sara and Sam's room. I feel like she's still here. Sometimes I have these . . . doubts. My situation was different from Sam's. He dearly loved his wife. I'm not . . ."

"Mom, Sam knows his own heart. He's moved on. He found you. You don't have to live here in this house if you don't want to. You have your own house but you need to ask yourself if Sam feels the same way about our house. Dad's room is the same. You didn't change a thing. Sam cleared all of Sara's things out of here. Hey, you could move down the hall to another room."

"I guess. It's time to go downstairs. Where's your veil? Amy, do you think I'll make a good grandmother?"

"The best. Mom, I know about Dad. I want to thank you for never telling me. I think if you had, I would have run amuck. Now, we're never going to talk about that again."

Tillie nodded. "Did something happen to the veil?"

"I'm not wearing it. I'm wearing this"—Amy said, plopping her purple hat on top of her curly head—"and this scarf," she said twirling the purple scarf around her neck. "Whatcha think, Mom?"

Tillie laughed so hard she cried. "I think you're going to give those California gals a run for their money. I hear the music. Sam's waiting outside the door to walk you down the steps and give you away to his son."

"Then let's do it."

She saw him standing next to the minister. She paused, waiting for him to see her. He turned, his eyes popping wide as both his fists shot in the air. Amy started to laugh as all the Seniors clapped their hands. She sashayed forward, twirling the end of the purple scarf this way and that. Gus howled with happiness as wedding protocol flew out the window.

This, he decided, just like the last two months, was a memory he'd keep with him for the rest of his days.

Ten minutes later, the minister said, "I now pronounce you man and wife. You may kiss the bride."

The Seniors clapped and hollered, whistled and stomped their feet.

"I promise to love you forever," Gus whispered in Amy's ear.

"And I promise to love you even more."

Comfort and Joy

Chapter One

Angel Mary Clare Bradford, Angie to her friends, looked over at her assistant, who was stacking rolls of colored ribbon onto spindles. Satisfied that the rolls of ribbon were aligned to match the spindles of wrapping paper, she turned away to survey her domain.

The thirty-foot-by-thirty-foot room with its own lavatory was neat as a pin because Angie Bradford was a tidy person. The room she and her assistant, Bess Kelly, were standing in was known as the Eagle Department Store gift wrap department.

Eva Bradford, Angie's mother, had a lifetime lease on this very room, thanks to retired owner Angus Eagle, something that rankled the current young department store head, Josh Eagle, Angus's heir.

Angie and Josh had gone to the mat via the legal system on several occasions. Josh wanted the lease canceled so he could open a safari clothing department. He claimed the paltry, three-hundred-dollar-a-month rent Angie paid for the gift wrap space was depriving the Eagle Department Store of serious revenue. Another set of legal papers claimed his father had not been of sound mind when he signed the ridiculous lifetime lease.

Angie countered with a startling video of Angus playing tennis and being interviewed by the *New York Times* talking about politics and his philanthropic endeavors on the very day he signed the lifetime lease. In a separate filing, Angie charged Josh Eagle was a bully, and presented sworn testimony that he repeatedly turned off the electricity in the gift shop as well as the water in the lavatory just to harass her. On occasion the heat and air conditioning were also turned off. Usually on the coldest and hottest days of the year.

Josh retaliated by saying Angie should pay for the electricity, water, heat and air conditioning. He said there were no free lunches in the Eagle Department Store in Woodbridge, New Jersey.

Judge Atkins had glared at the two adversaries and barked his decision: Josh Eagle was not to step within 150 feet of the gift wrap department. Angie was to pay an additional thirty-dollars-a-month rent for the utilities, and a new heating unit was to be installed at Eagle's expense.

At that point the Eagle-Bradford war escalated to an all-time high, with both sides doing double-time to outwit the other. The present score was zip-zip.

"So, are you going to the store meeting or not?" Bess asked as she gathered up her purse and jacket.

"Nope. I don't work for Josh Eagle or this store. I work for my mother. I'm just renting space from

Eagle's. It was toasty in here today, wasn't it?" Angie asked. It had been unseasonably cool for September.

Bess eyed her young employer and laughed. She'd worked for Eva Bradford for twelve years before Eva turned the business over to her daughter, 110 pounds of energy who was full of spit and vinegar, five years ago. Angie had jumped right into the business, played David to Josh's Goliath, and come out a winner. At least in Bess's eyes. With the Christmas season fast approaching, Bess knew in her gut that Josh Eagle would pull out all his big guns to try to get under Angie's skin and make her life so miserable she would give up and move out. She laughed silently. Josh Eagle didn't know the Angie Bradford she knew.

"Come on, boss, I'll walk you out to the parking lot. How's Eva today?"

Angie slipped into her jacket and hung her purse on her shoulder before she turned off the lights. She pressed a switch, and a colorful corrugated blind came down, totally covering the entrance to the gift wrap department. She waited a moment until she heard the sound of the lock slipping into place. She'd installed the sliding panel at her own expense, much to Josh Eagle's chagrin. She then locked the walk-through door to the gift wrap department. Not just any old lock, this was a special lock that Josh Eagle couldn't open with the store's master keys. She'd also installed her own security system with the ADT firm. Josh had taken her to court on that one, too, and lost, with the judge saying Angie was protecting her investment and as long as she wasn't asking him to pay for her security, there was no problem. Back then the score had been one-zip.

"Uh-oh, look who's standing by that big red X you painted on the floor!"

Angie looked ahead of her to see Josh Eagle glaring at her. "You're late!"

He was good-looking, she had to give him that. And he had dimples. Right now his dark brown eyes were spewing sparks. He was dressed in a power suit and tie, his shirt so blinding white, it had to be new. It was all about image with Josh Eagle.

Angie looked down at her watch. "Actually, I'm leaving right on time, Mr. Eagle. My lights are off, the heat has been turned down, the security system locked and loaded and my door is locked. It's one minute past six. The store closes at six."

"I called a meeting for six-fifteen for all department heads. That means you're supposed to be in the conference room promptly at six-ten. You're still standing here, Ms. Bradford. What's wrong with this picture? Well?"

Angie sighed. "How many times do I have to tell you, Mr. Eagle? I do not work for you. Judge Atkins sent you papers to that effect. I have copies in case you lost yours. What part of I-am-not-one-of-your-employees don't you understand?"

Josh Eagle looked like he was about to say something, then changed his mind. Angie started walking again, and when she got to Josh and he didn't move, she stiff-armed him.

"You touched my person," Josh said dramatically as he pretended to back away.

"Will you get off it already! Do you sit up there in your ivory tower and dream up ways to torment me? I did not touch you. I put my arm out so *you* wouldn't touch *me*. In case your vision is impaired, I have a witness. Now, I suggest you get out of my way and don't come down here again with your silly demands. This shop is off-limits to you!"

"Just a damn minute, Ms. Bradford. If you want to go to court again, I'm your man. I want to know what you're going to do about wrapping my customers' Christmas gifts this year. That's the main topic to be discussed at tonight's meeting."

"We've had this same discussion every September for the past five years. You had the same discussion with my mother for the five years prior to my arrival, and the outcome has always been the same. This year is no different. Pay me to wrap your customers' gifts, and we're in business. If you don't pay me, I cannot help you. I'm in business to make money just the way you are. Try to wrap your feeble brain around that fact, then get back to me or have your lawyer call my lawyer. Good night, Mr. Eagle."

Outside in the cool evening air, Angie dusted her hands together. "I thought that went rather well." She sniffed the air. "Someone's burning leaves. Oh, I just love that smell."

Bess opened her car door. "I think you enjoy tormenting that man. I agree he's sorely lacking in the charm department, but my mother always told me you can get more flies with honey than vinegar. The guy's a *hottie,* that's for sure."

"Ha! Eye candy. The man has no substance, he's all veneer. On top of that, he's greedy and obnoxious. With all that going against him, I wonder how he manages to charm that string of women he parades around all the time," Angie sniffed.

"His money charms them. Josh Eagle is considered a good catch. You know, Angie, you could throw your line in the pond. You reel him in, and all this," Bess said, extending her arms to indicate the huge parking lot and the department store, "could be yours!"

Angie started to laugh and couldn't stop. "Not in this lifetime. See you tomorrow, Bess."

"Tell your mother I said hello."

"Will do," Angie called over her shoulder.

Angie sat in her car for ten minutes while she played the scene that had just transpired back in the store over and over in her mind. Would Josh Eagle drag her into court again? Probably. The man had a hate on for her that was so over-the-top she could no longer comprehend it. In the beginning she'd handled it the way she handled every challenge that came her way: fairly and honestly. She fought to win, and so far she'd won every round. Remembering the look on Josh Eagle's face, she wondered if her luck was about to change.

Well, she would think about it later. Right now she had to stop for pizza and go to the rehab center on New Durham Road, where her mother was waiting for her.

Angie reached for her cell phone to call Tony's Pizza on Oak Tree Road. She ordered three large pepperoni pies and was told they would be ready in ten minutes. That was good, the pies would still be hot when she delivered them to Eva and the other patients at the rehab center.

On the ride to the pizza parlor Angie thought about her mother. A gutsy lady who had worked part time to help with the family bills. Back when she was young, with a family to help support, she'd worked three days a week for Angus Eagle, a man her own age whose wife deplored housework. Her mother had cooked and cleaned for Angus, and in doing so they had forged a friendship that eventually resulted, one Christmas morning, in his turning over the gift wrap department at his store to her with a lifetime lease.

Her mother never tired of telling her the story of that particular Christmas that changed her life, even though Angie, who was fifteen at the time, remembered it very well. Angus's wife hadn't wanted to be bothered wrapping presents for Josh and her husband, so she'd turned the job over to Eva. Each time her mother told the story, she would laugh and laugh and say how impressed Angus had been at her flair for gift wrapping.

It was always at times like this, when Angie grew melancholy, that she thought about her own life and why she was doing what she was doing with it. She'd gone to work on Wall Street as a financial planner, but five years of early mornings, late nights and the long commute was all she could take. Then she taught school for a couple of years but couldn't decide whether or not teaching was a career to which she wanted to commit herself. Five years ago, she'd happily given it up without a second thought when, after her aunt Peggy got into a serious automobile accident in Florida, her mother suggested that Angie take over the gift-wrapping business. Eva had rushed down to care for Peggy, knowing she was leaving her little business in good hands, and was gone four years.

After her aunt's passing, Eva had remained to take care of her sister's estate, returning to New Jersey only a year ago.

It was nice having her mother home again, in the big old house on Rose Street.

Angie giggled when she thought about all the young guys, the sons of friends her mother had invited to dinner on Sunday in the hopes one of them would be suitable for Angie. So far, she'd made a lot of new male friends, but none of them was what she considered blow-my-socks-off material.

As always, when she got to this point in her reverie, Angie's thoughts turned to her beloved father and his passing. It had been so sudden, so shocking, so mind-bending, it had taken her years to come to terms with her loss. How she missed the big, jolly man who had carried her on his shoulders when she was little, the same man who taught her to ride her first bike, then to drive her clunker of a car. He'd hooted and hollered at her high school graduation, beamed with pride at her college graduation and could hardly wait to show her the brand-new car he'd bought her. It was all wrapped up in a red satin ribbon. Oh, how she'd cried when she'd seen that little silver Volkswagen Jetta convertible. These days she drove a bright red Honda Civic, but the Jetta was still up on blocks in the garage on Rose Street. She planned to keep it forever and ever.

Angie dabbed at her eyes. It was all so long ago.

Twenty miles away, Eva Bradford sat in the sunroom of the Durham Rehab Center, waiting for her daughter. The television was on, but she wasn't listening to the evening news. Nor was she paying attention to the other patients, who were talking in polite, low tones so others could hear the news. Her thoughts were somewhere else, and she wasn't happy with where they were taking her.

Eva looked up when the evening nurse approached her with a fresh bag of frozen peas to place on her knee. She was young like Angie with a ready smile. "You know the drill, Eva, thirty minutes on and thirty minutes off." The nurse, whose name was Betsy, reached for the thawed-out bag of peas Eva handed her.

Eva wondered if she'd ever dance again. Not that she danced a lot, but still, if the occasion warranted it, she wanted to be able to get up and trip the light fantastic. Knee replacements at her age were so common it was mind-boggling. She looked around the sunroom and counted nine patients with knee replacements, one a double knee, four hip jobs and two back surgeries. Of all of them, she thought she was progressing the best. Another few days and she was certain she would be discharged with home health aides to help her out a few hours every day. She could hardly wait to return to the house on Rose Street in Metuchen.

Eva turned away from the cluster of patients who looked to be in a heated discussion over something that was going on in the Middle East. She did her best to slide down into the chair she was sitting on so she wouldn't have to look at Angus Eagle who, according to Betsy, had just been transferred from the hospital to receive therapy for a hip replacement he'd had a month ago. She knew the jig would be up when Angie arrived with their nightly pizza. At this moment she simply didn't want to go down Memory Lane with Angus or be put in a position where she had to defend her daughter's business dealings.

She hadn't seen Angus for a long time. At least five years—she really couldn't remember. She tried to come up with the exact year. In the end she thought it was five years ago, the same year her older sister, Peggy, a childless widow, had been in that bad car accident. She'd gone to Florida and stayed on for four years because her sister's health had deteriorated, and with no children to help out, it was up to her to see to her sister's comfort. Then, she'd stayed to handle all the legal matters, and sell the house, the furnishings and the car. She'd been home for a year now. She swiped at the tears that threatened to overflow.

Would Angie take care of her the way she'd taken care of Peggy? Of course she would. Angie had a heart of gold and loved her. She couldn't help but wonder who was going to take care of Angus Eagle. Not that hard-as-nails son whose mission in life was to make Angie give up the gift wrap department. Well, Angus could certainly afford in-home health care around the clock.

Eva looked up to see her daughter standing in the doorway holding three large pizza boxes, one for the two of them and two for the other patients. Angie was so kind. She watched as Angie handed two of the pizza boxes to Betsy and moved across the room to join her mother. Angie hugged and kissed her.

"How'd it go today, Mom?"

"Not too bad. I think I'll be out of here in a few days. Honey, Angus Eagle arrived today for additional therapy. He had a hip replacement a month ago, according to Betsy. He's sitting over there between Cyrus and Harriet. Don't look now."

"And this means . . . what?" Angie asked as she sprinkled hot peppers on the pizza, then handed her mother a huge slice. She chomped down on her own as she casually looked around. She had no trouble locating the elegant-looking Angus Eagle. At seventy years of age, he still looked dashing, with his snow-white hair, trim body and tanned complexion. It had been a few years since she'd seen him in the court-room alongside his son. How angry he'd looked that day. Today he looked like he was in pain. A lot of pain.

"Well . . . I don't know. I'm sure he hates us both. He's probably regretting giving me that lifetime lease. You know that old saying, blood is thicker than water. Josh is his son, so it's natural for him to side . . . whatever," Eva dithered as she bit down into her slice of pizza.

"Business is business, Mom. Isn't that what you always told me? Sometimes people make deals that go sour. As long as it's done legally, the way your deal was done legally, you live with it and go on. Josh and I had a rather heated exchange as I was leaving the store this evening. By the way, it's cold out in case you're interested. I think today was the first day that shop felt warm."

"What happened? Wait, look—is *he* eating *your* pizza?"

"Oh, yeah, and he looks like he's enjoying it. What happened? Well, Josh thought he could dictate to me. He called a meeting for six-fifteen for all department heads. I'm sure you remember he does that every September. He wants me to gift wrap his customers' packages. For *free*. I told him if he paid me, I would. It was a standoff. I have an idea. Want to hear it?"

Eva smiled at the excitement in her daughter's voice. She leaned forward to hear what she just knew was going to be a smashing idea. "What's he doing now?"

"Watching us. I am going to decorate the shop like a fairy land. Gossamer, angels, Santas, sleighs, Santa sacks. I'm going to gift wrap Santa sacks for the kids. I already ordered the red and green burlap. Colored raffia ties for around the sacks. I'm going to suspend some reindeer from the ceiling with wires. Bess said her husband will make us a wooden sled and paint it. The best part is the room is big enough to do all this. We'll get some publicity with the local paper. Parents will bring their kids to see it and, hopefully, shop. Extra business for Eagle's, but Josh won't see it that way, would be my guess. This is the part you might have a problem with, Mom, but hear me out, okay? I'm going to, for a price, agree to wrap purchases from other stores. On a drop-off, pick-up-later basis. I'll hire a few extra people, and we'll do it after hours, when the store is closed. Josh won't have a comeback because I pay my own utilities."

"Can you do that, Angie?"

"My lawyer said I could, so that's good enough for me. Josh will fight me, but that's publicity for me. I'm looking at it as win-win. You look worried, Mom. Are you seeing something I'm not seeing?"

"Well . . . You know me, I'm just a born worrier. If your lawyer says it's okay, then I guess it's okay."

Angie frowned. What was wrong with her mother? Normally, she'd be up for anything to make the shop prosper. She risked a glance in the direction of Angus Eagle. Caught staring, she offered up a wide smile. To her delight, Angus winked at her. *Now* that's *something I'll have to think about later.*

"How's that new company doing with your special order?" Eva asked.

"Mom, you won't believe it, but they came through

royally, and the price is unbelievable. One-of-a-kind baubles, artificial greenery that looks better than the real stuff, and it's been sprayed, so it even has a balsam scent. I ordered tons of stuff. Their ribbon is satin. Real satin, all widths. Our Christmas packages are going to be over the moon. And it's just a little cottage industry in a small town called Hastings, in Pennsylvania. They're going to start shipping the merchandise to the house next week."

Mother and daughter spent the next hour discussing a real tree versus artificial, paper wrap versus foil wrap and other unusual ways to wrap gifts.

A bell sounded in the hallway. Betsy appeared to take away the frozen peas. She chatted for a moment, asked Eva if she wanted to return to her room or stay to watch television. "Five minutes, ladies."

"I guess I better get going, Mom. I'll be back in the morning with the order from Dunkin' Donuts. Two dozen donuts, right? Same number on the coffees?"

Eva smiled. "Plus one more for Angus."

Angie picked up her jacket and purse before she hugged and kissed her mother good night. She was almost to the door when she saw Josh Eagle standing in the doorway staring at her. She was about to move past him when a devil perched itself on her shoulder. "Spying on me, Mr. Eagle? Or are you *stalking* me? Shame on you!" She said it loud enough so everyone in the room could hear.

"Don't flatter yourself, Ms. Bradford. I'm here to see my father."

Angie whirled around and pointed to the clock. "Well, that figures! You have three minutes to visit. Oh, is that a gift for your father? A Hershey's bar!

How kind of you. Money-hungry jerk," she hissed, before she sailed through the doorway and down the hall.

"Witch!" Josh hissed back, but loud enough to be heard by the patients. "Hey, wait a minute, you forgot your broom!"

Angie stopped in her tracks and turned around. "What did you just call me, you pompous, money-hungry, no-good pissant?" Venom dripped from Angie's lips as sparks flew from her eyes.

Josh Eagle immediately regretted his words, but he couldn't back down now. "I called you a witch and said you forgot your broom. You called me a money-hungry jerk. So now I'm a pissant. Well, it takes a pissant to know a pissant."

The captive audience gasped as they watched the scene unfold in front of them. Even Betsy, mouth hanging open, could only stare at the two hissing enemies.

"I called you that because I was too polite to call you what you really are. Now, if you don't get out of my way, you are going to be minus a very important part of your anatomy." To her chagrin, Angie realized her voice had risen several decibels. Stricken, she looked around at the patients staring at her. All she could think of to do was wave.

As one, the rapt audience gasped. They returned her wave, even Angus.

The final bell for visitation rang.

"Looks like you have to leave now, Mr. Eagle. You better stay 150 feet away from me, or I'll have you arrested," Angie said coldly.

"Oh, yeah?" Josh blustered.

"Yeah!" Angie shot back. She flipped him the bird

before turning on her heel and marching down the hall.

The audience gasped again.

"I'm afraid you have to leave now, Mr. Eagle," Betsy said. "Try to come a little earlier tomorrow. You better wait a minute—Miss Bradford did say 150 feet. She looked to me like she meant business. It won't look good for the center if she calls the police." Betsy eyeballed the distance down the hall. "Okay, you can go now." She reached out to take the Hershey's bar, but Josh shoved it into his pocket.

Eva did her best not to laugh out loud. She turned around when she heard something that sounded like hysterical laughter. Angus Eagle was laughing so hard one of the aides was clapping him on the back. She was stunned to hear him shout, "You got yourself a spitfire there, Eva!" She wished he would have said something she didn't already know.

The score for this round, if anyone was counting, was one-zip, with the point going to Angie.

Chapter Two

Josh Eagle, his shoulders slumping, entered the house through the kitchen. Delectable aromas wafted about the kitchen, thanks to Dolores, the day lady who had been with his family for the past twenty years. He knew his dinner was warming in the oven, but for some reason he wasn't hungry. The fact of the matter was he was too damn mad to eat.

As he yanked at his tie with one hand, he opened the oven door with the other and set his dinner plate on the kitchen counter. Maybe he'd eat later. First he needed a beer, and he needed to calm down. He carried a beer from the fridge and swigged at it as he made his way to the second floor. He stripped down. Within minutes he was in sweats and slippers. It took him a minute to realize he was cold. He marched out to the hall to turn the thermostat to eighty before he made his way downstairs to grab another beer.

Heat gushed from the two vents in the kitchen. At

least he would be warm while he drowned himself in ice-cold beer.

Josh sat down at the kitchen table and propped his feet on a chair as he swigged from the bottle in his hand. Who in the damn hell did that female think she was? He answered himself by saying she was the female who had him over a barrel. He stretched out a long arm to snag a chicken leg off his dinner plate and was just about to bite down into the succulent-looking piece of chicken when the phone rang.

Josh eyed the phone suspiciously. He didn't know how he knew, but he knew it was his father on the other end of the line. He might as well get it over with. He was a small boy again when he picked up, knowing full well his father was going to have something very profound to say. Something he wasn't going to like.

Josh looked at the caller ID. He squared his shoulders, clicked the ON button and said, "Hi, Dad."

"Good evening, son. I'm sorry we didn't get a chance to talk this evening. I was looking forward to a long chat."

"I'm sorry, Dad. I had a meeting. I'll come earlier tomorrow. Do you need anything?"

"No, I don't need anything, Josh. Is there anything you want to talk to me about?"

Well, hell, yes, there were at least two dozen things he wanted to talk to his father about, but the old man only pretended to listen to anything he had to say. Josh threw caution to the winds and said, "Since when do you ever listen to anything I have to say? So, the short answer is, no. Is there something you want, Dad? Like maybe my hide, a pint of blood?

Name it, and it's yours." His voice was so bitter that Josh could hardly believe it was his own. He heard his father sigh. He always sighed when Josh let loose with his feelings.

"You were pretty hard on that little gal, weren't you?"

"If you say so, Dad. Is there anything else? If not, I'm going to turn in early."

"Okay, I'll see you tomorrow, son."

"Actually, no, I won't be stopping by. If you need something I can have someone from the store drop it off. But now that you've brought it up, there is something I've been meaning to say. I guess this is as good a time as any to tell you that I'll be leaving the first of the year. I'm moving to London. I got a job at Harrods. I leave New Year's Day. You can have Eagle's back. I guess I'm not really giving it back to you since you never really relinquished your interest in the store to me the way you agreed to. The way I figure it is this: You'll probably have a week in January before you have to close Eagle's doors for good. Good night, Dad."

Josh tossed his beer bottles into a wire basket in the laundry room. As he made his way up the stairs he could hear the phone ringing. He knew it was his father calling back because he was in shock over his son's cold announcement. "It's been a long time in coming, Dad," Josh muttered as he settled himself in his small home office. He clicked on the computer and ran some stats. Nothing had changed since earlier in the day. Eagle's was still at the bottom of the list. Just a few months until Eagle's would have to close their doors. Well, come the first of the year, Eagle's Department Store would no longer be his problem. He was sick and tired of battling his father, sick and tired of batting his head against a stone wall. Eventually he would get over the shame of failing. He had a job waiting for him at the prestigious Harrods in London, where his expertise would be appreciated.

The phone at the end of the long second-floor hallway continued to ring. "Give it up, Dad, I have nothing more to say."

Josh climbed into bed and pulled up the covers. Then he climbed back out of bed to turn the thermostat down to sixty degrees. Back in bed, his last conscious thought before drifting off to sleep was that he had to apologize in the morning to the witch with the broom.

Eva knew that Angus was coming up behind her. She could hear his walker on the tile floor. Then again, they were the only two patients in the sunroom, so who else could it be? She steeled herself for Angus's sharp tongue and whatever he was about to say. She clicked the OFF button on the remote control. What was left of the evening news report disappeared.

"Do you mind if I sit down, Eva?"

"Not at all. It's nice to see you again, Angus. It's been a long time, five years if I'm not mistaken. How strange that we should meet up like this after so long."

Because she was a nurturer by nature, Eva wanted to get up to help Angus ease himself into the chair across from her, but these days it was a production to get herself up and moving. "Are you in pain, Angus?"

"A bit. How about you?"

"At times. I try to ignore the pain and just use the frozen bags of peas. They really do help. Other than the hip replacement, how are things?"

"Are you asking to be polite or do you really want to know?" Angus asked.

Eva thought she'd never heard a sadder voice. "Is there anything I can do, Angus?"

"Not unless you have a magic potion that will turn my son into a charming young prince. What was that all about earlier?"

Eva decided not to pretend she didn't know what her old friend was talking about. "Rivalry would be my guess. Two strong, bull-headed people pushing each other's buttons. How is the store doing, Angus?"

"According to my son, not well at all. He blames me. Says I'm an old fuddy-duddy. He says I have no foresight. He claims I'm locked in the past. He said the last time I had an idea was the day, almost twenty years ago, when I gave you the lifetime lease on the gift wrap department, and from that day on, it was all downhill. He doesn't like me much, Eva. Yesterday he called me a meddler."

Eva threw her hands in the air. "What did you do? Or should I be asking what *didn't* you do? Josh was always such a wonderful young man. How did it all go wrong? I don't understand any of this, Angus."

Angus leaned forward. "Look at me, Eva. I have something to tell you that is going to affect you as well as your daughter. My son just told me a few minutes ago when I called him that he's leaving the store the first of the year. He's accepted a job at Harrods in London. That means the store will be closing.

He's been telling me that for the past year but I . . . I just blamed him for not knowing what he was doing. I was . . . I was cruel about it, saying things like I made a mistake when I turned things over to him, that he wasn't up to the job."

"Oh, Angus, how could you do something like that?" How was she going to tell her daughter they would both be out of a job after the holidays with only her Social Security coming in?

"Because I'm a horse's patoot, that's how. Josh has been telling me for years that we had to stream-line the store, we had to keep up with marketing trends. He wanted to hire new buyers, be more main-stream. I fought him every step of the way. He wanted to restructure everything. That meant layoffs. I didn't want to deal with it. One time he actually called me a dried-up old fart and told me I deserved whatever happened with the store. He was right and I was wrong. And I'm not going to lie to you, Eva, but the gift-wrapping shop was always a thorn in Josh's side. He thought, and I'm sure he still thinks, that you and I had an affair that is ongoing. I think that's an-other reason he keeps going to the mat with your daughter."

Eva's thoughts were all over the place as she stared at her old friend. "I thought the store was doing well. How could I have been so wrong? What are you going to do?"

"What can I do? Josh's mind is made up—he's leaving because he's fed up. I have to admire his spunk. He gave it his best shot, and I just kept fouling up everything he did. Now all my chickens are com-ing home to roost."

"For heaven's sake, Angus, Josh is your son. You can't let him leave under these conditions. You have to make this right. There's nothing in this world more important than family. If you don't take a stand now, you'll never get Josh back. What's so hard about saying you're sorry, that you made mistakes? You can't just let Eagle's close their doors. Eagle's is an institution in this town. Shame on you, Angus Eagle. I'm going to bed now. I don't want to talk about this anymore. I have therapy at seven o'clock."

"Eva, wait. Help me out here."

"Oh, no. It doesn't work that way. You're the only one who can make this right. I'm willing to cancel that lifetime lease and renegotiate a new one. In fact, I insist. I'll call my lawyer in the morning."

"That's a drop in the bucket, Eva. The gift-wrapping shop was never about money. In the beginning it was a courtesy to our customers. You're the one who turned it into a moneymaker. Then Josh wanted to use the gift wrap department space to outfit a safari department. He said it was the 'in' thing. I'm ashamed to admit I laughed at him. Two days later, I heard a group of men on the golf course talking about all the gear they'd just purchased because they were going on safari. One of the men poked my arm and said Eagle's didn't even know what a safari was. Even then, I couldn't see it. I guess I *am* a dried-up old fart, just like Josh said I was."

"Yes, Angus, I guess you are just one big gas bubble. I certainly don't envy you."

Eva struggled to her feet as she leaned heavily on her cane. She knew she'd been sitting too long. She could hardly wait to get to her room so she could ring the nurse to ask for a bag of frozen peas. She moved off as she tried to figure out how she was going to tell her daughter what Angus had just shared with her.

Christmas this year is going to be bittersweet, she thought.

When Eva woke the following morning the first thing she saw was Angus Eagle standing in the open doorway. "How long have you been standing there, Angus?" she gasped.

"About an hour. You snore. I thought only men snored. Can I come in and sit down? I didn't sleep all night. I've been walking up and down the halls and I'm getting tired."

"For heaven's sake, come in and sit down. For your information, everyone snores, even children." Eva pushed the button on the remote to raise her bed. She wished she had a cup of coffee.

"I asked a nurse to bring us some coffee. I hope that was okay. Listen, Eva, you were always so grounded. I assume you still are. That's one of the things I always admired about you. I need your help and I'm not ashamed to be asking, either. For me to give in now, to give up total control when we're just months from closing our doors seems a bit silly to me. Josh won't buy into it. You know that old saying—too little, too late. You know as well as I do that the Christmas season revenues can carry a store for a whole year. We depend on that revenue. What should I do?"

"Angus, I know nothing about the retail business. My only claim to fame is I know how to gift wrap packages. I think you should talk to my daughter. She seems to have an eye and ear to the business. In the past she spent hours and hours telling me all the things wrong with the store. And I know for a fact she dropped dozens of suggestions in Eagle's suggestion box on the second floor because she thought if you had more foot traffic, she would have more gifts to wrap. We had a really bad summer; everyone was buying from the discount houses. That's something else you didn't take into consideration. They popped up all over town like mushrooms. For the record, all of Angie's suggestions were ignored."

Angus's voice was desperate when he asked, "Will your daughter talk to me?"

"Of course she'll talk to you. What kind of child do you think I raised? It's your son she won't talk to. But when I tell her he really isn't her enemy, that you are, well, I don't know for sure. There's no doubt about it, Angus, you're standing knee-deep in a mess. Of your own making, I might add."

"I know that, Eva. Help me out here."

"Put yourself in your son's shoes. What would you like your father to do? How would you handle it?"

Angus shrugged. "Josh said I never listened to him. It's true. All of a sudden, I'm going to listen now, when it's too late? Maybe there's a way to help him without him knowing I'm helping."

"Spit it out, Angus. How? I suspect you have some groveling to do first, my friend. Call him at the store. Ask him to come here to see you. That's a first step. By the way, Angus, how long are you here for?"

Angus grimaced. "Today or tomorrow. I've been here a week but I stayed in my room because I didn't want anyone to know I was here. I simply didn't want to socialize. I wish I had known you were here, Eva. When are you leaving?"

"Tomorrow, I think. I'll have a home health aide

for two weeks. She'll come by three times a week and help with my therapy. The rest is up to me. We can talk on the phone if you like."

"I'd like that. I really would."

"How are you going to get home, Angus?"

"I'll call a car service. I don't want to bother Josh. I'm surprised he hasn't moved out of the house. I'll have to stay out of his way."

"This is not right, Angus. Angie is going to come by this morning with donuts and coffee. She does that every morning. She can give you a ride home if they discharge you today. You can talk to her then."

Eva almost felt sorry for her old friend as he made his way to the door. Almost. Angus looked back, his face filled with pain. For some reason Eva thought the pain was more mental than physical. Once, this wonderful man had literally saved her financial life. Maybe with the help of her daughter, she could return the favor. How that would come about, she had no clue. *Well,* she thought briskly, *I can think about that while I'm having my therapy. Perhaps thinking about Angus will help to alleviate the pain of therapy.*

By nine o'clock Eva had finished her therapy, eaten a light breakfast, and showered before she slowly made her way to the sunroom, where she flopped down on a chair, her forehead beaded with perspiration from her efforts. She could hardly wait for Angie and the delicious coffee she was addicted to. Not to mention the donuts.

Eva looked around, acknowledging the other patients who were waiting for their turn in the therapy room. There was no sign of Angus. She didn't know if that was a good thing or not. She leaned back and closed her eyes, her thoughts going in all directions.

Fifteen minutes later, Eva's eyes popped open when she felt a light touch to her shoulder. "Morning, Mom. Did you have a good night?"

"I did have a good night. Angie, I need to talk to you. Pass out your donuts and coffee and hurry back here." Seeing the alarm on her daughter's face, she hastened to add, "It's not about me. I'm fine. Hurry, Angie."

A few minutes later, worry lines were etched on Angie's face as she settled herself next to her mother. She shook her head when her mother offered her a jelly-filled donut. "What? Tell me, Mom."

"It's the store, Angie. Angus and I spoke last night after you left. When I woke up this morning, he was standing in my doorway waiting for me to wake up. It's not good, Angie. Let me tell it all to you the way Angus told it to me. Don't interrupt me, either."

Angie listened, her facial expressions going from anger to disbelief to sadness. When her mother finished, the only thing she could think of to say was, "We can't let that happen, Mom. Eagle's is an institution. We can renegotiate the lease. Oh, God, I need to think about this. I thought Angus Eagle was a nice man. How could he have sabotaged his son like that? I feel terrible about the way I treated Josh. I need to give Mr. Eagle a piece of my mind."

"You need to do no such thing. What you will do is give Angus a ride home. He's finished with his therapy today and was going to call a car service. I volunteered your services, dear. You can talk to him on the way home."

"Mommmm!"

"Sweetie, we're all in this together. I don't want Angus to lose his son, and that's what will happen. Both of them have too much pride to admit when they're wrong. Because we're women, we can fix that. At least I think we can. All right, we're going to *try* to fix things. All those wonderful suggestions you had over the years might come in handy now. All you have to do is get Josh to think they're his ideas."

"Mom, you can't undo years of being in the red in a few short months. Yes, profits are greater during the holiday season, but that alone can't ward off the inevitable."

"I'll settle for a reprieve. For now, the gift wrap department belongs to Eagle's. We'll take 20 percent and the store takes 80 percent. This is just for now. I'll call our lawyer today to discuss it. We have two short months to turn things around before the shopping season begins."

Angie offered up a bitter laugh. "Mom, Eagle's merchandise is archaic. Where can they get new stuff in two months?"

"Where there's a will, there's a way. Think about something people can't do without. Then stock up on that. Fire sales, get rid of the junk they're stuck with or donate it somewhere. Get some glitter and sparkle in there. I know you'll come up with something, dear."

"Mom! When was the last time you experienced a miracle? That's what it's going to take to get Eagle's to soar again. I'm not . . . I don't think . . ."

"I don't want to hear anything negative. From here on in, we think positive. I know we can at least get it off the ground. If we can do that, then it's up to Josh to follow through. Now run along and pick up Angus and take him home. He is a nice man, Angie. He just didn't know how to let go, and he didn't trust his son enough to let him run with the ball. Unlike me, who trusted you completely. Angus is a man," Eva said, as if that was the only explanation needed.

Angie bit down on her lip. "Okay, Mom. I'll do what I can. I'll see you tonight. What do you want me to bring?"

"A hoagie would be nice."

"You got it." A moment later, Angie was gone. Eva closed her eyes and sighed mightily. She couldn't help but wonder if there was a miracle in Eagle's future.

Chapter Three

The following morning, Angie dressed with care. It was still cool, so she decked out in warm clothes—a plum-colored suit, sensible heels and a crisp white blouse. Light makeup that her mother said she didn't need, a spritz of perfume and she was ready to go toe to toe with Josh Eagle.

There was no point in kidding herself. She was nervous about the confrontation. More so since driving Angus Eagle home yesterday, a drive that had been made virtually in silence. Twice she'd bitten down on her tongue so she wouldn't say something her mother wouldn't approve of. Back in the recesses of her mind Angie wondered, and not for the first time, if Angus and her mother had ever had an affair. Lifetime leases didn't happen for no reason. No one was that kind, that good-hearted. Or, were they? Well, it was none of her business, so she needed to stop thinking about it. Easier said than done.

Angie ran her fingers through what she called her

wash-and-go hairdo. A month ago her mother had finally convinced her to cut off her long, curly hair in favor of a more stylish cut. Her mother said the new hairdo was becoming, and mothers never lied. Well, almost never. After two weeks of staring at herself in the mirror, she agreed with Eva's assessment.

Angie realized she was postponing the moment when she had to leave and get on with the day. For all she knew, without an appointment to see Josh Eagle, all this anxiety she was experiencing might be for naught. For naught—such an old-fashioned term. One her mother or Angus Eagle would use.

On the ten-minute ride down Route 1, Angie thought about her own precarious position at Eagle's. If the store closed, she would be out of a job. It might be months before she found another one. Being self-employed, she wouldn't be able to collect unemployment insurance. Her mother would have to start pinching pennies because the medical bills would be coming in shortly. Even with Medicare, her mother would be paying them off for months. With only Social Security coming in, their meager savings would be gone in the blink of an eye. Well, she couldn't let that happen. She'd always been an idea person, according to her mother. If there was ever a time to come up with a dynamite idea, now was it.

Angie slowed for a traffic light, then made a right onto Woodbridge Avenue. She drove down to the mall lot, left her car and entered Eagle's through one of the back doors next to the loading platform. Instead of going straight to her shop, she walked the floor. There were no customers in the store that she could see. The sales help were standing around chatting with one another. She wondered what happened to the rule of look busy even if you aren't. She winced again as she surveyed the merchandise, which looked like it had been hanging on the racks forever. Hopelessly outdated.

Was it too late to save this store? She glanced around again and nodded to herself. Well, she'd never been a quitter. But, as Bess would say, there's a first time for everything.

Angie walked back to the end of the store to the gift wrap department, rolled up the corrugated shield, unlocked the door and turned up the heat. In the little alcove at the far end of the room, out of sight, was a little station where she kept a coffeepot. She filled it and waited for the hot water to drip into the little red pot. She couldn't do anything until she had a cup of coffee. Coffee fortified her, made her brain cells do double-time. The moment she finished her second cup, she would march herself to Josh Eagle's office on the second floor. She had no clue what she was going to do or say when she got there. She'd always been pretty good at winging it. There was a lot to be said for spontaneity. She didn't believe it for a minute.

At the same time as Angie was waiting for the coffee to brew, Josh Eagle was pacing the confines of his office. He hated that he had to go down to the first floor and apologize to the witch with the broom. She looked like the type who might take a swing at him. His stomach started to curdle at the thought. Still, there was no reason for him to behave the way he had at the rehab center the other night. He should have sloughed it off and ignored the young woman with the sparks in her eyes. And, she was pretty. He told himself she could be pretty and still be a witch.

Josh diddled around for another twenty minutes before he squared his shoulders, straightened his tie and shook down the cuffs of his shirt. Now he was ready. His heart was beating way too fast. His mouth felt dry.

His cell phone rang, jarring him from what he was feeling. He looked down at the caller ID and saw that it was his father, who had come home yesterday and was asleep when Josh got home. He'd said everything he had to say to his father the night before. It was much too late to hear his repeated apologies of *I'm sorry, son. I didn't know, son.* Then a few more I'm sorries. No sense beating a dead horse. He ignored the insistent ringing and left his office.

He met her a foot away from the huge red X. He'd gone ballistic the day he'd seen that red X for the first time. The witch's biting words at the time still rang in his ears to this day. *Step one foot over that X, and I'll have you arrested!* He knew she meant every word of it. And that was three years ago. To date, he'd never stepped beyond the X. How childish was all this? Damn childish.

Josh took the initiative. "Ms. Bradford, I came down here to apologize to you for my rude behavior the other night. Not that I'm defending my rude behavior, but I have a lot on my plate right now."

"I know you do. I was on my way to your office to apologize to you. Would you like to . . . uh . . . go out to the food court and get a cup of coffee? Neutral ground, so to speak. If you're busy . . ."

Josh stared at the young woman. Did she just invite him for coffee? "Sure," was all he could think of to say. How brilliant was that?

They walked around the corner, down one of the long halls until they reached the food court, which was virtually empty this early in the morning. Neither said a word on the short journey.

"How do you take your coffee?" Josh asked.

"Black. It's not coffee if you doctor it up with cream and sugar."

"I feel the same way. Take a seat, I'll get the coffee." A black-coffee drinker like himself. Who knew?

The moment Josh sat down, Angie leaned forward and said, "We're going to cancel the lease. We can renegotiate it again after the first of the year if the store is still open. Until then, Eagle's gets 80 percent of the take, we get 20 percent. Look, let me finish what I have to say before I lose my nerve. My mother told me what you told your father. You're leaving the first of the year. I guess I more or less understand that. Speaking strictly for myself, I've never been a quitter, but that's me and, like you said, you have a lot on your plate.

"Your father . . . well, he's been wrong. Older people have a hard time . . . What they do is give generously and then they realize they lost their control. It's hard for them to accept the aging. . . . Help me out here, Mr. Eagle."

"First things first, let's stop with the Mr. and Ms. I'm Josh, and you're Angie. Okay?"

Angie smiled. Josh suddenly felt his world rock. "I . . . I know what you're saying. For the last ten years I've battled my father. He's stubborn as a mule. I had so many plans for the store, but he shot me down each and every time I presented something. I finally got to the end of my rope. There's nothing more I can do."

Angie sipped at the scalding-hot coffee. "Sure there is. Where are all the suggestions that were in the suggestion box? I used to slip one in that box once a week."

"You're the one who . . . I still have them all in my office. They were good suggestions. I ran each and every one of them by my father, but he vetoed all of them. I'm being kind when I say he's in a time warp."

"I know. I drove him home from the rehab center yesterday. He didn't say much to me, but he did open up to my mother, who in turn passed it all on to me, and I am now telling you. What a round-robin. Why can't people just say what's in their minds and hearts?"

"Why are you telling me all this?" Josh asked, suspicion ringing in his voice. "I thought you hated my guts."

Angie looked genuinely puzzled at his remark. "I don't hate you personally. I don't even know you. I hate what you did. I guess I should say I hate what you didn't do, but I didn't understand what was going on. I have ideas," she said quietly.

"It's too late, Angie. The store needs mega revenues for the Christmas season or the doors close in January. Dad . . ."

"You scared the devil out of your father, according to my mother. He's onboard now. You have carte blanche to do whatever you want. I have ideas," she repeated.

In spite of himself, Josh was intrigued. "It's the middle of September, Angie."

"That's almost two months until the Christmas

season kicks off. If we hunker down, with no interference, I think we might be able to make this a banner season. I'm game if you are." Angie waited, hardly daring to breathe, waiting for Josh's answer.

"I guess I owe my old man one more shot at it. If nothing else but to prove I wasn't a know-it-all. If, and it's a big *if,* we pull it off, I'm still leaving for London after the first of the year. I committed, and I never go back on my word."

"That's your decision, Josh. I, for one, would never try to talk you out of something if your mind is made up. I guess that's a holdover kind of thing from when I was a kid. I have a ton of stuff to do today. How do you feel about getting some Chinese at the Jade Pagoda this evening after the store closes? We could talk in detail and make a plan. That's if you're serious. If you are, check all those suggestions I bombarded you with. There's a game plan in there."

Josh propped his elbows on the table. "Did you just ask me to dinner? A date?"

Angie laughed. "Well, yeah," she said. "Now that we're . . . uh . . . friends, I thought . . ." She flushed a bright pink when she caught Josh smiling at her. "I never asked a guy for a date before. It's a little embarrassing."

Josh threw his head back and laughed, a sound that sent shivers up Angie's back. "Now you know a guy's worst fear. Asking a girl for a date is traumatic. I accept. I'll meet you by the loading dock at six-ten. Does that work for you?"

"Yes. I want you to think about something today. I'd like to see you close the store for two days. Get rid of all that outdated merchandise on the floor. Close off the second floor until we can decide what we're going to do, what we're going to specialize in. Like I said, I have some great ideas."

Josh felt his throat close up. "Close the store! In the middle of the week? That had never happened in the lifetime of the store. Are you sure you have a plan?"

"I do. It will work, too, as long as you don't fight me. Look, I'm giving up the lease. It's all yours. That alone should prove I'm on your side. Besides, I hate the thought of going job hunting. Do we have a deal?"

Josh gulped but nodded. Angie's hand shot out. He reached for it, marveling at how soft her hand was in his.

Josh smiled.

Angie smiled.

Throw your line into the pond and reel him in, Bess had said. Angie giggled all the way back to the gift wrap department, which she'd just given away.

The first thing she did when she walked behind the counter was to call her mother. "Josh said okay, but he's still leaving in January because he committed to Harrods. I'm hoping he might change his mind. We're in business, Mom. Listen, I'm going to have Bess pick you up and take you home. I have tons of stuff to do. You can work the phones when you get home. You okay with that? Okay, now listen up. . . ." She went on to detail the outline of her plan.

"Yes, honey. It all makes sense. I just hope you can do it all in two months. The vendors aren't all that co-operative at this time of year. Is it okay to tell Angus?"

"Sure. Your job is to make sure he doesn't waffle on us. Talk it up real good, Mom."

"Okay, honey. Congratulations!"

"Bess, instead of taking me home, take me to Mr. Eagle's house. It's just a few miles out of your way since it's on the corner of Plainfield Road and Park Avenue. Angus has a ramp, so I won't have a problem with the steps. Angie can pick me up later."

Bess raised her eyebrows but only nodded. Something was going on. She wondered when Eva or Angie would confide in her. She didn't like being kept in the dark. And now this visit to the Eagle home. Something was definitely going on.

"Just park in the back, Bess. The ramp is by the kitchen door. At least it was years ago, when Angus's father had to use a wheelchair. No, no, don't help me. I have to do this myself. I have my cane. Thanks for bringing me here, Bess. You're a good friend."

"Is there anything I can do, Eva?"

"Not right now, but very shortly there will be plenty for you to do. Have a nice day now. Go, go! I'm fine."

At the kitchen door, Eva used her cane to rap on the glass pane. When there was no response, she opened the door and stepped into the kitchen. She took a moment to look around. She'd spent a lot of time in this kitchen, catering to Mrs. Angus Eagle. The truth was, as Angie pointed out more times than she wanted to remember, she spent more time here than she did in her own kitchen. She suspected Angie still held that against her.

It was all so long ago.

"Angus, it's Eva," she called out. "Are you here?"

"I'm in the den. What in the world are you doing here? Are you all right? How did you get here? Good Lord, Eva, are you sure you should be out and about? Come in, come in. Sit down."

Eva could hardly wait to sit down. Once there she wondered how she was going to get up out of the depths of the deep, comfortable couch. She'd worry about that later. "I suppose I could have called you when I got home, but for some reason I didn't want to be alone. I thought since I'm clumsy by nature, I might fall or something. So I decided to come here. You're stuck with me until Angie can pick me up, which won't be till later this evening. Or, I can take a taxi."

"Nonsense. I'm grateful for the company. I was just sitting here thinking about how badly I've fouled things up. Josh still won't take my calls, and I was asleep when he got home last night. I've been calling him since eight this morning. My son can be very unforgiving. Is your daughter like that?"

"At times. When I was standing in your kitchen I was thinking about how angry she got when I had to cook dinner for your family. Then I would rush home and cook dinner for my own family, and it was always late. Then I had to rush back and clean up because your wife wouldn't do it. That meant Angie had to clear up my own kitchen. It's one of the reasons why she doesn't like you. She thought you took advantage of me."

Angus looked dazed. "I didn't know that, Eva. What I mean is I didn't know you went home to cook for your family, and then came back here. You should have said something. I would have cleared the dishes myself. There's no point now in me trying to make apologies to you for my wife. But I am sorry, Eva."

Eva stared at her old boss. "Angus, who did you think cooked my family's dinner those days?"

Angus threw his hands in the air. "I guess I never thought about it. You should have said something at the time. What do you want me to say?"

Eva snapped her fingers in Angus's direction. "Earth to Angus! Your wife told me if I complained to you, she would fire me. I needed the job. She was so demanding. I wanted to quit so many times, but my family needed the money I brought in."

"Eva, I am so very sorry. I didn't know. If there was a strain between you two, then why would my wife insist I turn over the gift wrap department to you? It doesn't make sense."

"She didn't want me around in the afternoon when she . . . when she . . . entertained. It was to ensure I never said anything. Fill in the blanks, Angus, and I am never going to talk about this again. Are we clear on that?"

"No, we are not clear on anything. When you imply something like that you need to . . . to explain *exactly* what you're saying. We're talking about my deceased wife here. Eva?"

"How many ways are there to say your wife entertained in the afternoons while you were at the store and your son was out somewhere or away. She did not entertain women with tea parties. I only ever saw one man and that was quite by accident, so I cannot give you a name. That's it, Angus. Now, leave it alone."

Angus rubbed at his jaw. By the stubborn set of

Eva's chin, he knew she had said the last word on the subject. "I didn't know. Something like that never occurred to me."

Eva picked up her cane and waved it around. "I didn't know, I didn't know. That's all you've been saying for several days now. What *did* you know, if anything?" she asked sourly. "Look at the mess you're in, and now I'm in the same mess because my daughter is going to be out of a job, and I'll be losing my share of the profits. 'I didn't know' is not good enough, Angus."

Angus felt his shoulders start to shake. He choked up and turned to Eva. "It's my only defense. I was so obsessed with the store, keeping it going, trying to stay ahead of all the upstarts coming into town. I didn't want to fail my father. I see now where I was wrong. I'll be honest with you, Eva. I don't know what to do. 'I'm sorry' more or less falls into the same category as 'I didn't know.' Can you help me?"

Eva leaned her cane against the sofa. "Was that so hard, Angus? Asking for help? This is the same position your son finds himself in right now. With a slight difference. He had the good sense to ask you for help, but you stomped on him. He's the one you have to talk to, not me. If you don't, you're going to lose him. Open your heart and your mind, and if he calls you an old fart again, suck it up. We're supposed to be older and wiser, the ones our children come to in need. I think that little ditty just reversed itself."

Angus forced a laugh. Eva thought it the saddest sound she'd ever heard.

"How'd you get so smart, Eva?"

"By trying not to do the things you did. I had to

think about my family. We weren't well-off like you were. We struggled for everything. More than once Angie had to wait weeks when she needed new shoes. There were a lot of things she couldn't have when she was younger because they cost too much money. My husband worked on an assembly line. We had a mortgage payment, car payments, appliance payments. Then we had to save for college. Until you leased me the gift wrap department, we barely made ends meet. I don't want to talk about this anymore, Angus. I want your word that you are not going to interfere with the kids when they do whatever it is they're going to do. Your word, Angus, or I'm leaving and will walk home, at which point I will collapse and my condition will be on your conscience."

"You drive a hard bargain, Eva. You have my word. I'm not going to like what they're going to do, am I?"

"Not one little bit!"

"Can you give me a clue, a hint?"

"Try this one on. They're going to close the store and get rid of all that stuff that came over with the ark."

"The merchandise? That represents money. What . . . What are they going to do with it?"

"My guess is there's going to be one heck of a super-sale followed by a bonfire somewhere real soon. Like I said, Angus, get over it."

"What the hell, okay. Want to stay for dinner? Dolores is still with me, so you know there's something delicious waiting."

"I'd love to stay for dinner."

"Do we have a date, then?"

"We do indeed have a date. Speaking of dates, Angie

and Josh are going out for Chinese this evening. I rather imagine the two of them will be venting to one another about the two of us," Eva said.

"Imagine that!"

"I think the two of them think you and I had an affair years ago," Eva said, her face taking on a rosy hue.

Eyes twinkling, Angus said, "Imagine that!"

Eva laughed. "Yes, imagine that!"

Chapter Four

The Jade Pagoda was bustling when Josh held the door for Angie. They were shown to a table into the back section of the room that was separated from the other diners by strings of silver beads—beads that tinkled as the servers walked in and out. It was a pleasant sound, as was the fountain that trickled over lava rocks in the middle of the room. A smiling Buddha holding a fortune cookie sat atop the fountain, welcoming all guests.

"I come here sometimes just to relax," Josh said, waving his arm about. "Win Lee told me if you rub the Buddha's belly he'll bring you good luck. For some reason, that little fat guy never worked for me."

Angie smiled. "Maybe it's because you aren't Chinese."

"Do you think?"

"No! I just said that to have something to say."

"Do you come here often?"

"After my father died, Mom and I used to come

every Friday night. When she went to Florida to help my aunt I stopped coming, mainly because I don't like to eat alone. When Mom finally came back we just never picked up where we left off. I agree with you, though, it is soothing and peaceful in here. People seem to whisper when they're here. Then again, they might have some top-of-the-line acoustics."

Josh held a chair for Angie before he took his own seat. "My mother wasn't one of those warm, fuzzy mothers. I used to hang out at friends' houses because I liked the way they interacted with their mothers. It sounds like you and your mother had a good relationship."

"We did. Sort of. Kind of. I hated you and your family for a long time," Angie blurted. "That . . . That probably colored my determination to fight you on the lease."

Josh looked so shocked at her words, Angie hastened to explain. "My mother spent more time at your house than she did at her own. Every time I needed her, she was at your house. Back then I didn't understand my family's need for money. I also didn't like it that my mother cleaned your house and cooked for you. Our dinners were always late. Then my mother would go back to your house to clean up after your dinner while I was the one who cleaned up ours. I wasn't always as kind as I could have been to my mother. Of course I regret that now. My dad did his best."

Josh blinked. He struggled to find something to say. "I guess I would have felt the same way. As a kid you just more or less take things for granted. I'm ashamed to admit I never thought about Eva in terms of having a family to take care of. She was just there sometimes. I'm sorry if that hurts your feelings, Angie."

"Well, that was then, this is now. We were both kids back then. You know what they say, you can't unring the bell. Isn't it ironic that we've come together like this? Your father with his hip operation, Mom with her knee replacement. If it weren't for that, you and I would still be battling one another. I guess everything happens for a reason."

"So we have a truce. At least for now."

"Yes. We have to make it all work. I think we can. Did you look over the suggestions I put in the box?"

"I did. Most of them are really good. I particularly like your idea to turn the gift wrap department into a Christmas wonderland. But the retail side of me can't quite accept the idea that for a fee you're willing to gift wrap merchandise from other stores."

"The idea, Josh, is, those customers will browse the store and buy point-of-purchase merchandise with the money going into Eagle's coffers. The gift wrapping is not going to be cheap, I can tell you that. Most of that money will now go into your coffers, too."

Josh nodded as he motioned to the waitress. He told her that they were ready for some green tea. "I sent out memos today. We'll close the store this weekend for two days. Three if we need an extra day. I also made arrangements for everything on both floors that has been marked down twice to go to Goodwill. Everything else will be sold below cut-rate to two different discount stores. This will get underway Friday night after the store closes. You might want to walk through the store to see if you think there's anything we can salvage."

"Get rid of it all. We're starting fresh. No holdovers. You also need to get an electrician to install some better lighting. A nice new, shiny tile floor will work wonders."

"I'm not a miracle worker, Angie. Two days, even three, it's a monumental task."

"Offer a bonus. Tap into your workforce. The salespeople have spouses who might like to make some extra money. Your new motto from here on in is, 'The Eagle Soars.' Start running ads in the local newspaper. Get some flyers made up. Hire some kid to put them on the windshields of the cars in the parking lot. Have a raffle every day. All entries have to have a sales receipt attached. That kind of thing. In order to make money, you have to spend money. You might need to close for two *weeks*."

Josh brought the little cup of tea to his lips. His gaze locked with Angie's. "Two weeks! Young lady, you're scary!"

"I'm going to take that as a compliment. A scary compliment. What did you do about laying off your staff?"

Josh leaned back in his chair. "It was hard, but I did it. I think a lot of the staff were more or less relieved. I laid everyone off for three weeks except for a few I knew we would need. I don't know why, but I thought some, if not most of them, welcomed the decision. Some of the staff are my father's age. Past retirement age, but Dad wouldn't let me lay them off. I checked all their files, and none of them are in dire need of money. They work to have something to do. I can't fault them for that."

"You might be able to use the grandmothers to man the day care I want to put in on the second floor.

Think about it, Josh. Mothers dropping off their children so they can shop! At thirty dollars a day with lunch and snacks, it would be a bargain. Of course you'd have some moms who just might want a few hours at a time. We'd work out a reasonable fee. I can see you taking in a couple of thousand bucks a day. The more activities you have for the kids, the more demand for the service. The kids would get a day with a real grandma who will read them stories, sing songs with them, rock the babies. Your dad and my mom will be perfect if we can get them to agree and at the same time still be in the loop. I already earmarked all the things on the floor that could go into the day care. I have a lot of friends whose kids have outgrown many of their things. I can ask to borrow them. Next year, if this all works, we could really do a bang-up job, but for now, I think this will work."

"My father is going to go nuclear!" Josh laughed. "Day care! Never in a million years would I have come up with that idea. You're right, you are an idea person!"

"Thank you, sir!"

The waitress showed up to take their order. Angie ordered a dish called Volcano Shrimp, while Josh ordered a sizzling seafood platter. Both now crunched down on hard noodles, a bit more relaxed with one another.

As Angie munched, she asked, "What did you think about my idea of having a really huge live Christmas tree in the middle of the floor? And the Santa with his sack of toys?"

"Great idea, but it will seriously deplete floor space. I'm still waiting to see what kind of merchandise we're going to be selling. Not to mention where we're going to get that merchandise. Vendors are notoriously cranky and in no hurry to get the deliveries to you during the year. They're worse over the holidays. I hesitate to ask this, but is there a Plan B lurking anywhere?"

"Plan B? More or less. Incentives. Cash on delivery. If the merchandise angle falls short of my expectations, I think we could more than make up for the revenues with services, like cooking lessons, knitting lessons, all kinds of hourly lessons. Kind of like the YMCA. I think I'd like some Chinese beer now."

"You like Chinese beer! Imagine that! I like it myself." Josh signaled the waitress and placed the order. When it arrived, he held up his bottle to clink it against Angie's. "What should we drink to?"

"To success, what else?"

Angie drank from the bottle, ignoring the glass sitting on the table. Josh seemed mesmerized by his dinner companion as she kept upending the bottle. He'd never dated a girl who really liked beer, much less drank it from the bottle. He grinned from ear to ear. He took a moment to wonder what it would be like to kiss those full red lips. He just knew in his gut he'd soar like an eagle.

Angie and Josh were the last to leave the Jade Pagoda. With way too much Chinese beer under their belts, Josh called for a taxi. "We can pick our cars up in the morning."

"What time is it?" Angie mumbled as she looked at the array of beer bottles on the table.

Josh peered at his watch. He knew he was snookered when he couldn't read the numbers. "Late," he said triumphantly. "Do you have to be home before . . .

before . . . the moon comes out?" Damn, he was witty tonight. And charming.

"I was . . . I think I was supposed to . . . Maybe I wasn't . . . Where is my mother, do you know?"

Angie was looking at him like he had the answer at his fingertips. He didn't want to disappoint his new friend. "I'm not sure. I'll help you look for her."

"That's wonderful. Thank you. I think she might be . . . you know, pissed that I forgot about her."

Josh pulled himself up to his full six-foot-two-inch height and said, "We *were* busy."

"Yes, we were. Why don't we walk home, Josh? We might see them on the way. Oh, I remember now, my mother is keeping your father company. That's not good. Oh, shit! My cell phone is off."

Josh burst out laughing and couldn't stop. Suddenly this peppery young woman he'd dined with, drunk with, was all too human. "How many times did she call?"

"Well, guess what, Josh? I can't really see those itsy-bitsy little numbers. A lot. And who's paying for this taxi?" Angie asked as it pulled up.

Josh stepped up to the plate. "Eagle's," he said smartly.

"Tell him to take us to your house. Then he can take me and my mother home. She is going to be so . . . so . . ."

"Pissed?" Josh asked, howling with laughter. "My old man is going to go through the roof. I need to move out and get my own place. I think he needs me, and that's why he likes me living with him. I bet your mother feels the same way. They're old. Old people think like that."

They got into the cab and Josh gave the driver his address.

"Nah, it's all a game to keep us in line. Those two are more independent than either one of us. If you had your own place, I could visit you."

Whoa. Josh leaned over and kissed her ruby-red lips. At least he thought they were ruby red. He didn't care if they were ruby red or purple.

"You're a good kisser," Angie said a long time later. "I think the driver wants you to pay him. Are we at your house? Time does fly when you're having fun, doesn't it? Yesireee, you are a good kisser."

"Damn straight I am. A good kisser. Not because I had . . . have a lot of practice," Josh said, handing the driver a twenty-dollar bill for the five-minute ride. "Keep the change," he said magnanimously.

"Wait for me, mister, I have to pick up my mother."

Walking up the driveway, Josh stopped and reached for Angie's arm. "Should we have a story? You know, why we're so uncaring, so negligent, so . . ."

"Drunk?"

"Egg-zactly," Josh said, roaring with laughter.

"No defense is the best defense. I don't really care. Do you care, Josh?"

"I don't think I do. Tomorrow I might."

Josh was about to open the kitchen door when it swung open. He looked up to see Eva Bradford glaring at him. His father's face defied description. A sappy expression on his face, Josh said, "Good evening, everybody." He made a low, sweeping bow. Not to be outdone, Angie did the same thing and almost fell on her face.

"They're both drunk," Angus said.

Josh straightened his jacket and looked over at

Angie. "They're worried about us while they've been here . . . noodling . . . canoodling . . . Oh, shit, messing around. Hrumph!" he sniffed. "Your chariot awaits, Mrs. Bradford. It's a taxi."

"Mom!" Angie looked properly horrified. "I knew it! I knew it! You two . . . You lied to me. You were doing what he said . . . noodling around," she said, pointing to Josh.

"We were not. You're inebriated, Angie. Shame on you!"

"Joshua, go to your room."

"Why should I? No! I'm moving out and Angie is going to come and visit me. When I move to England, she's coming to visit me there, too. So, Pop, what do you have to say to that?"

"Talk to me when you're sober, and I will have plenty to say. These ladies need to go home right now. You need to go to bed, Joshua."

Josh looked over at Angie and said, "He only calls me Joshua when he's really mad. Come along, fair lady, I always see my dates home. Do you want me to stay with you until I find an apartment?"

"Sure," Angie said agreeably. "Mom can stay here. Win-win. Works for everybody. I think I'm going to be sick."

Eva fixed her angry gaze on Josh, and said, "Young man, I am holding you personally responsible for my daughter's condition. Do something!"

Josh stepped up to the plate for the second time that evening. "And I and I alone accept that responsibility." He offered up a second sweeping bow and fell over, toppling one of the kitchen chairs. "The meter is running," he said as Angie bolted for the kitchen door.

"Do something, Angus!" Eva hissed.

"It's your daughter who's . . . Well, she's . . ."

"Your son got my daughter drunk. Don't deny it."

From his position on the floor Josh said, "No, no, she got that way all by herself. She had so many ideas." A moment later he was sound asleep on the kitchen floor.

Angus shrugged. Eva did her best not to laugh.

Angie came back and looked down at Josh. "He's not . . . dead, is he?"

"I'm thinking tomorrow morning he might wish he was," Angus said.

Angie sat down on the floor next to Josh. "Oh, I had so many ideas. Josh liked all my ideas." She untangled herself and laid her head on Josh's stomach.

"I say we just leave them here," Eva said. "I'll let the taxi driver go. You get some blankets and pillows."

"Then what?" Angus asked.

"Do you want me to draw you a map, Angus? Do you want to make your son out to be a liar? We're going to canoodle."

"Oh!" Angus wondered if Eva picked up on the anxiety in his voice.

And then she was back in the kitchen, a wicked gleam in her eyes.

Chapter Five

The sun was just making its way to the horizon when Josh stirred on the kitchen floor. He felt like a ton of bricks was sitting on top of his chest. Somehow, he managed to crank open one eye. A nanosecond later, his other eye flew open. He gasped. The woman wrapped around his torso stirred and mumbled something he couldn't quite hear. Josh moved. Then the woman moved and rolled over onto the floor. She was awake in an instant, looking around as she tried to figure out where she was and why she was lying on a strange kitchen floor. A tortured groan escaped her lips.

Josh groaned in sync as he struggled to sit up. His eyes were as wild-looking as his hair, which was standing on end. Angie didn't look much better.

"Ah, did we . . . ? What I mean is . . . Do you remember?" he finished lamely.

Angie rubbed her temples in an attempt to ease the

pounding in her head. "No, I don't think, and . . . No, I don't know," she said just as lamely.

"Why are we . . . ? We slept on the floor?" Josh asked this as though sleeping on the floor was one of the Seven Wonders of the World. "Why did we do that?" he asked as he got to his feet. He stretched out a long arm to pull Angie to her feet.

"Maybe because we were drunk?" It was a question and a statement.

Josh looked down at the floor to see the pillows and blankets. He cursed under his breath as he pointed them out to Angie. She looked away in embarrassment. "Are you sure we didn't . . . ?"

"I think I would remember *that*," Josh said, walking over to the coffeepot. He thought his head was going to pound right off his neck. He filled the pot, measured coffee and pressed a button. "Do you want some orange juice?"

"I didn't even brush my teeth. It feels like something is growing in my mouth," Angie said. "No on the orange juice. Oh, God, we left our cars at the Jade Pagoda. Now I have to walk there to get it. Damn. I look like someone who just . . ."

"Had a wild night of sex?" Josh asked.

"Stop saying that. We didn't . . . I'm almost . . . No, I'm sure we didn't. We never should have had that plum wine after drinking beer. This is all your fault, Josh. You said we couldn't insult Mr. Win Lee by refusing the complimentary wine."

"You guzzled half that carafe all by yourself. You even got sick. I did not get sick. I only pretended to drink the wine."

"Ha! My mother . . . Your father . . . They saw us. They covered us up. Where's my mother?"

"How should I know? You're her daughter, you should know where your mother is at all times. What kind of daughter are you, anyway?"

"The kind that doesn't know where her mother is. I bet your father . . . I bet he took unfair advantage of her with her new knee. My mother is naive and not the least bit worldly. Your father is a shark. Just like you." Oh, God, did she just say that?

"Are you accusing my father of attacking your mother? My father, who can barely walk, who just had a hip replacement? That father?" Damn, his head was pounding so bad he could hardly stand it. A shark! Damn.

"Ha! Your father's new hip and my mother's new knee are those *titanium* joint things. That probably makes them almost bionic. They can *walk*. If they can walk, they can do *other* things."

"My father would never . . ."

"Yeah, well, neither would my mother. Your father is a lot bigger than my little mother. She only weighs a hundred pounds. Your father must weigh two hundred. I rest my case. Oh, please give me some of that coffee before my head explodes. This kitchen hurts my eyes."

Josh poured coffee. "Do you always complain like this so early in the morning? What's wrong with this kitchen?" Josh asked, looking around the ancient kitchen.

"It's outdated for one thing, just like the store. I never saw a stove with legs. What the heck is that funky-looking round thing on top of your refrigerator? I don't see a dishwasher. Not that it's any of your business, but the only time I complain this early in the morning is when I'm hungover, which is almost never, and when my mother goes missing. Have you noticed we're fighting?"

"Everything works. We're not fighting, I'm discussing things and you're . . . Well, what you're doing is complaining."

Josh gulped from his coffee cup. Angie did the same. The word noodling came to Josh's mind. Wouldn't it be a hoot if his old man had more action going for him than he did? He started to laugh at the thought. He shared his thought with Angie, who, despite her pounding head, also started to laugh. Sometimes he was so damn witty he couldn't stand himself.

Behind the kitchen door Eva and Angus listened to their offsprings' mating call. At least that's what Eva told Angus it was. Angus just shook his head. "She's right about your kitchen; it's a disgrace. You need to get with the program, Angus."

Angus nudged the door open a sliver and let his gaze roam around the kitchen. "I like things I'm comfortable with, and I'm comfortable with this kitchen. Everything works just fine." Then, tongue in cheek, he said, "Your daughter doesn't really know anything about you, does she, Eva? You are not naive, and you're as worldly as they come, if last night was any sort of indicator. Does your daughter know how good you are at improvisation?"

Eva giggled. "That will be enough of that, Angus. What are they doing now?"

"My son is whispering in your daughter's ear. That could mean any number of things. I suggest we go back to our chairs and let them find us. Pretend to be asleep."

Twenty minutes later, Eva reared up from her chair. "I don't think it's going to happen, Angus. They aren't going to find us," she said, limping over to the doorway. They're gone. What time does your day lady come in? Do you think she can give me a ride home?"

"She's due right now. Of course she can take you home. Will you come back, or should I have her bring me to your house later on? Better yet, why don't I call a car service so we can have a driver at our disposal. Will that work for you, Eva?"

"Yes, I think it will. You have my cell phone number. Call me when your day gets under way."

Thirty minutes later Eva entered her own house. She stopped at the refrigerator for a bag of frozen peas, then made her way into the family room, where she settled herself in her favorite chair. She sighed with relief when the cold from the frozen peas seeped into her swollen knee. With the three Advil she'd just taken, she knew she would feel better in a little while. She leaned back and closed her eyes. Overhead she could hear the water gurgling in the pipes; Angie washing away the night's activities.

Soon after, Eva's eyes snapped open when she felt a presence near her chair. "Did you have anything to eat, dear?"

"No, but that's okay, I'm not hungry. I'll get a bagel or something in the food court later on. What are you going to do today, Mom?"

"Well, Angus said he was going to hire a driver and come over later. We're going to do our best to pitch in and help Josh with the store. I worry that Eagle's will go under. If that happens, Angus will be destroyed. Did Josh . . . Is he still planning on going to England after New Year's? Did he say?"

Angie perched herself on the arm of the sofa and stared at her mother. "He's still going. Mom, the guy tried for ten years to get Eagle's off the ground. I think I'd pack it in after ten years myself. His father is a selfish old man. You can tell him I said that, too. You stayed there all night, didn't you?" Her tone was so accusatory, Eva flinched.

Eva brushed at the hair falling over her forehead and adjusted the bag of peas on her knee. "I think I'm a little past the stage where I have to account to you for my whereabouts, Angie. Where I was or wasn't last night has nothing to do with our current situation. I'm sure you noticed I didn't say anything to you about how you spent your night or the condition you were in. Because, my daughter, you are old enough to make your own decisions, and you are accountable for your actions. Now, run along so you aren't late."

Angie bit down on her lower lip. She debated presenting an argument but didn't think she could possibly win any war of words with her mother. "Mom, where are all those cottage-industry magazines you subscribe to?"

"In the basement in the cabinet over the washing machine. Why?"

"I'm going to contact some of them. Everything for the most part is homemade. Small businesses like that have a hard time marketing their wares. I'm thinking . . . Now, this is just a thought . . . but maybe we can make this Christmas season a homemade, down-home Christmas. People love to buy things that

are made by hand. If any of those little businesses
have inventory, that will help us. What do you think?"

"I think it's a wonderful idea. I really do. I worry
that vendors won't be able to get merchandise to you
in time for the holidays. It might be too late, dear."

Angie stamped her foot. "No negative thinking,
remember? Anyway, we won't know if we don't try.
Josh wants to go off knowing he did the best he
could. Failure isn't an option at this point." Angie
pointed a finger at her mother and said, "Since you
seem to have the inside track with Angus Eagle, it's
your job to keep him out of our hair so we can make
it happen. The minute he sticks his nose into this ven-
ture, I'm outta there, and I feel confident in saying
Josh will flip him the bird and leave on the spot. Do
you think you can convey all that to Mr. Eagle?
While you're at it you should get him to work on that
kitchen of his. In case, you know, you ever want to
move in there."

A minute later, Eva could hear her daughter stomping her way to the basement. She made three trips carrying the boxes out to her car. One of the things she
loved about her daughter was that she always followed through on things. If there was a way to make
Eagle's Department Store soar, Angie was the one to
make it happen.

The second Eva heard Angie drive off, she picked
up the phone to call Angus. "I'm ready, Angus. Have
your driver pick me up; we're going to take a trip.
And, Angus, bring your check book. Where are we
going? To the Amish country, where we're going to
buy everything they have that's for sale. We're going
to eat homemade bread, homemade soup and home-

made pie for lunch. I'm excited, Angus. Almost as excited as I was last night. Like I said, I'm ready. I'll be waiting on the porch. I don't like to be kept waiting, Angus." A low, throaty, intimate laugh erupted when she heard Angus's reply.

Josh Eagle happened to be on the loading dock when Angie arrived. He was dressed in jeans, a UCLA sweatshirt and battered high-top sneakers. *Toss your line in the pond and reel him in.* He looked good enough to make a girl's head spin. Not that hers was spinning. Well, maybe it was revolving just a tiny bit. "Hi," she said brightly, as he reached out to take the box of magazines from her. She went back out to her car to get the other two boxes and they headed to her shop.

"What are you going to do with these?" Josh asked when he set the last box on the counter in the gift wrap department. Angie explained. She liked the sudden twinkle she saw in Josh's eyes. "Do you think it will work?" His voice was beyond anxious-sounding.

"A homemade, down-home Christmas! Isn't that what Christmas is all about? I'm almost certain it will work. I really am. But we need a campaign to go with it. I think you might have to call an advertising agency to get it off the ground. We're just two people, Josh; we're going to need help. I'm determined that you are going to go out of here with a bang. Along with your father's respect." Now it was her turn to sound anxious. "Are you having second thoughts about leaving?"

"No, not at all," he lied with a straight face. Suddenly the allure of the prestigious Harrods and going to England were losing their appeal.

"I know this is none of my business, but do you have an operating account to draw from? Do I have to run everything by you, or do you trust me to order things without your approval? How do you want me to arrange payment?"

"Yes, no and just charge everything to the store. I'll give you a corporate card. And, yes, I trust you. I have phone calls to make and several meetings with some of the old staff. The discount people are here to start moving all the merchandise. Alma Bennett is in charge of all that. The minute everything is out of the store, an electrician is coming in. And then the painters, who promised to do their work at night. A cleaning crew will be right on their tails to clean and polish the new floor. That's more or less behind-the-scenes stuff. Our real challenge is to get merchandise to fill the space. I'll call an advertising agency at some point this morning to get that going. You'll have to sit in on that meeting. How about lunch?"

"I'd love to have lunch with you. How about twelve thirty in the food court?"

"Works for me." His hands jammed into his jeans pockets, Josh started to whistle as he made his way to the second floor. He could hardly wait for lunch.

"Are those stars I see in your eyes, Angie?" Bess asked.

"Nope. Just new contact lenses."

"Yeah, right. Okay, what's up? What do you want me to do?"

Angie quickly outlined her plans, then told Bess everything that had transpired since she'd seen her last.

"Wow! Can we do it all in time? What about the vendors? They promise everything and give you zip."

"I know, I know, so we're going to insist on penalty clauses. We're also not really going to count on them. We're going to make this a down-home Christmas and try . . . I said *try,* to get up and running with the cottage-industry merchandise. Today you and I are going to scour these books, call the little companies and see what we can get here in time. We won't have to worry about gift wrapping today since the store is closed. Everything is on target with your husband and the decorations, right?"

"John is on it. He loves woodworking. He's made prototypes and is working off them. It will all be done in plenty of time. So tell me what's responsible for the sparks in your eyes. Is it Josh Eagle? *Wooeee,* you're blushing, Angie."

"I am not. It's . . It's really warm in here. Now, let's make some coffee and hit these magazines."

The morning passed quickly as the women consumed two pots of coffee while earmarking pages for further discussion. By noon, Angie's yellow legal pad was full of telephone numbers and notes on which merchandise she was interested in.

With one box of magazines to go, Angie washed her hands, fluffed up her hair and checked her lipstick, ready to meet Josh for lunch. "Do you want me to bring you something for lunch, Bess?"

"No, I brought my lunch. You do remember how to flirt, don't you, Angie?"

Angie stuck out her tongue in Bess's general direction, but in the end she had to laugh. "Do I look okay?"

"You look good enough to go fishing. Remember what I told you about tossing your line in the pond. Play it cool, and he's all yours. That's assuming you want him. From where I'm sitting, the guy is one heck of a catch. Go already. It's not nice to keep the boss waiting."

"Jeez, he is my boss, isn't he? That's going to take some getting used to. Are you sure I look okay, Bess?"

"You look fine, now go. Just remember to smile a lot. Pretend you're interested in what he has to say. You don't always have to be a know-it-all."

On the way to the food court Angie wondered how many women were waiting in the wings for Josh Eagle. She just knew he went for the long-legged modeling types with their glossy smiles, sun-streaked hair and designer clothes. And, according to Bess, who was up on all things Josh Eagle, if any of them had a brain, they'd be dangerous. Angie sniffed. Bess didn't know everything even though she said she did.

Josh was waiting for her by the Philly Cheese Steak booth, which probably meant that's what he intended to eat for lunch. He was holding a twin to the legal pad she was carrying. Ah, a business lunch. She smiled.

Josh waved the yellow pad. "Guess this means we're going to work through our lunch. I had a pretty good morning. How about you?"

"Bess and I made some progress. I want to run it

all by you before I make some calls this afternoon. I just want half a sandwich and a cup of coffee. And a brownie." She smiled. And smiled.

"Are you happy about something? You keep smiling. Is it anything you want to share?"

Angie made a mental note to slap Bess upon her return to the gift wrap shop. "Actually, I am. Happy, that is. I can see light at the end of tunnel, believe it or not. How about you?"

"You look pretty when you smile. You should do it more often. But to answer your question, I certainly feel a lot more positive than I did yesterday morning."

Angie didn't know what else to do because her heart was beating so fast, so she smiled. And smiled. Then she smiled some more. *I'm still going to slap you, Bess*.

Chapter Six

It was midafternoon when Angie pushed herself away from her tiny desk where she'd been making call after call in the hopes of saving Eagle's Department Store from closing its doors.

"How about a nice, cold soda pop?" Bess asked as she peered into the minifridge in the alcove where the coffeepot was located. Angie nodded.

Bess pulled over a stool and sat down next to Angie. She looked pointedly at the canvas bag at Angie's feet. Poking at the colorful bag with her foot, she asked, "You haven't told Eva, have you? Or Josh?"

Angie bit down on her lower lip. "I meant to tell Mom. I had it all planned, and then she up and decided to have her knee done. I didn't want to upset her. I don't . . . What I mean is, I don't think I owe Josh an explanation. As soon as Mom is in high gear again, I'll tell her. She knew this was not a forever job for me. I agreed to help out when my aunt died, then things went south. It's time for me to do what I do best, and this isn't it. Besides, she has you, Bess. It will all work out." Her tone was so defensive, Bess winced.

"Did you sign the contract yet?" Bess asked.

The contract Bess was referring to was an employment contract between Angie and the Sunnyvale, California Board of Education for Angie to teach the third grade starting next year.

"I have three more weeks before I have to submit the contract. I can overnight it. I know, I know, I will tell my mother before the three weeks are up. Don't go getting your panties in a wad, Bess. I know what I'm doing."

Bess pushed her granny glasses farther up on her nose. "I don't think it's so much that you'll be leaving as where you're going. Why couldn't you take a job around here? Why do you have to go all the way to California?"

Angie jumped off her chair. "See! See! You sound just like my mother. I'm thirty-five years old. It's time for me to do what I want. I stayed here after my dad died so Mom wouldn't be alone. I still live at home, for God's sake. What thirty-five-year-old do you know who still lives at home with their parents?"

"Josh Eagle," Bess said smartly. "I think he's thirty-seven, though."

"Well, he's leaving, too. I guess that makes us both late bloomers."

Bess mumbled something that sounded like, *"You just tossed your line in the pond, now you're going to let it sink to the bottom."* Angie ignored her and picked up the phone again to make another call.

* * *

Standing outside of both women's line of sight, Josh Eagle turned on his heel and left as silently as when he arrived. His shoulders were slumped, and he was dragging his feet.

Why should he care if Angie Bradford was leaving in January? He was leaving, too, so he wouldn't miss her. Would he?

The thought was so disturbing, Josh stopped in the middle of the main floor where all kinds of activity was going on. He felt like one of the mannequins as he watched the merchandise being wheeled out of the store on dollies.

The urge to throw his hands in the air and run as far and as fast as his sneakered feet would take him was so strong, Josh reached out to grasp the edge of one of the counters to hold himself in check.

Damn it to hell, he liked Angie Bradford. *Really* liked Angie Bradford. For some strange reason he suddenly felt like she'd betrayed him.

Josh made his way to his secret haven, the stairwell that led to the second floor. This was where he always went when things went sour with his father, or when he needed to get a handle on something. He sat down on the steps and looked at the hole in his sneaker over his big toe. He looked around at the gray stone walls that suddenly seemed as gloomy as his thoughts.

Josh knew what he should do, but did he have the guts to do it? For the first two years of his tenure at Eagle's, he'd spent a lot of time out here in the stairwell trying to decide if he should go toe to toe with his father. Out of respect, he'd never done that, and now here he was. He needed to go to Angie, tell her he'd overheard her conversation and ask her point-blank what her intentions were. She'd probably tell him it was none of his business, and he'd have to agree with her. But . . . And there was always a but . . . He liked her, *really* liked her. That's exactly what he should do. No doubt about it. Oh, yeah. So what if she told him it was none of his business? He was a big boy, he could handle a put-down.

Before he could change his mind, Josh banged open the door leading to the main floor of the store, where he retraced his steps.

As soon as he hit the small entryway to the gift department, Josh called Angie's name. Bess took one look at his face and excused herself.

"What's up?" Angie looked up from the notes she was making on her pad.

"Why didn't you tell me you were planning on leaving?" His voice was so cold, so gruff-sounding, Angie felt her heart kick up a beat. She immediately swung into her defense mode, crossed her arms over her chest and glared at the tall, good-looking man towering over her. "What?"

"You heard me. I came down here to talk to you, but you were talking to Bess and I didn't want to intrude so I waited. . . ."

"And listened to a private conversation. That's pretty sneaky in my opinion. I don't think it's any of your business, Josh. Which brings me to my next question. Why do you care what I do or when I do it as long as it doesn't interfere with the store?"

Josh hated the stubborn look he was seeing. He was all too familiar with that look. He'd seen it every time they met in court. He advanced a step and sat down on the stool Bess had vacated. He hooked his feet in the rungs and rocked back and forth. "I shouldn't care, but I do. I'm not sure why that is. I really didn't mean to eavesdrop. I'm sorry about that. And, you're right, Angie, what you do come January is none of my business. I guess I thought . . . When I told you about leaving, I guess I thought you should have told me about your plans, too. You really should tell your mother. Don't do what I did with my old man."

Somewhat mollified, Angie unfolded her arms and stared at the man sitting on the stool. She licked her lips. "I thought about telling you, but there was so much going on. I didn't want to add to your angst. I know I should have told my mother. If you were listening, then you know I didn't sign the contract yet. Maybe I'm dragging my feet. Maybe it's a mistake. Maybe a lot of things. For some reason I haven't been able to do that. I love the idea of going back to teaching. I love the kids. Working here was great, too, but Mom and I both knew it was temporary.

"You're leaving in January, so why should you care if I stay or go? For all either one of us knows, this little . . . plan we have might not work, and your father ends up having to close the store. It's all one big crapshoot, Josh."

"I like you!" Josh blurted. *Shit, did I just say that?* "I was hoping we could get to know each other better."

Angie's head bobbed up and down. She couldn't believe the words that popped out of her mouth. "I like you, too. I don't want to fight with you, Josh. I'm sick and tired of walking on eggshells. I do enough of that with my mother, and I'm sure you do the same thing with your father. Let's just get through the next few months and make decisions later on."

"But you said you had to sign the contract in three weeks."

Angie smiled and Josh's world tilted. "There will be other contracts, other jobs. I'm a good teacher. I've had other offers. The California one was just to get me on another coast. Truce?" she asked, holding out her hand.

Josh grinned as he grasped her hand. "Truce. How about dinner tonight?"

"Okay. You're going to come to my house, ring the bell with flowers in hand, a real date. Or is this business?"

"Nope, a real date. Flowers, eh? I think I can handle that. Does seven thirty work for you?"

"Yes, it works for me, but I was joking about the flowers."

The conversation was over but Josh didn't want to leave. "You should see what's going on out there on the main floor. I'm glad my father isn't here to see this. He hasn't called me today. That's not like him."

Angie started to laugh and couldn't stop. "My mother just called a little while ago. Seems your father hired a driver and, as we speak, the two of them are in the Amish country, where they are buying up all the quilts and whatever else the people are willing to sell. They rode from shop to shop in a buggy."

Josh sucked in his breath and for the life of him couldn't think of anything to say other than, "Uh-huh."

*   *   *

Eva settled herself in the town car, her legs extended. She flinched at how swollen and red her knee was. There was no doubt about it, she'd overdone it today. She could hardly wait to put the bag of crushed ice on her knee. They'd picked it up at a 7-Eleven store when they left the Amish country.

"How bad is the pain, Eva?" Angus asked, his voice full of concern.

"Probably as bad as yours. We're two old fools, Angus. At least I am. I didn't think this little trip through. I didn't realize we'd have to get in and out of the buggy so many times. I don't know what I thought. I'm sorry. Do you want some of my Advil?"

Angus held out his hand. He swallowed two of the tablets while Eva took three with the soda pop they'd also bought at the 7-Eleven.

"As soon as the ice and Advil kick in, we'll feel better. You have five weeks on me, Angus. I'm just eight days from surgery. Did you have trouble getting used to the pronged cane?" Eva asked, in the hopes that talking would take her mind off the pain in her knee.

Angus leaned back and closed his eyes. "Not at all. I had trouble with the walker. I felt like I was ninety years old. Tell me this damn trip was worth it, Eva. Just tell me that."

"It was worth it. Five hundred quilts! And all those jams and jellies. Even with all that *horse-trading* you did with the elders, I suspect we might have overpaid a little. The kids will have to mark them up considerably. Everyone wants a homemade quilt."

Angus opened his eyes, then reached for Eva's hand. "What's bothering you, Eva?"

Eva patted Angus's hand. "What makes you think something is bothering me?"

"Because I see something in your eyes. Sometimes if you talk about it, it helps a little. I'm a good listener, Eva."

"It's Angie. She thinks I don't know, but she's planning on leaving in January just the way your son is leaving. I was looking for something, and for some reason I thought it might be in her book bag. I wasn't spying. There was a teaching contract that she hasn't signed as yet. For a school in Sunnyvale, California. If you want the whole ball of wax, I need to work. If the store closes, I don't know what I'll do. My Social Security isn't all that much. My house is paid off, but the taxes are now more than the mortgage payment was. Angie wasn't really taking a salary, just money as she needed it. We have to pay Bess a regular salary. I'm sure that by January, if the store closes, my knee will be okay. I'll just have to find a job where I can sit part of the time. I just wish I had known about the store's difficulties before I had the operation. I would have put it off. The worst-case scenario is I'll sell the house and move into one of those garden apartments. I don't think apartment living will be too bad. Most of those apartments come with a little terrace. I might even get a cat for my golden years." Eva wound down like a pricked balloon.

Angus digested this information as his brain whirled and twirled. "You could move in with me, Eva."

"No, Angus, I cannot move in with you. Now, are you sorry you asked me what's wrong?"

"No, not at all. Good friends always share their

problems. If there's a way for my pigheaded folly where the store is concerned can be corrected, Josh will do it. I have so many regrets, Eva. I don't think Josh is ever going to forgive me."

"You don't know that for sure, Angus. This is no time for negative thoughts. Parents are allowed to make mistakes. It's human and it's normal. You do your best at the time. However, once our children come of age, there's no more room for mistakes. At least that's how I look at it. In many ways we've both been lucky. Your son stayed with you the way Angie stayed with me. That has to mean something. We can't be selfish now. Do you agree?"

"Yes, I agree. Maybe our answer is to just close the store in January." He watched as Eva nodded her head. For some reason he felt disappointed.

Eva's eyes opened wide. "So, what you're saying is we're quitters. You and I. You said if there was a way to turn things around, Josh would find it."

"I did say that. I don't know if it can happen or not. I'm trying to convince myself that Eagle's won't be closing its doors."

"Let's give them a chance, Angus. But only from the sidelines. All we'll do is offer encouragement and compliments. I think we can do that."

Angus squeezed Eva's hand. "I think so, too. How's the pain?"

"It's easing up. How's your pain?"

"I feel wonderful," Angus lied.

Bess covered her ears when Angie let out a shriek that almost split her eardrums. "What? What, Angie?"

But Angie was out the door calling Josh's name as she ran through the ground floor of the store. People turned to stare as they tried to figure out why the young woman was shrieking her lungs out. Josh appeared out of nowhere. Like Bess, he shouted, "What? What's wrong?"

"Wrong? Nothing's wrong. I have news. Good news! Wonderful news!"

"Come with me, my dear," Josh said, leading Angie to his private sanctuary in the stairwell. "This," he said, pointing to the steps as though they were His and Hers thrones, "is where I come to think and plan. Good place for good news, I'm thinking. What, what?" he all but shouted, his excitement palpable.

"Okay, okay," Angie said, sitting down on the second step from the bottom. She was aware Josh was holding her hand. She squeezed it. "I found this woolen mill in Portland, Oregon, that's going out of business. We can buy up their entire inventory. Their entire inventory, Josh! You can go online to see what I'm talking about. It's up to us to truck it here. The mill and the manufacturing end of it is all family-owned. The last surviving member of the family just sold out to a developer for big bucks. He was almost giddy that he could unload his warehouse in one swoop. All he wants to do is take his money and go. You need to call them right away and make an offer. They're expecting your call. Here's the number. The man's name is Samuel Eikenberry. Hurry, before he changes his mind, Josh."

"Stay right here. I have to go to the office for my cell phone. Wait for me. I want to make this deal in my . . . here on the steps. Will you wait?"

"Of course." A nanosecond later, Angie felt his lips brush hers.

"I promise to do better next time," Josh grinned.

"I'll hold you to it." *Oh, Bess, my line has a nibble*. Angie clapped her hands in glee at what had just transpired.

Twenty minutes later, Josh snapped the phone shut. His clenched fist shot in the air. "We have a deal, and Mr. Eikenberry is going to truck it here at my expense. I snapped up the offer. The latest styles, the best of the best and all wool. He asked if I wanted the blankets, and I said yes."

Josh's excitement was contagious. "You can never have enough blankets."

Then she was being kissed like she'd never been kissed in her life. Her world rocked, righted itself and then rocked again. "You didn't lie. You did do better. Wanna try for perfection?"

Josh was about to give her his definition of perfection when his cell phone rang. Thinking it might be Mr. Eikenberry, he answered it. His father's voice boomed over the wire. All he heard was five hundred handmade quilts; tons of jams, jellies, preserves; and two thousand Amish cookbooks. He laid the phone on the step and proceeded to show Angie his version of perfection.

When the couple came up for air they could hear Angus and Eva talking.

"I don't know what it is, Angus. It sounds like two cats fighting with each other. Of course, my hearing isn't what it used to be. What does it sound like to you?"

"Like someone is in pain and is moaning and groaning. Must be a bad connection."

Angie clapped her hands over her mouth so she wouldn't laugh out loud. Josh snapped the phone shut and reached for her again.

I've got the fish on the line, Bess.

Chapter Seven

Eva and Angus rocked contentedly in the rockers in what would be the temporary day care center for Eagle's Department Store.

"Isn't it amazing, Angus, how this all came together in three weeks? Angie did a wonderful job with all the vibrant colors, the mobiles and the colorful play tables and chairs. She got everything secondhand and just spruced it up. Speaking of my daughter, have you seen her?"

"You mean that harried, overworked young lady who is burning the candle at both ends? That daughter?"

"Yes, that one."

"She said she had to talk to Josh about an important matter. Something about Halloween items for this little center. I think I heard her say they were supposed to be delivered this morning and they didn't arrive. We lost three weeks of revenue, Eva. That's how long the store has been closed," Angus said, changing the subject. "It was supposed to be two days, then five days, then a week. Three weeks!"

"I know that, Angus. When the store opens next week, you'll make it up." Eva's voice turned anxious when she said, "You didn't say anything to Josh, did you?"

"No. I think he's waiting for me to lambaste him. I know, I know. Not a word. He knows what he's doing. At least that's what he's telling me a dozen times a day."

"Then believe it," Eva snapped. "Where is that daughter of mine? Stay here, Angus, I'm going to see if I can find her."

Angus waved her off and continued to rock in the new chair he had come to love. He wondered what it would feel like to rock a baby. Eva said he was going to love the feeling. Eva seemed to be right about most things, he thought happily. In a short period of time he'd come to trust her judgment completely.

Eva walked out to the main section of the second floor. Her startled gaze took in two things instantaneously. Her daughter looked like she was frozen in time as she stared at Josh Eagle and a tall woman who was kissing him. She blinked, and then pinched her arm as she walked up to her daughter to place a motherly hand on Angie's shoulder. She could see tears in the corners of her eyes. *This is not good, this is not good, this is not good. A mind's eye picture in real time will never go away.*

"I'm sure it's not what it looks like, Angie. She's probably someone he used to know. You young people tend to kiss hello, good-bye and everything in between. She probably just stopped in to see what's going on. Everyone in town wants to see what's going on. Come along, dear," Eva babbled.

Eva thought it was magical how her daughter could talk without her lips moving. "Really, Mom! How do you think she got in here when all the doors are locked? She called Josh 'darling' and was reminding him that they had a date for the Harvest Ball on Saturday. She pinched his cheek and was so cutesy cute she made my hair stand on end. Josh . . . Josh just smiled. He smiled, Mom. You're right, let's get out of here."

Josh took that moment to look in their direction. He looked so guilty even Eva had a hard time defending his actions.

Together, mother and daughter marched off, Josh calling their names. "Walk slower, Angie. I cannot run. And if you run, he'll know you're upset."

"Damn it, Mom, I *am* upset. I'm here busting my butt, working round the clock for that jerk so he can prove to his father that he knows what he's doing. We have a date on Saturday. Won't it be interesting to see how he wiggles out of it. I was starting to trust that jerk! Did you hear me, Mom?"

"Sweetie, I think the whole store can hear you."

"Guess what, Mom, I don't care! I'm going home. Don't worry, I'll be back at some point. If that Halloween stuff I ordered arrives, just unpack it. I'll see you later."

"Angie, I don't think going home . . ."

"Don't say it, Mom. Don't call me, either. I'm going to try and catch a few hours of sleep. I was here all night."

Eva, her heart heavy, watched her daughter as she made her way down the dim hallway that led to the

Eagle's loading dock. She looked behind her to see if Josh was anywhere in sight. He wasn't.

Angus had only to look at Eva's face to know something was wrong. "Do you want to tell me about it, or are you going to wear a hole in this new carpet?"

"Your son! He's a cad! He's out there on the floor kissing some long-legged woman who looks like she's been varnished, then shellacked. It seems he has a faulty memory. He has . . . I guess I should say, *had,* a date with Angie for Saturday evening, and that shellacked person stopped by to confirm her date with *your son* for the Harvest Ball on Saturday. I'm going home. You can have *your son* take you home. I don't know if I'll be back or not."

"Eva . . . wait!"

"Don't talk to me right now, Angus. Talk to that son of yours."

Angus heaved himself out of the rocker. He wondered how in a few short moments things could go from wonderful to terrible. He looked up to see the terrible end of things approaching at breakneck speed, a look of pure panic on his face. For some unexplained reason, the panicked expression on his son's face pleased Angus.

"Where's Angie, Dad? Did you see her? Is Eva here?"

"Is something wrong, son?" Angus asked.

"Hell yes, something is wrong. Angie caught—saw Vickie Summers kissing me. At least I think that's what she saw. Don't even ask me how Vickie got into the store. That woman can do anything she sets her mind to. I don't know how long Angie . . . What I mean is I don't know what she heard. . . . She wanted . . . She thinks . . . I'm not doing it. . . . She won't take no . . . Where the hell is Angie? I know her mother said something to you. You two are joined at the hip these days. What'd she say, Dad?"

A devil perched itself on Angus's shoulder. "You don't want to know, son. It will only upset you. You can't dangle two women on a string, Joshua. I think I told you that when you were sixteen, and girls were throwing themselves at you. You should have listened to me back then. Sit down, Joshua."

Josh recognized the iron command. In no way was it an invitation. He sat down in one of the rockers. "What? I think I'm a little old for a lesson on romance. Where did Angie go, Dad? She was pissed off, wasn't she?"

"No, son, she was hurt and humiliated. If the situation were reversed, how do you think you would feel?"

"Okay, okay, I get the point. Look, I didn't invite Vickie here. Like I said, I don't have a clue how she got into the store. I haven't seen her in . . . months. Actually, the last time I spoke to her was back in April. I did not invite her to the Harvest Ball. I didn't, Dad. That's the truth. Before I knew what was happening, she planted a lip-lock on me and I had a hell of a time pushing her away. That's when I saw Angie watching. If you know where Angie is, you better tell me, Dad, or I'm walking out of here and never coming back. I'm serious. She's my girl! I want to get to know her better. Hell, I think I want to marry her. I can't pull this off," he said, waving his arms about, "without her. Will you help me out already for God's sake?" Josh pleaded.

Lip-lock? It must be a new term for kissing. The devil on Angus's shoulder started a lively dance. Marriage. Maybe he'd get to rock in a chair with his very own grandchild. He just knew he was going to make a wonderful grandfather. Then he remembered the look on Eva's face and the way she'd said, *your son,* like he was the Devil incarnate.

Angus pulled his pipe out of his pocket and stuck it in his mouth. He chewed on the stem, his eyes on his son. "I'm too old to be offering advice. You're on your own, son!"

"That's it? I'm dying here, and you're telling me I'm on my own? What's wrong with this picture? Thanks for nothing, Dad."

Angus removed the pipe clenched between his teeth, and stared at it. "In my day, which was a lifetime ago, a fella would crawl on his knees, flowers in hand and the truth on his lips. If that didn't work, then the fella would throw a pebble at her bedroom window at night, and when she opened the window he'd sing her a song. Doesn't matter if the fella sounds like a frog. It's the thought that counts."

Josh was listening intently. "Yeah, yeah, what else would that fella do?"

Angus shrugged. "I never got beyond the singing part." He watched his son out of the corner of his eye and was pleased at what he was seeing.

"How far did you have to crawl?"

Angus wanted to laugh out loud, but he didn't. "Up the walkway, up the steps, across the porch and into the foyer. She kicked me out. I got two holes in my trousers for my efforts."

Josh looked down at his jeans. They were sturdy. *What's a few holes? I can always buy another pair.* "Thanks, Dad! I knew I could count on you. Take care of things, okay? I don't know when I'll be back."

Angus was so pleased with himself he made his way out to the loading dock, where he fired up his pipe and smoked contentedly. There was a lot to be said for experience.

Eva opened the front door. How quiet the house was. The first thing she saw was the brown envelope on the foyer table. It had enough stamps on it to go around the world at least three times. Eva's heart fluttered when she looked down at the address on the envelope. In a few minutes the mailman would be here to deliver the mail.

"Angie!"

"I'm up here, Mom. Do me a favor," she called down. "I see the mailman coming up the street. Give him the envelope on the table."

"Sure, honey." Eva picked up the envelope and slid it into the drawer of the table. The only way Angie could see the mailman was if she was sitting on the window seat in her room. Crying, from the way she sounded. Carrying out her charade, Eva opened the door a few moments later to accept the mail. She commented on the weather for a minute, then closed the door.

She called upstairs. "Angie, come down and talk

to me. You know I can't do the stairs comfortably. Please."

Eva was right, she saw as Angie descended the stairs and stood next to her—her daughter had been crying. "How about a nice cup of hot tea? Tea always makes things better. At least that's what my mother always said." She wrapped her arm around her daughter's shoulder and led her into the kitchen.

"I don't want to talk about this, Mom."

As Eva bustled about the kitchen, she said, "Well, I for one can certainly understand that. Men are so callow. They don't have the same feelings women have. I guess that might be a good thing. I think I would be remiss as a mother if I didn't point out to you that there are two sides to everything. You should ask yourself how that young woman got into the store. If she came uninvited, then you can't blame Josh for that. Ask yourself if Josh acted like he was enjoying the meeting. He looked kind of stiff to me, like he didn't want her there, but that's just this old lady's opinion. I didn't see him return her kiss. He just stood there. That's the way I saw it. You only heard the young woman say they had a date for the Harvest Ball. You didn't hear Josh agree, now, did you?"

"Whose side are you on, Mom?" Angie sniffed.

"The right side. I happen to think Josh is a stand-up kind of guy. He didn't beat around the bush the day he eavesdropped on you. He fessed right up, didn't he? It's when things fester that the problem gets out of hand. In short, my dear, I think you saw something you never should have seen. Having said that, it probably meant nothing. That's why you shouldn't have seen it—because you reacted without giving Josh a chance to explain or defend his actions. Now, drink your tea."

Angie picked at the fringe on the green-checkered placemat. "So what you're saying is I should go back to the store and wait for Josh to come to me and . . . explain what I saw."

"See! Now you're getting it! Yes, in my opinion, that's what you should do. If you don't, you'll always wonder what he would have said. You did tell me you really liked Josh. You told me you dream about him. He might be *the one,* Angie."

"She kissed him. You saw her. Kissing is . . . Kissing is . . ."

"Quite wonderful, depending on who is doing the kissing. I did not see Josh returning the kiss in question. There was no passion there that I could see. No reciprocity. That's about all I have to say, Angie. Think this all through, and don't throw away something on a jealous whim that could otherwise turn out to be wonderful."

The doorbell rang, cutting off whatever Angie's response was going to be.

"I'll get it, and then I'm going back to the store," Eva said. "Finish your tea. By the way, I won't be home for dinner this evening. Angus and I are going out for Japanese. He loves the knife show the chefs provide."

Outside, after Josh Eagle had run up to the Bradfords' front porch and rung the bell, he ran down the steps and out to the walkway, where he dropped to his knees. He sucked in his breath and proceeded to knee-walk his way to the Bradford front porch the moment the front door opened.

"Angie! Angie! Come quick! Hurry, dear!"

Thinking her mother fell or banged her knee, Angie barreled to the foyer. She almost screamed in relief when she saw that Eva was all right. She turned and looked where her mother was pointing. Her jaw dropped at what she was seeing. Josh waved. Angie, more or less, wiggled her index finger as she watched the man's progress. She could tell it was slow going for the tall man on his knees.

Eva tactfully withdrew and left by the kitchen door. She peeked around the corner of the house. He was still crawling. She laughed all the way to her car.

Angie walked out to the porch, her arms across her chest to ward off the October chill. By the time Josh reached the steps, Angie took pity on him and motioned for him to get up. "Do you mind telling me what you're doing?" There was a bit of frost in her tone that did not go unnoticed by Josh.

Josh struggled to his feet. "Angie, look, what you saw . . . It wasn't . . . It isn't what you think. Vickie is someone I used to know. And I didn't know her that well. I haven't seen or spoken to her since way back in April. She was looking for an escort to take her to the Harvest Ball. I have to assume I was a last resort because I never pretended to be anything other than a distant friend. She kisses everyone. I just found out that she bribed one of the workers with twenty bucks to let her into the store. If you hadn't turned tail and run, you would have heard me tell her I was seeing someone and had other plans for Saturday evening. So, are you okay with this? Please tell me you're okay with this so I don't have to do that singing thing under your window tonight." Josh wondered if he looked as exhausted as he felt. Would Angie take pity on him? Childishly, he crossed his fingers.

He was seeing someone and had other plans. That almost makes us a couple. It sounds like we are a couple. "I didn't know you could sing. Do you want a cup of tea or a beer? I can make some coffee."

"I'll take a beer and I can't sing. My father . . ."

"Offered you advice. Yeah, my mother stepped in and offered some, too. Okay, you're off the hook."

"Thank God! I'm going to have to guzzle that beer and get back to the store. Are you staying home?"

"No. I just got . . . miffed and came home. I did . . . I think I did something I might come to regret. I reacted and I . . . I signed that damn contract and it went off in the mail. The mailman came a little while ago, and Mom gave it to him."

Josh looked at her as though she'd sprouted a second head. "You were that angry? Damn, now what are you going to do? Are you sorry you sent it off?"

"Yes. Yes, a hundred times yes. I was going to call tomorrow and explain that I wouldn't be accepting the position. I never did tell my mother."

"Get your coat. Maybe we can catch the mailman. Do you know in which direction he goes when he finishes up your street? Never mind, you go one way and I'll go the other. It's still early so he won't be returning to the post office. If I find him first, he won't give it to me, so I'll call you on your cell. If you find him first, call me and I'll meet up with you."

Thirty minutes later the couple sat down on Angie's front steps. "He said Mom never gave him any mail. That has to mean she knows and kept the envelope or hid it. Parents are so devious," Angie groused.

"Oh, I don't know, sometimes they're pretty smart. Your mother saved your butt by not mailing that contract. My father gave me some shitty advice, but here we are with a better understanding of what's going on." Josh reached for Angie's hand and squeezed it.

"I think your father and my mother are going to end up together. They get along so well. And, they're great company for one another. Tonight they're going out for Japanese food. I'm okay with it, are you?"

"Yeah, you bet. My father is a different man these days. He hasn't given me one moment of grief as the bills come in. I think it's all due to your mother." This last was said so shyly, Angie smiled.

Angie held up her hand palm out and high-fived Josh. "To our parents!"

"To our parents and to *us*."

A red ring of heat popped up on Angie's neck. Then it crept up to her cheeks. She didn't know what else to do, so she smiled.

Chapter Eight

On a cold, blustery November day, everything Eagle swung into high gear. Announcers on the local airwaves invited shoppers to soar with the Eagle and avail themselves of the hospitality that was being offered by the Eagle family to all the families the store had served in the last hundred years.

Flyers and giveaways were handed out at all the mall entrances and parking lot to entice people into the store. There were flyers for the day care unit, flyers for the knitting and cooking classes. Flyers for sale after sale on just about every item in the store.

When the doors opened at ten o'clock, Josh, attired in a power suit and tie, stood next to his father to welcome and greet old and new customers alike.

Standing on the sidelines, Eva and Angie sighed with relief as shoppers flooded the main floor. They watched for a while, amazed and delighted that all their hard work was paying off with cash register activity. "I think we did okay, Mom. Now, if the merchandise keeps flowing in, and no one screws up, we just might make it through the holiday season and, if we're lucky, pay the bills and maybe show a tiny profit. If we're lucky," she repeated.

"Honey, we agreed, no negative thoughts. I have to get back to the second floor. We have a good crew to help with the kids. I'll see you later."

Angie meandered over to the cosmetics counter. She was pleased to see the free Vera Wang samples going like hotcakes and being followed up by sales. She looked around and realized the salesgirl had been right. Too much variety and people can't decide, so they walk away. Her advice had been to go with three manufacturers, and it now looked like she was right.

Josh had taken the salesgirl's advice to heart and instructed the few new buyers he'd hired to do the same thing. It looked like the strategy was working throughout the store.

Angie was so pleased with the way things were going, she gave herself a mental pat on the back as she walked the floor, hoping to hear comments or criticisms she could relay to Josh. She moved over closer to the door to better observe Josh and his father. How tired they both looked. But it seemed to her like a happy kind of tiredness.

Angie crossed her fingers that things would continue through the end of the year. Her eyes were everywhere as she continued to meander around, then made her way back to the front door, where she leaned up to whisper in Josh's ear. "Your father needs to get off his feet. Tell him to go up to the day care so he can sit down in one of the rockers. I can take his place if you like."

"I like. How's it going?"

"I think it's going very well. The big fishbowl for the nine o'clock drawing is almost filled. When school lets out, the kids will be here in droves in the hopes of winning the iPod. The safari department appears to be doing a brisk business. Cruise wear is beyond brisk. It's happening, Josh. How much longer are you going to do this meet and greet?"

"Not a minute longer. I want to check the stockroom. What's on your schedule?"

"I'm going to float around, check on Mom and your dad, that kind of thing. If Bess needs me in gift wrap, I'll help out. It's really working, Josh," she whispered.

"Because of you," Josh whispered in return. "When you're done, why don't you meet me in the stockroom?"

Angie wiggled her eyebrows. "That's one of the nicest invitations I've ever gotten. I'll be there. Wait for me."

Angie thought her heart would leap right out of her chest when she heard him say, "Forever if I have to."

Angie flew to the second floor. She skidded to a stop at the small desk to take in the scene in front of her. Angus and Eva rocking chubby babies, who were gurgling and cooing as Eva sang a lullaby. Angus looked so contented and peaceful, she felt a lump rise in her throat. Toddlers crawled through a maze of colored plastic tunnels, giggling and laughing. Infants in swings, their eyes following the mobiles overhead. Juice and cookies were being laid out on the play tables, after which it would be nap time. When she left the area her only thought was that the day care was going to net a profit. She couldn't wait to share her thoughts with Josh.

To the right and around the corner of the day care unit, a senior citizen was teaching six young mothers how to knit, her students paying rapt attention. The cooking class was all done via video and a large corkboard. The lesson today was how to bake a turkey for Thanksgiving. All was well there, too.

Now she could head for the stockroom. There was a bounce to her step that showed her excitement.

Angie opened a door that said NO ADMITTANCE and, underneath, EMPLOYEES ONLY. From far back in the room she could hear voices. Josh and a strange male voice. She didn't know why, but she tiptoed in the direction the voices were coming from. She peeked around a stack of sweater boxes. Bob McAllister, the general manager of Saks. What's he doing here in the stockroom? she wondered. As much as she wanted to spy and hear what was going on, she couldn't do it. "Josh!"

"Over here, Angie. Meet Bob McAllister."

Angie held out her hand. "Hello. We've met before. What's up?"

Josh laughed. "I just convinced Bob to take my job at Harrods. For obvious reasons, he doesn't want anyone to know until he can give his notice. That's why we had this meeting here in the stockroom."

Angie's head bobbed up and down. Josh wasn't leaving. He was staying. *Oh, thank you, God!*

"You guys did a hell of a job," Bob told her. "When Josh first told me his plan, I told him he could never pull it off. I'm happy to see I was wrong. If it means anything, you have the bulk of customers in the mall. Good prices, too. Great idea with only three choices per item. I've been trying to sell that idea to my people, but they won't buy in to it. See you around, guys. Let's have a drink before I leave, Josh."

"You got it."

And then they were alone. Josh reached for Angie and she stepped into his arms. "I love you, Angie Bradford. We're a team. This store is in my blood the way it was in Dad's blood. When I saw him writing out all those checks I knew he was investing in me, Josh Eagle, his son, not Eagle's Department Store. He finally moved beyond the store. These last few weeks he's turned into a real father."

"You should sneak up to the day care to see him rocking the babies. He looks so peaceful, so happy. Mom, too. I suspect they'll both make wonderful grandparents. We did good, Josh."

"We had a lot of help along the way. Eagle's is never going to be a Saks or a Neiman Marcus, and that's okay. We never aspired to be anything other than what we are—a family store where families come to buy merchandise because they trust us. Those families who shop at Eagle's grew up with us. We got off the track there for a little while, but we're back in business now. But, I can't do it without you, Angie. I'm not too proud to admit it, either. I want to marry you," he blurted.

Whoa. For the first time in her life, Angie was speechless. Because she couldn't make her tongue work, she simply nodded, her eyes glistening with happiness.

"If I kiss you, it's all over. You know that, right?"

Angie found her tongue. "Right."

"So . . . Want to help me open these boxes?"

"Sure."

The young couple worked in happy sync as salesperson after salesperson bounded into the storeroom to ask for more merchandise.

And before they knew it, the first announcement came over the loudspeaker that the drawing was about to be held for the winner of the iPod. They both ran out to the main floor just as Angus reached into the fishbowl to draw the winning number. "Annette Profit!" he said, holding up the winning entry. Annette Profit of Chez J's La Perfect Salon stepped up smartly and accepted the iPod. Angus hugged her and thanked her for shopping at Eagle's.

Five minutes later, when the last of the crowd disappeared, Josh locked the doors. The Eagles and the Bradfords walked back to the gift wrap department, where Angie handed out soft drinks.

"It was a hell of a day, son! I'm proud of you!" Angus beamed.

"No, Dad, you need to thank Angie and Eva and all those people who worked the floor. We aren't home free yet, but if we can keep up the kind of momentum we had today, I think we might coast right into the New Year in the black. By the way, I'm not going to England and I asked Angie to marry me."

"Wise man," Angus chuckled.

"Good choice," Eva said.

"It's time for us to leave," Angus said, getting to his feet. Eva followed him, leaving Josh and Angie alone. They looked at one another and then groaned because they knew they had three or four more hours of work before they could leave.

"I'm starved, Josh. Let's go out for a pizza and a beer and come back. We can both use a break. I haven't been outside all day. We can walk to the pizza parlor and clear the cobwebs."

Outside in the brisk air, Josh reached for Angie's hand. "Are we officially engaged or are we 'keeping company,' as Dad would say? I'm not really up on all the protocol on things like this. I never told anyone I loved her, and I sure never asked anyone to marry me before. . . . Are you *ever* going to say something?"

"I'm thinking. I like being engaged. That pretty much makes it official. No one ever told me they loved me except my mom and dad. For sure no one ever asked me to marry him. I guess we're starting off even. I was a little disappointed in our parents' reaction."

Josh laughed. "My father can be a sly old fox sometimes. He told me if I didn't act quickly, you were going to move on. He sounded so convincing I figured he and Eva planned it all out, and I had better pay attention. I was never the first guy out of the gate."

Angie stepped aside as Josh opened the door of the pizza parlor. "At least you got out of the gate; I never did. Let's get the works on the pizza. I want one of those apple dumplings, too."

"Whatever you want, it's yours."

Angie could hardly wait to call Bess to tell her what she'd pulled in on her line. She laughed to herself as she imagined what Bess would say. *"You pulled in the Big Kahuna! Way to go, Angie."*

Chapter Nine

Two days before Christmas, Angie woke at four thirty AM, more tired than when she'd gone to bed. *Just let me get through today. And tomorrow,* she pleaded. *Don't let me fall asleep standing up.* If she could just sleep five more minutes. Just five. She'd settle for three, but she knew she had to get up even though it was still dark outside. It had been Josh's decision to open the store at seven and close at midnight. Then there were two hours of getting things ready for the next day, the trip home and two hours' sleep. Still, she shouldn't complain, it was all working out perfectly.

Today was special, though. Bob McAllister had stopped by the gift wrap department late last night to whisper in her ear. It was her job to get to the store at six, open the doors and lead Josh to the food court, where all the general managers in the mall were holding their traditional private Christmas breakfast.

In the bathroom, bleary-eyed from lack of sleep,

Angie looked out the window as she waited for the shower to start steaming. As she raised the window she screamed, and then screamed again. "Snow!" She stuck her neck out the window to see if she could see what kind of accumulation there was down below. Her heart fluttered. Snow was every merchant's nightmare. Especially during the last week of Christmas shopping.

It was the shortest shower in history. In less than ten minutes, Angie was showered, dressed and tapping her foot impatiently as she waited for the coffee to run through the filter. "Snow!" The minute there was enough coffee in the pot, Angie poured, and then turned it off. She was out of the house a minute later and in her car. While it warmed up, she climbed back out to clear the snow off her windshield and back window. The little Honda was a marvel in snow and rain, so she had no worries about getting to the mall. She might even have a bit of an edge, traffic-wise, since it was just five o'clock. Another hour, and it would be a different story. As she made her way to Route 1, she listened to the local weather on the radio. Snow at Christmas was the kiss of death to every retailer. She wondered if Josh was up and had seen the snow. She wondered if she should call him, but she hated using a cell phone while she was driving. He would see it soon enough.

Twenty minutes later, when Angie blew into the mall on a strong gust of wind and swirling snow, Josh was waiting for her. The first words out of his mouth were, "This is going to kill us. The weatherman is saying six to eight inches. They're closing the schools. We need these last two shopping days like we need air to breathe. Damn! No one is here yet, so I made some coffee."

Josh reached for her hand. "I need to tell you again how grateful I am. I could never in a million years have pulled this off without your help."

"We'll find a way to make this work, Josh. It's the season of miracles. Come on, let's go get that coffee. Maybe we'll be able to think more clearly with some serious caffeine under our belts."

"There was no snow in the forecast. How'd this happen?" Josh demanded.

"It just happened, and we have to deal with it. Did you go home last night?"

"I went to the Best Western, got an hour's sleep and took a shower. I snatched a clean shirt off one of the sale tables, and here I am. I don't know when I've ever been this tired." Josh reached for Angie's hand and squeezed it. "I wonder if the managers' breakfast is still on."

"Trust me, it's still on. It's a tradition. We're low on merchandise, Josh."

"I know. Your cottage people promised a delivery for early this morning. They were going to truck it in overnight. Then we have to unpack, log it all in. If it even gets here. I'm thinking I might have to blow off that breakfast."

Angie reared up and spilled her coffee in the process. "Absolutely not! That breakfast is part of the way things are done around here. We're going to follow the rules and hope for the best. C'mon, let's go check the loading dock. For all we know, we could have merchandise piled to the rafters just waiting for us to unpack."

There was no erasing the doom and gloom Josh felt. "My father is going to pitch a fit. Somehow he's going to find a way to blame me for this snow. He knows how important these two days are. I know it. I feel it in my gut."

There was nothing for Angie to say, so she remained quiet. Somehow, though, she didn't think the elder Eagle would blame his only son for a snowstorm. At least she hoped not. And if he did, she knew she would have a few choice words for such an action.

Three miles away Angus Eagle was pacing back and forth in his old-fashioned kitchen, where Eva was calmly mixing pancake batter.

"Calm down, Angus, you can't control the weather. Something else is bothering you. Don't deny it, Angus. You're pulling on your ear, and you only do that when something is bothering you. Do you want to talk about it?"

"Yes, I guess I do want to talk about it. I'm almost broke, Eva. If I had stayed on top of things these past years I wouldn't be in this mess. It's all my fault for being so pigheaded. I didn't want Josh to start the year off in debt. So I've paid for everything as the bills came in. My personal funds are just about depleted. I wanted . . . It was . . . I can't ask you to marry me when I have nothing to offer. I thought . . . If I sell this old house and you sell yours, we could buy a smaller house or a condo. I think we could manage nicely and, if we're careful, we can live out our lives without . . . without depending on the kids. It was my intention to give the store to the kids if they got married.

"Now, with this snow, we're going to lose more revenue. I'll have to tap into the remains of my portfolio. I'm not complaining, Eva, I just want you to know where I stand. Can you see yourself roughing it with this old man?"

"Oh, Angus, is that why you've been so cranky these past few weeks? I'm all right with everything. How nice and yet how silly of you to be worried about me. It's the Christmas season, so let's get ready for a miracle, and if that was a proposal, I accept. Now, sit down before you wear out what's left of this horrible linoleum. How many pancakes?"

"Four!" Angus said smartly. "I have an idea."

"Let's hear your idea, Big Popper," Eva said as she slid a stack of pancakes on a plate.

Angus burst out laughing. "Promise me you will never call me that in front of the kids. I don't think they'd . . . uh . . . understand."

Eva's eyes popped wide when Angus leaned across the table to share his idea. "Oh, Angus, can you make that happen? That will surely be the miracle we need." She pointed to the seven-inch television on the counter and said, "Now they're saying twelve inches of snow. Never mind those pancakes, Angus, I'll eat yours. Get on the phone and work some magic."

The traditional Managers' Holiday Breakfast was already in progress when Josh and Angie made their way to the food court. Croissants, coffee and juice were being passed around as Bob McAllister, the president of the association, started to speak.

"We're going to make this short and sweet because we all have things to do to combat the weather none of us expected. As you all know, I'll be leaving the first of the year. I want to take a minute to thank all of you for your support over the years and to wish you all the best in the coming year. I'm turning the reins over to Josh Eagle, who I know will do the same fine job I've done in the past. . . . That was a joke, people.

"Moving right along here, all of us sitting here today want to congratulate Josh Eagle and Eagle's Department Store. We've been rooting for you every step of the way. You had us all chewing our nails wondering if you could turn the store around, and you did. Each and every one of us is proud of you and wish you and Eagle's every success. Did I also say we're all slightly jealous? We are. Utilizing the cottage industry was a stroke of genius and I for one applaud you."

Josh flushed at the round of applause.

"Having said that, Abrams' Trophies in the west wing made this up for you," Bob said, holding up a small bronze plaque. "It says, 'To Eagle's Department Store: the Most Innovative Store of 2007.' There's a card to go with it that every store owner signed. Congratulations, Josh!"

Josh stood, walked to the front of the gathering and reached for the plaque. "I don't know what to say other than thank you. Maybe someday I'll be able to tell all of you what this means to me. Not right now, though."

He looked to the back of the room to see Angie

waving her cell phone at him, an ear-to-ear grin splitting her features. She walked to the front of the room to hand the phone to Josh, who listened, his jaw dropping almost to his chest.

"People! People, wait a minute! That was my father. Maybe we aren't dead in the water after all. My dad called down to Edison and Piscataway and asked all his friends who have horse farms if they'd get their wagons out and hitch them up and bring them our way to transport shoppers. Eva Bradford called all the radio stations to announce our wagon train shopping solution. It's a plan, and it's under way. We're going to lose a few early-morning hours, but my suggestion is we all stay open around the clock. Good luck, everybody."

Josh whirled around to hug Angie. "Now where in the hell do you think my old man came up with this idea? Oh, who cares! Let's just hope it works."

"Oh, it's going to work. All people have to do is get to the central points and leave the rest up to us. Your dad saved the day, Josh."

Josh's eyes misted over. "Yeah, he did, didn't he," he said softly.

"Mr. Eagle! Mr. Eagle! Annette Profit here. I have the salon in the east wing." She held out her hand and smiled. "I just want a minute to tell you my mother used to bring me to Eagle's when I was little. It was always such a special treat. Especially when it was time to go back to school. Your dad always stood at the door and gave each one of us kids a free box of crayons and a tablet. On the Fourth of July he'd give us a gift certificate for a free ice-cream cone. At Easter it was a chocolate egg, and at Christmas it was a silver bell to ring so Santa would know where we lived. They were wonderful memories. Eagle's was a tradition. I'm glad you were able to turn the store around. Good luck, Mr. Eagle."

Josh was so choked up he couldn't get his tongue to work. He reached out to hug the young woman and smiled. He finally managed to choke out the words, "I'll bring that tradition back next year if you promise to bring your kids."

"Count on it, Mr. Eagle."

Angie linked her arm with Josh's as they turned to go back to the store. "That was so nice. I vaguely remember Mom talking about it, but the store was too expensive for us to shop. Mom did that discount thing. If it wasn't on sale, we didn't buy it. It's all about goodwill and family."

"These last few months have certainly been an eye-opener," Josh said. "I learned things about my father I never knew, I found the love of my life and I now know I can run this store."

Angie laughed. "I think I'm going to go back to the food court and find out if one of the vendors will be willing to honor hot chocolate vouchers for our customers. And those big fat sugar cookies for the kids. If Bess isn't busy, ask her to make up some vouchers and run them off. See if you can find someone to go over to the south wing where that huge candy store is. Buy up all the candy canes and hand them out at the door to the kids."

"Super idea! Where *do* you come up with these ideas? I think I'm going to be marrying a genius."

"I'm thinking you're right." Angie laughed again and waved her hand as she headed back to the food court.

* * *

It was the noon hour when Josh flipped on the television in his office. As local television cameras caught the wagon train heading for the mall he watched the unfolding scene with his mouth hanging open. Even the anchor seemed to be beside himself, his words running together. Josh turned when he felt a hand on his shoulder.

"Dad! How'd you get here?"

"I came on the first wagon. Eva is down in gift wrap. What do you want me to do?"

The lump in Josh's throat was so big he thought he was going to choke to death. "What you do best, Dad. What you did for years and years. Stand by the door and hand out treats—we have candy canes and vouchers for hot chocolate and cookies at the food court. Bundle up, Dad."

"You remembered I used to do that?"

Josh felt shame river through him. "No, Dad. Some lady came up to me and told me how you used to do that. She told me it was an event for her when she was a kid. I'm going to do that again. Want a job?"

Angus swung his scarf around his neck. "Depends on how much the job pays," he said craftily.

"I was hoping you'd do it for free."

"Sounds about right to me. You got yourself a new employee, son. See you later," Angus said, picking up the stack of vouchers. "Where are the candy canes?"

"In a big barrel by the front door. The candy people just delivered them."

Josh leaned against the door when it closed behind his father. His eyes were so wet he knew in a second that tears were going to roll down his cheeks. *It's not a bad thing*, he told himself. He knuckled his eyes before he opened the door, knowing in his heart that he was blessed. Maybe all this that was happening was the miracle everyone talked about during the Christmas season.

By four o'clock the mall was so busy that people were bumping into each other. Camera crews, photographers and reporters from all the local news channels contributed to the gala that seemed to be going on. Everyone was being interviewed. Only smiles and camaraderie could be seen.

The food vendors worked at breakneck speed to prepare food to be given to the drivers of the wagon trains. The coffee shop was almost out of coffee they were brewing by the gallon. And, one reporter put it, everything was free.

The primary channels ran with the story on the six o'clock news, referring to the event—the wagon train, the freebies the mall was giving out, along with the camaraderie of the shoppers—as Marketing 101 at it's best. By the time the eleven o'clock news came on, they were calling the wagon train a phenomenon. Within seconds the story flashed around the world via the Internet.

It was midnight when Josh walked to the front door to relieve his father. When he saw Angus being interviewed by CBS News he stepped back to listen. He knew he was eavesdropping, but he didn't care. The interview would play out in real time instantaneously.

"Now, you listen to me, young fella. What you're

seeing out there is not about money or the bottom line. This is about people coming together to help each other. Those farmers and their wagons aren't getting a penny for all their hard work. They've been out there bringing shoppers back and forth since early this morning. It's Christmas, son, a time when people help each other. Every merchant in this mall is my friend and my competitor. I want to help them as much as I want to help myself. But more important, we don't want to disappoint anyone and we want everyone to have a wonderful Christmas, especially the children.

"Mother Nature served us a hard blow today, but we all pitched in and did whatever we could to save the holiday. There aren't any shining stars here today. Everything is a group effort as you can see. You want a candy cane or a voucher for hot chocolate, young fella? It's time for my break now, so I'll be seeing you tomorrow. I don't want to be interviewed anymore."

And that was the end of that.

Josh grinned. "Guess you set them straight, huh?"

"Son, I didn't say anything but the truth. Now, if you don't mind, I'm heading upstairs to that rocking chair that has my name on it."

"Dad . . . I . . . I need . . ."

"No, you don't need to say anything. We need to talk more, son. Here!" Angus said, shoving a candy cane into his son's hand.

Eva wrapped an afghan around Angus's shoulders as he lowered himself gently into the padded rocking chair. A cup of hot chocolate found its way to his hand. "It's been a heck of a day, Big Popper. I just

saw your interview on TV. You were wonderful."
When he didn't answer Eva realized Angus was already sound asleep, so she removed the cup of hot
chocolate and drank it herself. As she rocked silently,
she realized she had never felt more peaceful, more
happy than she was feeling at that precise moment.
She reached over to pat the Big Popper's shoulder.

Life was wonderful.

Curled together with Josh in sleep in the gift wrap
department, Angie stirred and bolted upright. "Josh,
wake up! What about the horses?"

"What? What about the horses? What time is it?"

"They've been out there all day and night. That's
cruel. It's six o'clock."

"No, no, no!" Josh said, sitting up. "Dad got the
armory to donate the space. They've been rotating the
horses. It's warm in there. This is no Mickey Mouse
operation, you know. My old man covered all the
bases. Relax. Damn, my mouth feels like Dad's pipe
smells. Turn on the radio, Angie. I want to know
how much snow is out there." He knew he was babbling but couldn't seem to stop.

"Eighteen inches," Angie said as she filled the
coffeepot. "And it's still snowing."

"I'm going out to the main floor to check on things,
and I want to see how my father's doing. I won't be
long. Do you want me to get you anything from the
food court?"

"A sticky bun would be nice, and a toothbrush."

Josh laughed as he unfolded his tired bones. Satisfied that his father and Eva were sound asleep in the
rockers, he made his way to his office, where he went

online to check out the headline news. He was astounded to see that the mall had made the front page of just about every newspaper in the country.

The tiredness that seemed to have invaded Josh's body suddenly washed away. His step was light, his mood upbeat as he made his way out to the mall. He picked up two toothbrushes, some toothpaste, four oven-hot sticky buns and four cups of coffee.

Christmas Eve.

Josh realized he no longer cared if the bottom line at closing was red or black. All that mattered were his neighbors, his business associates, all the volunteers, and, of course his family. He thanked God for all the people who had come to his aid.

Singing "Jingle Bells" at the top of his lungs, Josh made his way to the second floor, where he handed out sticky buns and coffee to his father and Eva. He didn't miss a beat as he turned around and headed back downstairs to see the love of his life.

No doubt about it, Angie was the wind beneath his wings.

His mouth full of toothpaste in the small lavatory off the gift wrap department, Josh bellowed, "Angie, the cottage people came through. We have to unpack the merchandise. I guarantee we're going to be sold out before six tonight. We've been sending customers to other stores. All in the spirit of Christmas."

"I've been wrapping gifts for free. I hope you don't mind."

"Not one little bit," Josh said, biting into the still-warm sticky bun. "We better get our tails in gear, there are people waiting in line for their packages to be gift wrapped. It's just all so glorious. By the way, we made the front page of every newspaper in the country. We're even on the pop-up when you turn on the computer."

"That's great! Did they plow the parking lot?"

"They tried but gave up. It's still snowing, too. I have this suspicion we are going to be celebrating Christmas right here in the store."

Josh's suspicions turned out to be on the money.

The crowds at the mall started to thin out around four o'clock. By five there were just a few stragglers waiting to be picked up by one of the wagons.

At five thirty the loud speaker in the mall exploded into sound. "Promptly at six thirty, cocktails, compliments of Stephens' Liquors, will be served in the food court, followed by dinner, compliments of the vendors in the food court. One and all are invited to go caroling up and down the halls of the mall at eight o'clock. A silent midnight service will be held promptly at midnight. Sorry, folks," the tinny baritone said, "there will be no gift exchange because there's nothing left in the stores to exchange. Merry Christmas to one and all."

Holding hands, Josh and Angie walked to the front door of Eagle's, where Angus was operating the mechanism that would secure the store for the night. Josh thought he had never seen his father so happy.

"No more candy canes. Merry Christmas, son."

The pesky lump in his throat Josh thought was becoming permanent found its way to block his vocal cords once again. He wrapped his arms around his father and whispered, "Thanks for being my father. Merry Christmas, Dad."

Standing in front of the huge Christmas tree that

dominated the middle of the floor was Eva, who held her arms out to her little family. "Merry Christmas!"

Together, the Eagles and Bradfords walked out to the food court to a chorus of "Merry Christmas! Merry Christmas!"

Books by Bestselling Author
Fern Michaels

Available Wherever Books Are Sold!
Check out our website at **www.kensingtonbooks.com**

Romantic Suspense from
Lisa Jackson

See How She Dies	0-8217-7605-3	$6.99US/$9.99CAN
Final Scream	0-8217-7712-2	$7.99US/$10.99CAN
Wishes	0-8217-6309-1	$5.99US/$7.99CAN
Whispers	0-8217-7603-7	$6.99US/$9.99CAN
Twice Kissed	0-8217-6038-6	$5.99US/$7.99CAN
Unspoken	0-8217-6402-0	$6.50US/$8.50CAN
If She Only Knew	0-8217-6708-9	$6.50US/$8.50CAN
Hot Blooded	0-8217-6841-7	$6.99US/$9.99CAN
Cold Blooded	0-8217-6934-0	$6.99US/$9.99CAN
The Night Before	0-8217-6936-7	$6.99US/$9.99CAN
The Morning After	0-8217-7295-3	$6.99US/$9.99CAN
Deep Freeze	0-8217-7296-1	$7.99US/$10.99CAN
Fatal Burn	0-8217-7577-4	$7.99US/$10.99CAN
Shiver	0-8217-7578-2	$7.99US/$10.99CAN
Most Likely to Die	0-8217-7576-6	$7.99US/$10.99CAN
Absolute Fear	0-8217-7936-2	$7.99US/$9.49CAN
Almost Dead	0-8217-7579-0	$7.99US/$10.99CAN
Lost Souls	0-8217-7938-9	$7.99US/$10.99CAN
Left to Die	1-4201-0276-1	$7.99US/$10.99CAN
Wicked Game	1-4201-0338-5	$7.99US/$9.99CAN
Malice	0-8217-7940-0	$7.99US/$9.49CAN